LEVELING UP
CHOOSING PROVIDENCE - BOOK 1

JILL BURRELL

Cover Design © 2022 Kelli Ann Morgan at Inspire Creative Service.
Proof read by Aaron and Megan Walker.

Text Copyright© 2022 by Jill Burrell

All rights reserved. No part of this book may be reproduced in any form or by any electronic or mechanical means, including information storage and retrieval systems, without written permission from the publisher Cherry Creek Press®, except for the use of brief quotations in a book review. This is a work of fiction. Characters, names, locations, events, and dialogue in this book are products of the author's imagination or are represented fictitiously.

First edition: May 2022
Library of Congress Control Number: 2022904813

ISBN: 978-1-955507-08-0 (eBook)
ISBN: 978-1-955507-09-7 (pbk)

To my readers. Your support and words of encouragement make all the hard work of writing worthwhile

CHAPTER 1

*D*ebbie brought her Porsche to a stop in front of the Salvation Army donation bin. She climbed out and pulled the large garbage bag from the passenger seat. Taking a deep breath, she hefted it into the donation bin.

Good riddance.

Hopefully, someone would enjoy the expensive brand name clothing and shoes more than she had. Now that she was being honest with herself, she could admit they'd always made her feel a little self-conscious and uncomfortable. They reminded her of a time in her life that was full of censure and insecurities.

After pulling two more bags from the sports car's small front and back trunks, she took another cleansing breath and brushed off her hands as she mentally said farewell to that piece of her past. Although she didn't regret making changes, the lightness that filled her chest surprised her.

Five minutes later, she walked into Knights grocery store. She picked up a bunch of bananas and broke off three. She hated doing that, but there was no way she could eat six bananas before they turned brown.

Next, she dropped three apples into a produce bag. She'd grown so tired of throwing food away because she simply couldn't eat it all. It wasn't that she couldn't afford to waste the food, she could. She could afford just about anything, but that didn't change the fact she ate alone at her big dining table, watched movies alone in her theater room, and slept alone in a king-sized bed.

Debbie grabbed a small bag of salad and a cucumber. She didn't need the king-sized bed any more than she needed the massive eight-bedroom house she'd insisted on building two years ago.

Her phone chimed in her purse, bringing an end to her mental pity party. She pulled it out and read her sister Sheila's text.

You're coming to read with kids at the school tomorrow, right?
Yes, I'll be there.
Good, I promise you won't regret it.

Debbie hoped Sheila was right. She'd never considered participating in the program she'd been funding for the last four years, because not only did she not have any kids, reading with struggling students sounded painful.

At least, it would help fill her empty days.

I hope.

She'd had way too much time on her hands for far too long now. Heat filled her face as she recalled her emotional break down last month on her thirty-sixth birthday. She'd cried to her mom and sisters, confiding in them why her first marriage failed twelve years ago.

She couldn't have children. But she wanted more than anything to be a mom.

Her nephews' cheers about finally leveling up in their video game came from the playroom during her breakdown, and Debbie had tearfully insisted she wanted to *level up* too.

She had everything money could buy but not the thing she wanted most. A family of her own.

Her mom and sisters had surrounded her in a bubble of support ever since. They were determined to help her *level up* by constantly encouraging her to do things she'd never considered before, including applying to be a foster parent.

Debbie dropped her phone back into her purse, tossed a small bag of carrots into her cart, and pushed her shopping cart around the corner.

Crash.

"Oops. Look out," said a deep voice.

She looked up from the cart she'd just run into to find a pair of brown eyes looking at her. Despite the exhaustion on the man's face, he was handsome in a stocky-build, clad-in-denim-and-flannel kind of way. His heavy five o'clock shadow only added to his rugged good looks.

"Sorry, my fault. I wasn't watching where I was going."

"No problem. Have a nice night." He dipped his head and maneuvered his cart around her.

Debbie watched him over her shoulder, checking out his broad shoulders and trim waist as she pushed her cart forward.

Crash!

She let out a yelp as a display of candy-filled easter eggs toppled to the floor in front of her. Denim and flannel guy darted over to help her pick up the mess.

"Looks like you still weren't watching where you were going." A twinkle lit his tired eyes.

Heat flooded Debbie's face. "Apparently not." She wouldn't admit she'd been distracted by his backside.

He bent to help pick up the easter eggs rocking and rolling around her feet.

She dropped to her knees and filled her arms with the colorful sugar-filled orbs. The combination of fresh air, sawdust, and natural male musk hit her, and her attraction toward the man took root.

He was new in town, within the last year or so. She'd seen him at the soccer fields a few times when she went to her nephews' games.

If he has kids, he's likely married.

Too bad. He was one attractive man.

"Can you believe it's almost Easter?" His deep voice was warm, velvety, and mellow, reminding her of the feeling she got every time she sank into a warm bath.

Additional heat filled her cheeks.

Great. I probably look like a tomato. An awkward, clumsy tomato.

"I know. It feels like Christmas was just last week." She attempted to stack the eggs in the over-sized cartons. The first layer went fine, but the second layer didn't cooperate, and more eggs fell on the floor.

"Here," he said, "you hold the box, and I'll put the eggs in."

Debbie did as he suggested, catching her breath every time his arm brushed hers. After what felt like an eternity, but was probably only a few minutes, they stood and brushed off their knees.

"Thanks for your help. I never would have gotten them all stacked by myself."

"No problem." He smiled, and his eyes twinkled again. "Drive careful now."

Debbie laughed, letting herself watch him walk away for only a second before she tore her gaze away and carefully pushed her cart to the next aisle. The grocery store would be closing soon, so she needed to finish her shopping.

She was almost done with her list when her phone pinged again.

Gina Pratt's name lit her screen.

Debbie's hand trembled as her finger hovered over the text. It was either good news or bad news. She had done everything the social worker asked. She'd taken the required classes and childproofed her whole house. She already had twin beds because her nephews slept over occasionally, and she'd bought a crib. The only thing she hadn't done yet was buy a bigger vehicle that could accommodate kids and car seats, but she was planning on it. As soon as her brother Scott was able to accompany her.

Debbie wasn't sure she could handle it if the social worker told her she'd been denied. Becoming a foster parent with the prospect of being able to adopt was her only chance at becoming a mom.

Not true. She could adopt. In fact, she'd even started the process to adopt an infant, but that process was rarely fast and could be heart-wrenching when things fell through. She didn't hold out hope something would happen on that front anytime soon, since most women who put their babies up for adoption wanted them to go to homes with two parents.

Taking a deep breath, she tapped on Gina's message.

Congratulations, Debbie! Your paperwork is all in order and you have been approved to be a foster parent.

Debbie bit back the squeal that erupted from her, letting out only a small squeak. She didn't even try to fight the happy dance that had her tennis shoes tapping on the floor.

She checked to make sure she was still alone in the aisle before pulling her gaze back to read the rest of Gina's text.

When I bring you a child to foster, I'll try to bring everything they need. But it might be good for you to have a few diapers, formula, and bottles on hand.

Debbie's chest expanded with warmth.

Diapers!

She'd never bought diapers for herself before. She laughed out loud as she pointed her cart toward the baby section.

Of course, I've never bought diapers for myself.

But she'd never brought diapers to her home for a child she would be caring for either.

Adrenaline pumped through her veins as she brought her cart to a stop in the diaper aisle. She stared at all the packages, wondering which size she should buy. Which brand was best?

Knowing she was being impulsive again, but too excited to stop herself, she grabbed one box of each size of the most expensive brand. Sheila's kids got diaper rashes from the cheap diapers when they were babies. She pushed her cart to the next aisle, carefully balancing the boxes of diapers and pull-ups.

Tears filled her eyes as she stared at the binkies, bottles, and bibs. They were all so adorable. And just looking at them made her heart ache. If she was lucky, she'd get to foster an infant. She collected a variety of sizes and colors of bottles and pacifiers. Sippy cups came next, followed by baby wash and lotion.

She flipped open the cap of the baby lotion and inhaled.

Heaven in a bottle.

Knight's Grocery–the only grocery store in Providence–didn't have a large selection of baby stuff, but Debbie managed to find a couple of small fleece blankets and stuffed animals. She'd have to plan a bigger shopping trip to the Tri-Cities area soon. It could be some time before she actually got to foster a child, but she wanted to be ready when it finally happened.

"Attention customers, the store will be closing in ten minutes. Please make your final selections and bring them to the front of the store."

Debbie pointed her overflowing cart toward the registers. As she passed the feminine hygiene aisle, she remembered she needed tampons. She didn't have to buy them often because her cycle was so irregular, but her flow was so heavy, she hated being caught without them.

She propped a box on her loaded cart and headed to checkout, barely able to see around the stack of diapers. She rounded the corner and for the second time tonight ran into another shopping cart. The previous collision had been a mere tap compared to the bone-jarring impact of this cart crash. Boxes of diapers, bottles, baby wash, and tampons scattered across the floor. Several items from the other equally loaded cart toppled to the floor too.

"I'm so sorry," Debbie said.

"Forgive me. Are you okay?" The rugged, denim and flannel man stepped around his cart and studied her.

"I'm fine. I'm such a klutz tonight."

"I think this one was as much my fault as it was yours. I was hurrying to grab a few more things before the store closes."

The deep timbre of his voice sent a shiver skittering across her skin. It had been a long time since she'd felt this level of attraction for a man. Even the men she had pursued over the last couple years hadn't made her feel this aware. It certainly wasn't for lack of trying—on her part anyway. That's probably why they were all married to other women now.

Too bad Denim and Flannel was married. Although, she couldn't recall ever seeing his wife at the soccer fields.

"Obviously, I wasn't watching where I was going. Again."

"I'm not sure how you could over all of that." He chuckled as he eyed her cart.

"Yeah, I think I got a little carried away. I got some good news tonight, and I kind of went crazy."

"Congratulations." His eyebrows rose as his gaze shifted from the diapers to her flat stomach.

"Oh, um... I'm not pregnant."

A flush colored his cheeks. "Sorry, I just assumed..." His brow creased as he motioned to the boxes of diapers in her cart.

"Understandable." Debbie didn't offer an explanation, because it felt like too much information to share with a stranger.

He bent to pick up the scattered items, and she did the same. His masculine scent hit her again, and she had to keep herself from leaning closer and taking a deep breath.

Heat filled her face as she grabbed the box of tampons near his booted feet.

"Uh... I think those are mine." He held out his hand for the box she held.

She examined the pink box, spotting a yellow R for regular. Nope. These were not the tampons she had put in her cart. She handed them over.

"I mean, they're not mine. I'm buying them, but they aren't for me. They're for my daughter." Color flooded his face again, and Debbie couldn't help herself, she busted out laughing. He grabbed another similar pink box but with a green S. "I believe these are yours."

Her laughter died instantly. *Great.* Not only did this handsome stranger think she had some sort of diaper fetish, he knew she used super-sized tampons. That was way more information than anyone needed to know about her.

She snatched the box from his hand, and they fumbled around, gathering up the remainder of their items, both avoiding eye contact with the other. As soon as Debbie had all of her stuff, she apologized again and darted away as fast as she could while trying to make sure she didn't run into anyone else.

"Debbie? Is that you?" The gray-haired cashier looked Debbie over from head to toe as she loaded her groceries onto the conveyor belt.

"It's me, Sandy." Debbie smiled back. She'd gotten this reaction a lot lately.

"I almost didn't recognize you without–" Sandy stopped talking and looked down at the conveyor belt. "I mean, I don't think I've ever seen you without your jewelry."

Debbie laughed. "A lot more has changed about me than my jewelry."

Sheila and Joy had told her if she wanted to be a mom, she should look the part. They'd convinced her to trade in what they called the "bombshell look" for the "mom look"–jeans and a t-shirt. It hadn't taken much persuasion, because the heels Debbie had worn so religiously for the past few years were starting to cause back problems. So, she'd said good riddance to the low-cut, skin-tight clothing, and enough jewelry to buy food for a medium-sized country, and she donned yoga pants and sweatshirts. And she hadn't regretted it.

"I see that." Sandy's smile was back. "You look great. Different for sure, but you also look…happier."

Something interesting happened to Debbie when she changed her wardrobe. She no longer heard others' spoken and unspoken criticism, because she now looked like everybody else. She hadn't realized the stigma she'd placed on herself by dressing in expensive, revealing clothing and jewelry.

"I am happier, thanks for noticing."

"Good. I'm happy for you."

A few minutes later, Debbie pushed her purchases out to the dimly lit parking lot and froze.

There was no way all this stuff would fit into the two tiny trunks of her sporty little car.

This is what I get for being so impulsive.

CHAPTER 2

Austin watched the pretty redhead push her shopping cart toward the front of the store. At roughly five foot five, she could barely see where she was going around the stack of diapers.

He felt like a jerk for noticing that she was unnaturally busty for someone with such a slender waist. Her narrow hips didn't exactly have the soft rounded curves of a woman who'd just had a baby, but they were attractive nonetheless.

So why is she buying so many diapers?

The fluorescent light glinted off her red hair and he took note of its remarkable color. It was the most amazing shade of red, somewhere between dark burnished copper and ripe cherries.

After ensuring she was far enough ahead he wouldn't run into her a third time, he pushed his cart to the registers. He watched the total carefully as the cashier scanned his groceries. This was the first and biggest shopping trip of the month. He couldn't afford to go over budget.

He slowed his stride as he pushed his cart out to the parking lot and approached his truck.

Beside his king-cab pick-up truck stood the redhead with the front and back trunks and passenger door open of a gleaming red Porsche.

She shifted a box from the front of the car to the back only to take it out again, then muttered something about her family never letting her live this down.

Austin cleared his throat. "Do you need help?"

She spun around and shrieked, her hand flying to her throat.

"Sorry, I didn't mean to startle you." He took a step back so she wouldn't feel threatened. "You just look like you could use some help."

Her face reddened again in the dim parking lot lights, and a small flutter spiraled up from his stomach to his chest. She was even prettier when she flushed like that.

"Like I mentioned earlier, I got carried away. I didn't stop to think about how I was going to get all this home." She waved her hand toward the three boxes of diapers still in the cart.

Austin had never driven a Porsche before, but he knew there was no way the car's two tiny trunks and the single passenger seat would hold all her purchases.

"Um… yeah, I don't think it's going to fit in your car. Maybe you should call your husband to come pick it up."

"Oh, I'm not married. And I don't own a bigger car."

Not married.

Austin didn't know why but that tidbit of information both pleased and surprised him. She was a beautiful woman with gorgeous red hair, striking blue eyes, and an attractive figure. How had some man not snatched her up already?

She must be a single mom then, with a small child. If the diapers and baby paraphernalia were anything to go by. Sympathy pulled at him. He was all too familiar with how difficult being a single parent was.

"I could call my parents or one of my sisters, I suppose," she said to herself. "But then they'll never let me live it down."

"Live it down?" There was nothing wrong with buying groceries and stocking up on diapers.

"I tend to be impulsive, and they're always telling me I should stop and take time to think things through." She shrugged and propped a hand on her hip. "They're usually right. This just proves it."

Austin rubbed the tense muscles in his neck. It was late, and he was exhausted. He wanted to get home and spend a few minutes with his boys before bedtime. But he'd never been one to walk away from someone in need.

"Let's load all the diapers into my truck, and I'll drive them home for you." It wouldn't take that long to follow her home and unload a few boxes of diapers.

"Oh, that's nice of you to offer, but you don't need to do that. I'll figure something out."

"I don't blame you for not wanting a stranger to follow you home. Especially after tonight, when it probably seems like I'm stalking you. But I assure you, I mean you no harm. I'm just trying to help out."

The redhead turned away from him, talking to herself. "Rudy is on duty tonight. But he can't keep a secret for nothing." She swung back around and held her hand out. "My name's Debbie, and I would appreciate your help."

"Austin." Her soft hand felt dainty–almost fragile–in his.

"I'll gladly pay you for your gas and time."

"That's not necessary. Now let's get these boxes loaded into my truck."

He unlocked his doors and picked up two of the boxes of diapers, noting that they were different sizes. Her baby must be ready to outgrow size one diapers and would soon need size two.

He turned back to her car to grab another box. She pulled out the box she'd been trying to cram into the microscopic trunk of the sports car. The handle of a grocery bag caught on the box and came with it. The other edge snagged on something inside the car, tearing the bag apart. Her box of tampons landed at his feet again along with baby bottles and other baby stuff.

Austin bit back a chuckle and crouched to help her pick up the items. She leaned forward to snatch up the tampons, and they bumped heads.

"Oh, sorry. Did I hurt you?" He pulled back.

"What? No, I'm just embarrassed. I swear I'm not usually this clumsy." A rosiness took over her cheeks again.

"Don't worry about it. We all have those days." He caught a whiff of her perfume, picking up hints of violet, bergamot, and sandalwood. The scent was as elegant and expensive as her car. And unfortunately, all too familiar to him. Not *her* scent exactly, but he'd smelled his share of two-hundred-dollars-per-bottle perfumes in the past.

He helped her tuck the items they'd picked up into other grocery bags. Then he went back to moving the rest of the diapers to his truck while she loaded the remainder of her purchases into her car.

As he shoved the final box in the back seat, he realized it contained size five diapers. He looked at the other boxes again.

Debbie had purchased five different sizes of diapers, plus two different sizes of pull-ups for boys and the same for girls.

How many kids does this single mother have? And why does she drive a Porsche?

As he followed the flashy red sports car, he couldn't help thinking how out of place it looked in this small northwestern town full of pick-up trucks. One thing he couldn't figure out though, she didn't have an infant seat in the Porsche, but she'd bought enough diapers for a small army of infants and toddlers.

As Debbie headed north of town, he feared offering to help her might have been a mistake. How far out did she live?

Just as he picked up his phone to call Savannah to tell her he'd be even later than he'd thought, Debbie turned on her blinker.

When the Porsche turned into a driveway just outside of town, Austin braked. He let out a low whistle as he took in the size of Debbie's house. The two story rock and stucco home with under-the-eave lighting had six windows across the front of the house on the upper floor.

Of course, Debbie drove the most expensive car in the town, so it made sense that she lived in the biggest house in the county too. His chest tightened. It had been a long time since he'd been attracted to a woman. Any woman. Why, when he finally met someone who sparked his interest, did she have to be richer than he could ever dream of being?

He followed her up the driveway and parked off to the side as she pulled into the garage. He hopped out, intent on helping her unload her other purchases before carrying in the diapers.

She smiled at him as she opened the small back trunk. "I really appreciate this, Austin. I'll have to find some way to repay you."

"It's not a problem, really." He waited for her to pull out a couple of grocery bags before reaching for the remaining sacks.

The bag in Debbie's left hand caught on the same corner of the trunk as the bag that spilled in the parking lot, ripping it wide open. For the third time that night, Debbie's box of tampons fell at his feet.

Austin laughed out loud. "I swear those tampons don't want to go home with you."

Debbie's face flushed beet-red before she dropped to the ground. "Oh, my he— I mean, good grief." She kept mumbling as she picked up her groceries and tossed them back into the trunk.

He bent to help her then remembered bumping heads with her at the store and changed his mind. The hint he'd gotten of her perfume last time was alluring enough to make him want to pull her into his arms. But he'd learned a long time ago to keep his distance from women like Debbie.

He gathered all the bags in one hand and tucked the items she tossed back in the trunk into his arms. By the time she stood up, he held all the groceries in his arms, including the rogue box of tampons.

"It might be best if I carry them the rest of the way."

The embarrassment on Debbie's face turned to frustration as she stared at him. Then her face split in a grin, transforming her expression. She not only looked approachable, she looked downright beautiful.

DEBBIE GRINNED despite the heat radiating through her body. She had never been so embarrassed in her life. Of course, she'd never met a man who wasn't embarrassed to carry her feminine hygiene products and could joke about it. Her brothers and brother-in-laws would have disappeared a long time ago.

She couldn't remember the last time she managed to embarrass herself in front of an attractive man three separate times. Four if she counted the Easter eggs. She quickly circled her car and grabbed more groceries.

Austin waited patiently for her to open the door and flip on a light.

"You can just set everything on the kitchen counter."

He paused as he stepped into the kitchen, his gaze roaming around the large room. "Which one?"

Debbie's gaze followed his, trying to see the room from his perspective. Quartz countertops, state-of-the-art, stainless-steel appliances, and more cabinets than Debbie knew what to do with lined the room.

Yes, it was a much bigger kitchen than a single person needed, but Debbie had been optimistic when she built this house. She'd hoped one day, she'd have a family to fill it.

"Put them on the island." As she lifted some of the loose items from his arms, her fingers brushed the hair on his arm. Warm tingles shot through her hand.

She stepped back and let him set the remainder down himself. Even when she'd flirted with Sheriff Robert Winters last year and touched his hand or arm, she'd never felt that kind of electricity. That's why she'd eventually stopped pursuing him after his former girlfriend moved back to town.

That's what triggered her breakdown last month; she'd run into Robert and Jessie with their new baby at Charity's Diner. They both looked so happy, and she wanted that. She was so tired of pretending she was happy simply because she had all the money anyone could want.

It's just my luck that when I finally meet a nice, good looking man who interests me like that he's married.

He didn't wear a ring, but a lot of men who work heavy labor jobs didn't wear wedding rings. And Austin's broad shoulders definitely looked like they could handle heavy labor.

"I'll get the diapers from my truck." He disappeared out the door as soon as his arms were empty.

She carried in the remainder of her groceries then helped carry in the last of the diaper boxes.

Austin set his final armload on the stack he'd built beside the counter and looked around again. "So, um…how many children do you have?"

"I don't have any…yet." Debbie raised her chin daring him to find fault with her impulsiveness.

His brow furrowed as he scratched his jaw, creating a rasping sound against his stubble. "And you're not pregnant, yet?"

Yet? Pain shot through Debbie's chest. She gave a slight shake of her head.

"I guess, that explains why you don't have a car seat in your Porsche. Or why you drive a Porsche at all." His brow creased, and he shook his head as he looked at the stack of diapers and pull-ups. "So, who are these for?"

Debbie's cheeks warmed. "I um… I got word today that I've been approved to be a foster parent. The caseworker suggested I buy a few diapers to keep on hand. Just in case, you know?"

"A few?" Austin's eyebrows raised and it looked like he was holding back a grin.

"Did I mention I tend to be impulsive?"

"Right. Well, I guess it's a good thing you have plenty of space to store all of these diapers."

Debbie nodded. She had plenty of space for lots of things she didn't have. She also had plenty of things she didn't necessarily need, because she had no one to help fill up this house.

"I'd better get my groceries home." Austin stepped toward the door.

"Are you sure I can't pay you for delivering my diapers?"

He held up both hands, palms out. "That's not necessary. Congratulations on becoming a foster parent. I hope you get to foster lots of babies who will use up those diapers."

"Thanks, me too." She followed him to the garage door.

He turned back after stepping into the garage. "I know it's none of my business, but um…when you do get a child or children, it might be easier to take them places if you…had a car that was a little…more family-friendly."

"You're absolutely right." Debbie smiled at him. It was kind of cute the way he tried not to say something she might take offense to. "It's on my to-do list. And after tonight's fiasco, it's at the top of the list. I'll probably go buy a new car tomorrow."

His brow furrowed again as he gave a slight shake of his head.

Debbie knew the look well. She'd seen it often enough on the faces of her family. And she hated it. When she wanted something, she bought it. She didn't need to look for the best deal that fit her budget. Heck, she didn't even need a budget.

She'd grown tired of feeling like people judged her for spending her money. It wasn't like she was wasteful or anything. She always put the things she bought to good use. That's why she planned on turning the Porsche in when she bought another car. She'd miss it, but she didn't need two cars.

Austin waved and continued down the steps.

Debbie watched him climb into his truck before pushing the button to close the garage door. It's just as well he was probably married. She had a difficult enough time with her self-esteem; she didn't need some stranger–no matter how good looking and nice he was–judging her for her life choices.

CHAPTER 3

Austin looked in his rear-view mirror as he drove away from Debbie's house. Talk about extravagant. No wonder her family considered her impulsive.

He'd worked in construction long enough to know there was nothing impulsive about building or buying a house though. Especially a house that size. Of course, with the kind of money she seemed to have, maybe she hadn't needed to jump through as many hoops as most home buyers. She didn't sound like she'd have much trouble buying a new car tomorrow.

Must be nice.

The thought of her being independently wealthy made her a little less attractive. He shouldn't hold her financial status against her, but he'd been criticized… and burned by the wealthy too many times to count.

He shook off his somber mood and pushed Debbie's pretty red hair and blue eyes out of his head as he pulled into the driveway of his much smaller rental home.

His boys must have been watching for him, because they both ran out of the house before Austin stopped the truck. They wore pajamas, which meant they'd already had their baths. A lot of good it did, since they came out barefoot.

Austin opened his door and slid from the truck only to be enveloped in a double hug. He wrapped an arm around each boy and squeezed. Most boys weren't this demonstrative at ages seven and nine, but the last five years had been rough on all of them, and the kids spent too many hours alone.

Austin worked long hours with a lengthy commute. He hated it, and he hoped to someday get to the point where he didn't need to work so much to support his family. That wouldn't happen for a long time yet, thanks to Cheyenne.

"Daddy, guesssss what?" Cody said with a hiss.

"What, buddy?"

"I lost another tooth. Sssee?" He grinned, exposing his toothless front gums.

"Another one, already? Did Savannah have to help pull it out?"

She probably hated having to do that.

"Nope. It fell out when I wasss eating an apple."

Austin grinned. He hoped for Cody's sake, his top teeth grew in faster than the bottom two did. The poor kid had finally lost his lisp a few months ago after almost a year of waiting for his teeth to grow in. And now it was back.

He patted the boys' backs. "I'm glad my big strong helpers are here to carry in all the groceries."

By the time he got the boys loaded with the mega-sized packages of toilet paper and paper towels, Savannah had come out to help. He gave her a quick peck on the forehead then loaded her up with groceries. After a second trip for each of them, they all worked together to unpack the goods. The boys kept up a constant discourse about their day, often talking over each other, especially when they talked about the video game they'd played.

Austin loved his boys, and he loved that they liked to tell him about their day, but they sure were loud sometimes.

"You bought pudding!" Seven-year-old Cody jumped up and down hugging the pudding cups to his chest. "Can we have one tonight pleassse?"

"Please, Dad." Dallas's pleas joined his younger brother. He was two years older than Cody, but they were like peas in a pod.

There were a lot of things Austin couldn't afford to give his kids, and he didn't keep a lot of sweets in the house. But he made it a point to make sure they got dessert occasionally.

Leaning against the counter, he folded his arms. He pretended to glare at the boys while watching Savannah out of the corner of his eye. "That depends. Did you guys do your homework?"

"Yes," they chorused, heads nodding, while Savvy gave a thumbs up.

"Did you do your chores?"

More nods and another thumbs up.

"Did you eat all your dinner?"

"Uh huh."

"Were you good for Savvy?"

The nods this time were more hesitant, and Savvy waved her hand with the palm down in a so-so motion.

Even though the boys already knew he'd say yes, he leaned forward and stared them down. They stared back. They loved this game. He leaned a little closer and narrowed his eyes. They held his gaze, unblinking. His eyes began to burn, begging him to blink.

The boys were getting better at these staring contests. Pretty soon, they were going to beat him.

Cody blinked first. He groaned and rubbed his eyes, and Austin focused on Dallas's hazel ones, so like his mother's. Both boys got their mom's copper-colored hair too. Savvy's hair was lighter like Austin's mom's strawberry blond hair.

His thoughts turned to the pretty redhead he met tonight. Debbie had sparked something in him. An attraction he hadn't felt in a long time. Not since he first fell in love with Cheyenne. Apparently, he had a thing for wealthy redheads. He resisted the urge to frown since his kids were watching him. The last thing he needed was to fall for another spoiled-rich female.

Austin's eyes stung, and just when he was sure Dallas was about to give in, the punk smiled.

Could he see his dad wavering?

"Fine. You win," Austin said, squeezing his eyes closed.

The smile that lit up Dallas's face was worth admitting defeat. He was usually a serious child, so it was always nice to see him smile. The boys gave each other high fives and opened the pudding cups.

Austin heated the plate of food Savvy left in the fridge for him and joined the kids at the table. Macaroni and cheese and chicken nuggets–one of his least favorite meals nowadays. His boys loved it, and it was a good staple to keep on hand to tide them over until payday, but he'd love a juicy steak or hamburger once in a while.

They'd eaten cheap meals like this for far too long, but he tried to keep things simple for Savannah's sake. At sixteen, she carried a lot of responsibility, filling the role of mother to her younger brothers for the past five years.

He thumbed through the mail as he ate, spotting all the usual bills plus a statement from the hospital. He still owed six thousand dollars for Savvy's emergency appendectomy last fall and Cody's bout with pneumonia in December.

Thanks to Cheyenne maxing out not one but two credit cards before she left, he'd had to put the medical bills on a payment plan. He'd be paying them for some time still. He couldn't wait for the day he was debt free. Then he'd be able to give his kids some of the things they wanted.

He sent the boys off to brush their teeth while he finished his dinner, then he joined them for a story and prayers. When he returned to the kitchen, Savvy had just finished her homework.

She pushed the laptop toward him, knowing he'd need it to pay bills. A pink paper fell to the table as she tucked her books into her backpack and deposited it near the front door. Returning to the table, she picked up the paper, chewed on the inside of her cheek for a moment before frowning, then turned and dropped it into the trash can.

"Hey, Savvy, what was that?" Austin asked.

"Nothing. It's just some information about a summer art camp at Washington State University."

"And you weren't going to show it to me?"

"What's the point? I know we can't afford it, so…" She shrugged and started loading the dishwasher.

Austin hated that Savannah was so aware of their financial situation. But she'd been the one to help him figure out how to pay the bills online, and because Austin was a slow learner—except when it came to hands-on stuff—she'd had to help him for several months. She knew there was very little money left over after the bills were taken care of.

He retrieved the paper from the garbage can and sucked in a sharp breath. Without even reading the whole spiel concerning the camp, the amount of the tuition near the bottom leaped out at him. He resisted the urge to whistle.

Six hundred fifty dollars for an art camp!

His gaze roamed over the page. The tuition covered room and board for two weeks plus advanced art classes in several different areas. All in all, he supposed it was a good deal, but it was still a lot of money.

Savvy was right, they couldn't afford it. Especially, since he'd scraped the money together last month for the boys to play soccer this spring. But she was such a gifted artist he wanted to give her every opportunity to develop her talents.

His dinner set in his stomach like a lead weight. He hated wanting to give his children something, but being unable to afford it. Christmas the last few years had been the worst. He looked up to find Savannah watching him.

His throat grew tight. "It looks like a great opportunity."

A spark of hope lit her eyes as she turned away from the sink. "Ms. Jessie said that kids who participate in this program often end up getting a scholarship at WSU."

Scholarship? Savvy was only a junior; why was she thinking about scholarships already?

Because she's smart and she's a planner.

And college was only a little over a year away. His chest tightened at the thought. He wasn't ready for his little girl to grow up and leave home. Who would watch the boys when Savvy went away to school?

That sounded selfish, but he worried about it nonetheless.

And how on earth would he pay for college? If he was lucky, he'd get Cheyenne's debts paid off this year, but that wouldn't give him much time to save for college.

Fearing he was giving Savvy false hope, he put the paper up on the refrigerator with a magnet. "I can't make any promises, but I'll see what I can do." He took note of the deadline date.

How on earth will I come up with an extra six hundred fifty dollars in three weeks?

He already worked overtime as frequently as he could, hence the reason Savvy had to take care of the boys so often.

It had been years since he'd donated plasma, but maybe it was something he needed to consider again. It wouldn't give him six hundred dollars in three weeks though.

CHAPTER 4

"Do you want to come to church with us this Sunday, Debbie?" Joy's out-of-the-blue question echoed through Debbie's head again.

Her sister had sprung the question on her while she'd made freezer meals with her mom and sisters yesterday, and something had tightened in Debbie's chest. She'd felt the lack of church worship and fellowship in her life for some time now. Being angry at God for so many years hadn't done her any good. It had only made her more bitter.

Letting go of the resentment she'd harbored for so long wasn't easy though. And Debbie had said and done some things that had hurt others. Things she needed to make right before she could get right with God again.

She looked at the to-go containers on the seat beside her. Apologizing to Amy for the hurtful things she'd said to her years ago hadn't been easy, and Debbie had ended up ordering two pieces of chocolate cake before she'd found the courage to say what needed to be said.

Of course, Amy had graciously forgiven her. Hopefully, Jessie Winters would be equally understanding.

Debbie got out of her new Escalade and entered the high school amid the rush of teenagers pouring out. She probably should have waited, but she didn't want to miss Jessie. The art teacher had just returned to teaching this week after six weeks of maternity leave. If Debbie missed her here, she would have to go to Robert and Jessie's home to make her apology, and she didn't think she could handle that.

Not because she was jealous of Jessie winning Robert's heart in a matter of months when Debbie had tried for years. Okay, so maybe she was a little jealous. But it was because Jessie had a baby, and Robert had easily accepted the role of father, even though the child wasn't his.

That's what Debbie had hoped for all along; to marry a good man who wouldn't mind adopting a bunch of children. She figured that was the only way she'd ever get a family of her own.

Until her sisters planted the idea of becoming a foster mom in her mind. Being a single parent was not Debbie's dream, but if she wanted a family at this stage of her life, she couldn't sit around and wait for a man to show up.

Debbie made her way through the crowded halls to the art room. She stepped inside to find Jessie standing beside a pretty girl with strawberry blond hair, studying a canvas on an easel.

"I think you nailed it, Savannah. You could probably add a little more texture to the foam created by the waves here along the shoreline." Jessie pointed toward the bottom of the painting. "But it looks amazing."

Savannah tilted her head as she stared at the painting. "I thought I might have overdone it, but looking at the picture as a whole, I think you're right." The girl picked up her backpack and headed toward the door. "See you tomorrow, Ms. Jessie."

She smiled at Debbie as she passed by.

Debbie returned it, then turned to find Jessie watching her.

"Hi, Debbie. What can I do for you?"

Resisting the urge to pace and wring her hands, Debbie strolled farther into the room. "I never had a chance to congratulate you on the birth of your baby."

"Thank you?" Jessie looked as confused as she had last summer when Debbie showed up at the ranch to warn her off Robert.

Full of nervous energy, Debbie continued to wander, tapping her nails on the tabletops. Jessie made her way toward her desk at the front of the room. They looked like two felines circling each other.

Just spit it out already.

Before Debbie could form the words, *"I'm sorry,"* she found herself standing in front of the easel Savannah and Jessie had been studying. The striking image of an aged, wooden fishing boat laying on a white sandy beach and gently-rolling waves took her breath away. The contrast between the azure sky, cobalt water, and alabaster sand reminded Debbie of her time spent in Greece and other tropical locales.

A strong desire to have a similar image painted on the wall between her dining room and kitchen struck her. Debbie wanted to do something amazing there, but she hadn't been able to decide what.

"Is there a reason you're here, Debbie?" Jessie's voice pulled her attention away from the picture and the idea forming in her head.

"Yes, sorry. I got sidetracked by this painting. It really is amazing, isn't it?"

Jessie crossed the room again to stand beside Debbie. "Yes, Savannah is very gifted. I find it difficult to challenge her."

"I can see why." Debbie pulled her gaze away from the painting and turned to Jessie. She folded her arms over her chest to keep her hands from fidgeting. "I'm here because I owe you an apology."

Jessie's eyes widened, and she fell back a step.

"I should never have said you didn't deserve Robert and accuse you of keeping him as a back-up plan."

"You have nothing to apologize for—"

Debbie held up a hand. Her apology was getting hijacked again. Amy had tried to do that too. "I do. I basically said a relationship with you would hurt his chances of getting re-elected. I was rude to you, and you didn't deserve that. You were going through a lot."

Jessie smiled. "The truth is, you helped me realize that I needed to do whatever I could to ensure Robert and I got a second chance."

Debbie relaxed and let her arms fall to her sides. "Well then, you're welcome, I guess. Robert looks much happier since you returned to Providence than I've ever seen him. Marriage and fatherhood suit him, and motherhood suits you." She couldn't hide the tightness those last words caused in her voice.

"Thank you." Jessie ran her fingers along the back of a chair. "You know, after the choices I made years ago, I didn't think I deserved a second chance." She raised her head and looked directly at Debbie. "But I've come to realize everyone deserves to be happy."

Debbie sucked in a sharp breath as the words pierced her heart. She agreed with Jessie, but it wasn't always that easy. Especially if God had other plans for your life. She'd gone through all of the stages of grief when she found out she couldn't have children. Then she'd gone through them all over again when her first marriage fell apart thanks to her defective body.

She'd tried to find happiness in other ways, mainly by helping others. That's how she met her second husband. With his money, she'd been able to help a lot of people, and it had brought a measure of happiness, but it hadn't given her the one thing she wanted most.

"Are you happy, Debbie?" Jessie asked in a gentle voice.

Tears sprang to Debbie's eyes, and she looked away from Jessie's compassionate gaze. She was not typically an emotional woman, but something had shifted in her recently—on her thirty-sixth birthday, to be exact—and she found herself battling the insecurities she thought she'd overcome years ago.

Her biological clock had gone haywire years ago, but her physical body was screaming for some type of fulfillment she couldn't provide.

Debbie blinked away the tears, squared her shoulders, and raised her chin. She gave Jessie a tight smile. "Of course, I'm happy."

The look in Jessie's eyes said she didn't believe Debbie, but she smiled anyway. "Good, I noticed you've made some changes recently." She motioned to Debbie's clothing. "I like the new look."

Warmth filled Debbie's cheeks. Amy had made a similar comment. Had Debbie really been that bad?

"If you want people to notice you, then you need to stand out." Debbie

could still hear Sofia's high-pitched voice in her head. *"You're a wealthy woman now. You need to look and act like it."*

Sofia had been the one person to welcome Debbie when all of her second husband's friends criticized her for being skinny and plain. Debbie had thought she needed the expensive name-brand, skin-tight clothing—that was somewhat revealing—and her flashy jewelry to get attention. But she hadn't realized it made her look… What? Unhappy? Desperate for attention?

She smiled at Jessie. "Thank you. I'm trying to make some changes in my life, but in order to move forward, I need to make sure there aren't any regrets."

Jessie laughed. "I hear you. I was *full* of so many regrets when I first returned to Providence. It wasn't until I finally accepted that I can't change the past, and I only have power over my future, that I finally found peace and contentment."

Peace and contentment. They weren't quite the same thing as happiness, but it was close. At this point, Debbie would settle for feeling content.

She'd better change the topic before she grew emotional again. "I've been meaning to talk to you about commissioning a painting." It was one thing to leave a generous tip for Amy, but Debbie needed a different tactic to make amends with Jessie.

"Really? What do you have in mind?"

"I'm having a hard time narrowing it down." Her gaze returned to the seascape painting, and ideas filled her head as she recalled the traveling she'd done. A mural would be amazing but there were so many beautiful places in the world that she'd love to have paintings of on her walls. How would she narrow it down?

I could decorate each room in the house with a theme from a different country.

Debbie's breathing sped up as the idea took root. She'd done minimal decorating since she moved into her new house, because without a family it just didn't feel like home yet.

"I can't decide if I want you to paint something from France or Italy or maybe India."

"I've never been to India." Jessie pressed her hands to her chest. "But I loved Italy and France. So rich in history and art."

"I didn't realize you'd been to Europe," Debbie said.

"Years ago, yes." Jessie told Debbie about how she'd studied abroad for eighteen months, and as they continued to talk about their favorite places to visit, they realized they had been in a couple of the same cities around the same times.

As Debbie discussed what type of paintings she wanted Jessie to do, her gaze kept returning to the painting on the easel. A lightness filled her chest as she studied the artist's style and the vivid colors. A burst of adrenaline coursed through her veins as she pictured a little coastal village in Greece that had become one of her favorite places in the whole world. She knew exactly what she wanted her mural to look like. Tingling filled her hands and fingers as an urgency to go through her pictures filled her. She hadn't felt this excited since she got the text approving her as a foster parent last week.

But it could be weeks or even months before she got to foster a child. Waiting was driving her crazy already. This project would give her something to focus on now.

"What can you tell me about the girl who painted this?" Debbie pointed to the easel.

"Like I said, she's incredibly gifted."

"Do you think she could do something similar to this but on a much larger scale?"

Jessie nodded. "With a little guidance, I think she could. Why? What are you thinking?"

Debbie explained that she'd like to hire the girl to paint a six by eight foot mural.

Jessie explained some of the challenges and intricacies of such a project then added, "She might find it overwhelming, but I'd love to see her take on a project like this." Jessie walked to her desk with purpose and picked up a pink flier and handed it to Debbie. "I'd love to see her take advantage of this exceptional summer art program offered by WSU, but I'm not sure her family can afford it. She might agree to take on the project if you offer to pay for her tuition for the program."

Debbie studied the flier. Her gaze rested on the bottom line. Six hundred and fifty dollars. That was nothing to her but many middle-class families might find it difficult to pay. An idea began to take shape in Debbie's head, and additional adrenaline shot through her, causing a prickling feeling on the back of her neck.

"Do you mind if I hang onto this?" When Jessie shook her head, Debbie asked, "What's the artist's name?"

"Savannah Reed."

Reed. Was she any relation to Dallas Reed and his younger brother Cody? She'd only read with the fourth and second grade boys twice, but they were the cutest kids. She wanted to put little toothless Cody in her pocket and take him home. Debbie pictured their red hair and freckles and the strawberry blond who had smiled at her as she walked out of the classroom and decided it was a strong possibility.

Debbie smiled at Jessie. "I don't suppose you can tell me where she lives?"

"I'm afraid not, but it's a small town." Jessie grinned and winked. "I'm sure you can figure it out."

"Indeed." Debbie laughed as she made her way to the door.

CHAPTER 5

Debbie double checked the address on the red brick home to make sure she was at the right place before approaching the front door.

It wasn't ethical for Jessie to give her Savannah Reed's address, but it hadn't taken much asking around to find out the Reeds lived in one of Dwayne Saunders's rental homes. Providence was a small town, and her sisters knew everyone, including where they lived. Never mind that the Reeds had been here for less than a year.

Debbie smoothed down her blouse and slacks before fluffing her hair. Despite her eagerness to talk to Savannah, she'd forced herself to go home and change out of her jeans and t-shirt and put on something a little nicer. If she was going to play the part of a wealthy benefactress, she should look it.

She knocked on the faded yellow door, hoping Savannah's parents would be willing to let her participate in what might sound like a hair-brained idea.

Shouts came from behind the door. "I'll get it!" Followed by, "No, Imma get it!" Running feet pounded across the floor before a thud sounded against the door.

It opened, and Debbie looked down to see little Cody Reed with his brother, Dallas, right behind him.

"Hi, boys. How are you?"

"Miss Debbie?" Dallas's nose scrunched.

"Whatcha doing here?" Cody asked.

"I came to talk to your sister and parents." Debbie smiled down at the boys. Yep, she still wanted to stuff Cody in her pocket and take him home. Dallas too.

"Why?" Dallas asked. "Are we in trouble?"

"No, of course not." Did people show up at the door often to complain about the boys who were obviously rambunctious if the race to open the door was anything to go by. "Will you tell you mom and dad I'm here?"

Dallas turned away and yelled. "Dad! Savvy!" as Cody said, "We don't have a mom."

Debbie's heart broke for the adorable little boys. Now she wanted more than ever to take them home with her.

"Cody, why are you standing there with the door open?" A deep, semi-familiar, baritone voice sent a shiver of awareness skittering across Debbie's skin, and she tried to recall where she'd heard it before.

The door opened wider, and Debbie launched into the spiel she'd rehearsed. "Hi, we've never met but—" Heat rushed up her cheeks as she took in Cody's dad. Tall, broad-shouldered, and dressed in flannel and denim. Her heart picked up speed at the sight of the knight who came to her rescue last week. An attractive five o'clock shadow covered his jaw again. "Oh, I guess we have met."

It saddened Debbie that Dallas and Cody didn't have a mother, but she couldn't help the spark of excitement that came with knowing Flannel and Denim was single.

Stop it! Haven't you had enough rejection lately?

Being single didn't equal interest. No way would Debbie express interest in a man again, unless she was certain he wanted her for more than her money.

"Debbie?"

"Austin."

"How'd you know her name, Daddy?"

Austin looked down at his son, a quizzical look on his face. "Because I met her last week." He ruffled Cody's hair. "How do you know Debbie, buddy?"

"She reads with me at school and gives me Smarties. She's nice." He gave her a toothless grin, and Debbie's heart melted.

Could she somehow sneak him into her car when she left without his dad noticing? Maybe she could lure him in with the stash of Smarties she kept in her purse. Biting back a smile at the thought, she focused on the task she came here for.

"Mr. Reed—Austin, I have a job proposition for your daughter."

"You know Savvy, too?" Austin's brows rose.

Just then, the pretty strawberry blond walked into the family room. Her brow wrinkled at the sight of Debbie at the door.

"Not formally, no, but our paths crossed this afternoon at the school." Debbie's palms grew damp. Good thing she and Austin had already met. Otherwise she'd feel the need to shake his hand. She resisted the urge to wipe her hands on her slacks. "May I come in and present the job opportunity I have for Savannah?"

"Of course." Austin stepped back and waved her in although his brow hovered somewhere between curiosity and confusion.

As Debbie walked past him, the scent of sawdust, sunshine, and pine hit her, and a surge of attraction swept over her. She discreetly swiped her hands down her thighs as she took a seat on the couch. She couldn't understand where this sudden jumble of nerves had come from. It wasn't like she'd never made business deals before. She just hadn't done it with a man that she found so incredibly attractive. And for some reason, the prospect of him and Savannah saying no made it difficult to breathe.

Surely, she could find another artist to paint the mural that had become a sudden obsession. But she didn't want another artist, she wanted this gifted girl who now looked at her like she'd grown a second head. And she wanted to give Savannah the opportunity to take advantage of the art camp Jessie mehtioned.

Cody sat beside Debbie and stared up at her, melting her heart a little more. Dallas sat on the other side of her though not as close as his younger brother. Austin dropped into a nearby armchair, and Savannah carried a kitchen chair over and perched on it, still giving Debbie a wary look.

Debbie cleared her throat and pulled three photographs from her purse. "Savannah, I saw your painting at school when I stopped by to talk to Jess—uh Mrs. Winters. Your artwork is amazing. You are very talented, and I love your style."

Rosy spots colored the girl's cheeks, and she ducked her head as she gave a hesitant smile. "Thank you."

Debbie held the photos out to Savannah. "Do you think you could paint a scene similar to these on a much larger scale?"

Savannah's hand trembled as she took the photos. "How much larger?" Her eyebrows rose as she studied the pictures.

"I'd like you to paint a mural on my wall. Maybe six feet by eight feet or so."

Savannah sucked in a sharp breath, and her eyebrows rose even higher.

"Six by eight?" Austin leaned forward in his seat. "Savvy's never painted anything that large."

"I know. Mrs. Winters let me know that the process would be considerably different than a normal painting. She also said she'd be willing to help Savannah get the project started and guide her along the way."

"She did?" Savannah's head shot up.

Judging by the light in the girl's eyes, Jessie Winters was Savannah's hero.

Debbie nodded. "Mrs. Winters thinks this project would be a good challenge for you and help you further develop your skills."

"But a six by eight mural could take weeks, maybe even months, since Savvy's still in school." Worry lines creased Austin's tan forehead.

"I'm in no hurry." Debbie shrugged. "I'm willing to pay Savannah either an hourly wage or a contracted price. And I'll buy all the supplies, of course."

Austin shook his head and shot his daughter an apologetic look. "I'm afraid Savannah doesn't have time for a project that big. She has to take care of her brothers after school every day."

Debbie's breath hitched and a heaviness settled over her. She resisted the urge to fiddle with her purse strap. She didn't understand the overwhelming desire to have Savannah paint this mural, but she wasn't ready to give up yet.

She smiled down at Cody and Dallas. "Your kids are welcome to come to my house each day. I'd be happy to pick them up from school."

Cody put his hand on her knee, tugging at Debbie's heartstrings. She covered his hand with her own.

Austin shook his head. "They may look docile now, but they're normally quite rowdy. I doubt your house is kid friendly."

Debbie scoffed. "My nieces and nephews visit all the time. My house is quite childproof." Even more so since applying to be a foster parent.

Austin raked a hand through his hair. "Savvy does far more than just watch the boys. I work late on Mondays, Wednesdays, and Fridays, so she has to help them with their homework and fix dinner."

"I can help them with their homework, and I'll even fix dinner for you all."

Do I sound desperate?

She certainly felt it for some unexplained reason.

Austin shook his head. "I can't expect you to feed my family every day." He squared his shoulders and jutted out his chin.

"I don't mind, really. I'm offering because I love kids. And I enjoy cooking."

Austin's gaze narrowed on her face, and Debbie read the mistrust there. As though he tried to figure out what game she was playing.

Debbie held his gaze, keeping her chin high.

"Why me?" Savannah's quiet question broke the stare down that had developed between Debbie and Austin.

Debbie smiled at the girl. "Your painting struck something in me." Debbie pressed a hand to her chest. "You have a unique style that I love. You're very talented, and I like to encourage people to foster their talents. That's why I'm willing to pay you generously to do the painting."

Savannah looked at her father, a mixture of hope and trepidation filling her face. Austin's face still held a combination of distrust and indecision. The girl's gaze shifted to the kitchen where Debbie spotted a pink paper stuck to the refrigerator with a magnet.

Could the art camp be the key to getting Savannah and her father to agree to do the painting? If there was one thing Sofia taught Debbie about getting what she wanted, it was to use all the weapons at her disposal.

She pulled the flier Jessie had given her from her purse. "Mrs. Winters told me about the art camp at WSU. I'd be happy to pay your tuition for the camp as part of your payment."

Savannah's eyes widened. "*Part* of my payment? That art camp costs a lot of money."

Debbie gave Savannah a patient smile. "It is a lot, but you're a talented artist, and talent like yours doesn't come cheap." She mentioned the going rate she and Jessie had discussed for artists who did this kind of work, and Savannah's eyes grew bigger by the second. "In fact, in addition to paying for the art camp, I'd like to offer you a full-ride scholarship to the college of your choice after you graduate next year."

When Savannah gasped, Austin sat back in his seat with a heavy sigh, shaking his head. He crossed his arms over his chest and pinched his bottom lip.

Debbie thought the prospect of a scholarship for his daughter would please him, but he looked like a thundercloud now. Not only was the distrust still obvious on his face, his scowl now showed distaste.

Was it directed at her personally? Or the fact that she was willing to use her money to get what she wanted?

She looked back at Savannah but watched Austin out of the corner of her eye. "Or I could pay you an hourly wage if you'd rather. If the mural goes well, I may hire you to do some other projects, too."

Judging by the deep furrow between Austin's brows, that tactic didn't help.

Savannah held her dad's gaze as though they were having a private conversation in their heads.

Debbie resisted the urge to wipe her palms on her slacks again.

Finally, Austin leaned forward again. "I think Savvy and I need some time to discuss your...proposition. Can I get back to you in a day or two?"

Proposition? He made her offer sound like a bad thing.

Debbie's stomach sank. It wasn't a "no," but it may as well be. The animosity on Austin's face and body language told her he didn't care for her proposal.

Or maybe he just doesn't like me.

The lightness she'd felt this afternoon at the school dissipated, replaced by a heaviness that enveloped her whole body.

"I understand." She gave a curt nod then pressed her lips together as she pulled a small notepad from her purse and wrote her name and cell number. Ripping out the page, she dropped it on the coffee table before standing. "I look forward to hearing from you."

Austin sprang to his feet. "I'll walk you out."

Debbie flinched. Was he waiting to get her outside to tell her what she could do with her job offer?

∽

Austin wasn't sure why he offered to walk Debbie to her car other than the pretty redhead both confused and intrigued him.

She said she'd been approved to be a foster parent, so she must like kids, but in his experience, wealthy people had little tolerance for children. Why was she so adamant Savvy needed to be the one to paint her mural?

The waning sunlight glinted off Debbie's deep red locks, and he shoved his hands into his pockets to keep from reaching out and tangling his fingers up in her curls.

"I see you bought an SUV," he said to distract himself from her hair. His gaze roamed over the gleaming white Cadillac Escalade. Talk about one heck of a family car. How many children did she anticipate fostering?

Of course she had to buy the most expensive SUV out there. Only the biggest and best were good enough for people with money like she had. He still couldn't believe she'd offered his daughter a full-ride scholarship. Austin still didn't want to think about Savannah going off to college soon.

"Yeah, my brother Scott is a mechanic. He helped me find a good used one. He wouldn't let me buy new."

At least someone in her family has some sense. The SUV may be used, but he doubted it had more than twenty thousand miles on it.

Austin grinned. "Trying to keep you from being impulsive, huh?"

"Something like that." Debbie laughed. A light musical sound that made Austin's stomach do a nosedive.

She opened her car door, and he cleared his throat. "Why are you offering to pay my daughter so much to paint a mural?"

Debbie shrugged. "I told you, I really like Savannah's style."

"But why offer her so much?" He waved a hand. "I know you explained the going rate thing, but despite being gifted, Savvy's young and inexperienced with this kind of thing."

Debbie shrugged. "I can't explain it, but I just really want Savvy to do this painting." Debbie lowered her gaze as she pressed the toe of her shoe into the crack in the driveway. "Someone taught me years ago if you want something, you go for it. You know, make people an offer they can't refuse."

A bitter taste filled Austin's mouth and his stomach knotted. Of course, rich people got everything they wanted by throwing money around.

Debbie met his gaze as though daring him to find fault with her tactics.

He bit his tongue. He knew from experience how demanding and picky wealthy people could be. And he didn't want Savvy at the mercy of this woman. But could he withhold this incredible opportunity from his daughter?

"What if she doesn't do a good enough job?" That sounded horrible, like he didn't believe in his daughter's artistic abilities. She was extremely talented, but she'd never undertaken something of this magnitude. "I mean, what if you don't like the way the mural turns out?"

"She'll still get paid, if that's what you're worried about. In fact, according to the deadline on that flier I probably ought to pay her up front."

Austin didn't want it to look like he was only worried about the money. He was much more concerned about what this might do to Savvy's self-esteem if she couldn't please the wealthy redhead. "That's not what I meant. It's just that Savannah's never had a job let alone worked for someone like you."

Debbie's eyes narrowed. "What do you mean *someone like me?*"

Heat rushed up Austin's neck. "I didn't mean… Look, I've worked for wealthy people before, and I know they can be…particular about things."

"So, because I'm wealthy, you think I'll be picky and unreasonable?" When Austin ducked his head, Debbie went on, "I have no doubt I'll be pleased with Savannah's painting, but if it doesn't turn out like I hope, then we'll paint the wall and start over." She shrugged like it was no big deal.

"Just like that?"

"Just like that. But don't worry, I'd never be spiteful about it. I'd only paint over it if Savannah isn't happy with the way it turns out."

Once the project was finished, Savvy wouldn't have a reason to go to Debbie's house anymore, so she'd never know if Debbie decided to paint over it.

Austin looked up at the sound of a screen door closing.

His neighbor, Darrell Miller, walked out of his house carrying a bag of trash. Darrell raised a hand in greeting.

Austin returned the wave before turning back to Debbie. "I see. Well, I still need to give it some thought. I'll let you know in a day or two."

Debbie smiled, and Austin's heart jolted. She was a pretty woman, but when she smiled, her whole face lit up, and she was positively radiant. Like her red hair.

He watched her climb into her SUV and back out of the driveway.

After depositing his trash in the garbage can, Darrell wandered toward Austin. "Was that Widow Wheeler? I almost didn't recognize her without the Porsche and with the way she was dressed."

"Excuse me?"

"Oh sorry, Debbie Wheeler. Folks around here call her Widow Wheeler."

Widow?

Was that how she came by her money? Austin turned raised eyebrows to Darrell, hoping the man would explain further. Darrell was about as big of a gossip as there ever was.

"Well, we don't call her that to her face of course. But when she came back to town after her second husband—the wealthy one—died, she kept informing people she was a widow, as if we all thought she might have gotten her money by illegal means or something. Funny thing though, she went back to her maiden name of Wheeler, so Widow Wheeler sort of stuck."

"Widow, huh?"

Her second husband died, but why did her first husband let her go?

Maybe he wasn't wealthy enough to support the lifestyle she wanted.

That thought sure hit home. Austin's stomach turned sour.

Debbie may be pretty, but she had expensive tastes. Her new SUV proved that. Austin learned a long time ago that not only could he not support such a lifestyle, he had no desire to live that way.

"Yeah, it's been about four years since she came back to town," Darrell said, interrupting his thoughts. "And she's been on a quest ever since to find husband number three."

A sudden chill filled Austin. "Why do you say that?"

Did Debbie have ulterior motives in asking Savvy to paint a mural? Is that why she was so eager to have the kids come to her house after school? So Austin would have to come pick them up. He thought back on their multiple run-ins with each other at the grocery store a few days ago. Had those been planned?

No, they were accidents.

And as much his fault as it was hers, especially the second one. Surely, Debbie wouldn't use his daughter to get to him. But hadn't she said if she wanted something, she went for it? All she had to do was make people an offer they couldn't refuse. And she'd done that with Savvy. He'd seen the wheels turning in his daughter's mind, despite the trepidation in her eyes. She wanted to do this painting.

He shook his head. Why would Debbie be interested in him? Just because he found her attractive didn't mean she thought the same of him. Besides, he certainly didn't have anything to offer her.

"Yeah, she's flaunted all her assets, if you know what I mean..." Darrell waved his hands in a curvy, hour-glass motion in the age-old sexist action used to denote a woman's figure. "...in pursuit of one man after another pretty relentlessly over the years, but most of the eligible bachelors are married now."

Austin didn't know what to think of Darrell's implications concerning Debbie. What exactly was he saying? No way would he let his daughter hang around a woman who used her body to—

"Maybe she finally gave up trying to find a husband and that's why she's dressed so normal. Gotta say I almost didn't recognize her without all the jewelry and sexy clothing."

Sexy clothing?

Austin wished his talkative neighbor would shut up now. If Darrell hardly recognized her, how did she usually dress?

He pictured the rose-colored blouse Debbie wore today. It wasn't as form-fitting as the t-shirt she wore at the grocery store last week, but it—coupled with the expensive slacks—definitely accented her figure. Neither outfit could be considered revealing or inappropriate in any way.

Debbie had been sweet and kind with the boys, but before he agreed to let Savvy paint the mural, he needed to make sure Widow Wheeler wouldn't be a negative influence on his impressionable teenage daughter.

CHAPTER 6

Austin parked his truck in Debbie's driveway. Her house—or rather mansion—looked much larger in the daylight than it had last week when he drove her diapers home for her. He studied the steep pitch of the gabled roof.

Glad I didn't have to shingle that.

A grin pulled at his lips as he recalled Debbie's frustration over the box of tampons that had repeatedly fallen at his feet. She was cute when embarrassment colored her cheeks.

Shaking his head, he climbed from his truck and raked his hands through his hair then turned to check his reflection in the truck window to make sure he hadn't messed it up. He wasn't trying to impress Debbie, but he had to discuss a delicate topic with her. Showing up looking disheveled wouldn't help.

He made his way to the front door, smoothing down the front of his shirt, before pressing the doorbell. He wore a flannel shirt—his typical October through April attire—but at least it was clean.

It had only been twenty-four hours since Debbie came to his house and Savannah had hounded him all afternoon to make a decision. Last night, she'd been reluctant because she wasn't sure if she could do what Debbie wanted, but after talking to Ms. Jessie, who promised to help her get started and guide her, Savannah was eager to start the project. She'd called him at work half a dozen times this afternoon to see if he'd made a decision yet. Repeatedly, insisting she could do it and was eager for the chance to earn the money for art camp.

But Austin needed to figure out what kind of woman Debbie was. Was she the woman he met at the grocery story, who got carried away buying diapers? Or was she the woman people called Widow Wheeler, who was looking for her next husband?

The door opened, and he sucked in a sharp breath. There stood Debbie in a flowing white skirt and a pretty blue blouse—Savannah would probably call the color cerulean or something equally exotic. All Austin knew was it made her blue eyes look almost electric. She was gorgeous.

His heart skipped at the sight of the mass of red curls surrounding her face. Again, he marveled that this woman was single.

"Hi, Austin." Debbie smiled, and his heart raced a little faster.

"Hey." His voice squeaked. He cleared his throat. "I mean, hi."

Her face fell. "I've been waiting for a call or text. But you coming to see me in person means you probably don't have good news for me."

Austin scratched his neck. "Not bad news necessarily, but I do have some questions before I agree to let Savvy work for you."

He wished he could afford to pay the tuition for Savvy's art camp himself and not subject his daughter to working for the wealthy redhead. What if she turned out to be critical and demanding, like Cheyenne's parents?

Debbie stepped back and opened the door wider. "Of course, come in."

"Are you sure? You look like you're getting ready to go somewhere. I can come back another time."

Anything to delay the awkward conversation he needed to have with her.

Debbie waved a hand. "Oh, I'm not going anywhere. I'm just having a good hair day, so I thought I'd dress up a little."

His gaze jumped to her hair again. She was definitely having a good hair day.

"I'll try not to take up too much of your time." Austin stepped inside, resisting the urge to fidget by clasping his hands together behind him.

His gaze roamed over the wide entryway, from the hardwood floors to the vaulted ceiling with an expensive Crystal chandelier. A wide staircase swept up one side of the entry to a balcony on the second floor.

Debbie closed the door and led him past a sparsely decorated sitting room with an arched doorway to the kitchen where he'd deposited the diapers last week. "Will you join me for a treat?"

"Oh no, that's okay." Austin stepped back.

Again, his gaze wandered around the room. Custom oak cabinets, gleaming countertops, crown molding. No expense was spared on this house.

"Please save me from myself. I got carried away yesterday and ordered two pieces of chocolate cake at Charity's Diner. It's so rich, I'll never be able to eat them both." She crossed the kitchen to the fridge and pulled out two take-out containers.

Within minutes, Austin was seated across from Debbie at the small table in the breakfast nook with a fat slice of chocolate cake and a glass of milk. A wall of windows let in the evening light, giving the area a soft, almost romantic glow. He wished Debbie had insisted they sit at the larger, much wider mahogany table he'd glimpsed in the next room.

"So, you said you have some questions for me?" Debbie poked her fork into the cake.

He fiddled with his fork, dreading the topic he needed to discuss with her. Before he could find the words to broach the subject, she put a bite of cake in her mouth.

"Mmm..."

The unexpected sound created an awareness in Austin he hadn't felt in years. His gaze lingered on her face. Her long eyelashes fluttered closed, resting on her cheeks, and her pink lips pursed.

She opened her eyes to see him staring at her. "Sorry, this cake just gets me every time. It's amazing—so moist and rich."

Austin tore his gaze away and forced himself to take a bite. His own eyes drifted closed when the decadent chocolate hit his tongue. "Mmm... That *is* good."

He hadn't tasted anything that rich and delicious in years.

Debbie laughed. "See, I told you."

Austin took another bite, barely suppressing a moan of his own, before he cleared his throat and brought up the subject he needed to discuss.

"Savannah is eager to tackle your project, but I have some...reservations."

"As any good parent should. I'm happy to answer any questions you have." She put a hand to her chest. "I'm an open book."

Austin put down his fork and scratched his neck. "I've um...heard some things about you that concern me about...what kind of influence you might have on my daughter."

Debbie's eyes widened, and her fork fell from her hand, clattering against her plate. Rosy spots filled her cheeks, reminding Austin of the doll his little sister had when they were young.

Her chin rose a fraction, and she gave a tight smile. "I know what people say about me, and most of it's conjecture. They call me a fake because I look so different now than I did when I left town at eighteen."

"A fake?" Austin hadn't heard anyone call her that.

Debbie squared her shoulders. "I was a late bloomer." She pointed at her head. "My hair was a much lighter color when I moved away. It darkened up during my early twenties. People think the color comes from a bottle, but it doesn't." She pointed to her eyes next. "They say the same about my eyes."

He looked into the eyes that matched her vivid blue shirt. "They think you wear contacts?"

"Yes, because my eye color varies from day to day, depending on the color of my shirt. But I don't wear contacts." Pink tinged her cheeks again. "Okay, so my eyelashes *are* fake, but that's only because I hardly have any eyelashes at all."

Austin studied her lashes. At least they weren't ridiculously long like some women wore. Like Cheyenne always wore. Debbie's lashes were the perfect length and thickness to emphasize her gorgeous eyes instead of detracting from them. She wore little makeup; her blue eyes with flecks of green in them were striking enough without it. Her eyes reminded him of pictures he'd seen of the Caribbean ocean.

His mouth went dry as he acknowledged how attractive Debbie was. He sat back in his chair and drew in a slow, steady breath. The last thing he needed was to get messed up with another pretty redhead. Especially a wealthy one.

Debbie must have just been getting warmed up because she kept talking. "And yeah, my nails are fake obviously, but come on, what woman doesn't like having pretty nails? And it's not like they're so long I can't function."

He glanced at her delicate hands as she displayed her nails. Her pink-tipped fingers were no more extravagant than her eyelashes. Just long enough to make people notice and wonder if they were real or not.

Cheyenne had often insisted on having acrylic nails. But she'd worn hers so long it hampered her ability to do things like change diapers and wash dishes.

"Okay, so maybe I am a big fat fake," Debbie said in a dejected tone. She pointed to her chest. "Because these are fake too."

Austin choked on the bite of cake he'd just put into his mouth. Tears streamed down his face as he tried to get his coughing under control. Did she really just say that?

"I mean, I was a late bloomer, but I certainly didn't bloom that much. I had a good reason for getting an enhancement though. It wasn't just because I was vain."

Do not look. Don't look at her chest.

Stunned by her frankness, he found his gaze dipping to her ample bust-line. Though not overly large, she was definitely bustier than most women with such a slender waist. Heat filled his cheeks when he realized he was staring, and Debbie had stopped talking.

He raised his gaze to her face. Her animation and the hint of haughtiness she'd displayed earlier had dimmed.

He should say something, but *"they look nice"* didn't sound appropriate. "I...uh."

"I've never been happy with my figure. I mean, my younger sisters inherited my mom's curves. It wasn't fair. Why did I have to be the only flat-chested female in my family?"

Austin raised a hand to stop Debbie. This was not the direction he thought this conversation would go. "I don't need to know—"

"No, it's fine." Debbie waved away his protest. "It's not like it's a secret, and I did say my life was an open book. So if it helps you make up your mind about letting Savannah paint my mural, then I'll tell you whatever you want to know."

Austin couldn't think of a way to circle back to the negative influence thing again without offending her.

Debbie cleared her throat and started talking again. "Seven years ago, I married a very wealthy older gentleman."

Austin's interest piqued. "How much older?" The words were out before he could stop them.

Debbie raised her chin again, her gaze narrowing, as if she knew her response wouldn't be well-received. "I was twenty-nine, and he was sixty-eight. It was a marriage in name only, and contrary to what people believe, I didn't marry him for his money."

Austin resisted the urge to let out a long whistle.

Talk about older alright.

Debbie pushed cake crumbs around her plate with her fork. "I had my reasons for marrying him, but most people don't understand them, so I don't bother sharing them anymore." She gave a tight smile. "People called me Peter's trophy wife. Except I wasn't much of a trophy. I was skinny, plain, and flat-chested. I was frequently criticized and ridiculed in Peter's social circles. But he had a good friend whose wife took me under her wing. And yes, Sofia was a trophy wife. At the advice of Sofia, and with Peter's encouragement, I had surgery. And I've been much happier with my figure ever since."

Austin couldn't fault Debbie for getting augmentation to help her self-esteem, but he still saw uncertainty in her eyes each time she squared her shoulders and raised her chin in that haughty air he'd seen from rich people too many times to count.

If not for the money, why did she marry such an old man? It obviously wasn't for an intimate relationship if it was in name only.

And why on earth is she telling me all of this?

Austin shoved another bite of cake into his mouth before scratching his neck again. "I haven't heard anyone call you fake, and although I'd heard you'd been married twice, I didn't need to know any of that other stuff."

"Oh." Another flush covered Debbie's cheeks. "Apparently, I'm a little too talkative, as well as impulsive."

Austin forged on, coming straight to the point. "I've heard you're looking for husband number three, and I just want you to know you're barking up the wrong tree."

"What?" Debbie sprang to her feet. "You think I want to hire your daughter to get your attention? What an arrogant assumption!"

Austin came to his feet too. "I'm not saying I'm some great catch, because I'm not. I'm far from perfect. But I've heard that in recent years, you've thrown yourself at one man after another in town trying to find husband number three. I won't allow my young, impressionable daughter to work for someone who has questionable morals."

Debbie gasped and stared at him wide-eyed, but he pushed on. "If my kids are going to spend time in your home, I need to know they aren't going to encounter...something inappropriate."

Debbie's eyes flashed with anger. "How dare you come into my home and accuse me of being a—a floozy?"

Austin softened his voice. "I'm not accusing you of anything." Except he kind of had. He shook his head. "I simply want to make sure I'm not sending my kids into an environment they shouldn't be in."

"I think it's time for you to leave." Debbie turned toward the front door.

"No wait. I'm sorry." He grabbed her hand.

Electric shocks raced up his arm. He let go of her and shoved his hands into his pockets.

"Look, I didn't mean to come in here all accusatory. I'm just worried about protecting my kids. They've been through a lot."

"I understand." She sighed. "Child Protective Services has deemed me fit to be a foster parent, so that should tell you there's nothing to worry about." Debbie's shoulders slumped as she lowered her gaze to her hands. She picked at her nails. "As for me throwing myself at some of the men in this town..." Color flooded her face and neck clear to the open collar of her blouse. "I may have flirted with a few men in recent years, expressing my interest. And unfortunately, I don't have much of a personal bubble, so I probably appeared kind of forward, but I never threw myself at them in the way you're insinuating." She covered her face with her hands. "Okay, that's not entirely true. I did kind of throw myself at Ja—one guy. But in my defense, I wasn't really myself that night."

"What do you mean?"

Debbie sat back down at the table, so Austin joined her. She stared at the wall behind him as she spoke. "I'd finally gotten a date with one of the guys I'd been interested in, but I came down with a horrible cold the day before the date. I didn't want to cancel because I was afraid I wouldn't get another chance to go out with him. So I took some heavy duty cold medicine. A double dose. I should have known better, because most medicines make me a little loopy as it is, but then I realized I'd accidentally taken the night-time stuff. Well, I didn't want to sleep through our date, so I drank a five-hour energy drink."

She propped her elbows on the table and hid her face in her hands again. "The whole night is a little fuzzy, but I'm pretty sure I said and did some things I'm not proud of. Fortunately, Ja— my date was a gentleman and nothing happened."

Austin bit back a grin as he pictured a tipsy and hyper Debbie throwing herself at her date. The man must have been a saint. His smile faded as he recalled the way Cheyenne had thrown herself at him again and again. Austin hadn't remained a saint for very long. He meant it when he said he was far from perfect.

Debbie dropped her hands and with an air of defeat, looked him in the eye. "In an effort to clear the air, and squelch any other rumors you may have heard about me, I will admit that I used to wear much more…revealing clothing. A carry over from Sofia's influence and the desire for attention." She tapped her nails against the table. "I don't dress like that anymore. In fact, I've recently revamped my wardrobe and undergone something of a makeover." She tucked a lock of hair behind her ear as she squared her shoulders again, but Austin could still read the uncertainty in her eyes. "I promise you won't regret letting your children be in my home and around me."

If Child Protective Services found her acceptable to be a foster parent, then Austin was probably putting too much stock in Darrell's ramblings.

He grinned as he looked around the spacious kitchen. "No, but you might. The boys can be pretty rambunctious."

CHAPTER 7

*D*ebbie danced and hummed as she mopped the hardwood floors of the kitchen and dining room. A thrill of energy zinged through her as she skirted around the drop cloth spread around the section of wall where Savannah would start painting today.

Technically, she'd already started. Last Saturday, Debbie accompanied Jessie and Savannah to the Tri-Cities area to buy the supplies for the mural. Later that afternoon, they'd whitewashed the wall, then they'd both come over yesterday evening to mark a grid that would help Savannah proportion the painting properly.

Debbie wiped her brow. She'd worked up a sweat cleaning her already clean house, but so much nervous energy flowed through her today, she couldn't sit still if she tried.

No, not nervous energy. Excitement. She couldn't wait for Savvy to start the painting, but she especially looked forward to having Dallas and Cody here all afternoon.

She smiled as she remembered the shy smile and wave Cody had given her at church yesterday. She would be equally excited to see their father this evening if he hadn't accused her of hiring Savvy because she had designs on him. Sure the man was handsome, but he obviously had an ego the size of Mt. St. Helens.

Her blood still grew hot at the insinuation. She used to think she needed a man to have a family, but she'd decided a while ago not to base her happiness on anyone else. She didn't need a man to foster and hopefully, to adopt. That didn't mean she wouldn't love to have a man at her side, but it wouldn't be arrogant Austin Reed, no matter how attractive he was.

An hour later, she headed to the kitchen intending to set out the lasagna she'd made with her sisters last week to thaw for dinner. Then maybe she'd whip up a batch of cookies for an after school snack for the Reed children before taking a shower and getting ready to pick them up.

Her phone rang before she reached the freezer. Debbie's heart leaped to her throat at the sight of Gina Pratt's name on her screen. She sent up a little prayer, "Please let this be a good call," as she answered the phone.

"Hello?" Debbie's heart remained lodged in her throat as she and Gina exchanged pleasantries, then Gina got to the point.

"I have a little three year old boy who needs a place to stay for a while, maybe even as long as a couple of weeks. Can you take him?"

Tears filled Debbie's eyes as she sank onto a barstool. Her heart raced so fast she struggled to breathe. "Yes, absolutely. I can take him."

She placed a hand on her chest and sucked in a deep breath, trying to calm herself.

"Fantastic. I'll be there in about thirty minutes with Noah."

"Okay." It was all Debbie could do to make her voice sound normal.

Gina ended the call, and Debbie raced to shower before Noah—what a cute name!—got there.

Twenty-five minutes later, she was still fluffing her damp hair when the doorbell rang. Debbie hurried down the hall, then forced herself to slow her stride and her breathing before she opened the door.

She sucked in a sharp breath at the sight of tall, slender, forty-something Gina standing there holding a duffel bag and a small dark-haired boy with the biggest brown eyes Debbie had ever seen.

Noah had the thumb of one hand in his mouth and the other wrapped around a lock of Gina's long blond hair.

Debbie waved Gina in and guided them down the hall to the playroom, where she hoped to distract Noah from the fact he was about to be left with a stranger.

Still holding Noah, Gina sat on a sofa. She rubbed his arm. "Noah, this is Debbie. You get to stay with her for a few days. She's really nice."

Debbie's heart pounded out an erratic pattern against her ribcage as she sat nearby.

"Want my mommy." Noah's eyes filled with tears, and Debbie's heart ached for the sweet little boy.

"I know you do, sweetie, but your mommy has to stay in the hospital for a few days. She asked me to find someone really nice to take care of you while she's there."

Debbie slowly reached out and gently stroked Noah's arm. "Hi, buddy. I'm so glad you're going to stay with me. We're going to have so much fun."

Noah turned his head into Gina's chest and pulled the lock of hair he clung to close to his face.

Gina gave Debbie an apologetic look then shifted to the floor with Noah to sit by the toy cupboard.

Debbie joined them and pulled out blocks, cars, and animals for Noah to play with. Her nephews had mostly outgrown these toys, but Debbie kept them around, hoping someday she'd have kids of her own that would play with them.

It took twenty minutes for Noah to finally slide off Gina's lap and engage with Debbie. During that time, Gina filled Debbie in on the situation. "Noah's dad hasn't been a part of the picture since right after he was born, and his mom was in a serious car accident this morning. She's in serious condition. His grandmother will be flying in from Georgia, but she's a caregiver for her disabled aunt and needs time to make some arrangements. She may not get here until next week."

Debbie sent up a little prayer for Noah's mom, as her heart broke for the little boy.

Thirty minutes later, Gina left Noah with Debbie. Equal parts excitement and apprehension filled her as Gina disappeared.

Fat tears fell on Noah's cheeks. "Want my Mommy."

Debbie gathered him into her arms. "Shh… It's going to be okay, sweet boy."

When Noah refused to be distracted by toys again, she curled up on the couch with him and turned on a movie. After thirty minutes of crying, the poor boy grabbed a lock of her hair and fell asleep in her arms.

Debbie's heart pounded extra hard for half a dozen beats before settling down. She continued to hold him, gently stroking his baby-soft skin. She felt bad for the circumstances that brought Noah to her, but her heart swelled at being given the opportunity to care for this precious little boy.

Sometime later, Debbie's phone chimed with a reminder. Disoriented, she opened her eyes. It took her several long seconds to realize she'd dozed off too.

He stirred when she pulled her phone from her back pocket. She checked her screen to find the reminder to pick up the Reed children. Gasping, she sat up straight. She was supposed to pick them up in fifteen minutes.

She got to her feet, still cradling Noah and hurried to find her purse. When Noah got teary-eyed and wrapped a fist in her hair again, she shoved a juice box, a package of goldfish crackers, and some Smarties into her purse.

Hurrying out into the garage, she remembered she'd told Gina she already had a car seat for Noah. A car seat that still sat in a box on the shelf in her garage. She opened the door of the Escalade and set him inside, then grabbed the box with the car seat and ripped it open, breaking a nail in the process. She bit back the swear word that flew to her lips. Just one of the many changes she was trying to make.

Noah started crying, so Debbie opened the package of goldfish and set him on the leather seat to eat his snack while she buckled the car seat into place. It took a lot longer than she expected because the safety restraint system wasn't that easy to figure out.

By the time she was ready to buckle Noah into the car seat, goldfish littered the seat and floor. Many of them crunched to pieces.

Debbie bit her tongue to keep from cussing again. She could clean the SUV. There was no point in getting upset with a child who had been through so much today.

She finally got him buckled in and the goldfish cleaned up, mostly, then remembered that Austin said Cody still needed a booster seat. Debbie grabbed another new box off the shelf and ripped it open, being careful not to break another nail.

Noah cried all the way to the high school, where Savannah waited outside, looking stressed. She made it a point of checking the time on her phone before climbing into the SUV.

"I know," Debbie said. "I'm so sorry I'm late. My afternoon got derailed."

"Whatever, let's just hurry to pick up my brothers before they call my dad."

∼

DEBBIE CARRIED Noah into the house with the Reed children trailing behind her. Fortunately, Noah stopped crying when they picked up Dallas and Cody. Dallas playing peek-boo and pulling silly faces at Noah helped.

She gave them a quick tour of the house, making sure they knew where the bathrooms were, and that the dining room where Savannah would be working was off limits. She hoped their excitement over the game and theater rooms downstairs would provide incentive for getting their homework done quickly.

"Okay, do you guys want to do your homework first or have a snack?"

"Snack!" Dallas and Cody shouted in unison.

"Snack it is. Go wash your hands."

"I better go make sure they actually use soap," Savvy said as she followed the boys down the hall.

Debbie washed Noah's hands at the kitchen sink then put him down so she could cut up some apples. He immediately wrapped an arm around her leg and stuck his thumb in his mouth.

"Hey, buddy." She picked him back up. "It's okay. I'm not going anywhere. Do you want to be my helper?"

Noah gave a solemn nod.

Debbie grabbed a bag of apples from the fridge and pulled a stool over to the sink for Noah to kneel on. "Can you help me wash these?"

"Me do it." He grabbed the apples from Debbie and dropped them in the sink.

Less than five minutes later, Noah's shirt was soaked and so was Debbie's. Two of the apples had fallen on the floor more than once, and Noah now wore peanut butter from ear to ear.

That boy had the fastest hands Debbie had ever seen, and he wanted to do everything by himself.

Cody and Dallas thought Noah was hilarious and kept laughing at him, which made Noah ham it up even more.

It was all Debbie could do to keep Noah busy with play dough that ended up everywhere while she helped the boys with their homework.

She'd never been so eager to tell someone to go play with toys.

"Dallas and Cody, you guys keep an eye on Noah, please," Debbie said before making her way back to the kitchen to clean up the play dough.

Savannah poked her head around the wall of the dining room. "I wouldn't count on Dallas and Cody keeping a very good eye on Noah."

"Good to know. I'll check on them in a minute. After I clean up this mess."

"Who is Noah, anyway?"

"I'm fostering him. His mom was injured in a car accident this morning and needs someone to take care of him for a while."

"Where's his dad?"

Debbie shrugged as she swept up play dough. "I guess he's never really been in the picture."

"Oh." Savannah's gaze dropped to her paint splattered hands, and Debbie stopped sweeping, wondering—not for the first time—where the Reed children's mother was.

Asking outright seemed insensitive. Debbie could tell Austin worked hard to provide for his family and meet his children's needs, but sometimes a girl just wanted her mom. Boys too for that matter, if Cody's attention the other night was anything to go by.

Savannah returned to her painting, and Debbie decided to let the subject drop. Maybe, with time, she could get the girl to trust her.

Once the floor was clean, Debbie checked on the boys. They had moved from the game room to the playroom, and it was already a mess, but they played nicely together, so she let it go. Debbie returned to the kitchen to start dinner.

Dinner!

"Oh no! I forgot to set the lasagna out of the freezer!" She hurried to the freezer to pull out the biggest of the foil pans she'd brought home last week.

Savannah poked her head around the corner again. "Everything okay?"

"I hope so. What time does your dad usually get home on Mondays?"

"About seven or seven-thirty."

Debbie checked the clock then read the 3 x 5 card taped to the top of the lasagna. It would be cutting it close, but it should get done in time.

She turned on the oven and shoved the lasagna in without waiting for it to preheat. After double checking that she had all of the makings for a salad, she hurried down the hall and checked on the boys again. Dallas and Cody had discovered the Xbox console hidden in the cabinet. They now played a video game while Noah jumped on the couch and cheered them on.

Normally, Debbie didn't tolerate that kind of behavior, but she was relieved that the little boy felt at home and no longer cried for his mom. She returned to the kitchen again, intent on making the cookies she didn't get to earlier. Thank goodness she had more than one oven.

Quite some time later, she heard Cody yell, "Ready or not, here I come."

They're playing hide-n-seek. How cute.

She just hoped they stayed out of her closet. That was one place she didn't want trashed. Most of the rest of the house was pretty kid-proof.

She'd just slipped the last pan of cookies into the oven when Dallas and Cody walked into the kitchen with hands tucked behind them and heads hung low.

Debbie had seen that look too many times to count on her nephews' faces. Her stomach plummeted. "Oh no, what happened?" All kinds of scenarios flashed through her mind from broken toys, to spilled soap, to someone bleeding.

"We lost him," Dallas mumbled, and Cody nodded, looking like he might burst into tears any second.

"Lost who?" Then it dawned on Debbie that Noah wasn't with the boys. Her stomach dropped even lower as a vice squeezed her heart, stealing her breath. "Where's Noah?"

Both boys shrugged in sync. "We don't know," Dallas said at the same time Cody said, "We can't find him."

Savannah stepped out of the dining room wide eyed, wiping her brush on a cloth. "You guys were supposed to keep an eye on him!"

"We did, but he's really good at hide-n-seek, and we can't find him." Now Dallas looked like he might cry too.

"It's okay, boys," Debbie said in a voice that sounded much calmer than she felt. "We'll all work together to find Noah, okay?" She looked at Savannah who nodded and set her brush and rag down.

Debbie stepped toward the hall. "Noah, it's time to come out now, buddy! The game's over. You won!"

Thank goodness the door to the swimming pool is locked.

Debbie froze halfway down the hall as an icy chill swept over her. She pressed a hand to her roiling stomach.

Wait. I locked it this morning, didn't I?

She turned to Savannah. "Help the boys search each room. I'm going to check to make sure the door to the pool is still locked."

"You have a pool?" Cody asked with a shout. "Cool!"

Savannah grabbed Cody's arm. "We are not swimming right now. We have to find Noah."

Debbie hurried out to the garage as Savannah herded her brothers down the hall.

Reaching the door to the pool, she twisted the knob.

Locked.

Relief washed over Debbie. She grabbed the key from the small hook near the top of the door frame and unlocked the door. It was impossible for Noah to get into the pool area without the key, but she needed to be sure. She'd never forgive herself if something happened to him.

She spent several long minutes searching below the surface of the water in the pool and the hot tub before heaving a sigh of relief. She checked behind the stack of inflatable tubes in the corner, and under the lounge chairs along the far side, then she checked under the wicker patio set on the other side near the hot tub before leaving the pool area.

After locking the door again, she joined the others in the house.

Spreading out, they searched each room, then Debbie and Savvy went back and re-checked the rooms Dallas and Cody had checked.

Then they checked all over again, emptying closets and lying on the floor to check under the beds. Debbie searched every inch of her closet, since the boys had left it in only mild disarray. With each passing second, her chest grew tighter.

Savannah's face looked as grim as Debbie felt by the time they gathered back in the kitchen. "Where could he have gone?"

"I don't know. We've searched every inch of this house." Debbie's stomach hardened as she looked at the front door. Had he gone outside?

Savannah's gaze followed hers. "I'll check the backyard, you check the front. Dallas, come help me. Cody, go with Miss Debbie."

Still on the verge of tears, Cody slipped his hand into hers. "We made a rule of no going outside," he said in a small voice.

Debbie was on the verge of tears herself, but she squeezed his hand anyway. "I know, honey, but sometimes little kids don't always obey the rules. Don't worry, we'll find him."

I hope.

CHAPTER 8

Austin yawned as he turned into Debbie's driveway. Afraid of how horribly his boys might have behaved, he wished Savvy had her own car, so she could bring the boys home, and he wouldn't have to face Debbie.

It was bad enough he didn't care for wealthy people, but pretty, rich women always rubbed him the wrong way. Especially when they used their looks and money to get what they wanted.

Debbie had assured him she wasn't after him, but having to come to her house every day to pick up his kids was more contact than he wanted to have with the attractive widow. Because as much as he disliked wealthy people, Debbie always made his heart rate pick up a little.

He'd already had a long talk with Savvy about how wealthy people could be difficult to work for and how she needed to stand up for herself. He'd also made sure she knew he was behind her all the way. No matter what.

He wasn't sure how they'd work things out if this job went south since they had already registered Savvy for the art camp with Debbie Wheeler footing the bill via her credit card.

He'd also lectured the boys on how to behave. The last thing he needed was for them to break a three-hundred-dollar bottle of perfume or something. He recalled the way Cody put his hand on Debbie's leg a few days ago and looked at her with more adoration than Austin had ever seen on the boy's face. The kid was hungry for female—specifically motherly—attention. That was his biggest regret about moving away from his parents in Boise.

He climbed from his truck and walked to the front door. As he raised his hand to knock, the door burst open.

"Oh, Austin." Debbie grabbed the front of his shirt in both fists. "Please tell me you didn't see a little boy out on the highway."

"What?" Austin's blood turned cold, and his thoughts jumped to his boys.

"We lost him, Daddy." Cody tugged on his sleeve, and Austin remembered to breathe.

With his heart racing for a much different reason than he'd expected, he grabbed Debbie's shoulders. "What happened? Where's Dallas?"

Her head jerked back. "Dallas? He's fine. He's checking the backyard with Savannah. But we can't find Noah."

Sighing, Austin released Debbie. "Who's Noah?"

Tears gathered in her eyes. "He's the cutest and busiest little boy. Gina, the social worker, only brought him to me this afternoon, and I've lost him already. I'm the worst foster parent ever!"

Understanding dawned on Austin as the tears fell onto Debbie's cheeks. He wrapped an arm around her. "What happened? How old is Noah?"

"He's only three. The boys were playing hide-n-seek with him, but now we can't find him."

"We found him the first time, Daddy, but then he hid real good, and now he's lost." Cody's voice wavered.

Austin picked up his son. "He's got to be here somewhere. How about I help you look for him."

"I bet you find him. You're the best at hide-n-seek." Cody wrapped his arms around Austin's neck and squeezed. The gesture usually made Austin feel ten feet tall, but today, it did nothing to dispel the sense of dread filling him.

He joined Debbie and Cody as they searched the front yard, all the while hearing Savvy and Dallas calling Noah's name from the backyard.

When they came up empty-handed, he feared Debbie might faint on him. She kept one hand pressed to her stomach—as though she might throw up—and the other fluttered around her neck—as if the collar of her blouse choked her.

He put his arm around her again and guided her into the house. "Hey, it's going to be okay. We'll find him. How long has he been missing?"

Savvy and Dallas entered the back door as he guided Debbie through the front. Dallas ran and gave him a hug. He looked as upset as Cody.

Debbie and Savvy shared a grim look. Debbie spoke first. "Boys, how long did you look for Noah before you came and got help?"

They both shrugged then spoke at the same time.

"Forever," Cody said.

"A long time, cuz we didn't want to tell you we lost him." Dallas looked down at the floor.

"He's been missing for at least twenty minutes—" Debbie's voice broke, and she clutched her neck again. "I have to call the social worker and tell her I lost the very first child she entrusted to me. I'll never get to foster again."

Austin recalled all the diapers Debbie bought at the mere prospect of becoming a foster parent. The woman was passionate about children. The little boy had to be here somewhere.

"No, you're not calling the social worker yet. We're going to find him. Debbie, get in your car and drive one mile either direction on the highway. Go north first. I came from the south and I didn't see anyone, but check that direction too. He's only three, he couldn't have gone very far. Savvy, take the boys outside and check the front and back yards again. Check under every bush. I'll search the house again."

Everybody nodded and headed in their assigned directions. Austin worried maybe he shouldn't let Debbie drive in her current emotional state, but he was the only one who hadn't checked the house yet. He could be more thorough because he hadn't ruled out any closets or cupboards already.

He started in the kitchen, searching the largest pantry he'd ever seen and every low cupboard, then he stopped and made himself search the high cupboards too, even though it was unlikely the boy had hidden in any of them. After searching the kitchen, dining area, and laundry room, he passed through a family room that had nothing more than two full-sized leather sofas, an end table, a TV mounted on the wall, and a fireplace.

Heading down the hall, he found himself in what could only be the master bedroom, judging by its enormous size and the king bed. Not to mention the hint of a delicate and somewhat exotic perfume that hung in the air. Another fireplace lined the wall shared with the family room. Trying not to let himself get distracted by the lavishness of the house, he searched the spacious master bath with it's fancy glass shower and sunken tub then soon found himself in Debbie's closet. To her credit, it wasn't packed as full as he expected it to be, but it was easily as big as his own bedroom. It'd take a lot of clothes to fill this closet.

Focus.

He swept the hanging clothes this way and that, making sure there wasn't a little boy hiding behind them. He didn't bother to take note of brand names because he could care less about such things, but there was no doubt in his mind her clothing and shoes were of the highest quality. He spotted a safe in the wall behind her blouses.

Good. Now I don't have to worry about the boys getting into Debbie's valuables.

He continued his methodical search room by room, noting the disarray in the playroom and wondered how much of it was his boys' fault and how much was a result of the frantic search for Noah? The final room on the main floor was an office with minimal furnishings.

His search upstairs passed quickly since most of the bedrooms were empty. After checking what felt like a dozen rooms but was probably only eight—he'd lost count after the sixth bedroom—he hurried down to the basement.

The poor little boy was no doubt missing his parents and his own home. If he'd found a spot that made him feel secure, he might not want to come out.

Keeping that in mind, Austin remained thorough in his search, taking his time, despite the anxiety coursing through him for the little boy's safety. His brows shot up when he flipped on the light of a home theater room with nearly a dozen leather recliners laid out in a stadium-style seating formation. His mind reeled at how much money Debbie must have spent on this house.

Once again, he pulled his mind back to the task at hand and inspected the room carefully before moving on. The next room, a home gym with a wall full of mirrors and half a dozen pieces of equipment, gave him pause again.

Is this how Debbie stays so slender?

Shaking his head, he moved to the last room. A game room? Pool, ping pong, and air hockey tables occupied half of the room. The rest was simply empty space except for an arcade style basketball game.

Chest tightening, he returned upstairs and wandered down the hall. His eyes rested on the open bathroom door. He'd only given the bathrooms a cursory glance by pushing back the shower curtain. Maybe he should check them again. Stepping into the bathroom, he discovered a closet behind the bathroom door that he hadn't seen earlier.

A surge of hope shot through him. He opened the door to find the shelves of the small closet mostly empty. Nothing more than a few bottles of body wash and shampoo, toilet paper, and a humidifier. His stomach sank.

Okay, Debbie was right to worry.

Before stepping from the bathroom, he opened the cabinet under the sink. That had been Cody's favorite hiding place when he was little. A stack of blue and black striped towels filled the small space. He'd started to close the cabinet when it hit him that something was off about the striped pattern.

He looked closer, spotting dark brown hair on the top of the pile. A striped blue and black shirt matched the towels almost exactly. No wonder no one had spotted Noah. He blended in.

After calling Debbie, he pulled the sleeping boy from under the bathroom sink.

Little Noah squirmed and cried.

"It's okay, buddy. I'm not going to hurt you." Austin carried Noah into the kitchen to the smell of burning sugar.

He sat Noah on a kitchen chair and rushed to the oven. He opened the door, and smoke poured out, burning his eyes. He grabbed the hot pads off the counter, and pulled a pan full of little black discs from the oven. He dropped the cookie sheet on the stove top and slammed the oven closed.

A high-pitched, beeping filled the kitchen, creating a deafening echo throughout the house, and chaos ensued.

Noah's cries grew louder, and he clapped his hands over his ears.

Debbie walked through the garage door and rushed to Noah, sweeping him up into her arms.

Savvy and the boys came in through the back door and added their screams to the ear-piercing screech of the fire alarms.

Noah still sobbed against Debbie's chest. Tears rolled down her own cheeks as she comforted him.

Austin grabbed a hand towel and climbed onto the counter to better reach the smoke detector up on the vaulted ceiling. The closer he got to the annoying little device, the more his ears rang. He waved the dish towel as though swatting at a swarm of pesky flies.

Savvy finally clapped her hands over her brothers' mouths.

Just when Austin thought his arm might fall off, the beeping ceased in the kitchen then gradually tapered off throughout the rest of the house.

Noah's cries turned to soft whimpers.

Jumping down, he looked around. Everyone stared wide-eyed, looking shell shocked.

He turned to Debbie. "Well at least you know your smoke detectors work."

Debbie gave him a tight smile and a short snort that couldn't quite qualify as laughter.

"Too soon?"

She set Noah on the chair and walked over to Austin. Rising up on her toes, she wrapped her arms around his neck.

He tensed. She meant it when she said she didn't have much of a personal bubble.

The scent of her perfume hit him as he relaxed. It reminded him of the expensive perfumes Cheyenne used to wear. Probably something like Christian Dior. Not the most expensive perfume out there but pricey, nonetheless.

"Thank you. I don't know what I would have done if I'd had to call Gina to tell her I lost Noah." Her soft breath tickled his ear, sending a current of electricity through him.

He patted her back then stepped away, disengaging himself from the woman who smelled almost as good as she looked.

"Looks like your first day as a foster parent is off to a good start." He made another joke, hoping Debbie didn't detect the breathlessness in his voice.

She rolled her eyes and let out a soft chuckle that ended much too soon. "It can only get better from here, right?"

Loud beeping filled the kitchen again.

Debbie clapped a hand over her mouth and rushed to a second oven. "I totally forgot about dinner. I hope it didn't burn too."

"Yay! Dinner! I'm starving!" Cody jumped up and down.

"Cody! What did I tell you about using your inside voice?" Austin asked.

"Sorry, Daddy." Cody lowered his voice. "But Debbie said we could have cookies after dinner."

"Sorry, buddy, the cookies burned," Austin said in a serious voice.

When Cody's face fell, Debbie swatted Austin's arm with the dishtowel he'd only minutes before been waving. "Only the last batch burned since I forgot to set the timer. We still have plenty of good cookies."

Austin raised a finger before the boys could start cheering. "But only for good little boys who clean up the toys they played with."

"Ah man!" Dallas and Cody cried in unison.

He shooed the boys out of the kitchen with Noah between them. "And keep an eye on Noah this time."

As Debbie took something out of the oven, and Savvy headed to the sink with her brushes, he opened the front and back doors to air the house out. He needed to put distance between him and Debbie. The domestic scene was something he could get used to, without the panic of missing kids and screeching smoke detectors, of course.

"Oh no. It's still frozen in the middle," Debbie said as he stepped back into the kitchen.

Savannah turned from the sink. "What is it?"

"Lasagna. My mom's recipe. I don't understand why it's not done."

A hint of garlic and tomato finally permeated the burned cookie smell, and Austin's stomach rumbled. He wanted to echo Cody's sentiment of, *"I'm starving."*

Debbie studied a pink 3 x 5 card. "Shoot, I was supposed to bake it at 425 degrees, not 350."

"Can't you just put it back in and bake it a little longer?" Savvy asked.

"I can, but it could take a long time to finish baking. The kids are hungry now." Debbie tucked the foil back around the pan. "I'll stick it back in and finish baking it. We'll eat it tomorrow and I'll come up with something else for dinner tonight." She opened the oven again.

Austin opened his mouth to tell Debbie he'd take his kids home and feed them, but her gasp stopped him. He stared as the foil pan in her hands buckled and folded. Noodles, sauce, and meat spilled across the open door and into the bottom of the oven.

"Oh my he— I mean, good grief. What else can go wrong today?" Debbie dropped the deformed lasagna pan back on the stove top and beckoned to Savannah. "Hand me some paper towels please."

Austin grabbed the garbage can he'd spotted earlier in the pantry and brought it over to the oven. "Do you want me to clean it up?"

"No, I can do it."

With her hands clad in bulky oven mitts, Debbie wadded up the paper towels and reached into the oven to wipe sizzling sauce off the element.

"Be careful, don't burn yourself."

"I am being careful." Irritation tinged Debbie's voice.

The paper towel she touched to the element burst into flames. Debbie shrieked.

Savannah screamed.

Austin's heart leaped to his throat. He reached out to help Debbie then froze. He didn't have oven mitts.

Debbie looked up wide-eyed, her face full of panic.

"Throw it in the sink!" he yelled.

Debbie turned with the flaming paper towel toward the sink where Savannah stood frozen.

"Move, Savvy!" Austin swung his arm as if the motion would make his daughter move faster.

The flames in Debbie's hands grew larger.

Savvy gaped at Debbie for two long seconds before lurching sideways.

Austin sighed when Debbie dropped the paper towels into the sink and doused them with water.

She turned with the oven mitt pressed to her chest and looked at him and Savvy with wide eyes. "First the cookies and now that. I promise I'm not always this big of a disaster in the kitchen."

Beep! Beep! Beep!

The fire alarm screamed again, and Austin burst into laughter.

Debbie scowled and shook her head.

Three little boys raced into the kitchen with hands over their ears as Austin hopped up on the counter again.

Debbie tossed him the dish towel, and he waved it like the head flag twirler in his high school color guard.

Once the house quieted again, Savannah finished cleaning her brushes and shooed the boys back to the playroom.

Austin stifled a few chuckles and helped Debbie clean up the mess in the oven. They decided to finish cooking what was left of the lasagna tomorrow.

A few minutes later, Debbie dug through her freezer. "I know I have ground beef in here somewhere."

"Listen, I can just take my kids home and fix them something."

She pulled her head from the freezer. "No. I promised to feed your family dinner, and I'm going to do exactly that." She pulled out a package. "Aha. See. All I need to do is defrost this and boil some noodles. I've got canned spaghetti sauce—don't tell my mom—that will make this go fast, I promise."

Austin should remind her it was almost his boys' bath time already, but they'd be mad if he made them miss out on spaghetti—their favorite—to go home and have a sandwich. Not to mention the cookies.

"Fine, what can I do to help?" He took off his dirty work shirt and draped it over a chair, leaving him wearing a snug white t-shirt.

Debbie stared at him, seemingly at a loss for words.

Warmth flooded through Austin as he took a minute to appreciate her skinny jeans and green blouse. Her eye color really did change with her shirt color. Today the Caribbean blue eyes looked more like velvety moss; moody and dramatic.

Was she as attracted to him as he was to her?

Debbie sucked in a sharp breath and turned away. Standing on tiptoe, she pulled open the cupboard above the microwave. "Can you reach the olive oil for me, please?"

Austin stepped closer and leaned into her space.

She took a small step back.

Locating the olive oil, he pulled it down and handed the almost full bottle to her. Remembering the electric shock he'd experienced when she hugged him, he jerked his hand back to avoid touching her fingers. But Debbie didn't have a firm grip on the oil yet.

The plastic bottle fell to the floor, bounced the cap off, and launched oil six feet into the air before landing on its side and spilling its contents at their feet.

Debbie gasped, her face registering shock. Streaks of olive oil ran down her cheeks.

Austin stammered. "Wha— I'm so sorry. I thought you—" Olive oil ran down the side of his nose onto his lips. He fought the urge to gag.

He bent to pick up the bottle.

Debbie spun around and grabbed the roll of paper towels. "I should buy stock in this stuff."

She threw a handful of squares at him, grabbed more to wipe her face, then dropped to the floor and began swiping with frantic motions. "I can't believe this!"

He knelt to help her clean up the mess that was all his fault.

Debbie's pace slowed, her shoulders slumped, and she made a strange gurgling sound.

Oh no. She's been pushed past her breaking point.

He hated comforting women when they cried. He never knew the right things to say. His mom always told him he didn't need to fix everything, sometimes women just needed someone to listen, but that was hard to do when all they did was cry.

He placed a gentle hand on her back. "Hey, it's okay."

She looked up at him with tears streaming down her face. She made a strange hiccupping sound before finding her voice. "My sisters..." she gasped for air, "always complained about days like this." Another hiccup-snort sound escaped her. "And I envied them." Her breathing shifted, and she dissolved into full-bodied laughter.

The rich musical sound made his heart hammer against his ribcage.

She's not crying. She's laughing.

Relief flooded over Austin, and he joined her, letting all of the stress of the past forty minutes dissipate.

Cheyenne would have been in tears over the burned cookies and spent the rest of the evening in her room decompressing. But Debbie kept insisting on fixing his family dinner, despite the stress of her first foster child going missing, burned cookies, and nearly starting her kitchen on fire. This woman was persistent.

Still giggling, Debbie continued wiping at the oil.

"I think you're just spreading it," he said with a chuckle.

She sat back on her heels. "You're right." Using her middle fingers as a spindle, she unrolled the paper towels.

Austin guided them until they spread across the entire spill, then he grabbed the trash can again.

Together, with the occasional giggle, they cleaned up the remaining oil.

"How long do you think it will take me to get the greasy residue off the floor?"

"Maybe we should let the kids come in and skate around in their socks?"

Debbie threw back her head and laughed again. When she finally sobered, she said, "You know what? I give up." She stood and pulled her cell phone from her back pocket.

By the time he returned the trash can to the pantry, Debbie was speaking into her phone. "Hi Susan, I need to place an order to be delivered please. I'll pay extra if you put a rush on it."

Debbie turned toward him. "What do you want on your hamburger? And would the boys rather have chicken fingers or hamburgers?"

Debbie is ordering hamburgers?

He didn't blame her for giving up on fixing dinner. At this rate, she'd burn the house down. His amusement fled. Cheyenne always DoorDashed dinner when she didn't feel like cooking. Whether they could afford it or not. But to his knowledge, the little town of Providence didn't have DoorDash.

"We can just fix sandwiches. You don't need to order out." Although sandwiches didn't sound at all appetizing since that's what he had for lunch every day.

She covered the end of her phone and grimaced. "I don't have enough bread. I didn't get to the grocery store on Saturday because I went shopping with Jessie and Savannah. Please just let me order dinner, and don't make a big deal of it." She gave him a pleading expression.

He stared at her for a long moment, chewing on the inside of his cheek. He didn't want her buying his family dinner, but she didn't need a fight on top of everything else tonight. He forced himself to relax then nodded. "Fine."

"So, what do you want on your hamburger?" She grinned, and his heart skipped a beat. It seemed to do that every time she smiled at him.

His mouth watered. He couldn't remember the last time he had a juicy bacon cheeseburger. And his boys were going to be ecstatic about chicken fingers and French fries. He rarely took his family out for fast food, let alone to a sit-down restaurant, because he simply couldn't afford those kinds of extravagances.

As Debbie rattled off a credit card number a few minutes later, he couldn't help making comparisons between her and his ex-wife. Cheyenne grew up with money and Debbie married into it, but they both spent it very lavishly. They both had huge houses and liked expensive perfume and clothing. Debbie may have revamped her wardrobe, but she still wore designer jeans.

One thing that surprised him, however, was the absence of servants. He'd expected to see at least one person who was hired help here at the house this evening. He hadn't anticipated her actually cooking for his family herself.

Austin had just entered the kitchen again twenty minutes later, after making sure the toy room and other rooms were straightened up, when the doorbell rang. He watched Debbie pull a hundred-dollar bill from her purse before heading to the door.

His eyes widened as he followed her to help carry in the food. Well, there was another difference between Debbie and Cheyenne. Debbie was much more generous than Cheyenne.

The blond teenage boy's eyes lit up when Debbie handed him the hundred-dollar bill. "Are you sure, Miss Debbie?"

"Absolutely, Eli. Thank you so much." Debbie smiled, and the boy returned it.

"Anytime!" Eli stepped back. "Seriously, anytime you need any kind of delivery, let me know."

"I will, Eli. Thanks again."

Debbie closed the door, and as they made their way to the kitchen, Austin asked, "Do you always tip that generously?"

Rosy spots colored her cheeks. "Not usually that generously."

"Why such an extravagant tip tonight?" He asked in a tight voice.

If she was trying to impress him, she'd failed. Watching her throw money around wasn't near as impressive as her persistence. It just proved his point that rich people thought they could say and do anything they wanted as long as they flashed enough money.

"Because it was Eli." She said it like it should mean something to Austin, but it didn't. "If Susan had sent any other busboy to make the delivery, I'd still have given a generous tip, but not as much as I usually give Eli."

"What makes Eli special?"

Debbie shrugged. "He's the oldest of six children, and he'll be going off to college in the fall. He's working three part-time jobs to save money."

"Oh." The tip still seemed excessive, but Austin had to admit he was more than a little impressed by the reason for her generosity.

Offering Savvy a full ride scholarship for painting a mural was apparently the kind of thing Debbie did every day. It put her so far outside his league he could never hope to measure up.

Why did that thought give him indigestion before he'd even eaten dinner?

CHAPTER 9

Austin slowed his truck as traffic came to a standstill. He smacked the steering wheel with his palm. He was late getting away from work as it was, now he'd likely spend another hour in traffic.

Picking up his phone, he called Debbie.

"Hello." Her breathless voice on the other end of the phone sent a ripple of warmth through him.

"Did I catch you at a bad time? No more fires or missing kids, I hope."

Debbie laughed, and his stomach did that dip it liked to do at the light, musical sound of her laughter. "No, thank goodness. We just came in from the pool. You should have seen how fast your boys did their homework at the prospect of swimming."

"Pool?" Alarm filled him. His boys knew how to swim—he'd seen to that—but they weren't strong swimmers. "I sent soccer clothes with my boys, not swim suits."

She chuckled again. "Which they are getting on right now. I keep swim suits on hand for my nephews. It wasn't a problem finding something to fit your boys."

A muffled sound filled the phone followed by, "No, Noah, that's for dinner. We have to get dressed before we eat." More muffled sounds, then Debbie huffed. "Sorry about that."

"Sounds like you have your hands full, so I'll make this quick, but first let me apologize."

"For what?"

"For the favor I'm about to ask you." Austin let out a sigh before explaining. "I got hung up at the construction site, and now I'm stuck in traffic."

"Bummer. I'm guessing you need me to get your boys to their soccer game?" Debbie's voice sounded more cheerful than Austin expected.

"Could you please? I hate being late for their first game, but I'll get there as soon as I can."

"Sure. I can do that. I was planning on going to my nephews' game this evening anyway, so it's not a problem." More muffled sounds filled the line along with Debbie saying something to Noah again.

Austin smiled. She sure had her hands full with that little ball of energy. Noah made Dallas and Cody look docile. At dinner last night, she put Noah back in his seat six different times before she finally gave up.

Debbie's strained voice came back on the line accompanied by Noah's cries. "Sorry, Austin, I need to go. What time are the boys playing? And what field will they be on?"

Austin checked the schedule on his phone as the traffic crept along at a snail's pace. He gave her the information then laughed as she hung up to more cries of, "Noah, stop!"

Did Debbie regret becoming a foster mom yet?

Fortunately, traffic cleared up a short time later, and Austin made better time than he expected. He was still late, but not as late as he thought he'd be.

Austin appreciated the huge recreation complex as he crossed to join Debbie on the sidelines of field three. For a small town, Providence had a top-notch community center, city pool, and recreation complex.

Something tightened in Austin's chest as he spotted Debbie tying

Cody's shoe. In order to keep the kids on the same team, so that he only had to worry about games twice a week instead of every night, he had Dallas playing down an age group and Cody playing up.

Debbie patted Cody's head before sending him back out onto the field. Then she darted down the sideline to get Noah who'd used the distraction to escape.

An empty camp chair sat beside her. Had she brought it for him?

The domestic scene warmed him but also made him a little nauseous too. It was bad enough he found Debbie so attractive, he didn't want to admire her thoughtfulness or the way she treated his children with more care and concern than their own mother had.

He stepped up beside her. "Thank you for getting the boys here."

Debbie looked up in surprise. "Hi. You got here sooner than I expected."

"Me too. Traffic didn't end up being as bad as I thought it would." He motioned to the chair beside her. "Do you mind if I sit down?"

"Go ahead." She pointed to a folded chair behind her. "I brought that one for you, but you may as well sit in Sheila's chair."

He hesitated before sitting. "Sheila?"

"My sister." She pointed to a redhead on the far side of the field. "I don't know why she even bothers to bring a chair, because she never sits at these games. She walks the sidelines the entire time." Debbie laughed. "She says she does it because she needs the exercise, but it's really so she can yell at her boys better. Never mind that her husband is their coach."

Just then, the woman on the other side cried, "Get it, Easton! Go, go, go." She looked downfield at another boy who looked identical to the first. "Weston, go help your brother!"

Austin laughed. "She named her twins East and West?"

Debbie rolled her eyes. "Yes, and she mixes their names up all the time. She's been known to call them things like Eat and Wheat. My favorite, though, is Easy and Wheezy." She grinned. "Those are the nicknames I use for them."

"Please tell me their last name isn't North or South."

"No, thank goodness. It's Lowery." Debbie pulled a wiggly Noah back onto her lap. "Speaking of names...I've noticed everyone in your family is named after a city. Was that intentional?"

"Yes, by my ex-wife. Her name was Cheyenne. She insisted since she and I were both named after cities that we needed to do the same with our kids."

"How long have you been divorced?"

"Five years."

Debbie pressed a hand to her chest. "So Cody was only two when she left?"

Austin's mouth went dry as his stomach hardened. "What makes you think she left?"

"Because you have custody of the kids. From what I've heard, if the mom wants custody, she usually gets it. Or shared at least."

"How do you know we don't share custody?"

"When I came to your house last week, and your boys answered the door, I asked to talk to their mom and dad. Cody said 'we don't have a mom.' That left me curious as to what happened to her." She said it with a shrug, as though it wasn't a big deal, but there was a tautness in her posture that was anything but casual.

Austin couldn't fault her interest. He was equally curious about her former marriages.

Why had her first husband divorced her? And if she didn't marry her second husband for money, why did she marry him? And why did she change her name back to her maiden name?

He wasn't ready to discuss with Debbie all the ways Cheyenne had betrayed and hurt him, so he wasn't about to pry into her private life.

He changed the subject. "Where's Savannah?"

"She decided to stay at my house to paint. Said she'd catch the boys' game on Thursday."

"And you're okay with her staying there alone?"

Debbie laughed. "She's sixteen. And she's been tending your boys for how long?"

Austin shook his head. "No, I just meant... You don't know her that well. I'm surprised you trust her to be there alone."

Debbie's eyes twinkled as she grinned. "Is there something I should know about your daughter? Is she a kleptomaniac or something?"

"No, of course not. It's just that people like you—"

"What do you mean by people like me?" Debbie turned narrowed eyes on him.

He raised a hand to ward off her ire. "I only meant that...most people are particular about their possessions and aren't usually very trusting of others."

Her brow furrowed. "Well, I'm not like that. Besides, there's nothing in my house that isn't replaceable."

That's easy for Debbie to say. Didn't Darrel say he almost didn't recognize Debbie without all the jewelry? She probably had more diamonds and other precious gemstones than even Cheyenne's mom. It's not that he didn't trust his daughter, but he was glad Debbie had a safe. He hated how he couldn't seem to separate Debbie from his experiences with Cheyenne's family.

He watched the action on the field while he searched for a change of subject.

Two young teenage girls stepped up to Debbie's other side with another younger girl, and Austin heaved a sigh of relief.

"Aunt Debbie, we're taking Mia over to the playground," the taller girl said. "Do you want us to take Noah?"

Hearing the word playground, Noah squirmed with renewed vigor. "Wanna play."

Indecision filled Debbie's face as she struggled to keep hold of the little boy until he looked up at her with pleading eyes. "Pleease."

"We'll keep a close eye on him, we promise," the shorter girl said.

"By close eye, you mean you won't take your eyes off him for a second, right? Because he loves to run off, and he is fast." She tightened her hold as Noah started to slide off her lap. "Noah, listen to me. You stay with Lizzy and Brooklyn, okay?"

"'Kay." The boy was gone as soon as Debbie's hold loosened.

The three girls ran after him, and Debbie sank back into her chair with a sigh.

Austin chuckled. "So how's the foster parent thing going?"

She laughed. "Both fantastic and horrendous. I've never met a kid with so much energy. I mean, my nephews can be pretty hyper, but Noah is worse than the four of them put together." She pushed her hair back over her shoulder, revealing a long slender neck. "I took him grocery shopping this morning. Talk about a fiasco. Being a foster parent is not quite like I expected it would be, but I love it." Her smile lit up her eyes, and Austin's heart rate kicked up a notch.

Debbie's devotion to the busy foster child was admirable. He was still trying to convince himself to look away a long moment later when Debbie gasped and jumped to her feet.

Austin's gaze followed hers to the center of the field where Dallas lay sprawled on the grass. He was out of his seat and halfway to his son when Dallas rolled over and pushed to his feet.

Austin stopped, watching Dallas carefully.

Dallas looked at his dad as he rubbed his knee. A strained look crossed his red face, and Austin could tell he fought the tears. At nine years old, Dallas tried so hard to act mature, but he was still just a little boy. Austin tried not to baby his kids, but as far as boys were concerned, there was a fine line between showing concern and smothering.

"That's the way, Dallas." Debbie's voice came from a few paces behind Austin. "Shake it off, buddy. You're going to be fine."

Dallas's gaze jumped to Debbie, and he gave her a shaky smile and a nod. Then he turned and raced down the field.

Debbie understood that Dallas needed validation but didn't want to be coddled in front of his peers. Again a surge of admiration shot through him.

Austin returned to the sideline and kept his attention on the field for the remainder of the game. His distraction with Debbie was not the reason Dallas had fallen and gotten hurt, but he couldn't let his admiration for the fiery redhead who'd dropped into their lives so unexpectedly distract him from giving his children the attention they deserved. He needed to focus on his kids and not let this woman who seemed too good to be true make him want things he was better off without.

His resolve weakened a few minutes later when Debbie leaned toward him pressing her shoulder against his. A current of electricity surged through him, making him aware of her subtle feminine scent.

"Check out these pictures Noah helped me take of the boys before the game."

Austin laughed at the multiple pictures where Dallas and Cody had their heads or half of their faces cut off.

"Oh this one turned out good. I'll send it to you."

His phone pinged with text after text as Debbie continued to find good poses of his sons.

He sucked in a deep breath when she finally leaned away and focused back on the game. It had been a long time since he'd been so aware of a woman. It's not like he planned to be single for the rest of his life, but he wasn't ready to think about remarrying yet.

He sprang to his feet when the final whistle blew. He needed to get his boys home, give them their baths, and get them to bed. And he definitely needed to put some distance between him and Debbie. The more time he spent with her, the more he longed for the domestic scene that surrounded him. One where he wasn't a single father struggling to make ends meet. Wishing every day he could give his kids more.

Despite his urgency to get away, he helped Debbie carry the camp chairs back to her SUV while she wrangled Noah. As soon as the little boy was secured in his car seat, Austin pointed his boys toward his truck.

"Let's go, boys. It's bath time and bedtime."

"Ah, but Miss Debbie promised us ice cream after the game," Cody whined.

Austin's eyebrows rose as he turned to Debbie, all feelings of admiration gone. Disbelief shot through him.

She'd promised his kids what?

Debbie's cheeks colored. "I said *maybe* we could get ice cream. Bbut your father said it's bath time, so we'll have to get ice cream another time."

His frustration settled into a scowl. She hadn't argued with him but she'd still made him out to be the bad guy.

"Another time, guys. It's too close to bedtime for ice cream tonight." The boys tended to have nightmares when they ate too much sugar right before bed.

"Ahhh."

Amid the protests, he herded his boys to his truck. He was about ready to climb in himself when Debbie called his name. He turned to see her hurrying toward him.

She handed over the boys' backpacks with one hand and a foil covered plate with the other. "Here's your dinner."

And the admiration flooded right back, coupled with appreciation. He couldn't believe the pendulum of emotions she triggered in him.

"Thank you. You didn't have to do that." He was glad she had though, since he wasn't sure what he would have scrounged up to eat at home.

She waved away his thanks. "It's just the scrambled lasagna from last night. It turned out pretty good despite everything."

Austin smiled at the memory of last night's fiasco. He dipped his head. "I appreciate it. I'll follow you home so I can pick up Savvy."

"No, don't bother. I'll drive her home so you can get your boys into the bath. Wouldn't want to delay their bedtime. Especially on a school night." She winked.

He hadn't fooled Debbie. He'd refused to take his boys for ice cream simply because she'd made the promise without consulting him first. It was a matter of principle now.

As he started his truck, Cody said, "Did you know Miss Debbie has a swimming pool, Daddy?"

"No, I didn't, bud." But it didn't surprise him.

That was another thing. Debbie didn't even consider asking him if it was okay to let his boys swim. What if they didn't know how to swim? She had willfully endangered his boys.

"She made us *all* wear floaties because she said she couldn't keep an eye on both of us and Noah." The disapproval was clear in Dallas's voice. He hated being treated like a baby.

Okay, so maybe Debbie hadn't endangered his kids, but it still rubbed Austin wrong. The fact that she had a pool at all put her in an entirely different league from him. A league he wasn't comfortable with.

Austin's grip on the wheel tightened during the short drive home as the boys told him about their afternoon. He heard so many variations of "Miss Debbie this" and "Miss Debbie that" the widow should qualify for sainthood.

Thirty minutes later, he'd finished the amazing lasagna—along with the cookies Debbie had tucked into a baggie under the foil—and sent the boys to brush their teeth when Savannah walked through the door.

She stood in front of Austin with her hand on her hip, scowling. "Why did Debbie insist on searching my backpack before dropping me off?"

He felt the color drain from his face. Would Debbie have searched Savvy's backpack anyway or had she done it because he'd cast doubt on his own daughter? How did he tell Savvy it was his fault?

"Listen, honey—"

Savannah burst into laughter. "You should see your face, Dad. That was priceless. Debbie dared me to say that. She even joked about giving me twenty bucks if I recorded your reaction."

He forced a laugh. Apparently, the widow had a sense of humor after all. Maybe he deserved that for accusing Debbie of being like all other rich people. She wasn't particular about her possessions, but she still shouldn't have promised his kids something without checking with him first.

"Since when are you two so chummy?"

Savvy shrugged. "She's pretty nice. I mean, she's offered me a full-ride scholarship—besides paying for the art camp—just for painting a mural on her wall."

Savvy's admiration for Debbie came through as loud and clear as Eli's had last night.

That's the last thing he needed; his daughter idolizing Debbie. The higher Savvy placed Debbie, the farther her idol would fall and the more it would hurt Savvy when she did.

Debbie was generous, but in his experience, the people who gave the most, expected the most. Sometimes to unrealistic levels.

CHAPTER 10

*D*ebbie brushed the perspiration from her brow as she wiped the last of the peanut butter off the cabinets. She'd only left Noah alone with his snack for a few minutes while she gathered the laundry, but somehow, he'd managed to not only slather his body in his favorite food, he'd painted the front of several cabinets and the floor in the creamy substance.

Between two nights ago and this morning, Debbie needed to request the cleaning company that came every two weeks do a degreasing, steam-cleaning treatment on her hardwood floors.

Her phone rang as she took Noah to the bathroom.

She hurried to the kitchen and grabbed it off the counter. Sheila's picture showed on her screen.

"Oh shoot." Debbie answered the phone. "Hi, Sheila, I'm so sorry. I forgot to let you know I wouldn't make it in to read with the kids today." She took Noah's hand and guided him down the hall.

Sheila chuckled on the other end of the line. "I figured you wouldn't make it after I met that cute little ball of energy last night. How's it going?"

Debbie repressed a shudder as she recalled the panic she experienced at finding Noah on top of the stove yesterday after she made a quick trip to the bathroom. The busy little boy had turned two burners on. She'd never been so grateful she'd spent the extra money to get an induction cook top that required special pans with a magnetic base in order for the burners to heat.

Debbie opted to share the story that didn't make her sound like a total failure as a foster parent. "Well, I'm giving him a bath after he tried to use peanut butter as a moisturizer and finger paints."

She put Sheila on speaker and set her phone on the counter before turning the water on in the tub.

Noah practically dove in before she could get his clothes off. As it was, he still made it into the tub before the water got warm.

"Cold!" he shrieked.

Debbie gave him an I-told-you-so look as he stood at the back of the tub shivering.

The boy loved water!

"That reminds me of the time the twins got a hold of the Nutella. Talk about a mess! Oh Deb, I'm so glad you're getting to foster already."

Already?

The last month and a half—since Debbie's breakdown and starting the fostering process—had felt like an eternity.

"Me too," she said as she dumped bubble bath into the tub. Hopefully the bubbles would help get the rest of the oily residue off Noah.

"So, I saw Austin Reed sitting by you at the soccer game last night. What's going on there?" Sheila's voice had that tell-me-everything tone.

"Nothing's going on." Debbie tossed in a couple plastic boats and squirty fish in the water before sitting down on the rug by the tub. She explained to Sheila how she'd hired Savannah to paint a mural and by default, ended up taking care of the Reed kids every afternoon and the circumstances that led her to be at the soccer fields.

She tried not to let her excitement over having the Reed children here every day show in her voice. Nor did she mention feeding them dinner every evening, because she didn't want to tell Sheila about that disastrous first night as a foster mother.

"You two sure looked cozy at the game."

"That's because he sat in your chair," Debbie said.

If Sheila's chair hadn't been there, and Austin had set up his own, would he have set it close to hers?

"I know, but you guys talked all through the game."

Not the whole game. Something changed in Austin's demeanor after Dallas's fall. It was almost like he was mad at her for telling Dallas he was okay and to shake it off.

"If he's coming to pick up his kids every evening, you should offer to feed them dinner. It would give you a chance to get to know him better." Sheila's voice now carried a scheming tone. "Isn't the quickest way to a man's heart through his stomach?"

Noah aimed a fat blowfish at Debbie and squirted a steady stream of water right at her chest.

"Noah, no. Squirt it at the wall." Debbie focused back on her phone call after Noah changed his aim. "I am feeding them dinner. Which reminds me, I need to put the roast and potatoes in the Crockpot as soon as I get Noah out of the tub."

"Pot roast. Good choice. Not something a single father likely makes very often. He'll be very impressed. What are you doing for dessert?"

"Dessert?" Yes, Debbie made cookies on Monday because she was so excited to have the Reed children here, but did she need to make dessert every night?

She recalled Austin's scowl last night when Cody told his dad she'd promised them ice cream after the game. She'd seen that look often on her sisters' faces when she gave her nieces and nephews a treat or a gift without checking with their mothers first.

More than once, she'd heard things like "Maybe I should leave them with you and make you put them to bed," or "You're not a mother, so you just don't understand."

Whenever she heard the first one, Debbie always wanted to cry, "Okay!" She was so lonely in her house that she loved having her nieces and nephews sleep over. It didn't happen near as often as she'd like.

Whenever she heard the second statement, she simply cried. No, she wasn't a mother, she didn't understand sleepless nights with sick kids or hurting because your kids were upset. But she wanted to.

Noah dive-bombed a boat, splashing water everywhere, including on Debbie, effectively putting an end to her pity party.

Joy and Sheila had been more careful about the things they said since they'd found out Debbie couldn't have children. And Debbie tried to make sure she got their permission before giving their kids a gift or sweets.

Debbie knew she'd overstepped the bounds last night by promising the boys ice cream without asking Austin first. She needed to remind herself being a temporary foster mother wasn't the same thing as being a mother. And as much as she loved the Reed children, she wasn't their mother.

"Yes, dessert. You want to impress Austin, don't you?"

Do I?

She couldn't stop thinking about the handsome man. He'd taken every disaster Monday night in stride and didn't get upset or stressed out. He'd simply laughed as he helped her clean up one mess after another.

She'd caught him staring at her a couple times and got the feeling he found her attractive. But then other times, he scowled, and his expression was filled with disapproval. And the way his lip curled every time he said *"people like you"* told her he had a passionate dislike for wealthy people.

"I don't think Austin likes me all that much," Debbie said, trying to hide her disappointment. Because a patient and attentive man like Austin was exactly the kind of man she wanted.

"It sure looked like he liked you last night while you guys were talking."

"Yeah, well, he's made it pretty obvious he doesn't care for my money."

"Pride."

"What?"

"Men are prideful. I suppose we women are too, to an extent. But men are worse. I'm sure he's intimidated by the fact that you're so wealthy."

Debbie wouldn't argue that Austin was prideful, but the frosty glare he gave her last night looked more like censure and resentment. He didn't like what her wealth stood for.

Or maybe he just doesn't like me.

That thought caused a twinge in her chest, because Debbie found him very attractive. But she had been disappointed and rejected by handsome men too many times to count. She refused to base her happiness any longer on a man's acceptance of her. Which was a shame, because she loved Austin's children.

That's why she'd suggested ice cream after the soccer game last night. She'd been so thrilled to be participating in such a normal family activity that she wanted to make the most of it.

Noah capsized another boat, splashing water three feet in the air, the bulk of which landed on her head, effectively ending her sidetracked thoughts.

"Sheila, I need to go before Noah floods my bathroom."

Debbie disconnected the call and pulled a towel from under the sink where Austin found Noah hiding.

Austin may be helpful and patient, but she didn't need a man in her life who made her feel guilty for being wealthy.

DEBBIE LIFTED the lid off the crock pot and inhaled. The pot roast and veggies would be ready right on time. She'd quickly learned the lesson her sisters had talked about for years. Dinner went much smoother when she started it early in the day. Before she picked up the Reed children.

She walked down the hall and checked on the boys in the playroom. She'd also learned that promising the boys they could swim after their homework was done got them to do that undesirable task without complaint. It also used up a lot of energy, so they were content to play quietly until dinner.

Debbie thought she'd never get Noah out of the pool this afternoon though. That kid loved water. Carrying him kicking and screaming from the pool and fighting to get the chlorine washed off and get him dressed again had completely exhausted her.

She grinned as she wandered into the dining room. Savvy had made a lot of progress, but the image was still mostly big patches of color with few discernible images. Debbie knew what the outcome would look like, though, and it excited her.

"How old were you when you started painting, Savannah?"

The girl shrugged. "I don't remember. I've just always loved color in every form. I remember playing with sidewalk chalk for hours at a time when I was young." A slight dimple appeared in her cheek when she smiled. "And I went through a dozen coloring books every year. Finger paints were always a favorite too." Her smile faded. "Until I got in trouble for painting on my grandma's wall. I didn't touch paints of any kind after that, until about five years ago."

Five years ago.

Wasn't that when Austin got divorced? Did her aversion to paints have something to do with her mother? Debbie's interest concerning Savannah's mother piqued but she didn't want to bring up such a sensitive topic.

Instead, she asked Savannah about her favorite classes, then their discussion shifted to friends and boys.

A tell-tale pink flooded Savannah's face as she said, "No, I don't have a boyfriend."

Debbie laughed. "Something tells me there's a certain someone you would like to have as a boyfriend, though."

The color staining Savannah's cheeks deepened. "Yeah, but…"

"But what?"

Savannah wiped her brush on a rag and shrugged. "There's this cute guy named Caleb in my math class."

Debbie leaned forward and grinned. "Does he know you like him?"

"I don't know. I don't think so. I mean I certainly haven't told him."

"Do you think he likes you too?"

Savannah grinned. "He moved seats and started sitting by me a few weeks ago."

"Ooh, that sounds promising."

Savannah dropped into a chair. "But my best friend, Rainey, spoke dibs on him months ago."

"Spoke dibs on him, how?"

"She's been crushing on him ever since he was in her biology class last term, even though they don't have any classes together anymore."

"I'm guessing she doesn't know you like him too?"

"No, and I feel bad because he asked me for my number a while back and he's texted me a few times. But I can't tell Rainey. I'm afraid she'll hate me, and I don't want to lose her as a friend."

Debbie had never met Rainy, but she didn't blame Caleb for being interested in Savannah. She was a pretty girl with high cheekbones and thick red hair with natural golden highlights. Savvy only wore minimal makeup—mascara and lip gloss—but it was enough to accentuate her big brown eyes and full pink lips. She had a confidence Debbie would have loved to have at that age.

"That's a tough situation, but if she's really your friend, I bet she'll understand. I mean, it's not your fault Caleb likes you."

Savannah frowned. "It's not like it matters. I mean, my dad probably wouldn't let me go out with Caleb anyway."

"Why? Doesn't he approve of him?"

"He's never met Caleb." Savvy stared at the brush in her hand. "He's just really protective, and I don't think he likes the idea of me dating, no matter who the guy is."

"Are you and your dad close?"

Savannah shrugged. "I guess so. He relies on my help a lot, and he's all I've got."

"You don't ever spend time with your mother?"

Savannah turned back to her painting. "No, she hasn't been around in years."

Debbie caught her breath as an ache filled her chest. How could Cheyenne not want to be there for every little event in her children's lives? As far as Debbie could tell, Austin was a good father, but there were some things girls didn't want to discuss with their dads.

"Listen, Savvy, if you ever need someone... I mean another woman to talk to about friends or girly things, I want you to know I'm here."

Savvy gave a sad smile. "Thank you. Ms. Jessie said the same thing."

Debbie stood and stepped closer to Savannah. "We mean it." She waited for the young girl to look at her. "It would totally make my day if you wanted to discuss your problems—or anything really—with me."

Savannah smiled, and Debbie felt an unexpected connection with her.

"Just don't ask me for help with science. I hated that subject in high school, and it didn't get any better in college."

Savannah laughed. "Me too."

Dallas and Cody came running into the dining room. "We lost him again!" they said in unison.

Heart in her throat, Debbie sprang to her feet. "Noah? Were you playing hide-n-seek again?"

The boys shook their heads.

"He just disappeared while we were playing Minecraft," Dallas said.

"Did you check under the bathroom sink?"

"Yes, but he wasn't there." Cody waved his arms in a circle. "We looked everywhere!"

Not again.

Debbie recalled the tantrum Noah threw when she brought him in from the pool earlier. A cold chill swept over her as she struggled to draw in a full breath.

I locked the door, didn't I?

She raced out to the garage on legs made of jelly. Her chest constricted at the sight of the overturned trash can in front of the work bench near the door to the pool. The empty hook where the key belonged sucked the air from her lungs.

The door to the pool stood open an inch, key in the lock.

With her heart racing at a manic pace, and her ears ringing, Debbie fought against the drag of feeling like she moved in slow motion.

She pushed her way into the humid room.

Noah stood at the pool's edge near the four-foot depth.

"No, Noah. Swimming time is over." Debbie barely got the words out before the lively little boy, who'd tested and tried her patience more times than she could count over the past few days, jumped into the water.

"No!" The collective shout came from the Reed children who'd followed her out to the garage.

Debbie couldn't have cried out if she'd wanted to, she couldn't even breathe. Frantic to get to Noah, she ran and dove in.

CHAPTER 11

Austin lifted his hand to knock on Debbie's front door. At the cry of, "No!" from inside the house, he changed his mind about knocking and threw the door open, grateful it wasn't locked.

With his heart in his throat, he hurried inside toward the sound of his children's panicked voices shouting, "Hurry," and "Get him." Then Savvy's words filled Austin with dread. "Is he breathing?"

He bolted through the garage door that stood ajar. His gaze scanned the garage big enough to accommodate at least four cars. Additional noise drew his attention to another open door.

Austin stepped into what was undoubtedly a pool house. A wall of windows let in light that reflected off the water, momentarily blinding him. He focused on his three kids hovered at the edge of the pool, watching as Debbie made her way to the steps at the shallow end. She hugged a squirming Noah to her chest.

Austin's mind raced as he took in the scene. Noah wasn't wearing a floaty.

Wait. Debbie and Noah are fully clothed.

Had the kid jumped in without Debbie's knowledge? Why hadn't she locked the door? She should be more careful and keep it locked if they weren't swimming.

Debbie stepped out of the water and staggered.

Savvy hurried to Debbie's side and put a hand on her arm. "Are you okay? Do you want me to take him?"

"No." The word was little more than a whisper. Debbie's arms tightened around Noah.

She walked several paces, her gait unsteady, and dropped onto a padded wicker chair. She pressed her forehead against the top of Noah's head.

Savannah followed and crouched down in front of them. Her voice was harsh when she spoke. "Noah, that was a big no-no. Do you understand? You could have drowned."

Austin's gaze jumped back and forth between Debbie and his kids. Savvy clearly thought Noah was in the wrong, but if Debbie had kept the door locked, this wouldn't have happened.

He was about to step forward and say so when Dallas spoke up. "Yeah, Noah, it's dangerous. That's why the door was locked."

The door was locked?

How did the little rascal get in then?

Cody noticed him standing there and rushed over to grab Austin's hand. "Daddy, Noah jumped into the pool all by himself."

Debbie lifted her head. Rivulets of water ran down her pale face, taking her mascara with it. Judging by the glassy sheen in her bright blue eyes, the moisture on her cheeks was more than pool water. Austin felt bad for thinking the worst of Debbie. Good thing he hadn't voiced his opinions.

Austin crouched down beside Savvy. "What happened?"

"Noah disappeared, again," Cody said.

Debbie shook her head. "H-He climbed up on the workbench and got the k-key off the hook."

Talk about a resourceful child!

Debbie got more than she bargained for with this kid.

Noah turned and looked at Debbie's face. "You look scary."

Austin's kids burst into laughter, but he couldn't join them. Debbie did look strange with black streaks of mascara making their way down her cheeks, but there was nothing funny about the paleness of her face.

Debbie didn't crack a smile. She simply stared at the water and scowled. A shiver shook her body.

Was it because she was wet and cold? Or because she'd processed what the outcome might have been had she been even one minute later?

"Here, let me take Noah. I'll get him changed while you go take a warm shower."

Debbie didn't protest when he pulled the child off her lap. She stood with a blank stare, and he motioned for her to go ahead of him. She walked with stilted movements as they exited the pool area.

Austin watched as she paused in the doorway to pull the key from the lock with trembling hands. His gaze followed hers when she looked up at the hook near the top of the door frame. He still couldn't believe Noah had climbed up there.

Debbie closed her hand around the key so tightly her knuckles turned white. When she didn't move, he wrapped his arm around her shoulders and guided her toward the house.

"Make sure the door's locked, Savvy."

With a shivering Noah on his hip soaking his own clothes, Austin guided a trembling Debbie down the hall, becoming more aware by the second how thin the pale pink t-shirt was that clung to her body.

He paused outside the master bedroom waiting for Debbie to enter.

She didn't move.

Austin shook her shoulder and looked into her eyes. "Hey, it's okay. Noah is fine. You saved him."

Tears spilled onto her cheeks. "But it's all my fault. I shouldn't have taken my eyes off him."

"You have to turn your back sometimes or you'd never get anything done."

"Tell me about it." She brushed a wet lock of hair out of her eyes with a hand that still trembled. "He dumped out a whole container of rice while I showered yesterday."

Noah's little body shivered in Austin's arms. "You're both freezing. Go get warm and dry, and I'll take care of Noah. You can tell me more about his crazy antics over dinner." He smiled, hoping to distract her from the heavy thoughts weighing on her mind.

She didn't smile, but thankfully, she walked into her room and closed the door.

Twenty minutes later, Austin had Noah dressed after giving him a warm bath. He'd put pajamas on him, figuring it was almost bedtime anyway.

Ten more minutes passed, and Debbie still hadn't come out of her room.

After the third time of pulling Noah off the counter and out of the pantry, Austin finally gave the kid a sippy cup of milk and a package of Goldfish crackers.

Dallas and Cody walked into the kitchen.

"I'm hungry." Cody held his stomach in a dramatic fashion. "Is dinner ready?"

"Um..." Austin wanted to say yes, because something smelled amazing, but there was nothing on the stove, and the ovens only showed the time. No temperature or timer.

Savannah rounded the corner from the dining room and pointed her paintbrush toward a crock pot on the counter. "I'm sure dinner is done, but shouldn't we wait for Debbie?" She looked toward the hallway.

His gaze followed hers. Did Debbie always take this long to get ready? Or was she still upset over what happened with Noah?

Austin put the boys to work setting the table, hoping to buy some time. By the time Savannah finished washing her brushes, Debbie still hadn't appeared. Feeling awkward, Austin carried the crock pot to the table and started dishing up the boys plates.

The pot roast and potatoes smelled heavenly, and Austin's stomach growled so loud Dallas and Cody laughed. On the days he worked late, he was always famished by the time he got home.

He paused his actions when Debbie walked into the dining room, wearing leggings and an oversized red t-shirt. The woman looked beautiful no matter what she wore. It didn't matter that her thick hair was still wet and she wore no makeup on her red-rimmed eyes.

Were they still red from crying at the poolside? Or had Debbie shed more tears behind her bedroom door?

"I hope you don't mind us helping ourselves. The kids were hungry."

"That's fine. I'm glad you did." She waved away his apology. "I'm sorry I took so long, I just needed..." She wrapped her arms around herself and shrugged.

Austin studied Debbie. He'd seen a glimpse of insecurity in Debbie's eyes before, but now, her whole posture screamed self-doubt and uncertainty. She looked so different from the confident woman who showed up at his house last week, offering Savvy a job and a scholarship.

She looked vulnerable.

Austin set Cody's food in front of him and turned to Debbie. "Is everything okay?"

"It's fine. I'm fine." She slid into her seat and smiled, but it didn't reach her eyes.

Austin dished up a plate and put it in front of her. He watched her from the corner of his eyes while they ate. Her gaze rarely left her plate except to linger on Noah occasionally. She pushed her food around, eating only a few bites.

When dinner wrapped up, Austin reminded the boys to take their dishes to the sink where Savvy helped them rinse their plates and load them into the dishwasher.

"Hey." He touched Debbie's arm. "Are you sure you're okay?"

She stared at his hand for a long moment before raising her gaze to meet his. Before she could speak, Cody came running back to the dining room. "Can we have ice cream now?"

Debbie turned to Cody and smiled. It still didn't meet her eyes. "Only if it's okay with your dad."

Had she intentionally promised his kids ice cream for dessert because he'd vetoed it last night? He was frustrated with her, but one look at her strained face and he didn't have the heart to say anything.

He looked at his son's pleading faces then bit back a laugh at Noah's matching expression. A sensation of warmth spread through Austin's chest. The trust in the big brown eyes Noah turned on Austin made him feel warm and gooey inside.

He grinned at Debbie. "Look at all of those puppy dog eyes. They're kind of hard to say 'no' to. But I wonder, do you have any chores that need to be done while I think about whether the boys deserve ice cream."

That earned him half a smile. He recalled the way she laughed so hard she cried two nights ago while they cleaned up the spilled oil. Debbie may say she was fine but she was lying.

She picked up her plate and scraped the food into the garbage. "Austin, will you take the boys to the playroom and make sure it's clean? Savvy, you can help me dish up the ice cream."

Austin hesitated as the boys ran down the hall. He considered asking Savvy to swap tasks, so he could talk to Debbie. Her behavior worried him.

But Debbie wouldn't meet his gaze, and he had a feeling she wanted to get rid of him on purpose.

The boys made short work of cleaning up, and Austin soon found himself seated at the table next to Debbie again.

She was still as quiet as she'd been throughout dinner despite the kids' excitement over adding their own chocolate syrup and sprinkles to their ice cream. And though she served herself a single scoop of ice cream, she let most of it melt in the bowl.

When the dessert bowls were licked clean and loaded into the dishwasher, Austin told his kids to grab their backpacks and get in the truck.

"Wait." Debbie picked Noah up and followed them to the door. "Dallas and Cody, thank you for all of your help with Noah. If you boys hadn't realized he was missing this afternoon—" She choked on her words.

Dallas shuffled his feet. "If we had watched him better, he wouldn't have gotten into the pool."

Cody hung his head too. "Sorry we lost him, Miss Debbie."

"I'm glad you told me when you did." She patted Cody's head. "Noah broke the rules. So he won't be allowed to swim tomorrow. But because I can't take him out to the pool, I won't be able to keep an eye on you boys either. So no swimming tomorrow, okay."

Both boys' faces fell.

Dallas's shoulders slumped, and Cody let out such a dramatic sigh Austin almost laughed out loud.

Instead, he winked at Debbie. "You're doing the right thing."

Debbie didn't look convinced. "Maybe, but now I've got to figure out how to entertain this guy all day tomorrow." Still holding Noah, she stepped out onto the porch as Austin and the kids walked out.

She acted like she didn't want them to leave. No doubt she felt overwhelmed by having to take care of Noah.

He paused on the sidewalk and studied her again, glad the kids continued on to the truck. "Are you sure you're okay?"

Twin creases furrowed her brow as she fidgeted with the hem of Noah's shirt. She shrugged. "I will be." She smiled, but it still didn't light up her eyes.

Debbie needed assurance and maybe some comforting. Judging by the way she embraced him after he found Noah the other day, she could probably use a big hug too. But they barely knew each other. It wasn't his place to offer to hold her.

His truck horn honked.

Austin scowled at Dallas who leaned over the seat.

"You'd better go, or Dallas might drive away without you."

Austin walked backward. "Call me if you need anything, okay?"

On the drive home, he gave his boys a lecture on patience and manners while a restlessness consumed him. Like he'd forgotten to do something important.

The feeling increased as he sent the boys off to get ready for bed. His thoughts kept returning to Debbie and how terrified she must have been to find Noah in the pool. He wished he could help her somehow. Do something to restore her confidence in herself as a foster parent.

When the restlessness still hadn't dissipated after reading the boys a bedtime story and tucking them in, Austin knew he needed to do something.

But what?

Then an idea came to him. He turned to Savvy who sat at the kitchen table doing her homework. "I've got to run an errand. Listen for the boys, please. And get yourself to bed by ten if I'm not back by then." He dropped a kiss on the top of her head before walking out to the small garage to find what he needed.

CHAPTER 12

Debbie stayed by Noah's bed extra long that night to make sure he was sound asleep before leaving his room. She still reeled from the events of that afternoon and hardly dared take her eyes off him.

She'd hidden the key to the pool up in her closet, so there was no chance of him getting it and sneaking off to the pool again. But there were so many other ways the active and inquisitive little boy could harm himself despite the extensive childproofing she'd done.

The doorbell rang as she walked out of his room.

She glanced at the clock on the stove as she passed through the kitchen. Nine-thirty.

Who's visiting this late?

Her sisters often stopped by late at night after their kids were in bed, but they usually texted or called first.

Hopefully, whoever it was wouldn't stay long. She was exhausted and needed to get some sleep so she could keep up with Noah tomorrow.

She opened the door to find Austin standing on her porch with a grocery bag in his hand. Her heart leaped in her chest. There was something about the rugged construction worker that did funny things to her insides.

"Austin?" She motioned for him to come inside. "Did one of the kids forget something?"

"No, I'm here because I thought you could use…" He shoved his hand in his pocket and pulled out a key chain. After rattling it a bit, he shoved the keys back into his pocket.

Austin usually acted so confident, she couldn't help but laugh at his odd behavior. "Use what?"

He shrugged. "I don't know. I was worried about you. You had a traumatic experience, and I wondered if you needed…someone to talk to or…" He shrugged again. "A shoulder to cry on."

Debbie wrapped her arms around herself as the fear and desperation she'd experienced earlier this evening flooded over her. "Was it obvious how rattled I was?"

He grinned. "Kind of."

They stood in awkward silence as Debbie chided herself for not hiding her emotions better. She'd always hated how she wore her heart on her sleeve. When she'd tried to prove she belonged in Peter's circles, the only way she'd been able to hide her feelings of inadequacy was by acting aloof and haughty. She hadn't been able to pull that off this afternoon, though. She'd been too upset.

"So do you?" Austin said

"Do I what?" Debbie pulled herself from her thoughts.

"Do you need someone to talk to?"

"Does that mean the shoulder to cry on is no longer an option?" She teased.

"Not if that's what you want, I mean need."

A twinge of sadness hit Debbie at the way he corrected his words. It reminded her Austin didn't approve of her and her money. He was willing to help a friend in need, but wasn't about to go around handing out hugs.

That's what Debbie really needed.

She needed someone to hold her and tell her she wasn't a failure, that she could learn to be a good mother. And she needed someone to promise her she'd eventually have a family of her own. Preferably sooner than later.

She walked into the sitting room and dropped onto the love seat. "What I need is someone to tell me I'm not a complete screwup."

Austin sat beside her, setting the bag he carried on the floor. "You had the door locked, Debbie. You did everything right, but sometimes, things still go wrong."

The warmth of his body beside her simultaneously soothed her and made her hyper aware of his muscular build and masculine scent. "I should have known better than to leave the key hanging in plain sight. I just didn't want to misplace it."

"You had no idea Noah would climb up and get it, let alone figure out how to actually open the lock with it."

"I did, actually." Debbie frowned. "I found him up on the stove yesterday after I left him for two minutes to go to the bathroom. He'd turned two of the burners on." Her heart rate skyrocketed like it did yesterday when she found Noah. She sucked in a deep breath and rubbed her forehead. "If I hadn't spent the extra money on a stove with an induction cooktop, Noah would have burned himself."

"Wow, he's a busy little boy." Austin nudged her shoulder with his. "One of the first lessons you have to learn as a parent is that no matter how badly you want to, you can't protect your children from everything."

"I know, but I'm so afraid he's going to end up getting hurt on my watch, and Social Services will take him away from me." She pressed a hand to her chest. She'd only had Noah a few short days, but he'd taken up residence in her heart.

Austin cleared his throat. "Why don't you have any children of your own?"

Willing herself to act nonchalant, she put her hand on the armrest and drummed her nails. The muted sound they made against the fabric wasn't nearly as satisfying as it was on a hard surface. Whenever Debbie felt uncomfortable, she directed her attention elsewhere. Her acrylic nails had become her diversion. She either studied them or tapped them. And if she was really stressed, she picked at them.

"I'm sorry. I don't mean to be nosy." Austin scratched the stubble on his chin. "It's just that you seem to really love kids. I'm surprised you don't have a bunch of your own."

"I do love kids, and I wish I had a houseful of them."

"Be careful what you wish for because you have a *really* big house." Austin grinned, and her insides turned to jelly.

Balling her fist until her nails dug into her palm, Debbie decided to confide in him. "But I can't have children."

Austin's brow furrowed. "I'm sorry to hear that. It must be very difficult for you, loving children the way you do."

Debbie nodded then dropped her gaze to her hands. "It is. I've tried to make peace with it over the years. Every once in a while I think I've succeeded. Then out of the blue, the desire to be a mother hits me, and it's so strong—" That old familiar, burning sensation rose up in her chest, sucking the air from her lungs.

It was always like this. The longing hit so hard and fast, Debbie thought she might suffocate.

Austin's calloused hand covered hers. He gave a gentle squeeze.

Debbie sucked in a deep breath, feeling like she'd surfaced after being under water for an eternity.

"I can't imagine how difficult that must be," he said in a quiet voice. "The first time Cheyenne and I separated, Savannah was only three, and it drove me crazy to be away from my daughter. To not be there to kiss her booboos and tuck her into bed every night."

The first time they separated?

Had Austin's relationship with Cheyenne always been tumultuous? He sounded like he missed his daughter more than he missed his wife.

Debbie kept talking. Maybe if she shared her loss with him, he'd be willing to tell her more about what happened between him and Cheyenne. "I went through a pretty serious depression when I found out my chances of getting pregnant were slim."

"I assume this was with your first husband?"

"Yes, Keith and I were high school sweethearts and got married shortly after graduation. We moved to Seattle so he could go to college. I worked two jobs to help put him through school. After he finally graduated, I wanted to start a family. We tried for a year with no success, so I went to a doctor. Several months and a whole bunch of tests later, I found out I had Endometriosis and Polycystic Ovarian Syndrome. If I was fortunate enough to get pregnant, I'd likely end up miscarrying."

Debbie studied Austin's strong hand that still covered hers for a moment before continuing. "We sunk ourselves in debt trying fertility treatments. Not only did infertility put a strain on our marriage, our financial problems became a constant source of contention between us. I reached the point where I was so desperate to be a mother that I suggested adoption even though we couldn't afford it." She gave a mirthless chuckle. "You'd have thought I suggested kidnapping a child by Keith's reaction." She dug her nails into the seam of the fabric on the armrest. "He didn't want someone else's child. He wanted his own. He was the last male in his family line. It was his responsibility to carry on the family genes."

Debbie fell quiet as she relived the pain that filled her when Keith insisted they use a surrogate. That way the child would be biologically his. Having a son had come to mean more to him than she did.

Austin squeezed her hand.

"We ended up getting divorced shortly after our sixth anniversary." Debbie let out a heavy sigh. "Keith remarried a year later and now has four daughters."

"There comes a time when you have to call it quits," Austin said quietly as though he hadn't heard the comment about Keith's daughters.

Before she could ask what made him and Cheyenne realize it was time to call it quits, he spoke again. "Is that why you married the older man? Because he wouldn't expect you to have children?"

As much as she loved the contact, she pulled her hand from Austin's. She didn't detect the disapproval she usually heard from most people concerning her marriage to a man thirty-eight years her senior, but Austin despised her money and therefore wouldn't approve of her marrying Peter.

"Not exactly. It was nice that there wasn't that expectation, but that's not why I married him." She cleared her throat. "After my divorce, I spent five lonely years away from my family, working my way through nursing school. Sure, I dated a little, but I couldn't face the same rejection I experienced with Keith, so I never let myself get too involved with anyone." She traced the floral pattern on the sofa with her fingernail.

"I met Peter after he'd been diagnosed with stage four non-Hodgkin lymphoma. He'd already gone through chemotherapy and had been in remission for two years, but the cancer returned with a vengeance. He refused to suffer through chemo again, so the doctors gave him medicine to slow the growth of the cancer cells and gave him less than a year to live."

"His daughter, Fiona, hired me to take care of him because she couldn't be bothered. She wanted to put her father into a care center where someone else could worry about him. But Peter refused to spend his final days in a care center. He wanted to enjoy some of the wealth he'd amassed and do some traveling before he died. I became his caretaker and travel companion."

"So why marry him? Couldn't you just travel with him as his nurse?"

"Fiona was a despicable person. She was absolutely awful to her father. Peter blamed his wife for spoiling her."

Austin gave a grunt that Debbie couldn't interpret, so she kept talking. "About a month after I started working for him, he and Fiona had a big fight about something, and Peter decided he didn't want Fiona to inherit all of his money." Debbie shook her head as she recalled how horrible Fiona was. "It's not like she needed it. I mean her husband was plenty wealthy. Anyway, he proposed to me."

"Just like that?"

"Just like that. I thought he was joking, and I laughed at him. But then he told me he was serious. I laughed again and told him he'd better stop talking crazy or Fiona would have him declared insane. He said he'd worry about Fiona and asked me to marry him again."

"So, you said yes?"

Debbie shook her head. "I said no."

"Why?"

Debbie stared at Austin wide-eyed. "Hellloo, he was almost forty years older than me. What would people think? What would my family think? If I said yes, everyone would assume I did it for the money. I'm not going to lie, the thought of being independently wealthy sounded great, but in the month I'd worked for Peter, I realized having money hadn't made him happy, or Fiona, for that matter."

"So why did you finally say yes?"

"It wasn't until two weeks later, when Peter had an especially difficult day, that I finally agreed to marry him."

"What happened that day that changed your mind?"

"I called Fiona to let her know her dad wasn't feeling well and that he wanted to see her." Debbie snorted. "She very rudely pointed our that she couldn't just drop everything any time her dad ran a little fever. Apparently, lunch at the tennis club with her friends was more important than her father." Debbie rolled her eyes. "I think she thought she'd hung up, but I heard her tell her friends, 'He's so needy. I can't wait until he kicks the bucket. I'm half tempted to ask his doctor to switch out his medicines for placebos, so this can all be over quicker.'"

Austin's eyebrow shot up. "Are you serious?"

"Yes, but as much as she ticked me off, that's not why I agreed to marry Peter."

"What made you finally agree?"

"Peter was so scared that day that he was going to die alone. If Fiona had her way, he would have." Debbie blinked back the tears that surfaced with the memory of the lonely, broken, old man. "I had spent the last five years alone and figured since I couldn't have kids, I'd probably end up dying alone too." She shrugged but knew the action looked as stilted as it felt. "I married him, hoping that someday down the road, someone would be there for me, so I wouldn't have to die alone."

Austin stared at her with arched brows. "So it really wasn't about the money."

Debbie smiled. "There are definite perks to being wealthy." Her smile faded. "But it doesn't bring happiness."

At this point, Debbie wondered if she'd ever find that elusive unicorn.

"No, I don't imagine it does."

"That's why I moved back to Providence. To be near family." She shook her head again. "And to get away from all the leeches who came crawling out of the woodwork offering to help me manage my fortune."

Austin shook his head. "So, what happened with Fiona? Did she contest the will?"

"She tried, but it was solid. It's not like Peter left her out completely; he left her several million dollars."

Peter whistled.

"She spread all kinds of horrible rumors in the influential circles about how I'd stolen her inheritance. I finally made a deal with her. I told her I'd give her Peter's entire estate—house, cars, everything—if she'd stop badmouthing me."

Austin snorted. "And you think she stopped? People like that only care about getting what they want. She probably went right back to telling lies about you as soon as you'd signed the titles."

Debbie shrugged again. "Probably, but I don't care. I packed up my original belongings plus a few gifts Peter gave me, and I left. I'd rather surround myself with people I know who care about me than phony, pious snobs."

"Agreed." Austin said the word with such conviction, Debbie figured he'd been burnt a time or two by wealthy people.

Was that why he disliked her? Because he assumed she was like all the wealthy people he'd known?

He grabbed the bag at his feet. "I thought you might like me to replace the lock to the pool with this." He pulled out a brand new lock with a double-sided keypad.

Debbie took the package and studied it.

Austin's shoulder pressed against hers as he pointed out each of the features. "It's keyless so you don't have to worry about someone finding the key. It's got a keypad, so only you will know the code. And the best part: it's got a smart lock, which means it will notify your cell phone if the door is opened."

"Where did you get this? The hardware store was closed by the time you left here."

Austin leaned forward, propping his elbows on his knees. "I bought it years ago, but never got it installed. It's just been sitting in my garage since we moved to Providence."

"Why is it double sided? I mean I don't really need a key pad on the poolside."

"I needed it to keep children from sneaking out of the house."

Debbie laughed. "Were Dallas and Cody that bad? I know you said they could be rambunctious, and I've seen the excess energy in them, but compared to Noah, your boys are angels."

Austin popped his knuckles. "It was really only for Dallas. He used to sleepwalk when he was a toddler. I found him outside more than once."

"Oh no." Debbie pressed her fingers to her lips. "That's so dangerous."

"Tell me about it. It scared me to death. I had to sleep on the couch so I'd know if he was trying to leave the house."

"Why didn't you ever install the lock?"

Austin popped his knuckles before answering. "Cheyenne le— We separated about that time, and I moved into my parents' house for a while with the kids. Shortly after the move, he stopped walking in his sleep."

"Just like that? That's so weird. You'd think the separation and the move would add more stress and make the sleepwalking worse."

Austin stared down at his hands. "Yeah."

Questions raced through Debbie's mind. Why did Dallas suddenly stop sleepwalking? Why did Austin end up with the kids? Had he been about to say Cheyenne left them?

A sharp piercing pain shot through her chest for Austin and his children's sake. Did Cheyenne have something to do with Dallas's sleepwalking like Debbie suspected she did with Savannah's refusal to paint again until five years ago?

She wanted to ask Austin all her questions, but there was something about his hunched shoulders that made her hold her tongue. So much for thinking if she shared her life story with him, he'd do the same.

"Well, what tools do you need to install this?"

Austin stood. "I'll grab what I need from my truck."

He was back within a few minutes, and Debbie followed him out to the garage, wishing she wasn't so attracted to this man who seemed so averse to trusting her.

AUSTIN LOOKED around Debbie's garage as he removed the screws from the current lock. "You kept the Porsche when you bought the Escalade, huh?"

Debbie leaned against the nearby work bench. "I wasn't planning on it, but my brother reminded me that the Escalade would be quite the gas hog when I don't have a foster child."

Not that she couldn't afford the gas. Austin focused on the note of sadness in her voice. For someone who wanted a family so badly, having to wait for foster kids to come in and out of her home must be torture.

Life was so unfair sometimes. Often, the women who didn't want kids and didn't make good mothers had no problem getting pregnant, and the women who wanted them and would make excellent mothers couldn't have them.

He grinned at Debbie. "Right, you're the impulsive one. Your brother...what was his name again?"

"Scott."

"Scott the mechanic is your voice of reason. Your sister Sheila is the uptight one."

Debbie laughed. "Oh, Sheila would smack you for calling her uptight. But yes, she can get pretty competitive and intense, especially at sporting events. She runs the reading program at the school, and she's great at motivating the kids."

Austin pulled the old lock from the door and used his knife to cut open the plastic on the new one. "Okay, we'll call Sheila the competitive one. Do you have any other siblings?"

"There's another sister between me and Sheila named Joy. Now she's uptight! She is the ultimate organizer and planner. She runs the meals on wheels program for the senior citizens here in Providence."

Austin nodded. "Joy the organizer. Any more siblings?"

"Rudy is the youngest." Debbie pursed her lips. "He's a sheriff's deputy. He's the most talkative one in the family."

Austin reached out his hand for the screws Debbie held. When her hand touched his, a zing of warmth shot up his arm. It was all he could do not to jerk away. He'd cursed himself earlier when he held Debbie's hand to comfort her. The contact sizzled with electricity. He'd half expected her to pull away, instead she'd sighed and almost melted against him. When she finally pulled her hand from his, disappointment had rushed through him.

"Okay, let's see if I've got it down. Debbie the impulsive one—"

Debbie punched his arm.

"Ouch. What did you do that for?"

"Just because I'm impulsive once in a while does not mean you…" She jabbed his chest with her finger nail. "Get to call me that. I'm a lot of other things too."

Austin grinned. Who knew Debbie was so feisty?

"Okay. So what other attributes define you?"

"Well, I…" Debbie frowned and looked at her Porsche for a second before studying her fingernails.

"Never mind. I stopped explaining my life choices to others a long time ago."

Austin straightened. He'd hit a sensitive spot.

He met her gaze. "Hey, I'm sorry. I'm just joking around, trying to get to know you and your family better." He changed the subject. "If I was you, I'd have kept the Porsche too." If money wasn't an issue, that is. "I'll bet it's fun to drive."

Debbie smiled the first real smile he'd seen all evening. "It is fun."

"You'll have to give me a ride in it sometime."

"Or I could just let you drive it. Driving is more fun than riding."

Yeah, but it would make him that much more envious of what Debbie had.

When Austin finally had the new key-pad lock secured, they spent a few minutes setting the code and installing the app that would alert Debbie's phone if the door was opened.

As he followed her back into the house, Austin found he didn't want to leave yet.

"Um, could I have a drink of water?"

"Sure." Debbie grabbed a glass from the cupboard and handed it to him.

As he filled his glass with cold water at the fridge, he racked his brain for something to say. Something that might prolong his departure. His gaze landed on a thick booklet sitting on the corner of the counter. A picture of an elaborate gazebo filled the cover.

Before he could ask about it, ice cold water hit his fingers then splattered on the floor. "Oops. Sorry."

Laughing, Debbie grabbed a handful of paper towels. "I think someone is trying to tell me it's time to invest in Bounty."

Austin chuckled as he wiped up his mess. "Yeah, you've used more than your share this week."

"You have no idea." Debbie grabbed her phone off the counter. "Look at what Noah did yesterday while I was gathering the laundry."

She held her phone out for him to see the little boy covered in peanut butter. Not only was Noah covered, the floor and the cabinet behind him had generous smears.

Austin laughed. "Was he eating it or finger painting with it?"

"He wanted a snack." Debbie swiped to another picture of Noah surrounded by Froot Loops cereal.

Austin laughed. She sure had her hands full with that kid.

"Cody did that same thing with Lucky Charms when he was two. Is Noah always hungry? After I got him dressed this evening it was all I could do to keep him out of the pantry."

"With as much energy as he has, he probably has a really high metabolism. The only time he's not getting into the pantry or cupboards is when he's swimming." Her eyes squeezed shut, and a shudder shook her body. She wrapped her arms around herself.

"Noah's fine, Debbie." He pulled her into his arms. "You saved him. And we've taken measures to make sure it doesn't happen again."

Debbie wrapped her arms around his waist and pressed her forehead into his shoulder. She sniffed a few times as her body relaxed into his.

Austin hadn't held a woman besides his mother for five years, and those had only been brief hugs. Holding Debbie was way different than hugging his mom. She felt small and fragile in his arms. Soft and warm. Electricity tingled along each of his nerve endings.

He shouldn't enjoy this so much. He and Debbie were nothing alike. So, maybe she wasn't the vain, arrogant, rich person he thought she was, but it didn't change the fact that her money made him feel like a poor nobody.

She'd never be happy living in a modest three-bedroom home—the only kind he could afford right now. Actually, he couldn't even afford that. That's why he was renting. And he could never handle her lifestyle.

Debbie seemed to need this hug, so Austin let her decide when to end it. He'd just enjoy it while it lasted and then pretend it didn't affect him so strongly. Because no matter how pretty Debbie was and how much he'd like to lift her chin and kiss her, he couldn't get over his feelings of inadequacy.

Debbie finally loosened her hold and leaned back but didn't step away. "I guess I needed that. Thank you."

Austin's gaze went straight to her lips, the urge to kiss her stronger than ever. He released her and stepped back. "You're welcome." His words came out breathless. He cleared his throat and forced his gaze away from her full lips and beautiful blue eyes. He picked up the booklet with the gazebo on the cover. "Are you thinking about putting in a gazebo?"

"I am. It was delivered a few weeks ago. But my dad gave himself a hernia trying to unload it alone. So it's going to have to wait a few months. My brothers said they'd build it, but no offense to them, even though they provide great muscle, they aren't exactly builders."

"I'll help them." Austin flipped through the pages of the book. "This looks like a piece of cake."

"You don't have to do that."

"You do realize I'm a builder, right? I've worked in construction since I was seventeen."

"That's kind of you to offer, but I couldn't ask that of you."

"Why not? You're feeding my family every night. It's the least I can do." He tossed the booklet on the counter. Doing this for her would make him feel less like he was taking advantage of her generosity. "I don't work this Saturday. I bet we could knock this out in a day. If your brothers are free, that is."

"You shouldn't have to work on your day off."

"I don't mind. I imagine Savvy's going to want to spend the day painting, and Dallas and Cody love helping with this kind of thing." Austin grinned. "They'll probably burnout half-way through, so you might have to help entertain them the rest of the day."

"I think I can handle that." Debbie grinned so big her eyes lit up. "I'll see if my brothers are available on Saturday."

"Great. I'll see you tomorrow after work." Austin headed for the door. He needed to leave before he pulled Debbie into his arms and complicated the friendship they'd managed to build despite their differences.

CHAPTER 13

Austin put a hand on Dallas's shoulder as he slid down from the back seat of the king cab truck. "Hold on, buddy." He waited for Cody to jump down and stand beside his brother. "Listen, today's going to be a long day, and you guys are my helpers, unless Miss Debbie needs your help with Noah. Don't forget to use your manners and obey Miss Debbie and her brothers who are going to be here helping." He held up a finger as Dallas nodded and turned away. "No swimming unless Miss Debbie says it's okay."

"Okay, Daddy. We'll be real good, we promise." Cody bolted to catch up to Savannah who was already at the front door.

Dallas ran after Cody.

By the time Austin reached the front door, he was surprised to see his kids still standing on the porch. "Did you ring the doorbell?"

"Twice." Dallas and Cody said in unison.

Austin glanced at his watch. It was almost eight. He'd planned to be here by seven-thirty so he could look over the instructions before Debbie's brothers arrived, but the boys didn't want to get out of bed this morning. Until he reminded them they were going to Miss Debbie's house today. Then they'd been so excited, he could hardly get them to stop and eat a bowl of cereal.

Austin reflected back on the past two days. He'd made it home on Thursday in time to eat dinner before taking the boys to the soccer game. When they prepared to leave, Debbie asked if she and Noah could come watch.

Dallas and Cody said, "Yes," before Austin could find a reason to say, "No."

With Savannah there to help keep an eye on Noah, Debbie and Austin had plenty of opportunity to cheer the boys on and talk about their days.

Almost like a married couple.

Debbie took dozens of pictures, appearing much more relaxed and cheerful than she was after the pool incident.

Despite Debbie sending him a picture yesterday of Noah's drawings in marker on the wall—accompanied by an eye-rolling emoji—there had been no disasters at dinner last night.

In fact, dinner—consisting of mouth-watering meatloaf and mashed potatoes—had been a nice normal meal with plenty of chatter and laughter from the kids. Exactly the kind of evening Austin could get used to.

At least Noah hadn't colored on the same wall as Savannah's painting, and thankfully, the markers were washable. He admired Debbie for her patience and dedication in taking good care of the lively little boy.

Cody rang the doorbell again before Austin could stop him.

Austin and Savannah exchanged concerned glances as they continued to wait.

Finally the door opened, revealing a rumpled Debbie with swollen eyes still wearing yesterday's clothing.

Austin stepped past his kids. "Debbie, what's wrong?"

"Noah's gone." Tears instantly flooded her eyes.

"What?" Austin pushed his way into the house. "How long has he been missing? Have you checked the pool?"

"He's not missing. Gina came and took him last night." Tears welled up in Debbie's eyes.

"Why?"

It wasn't right. Debbie had been an amazing foster parent.

"His mom came home from the hospital yesterday." Despite the good news, Debbie's voice remained mournful.

Austin couldn't help himself. He pulled Debbie into his arms. "I'm so sorry."

He motioned for Savannah to take the boys somewhere else as he guided Debbie into the sitting room. They'd probably end up in the playroom, and he'd have a devil of time dragging them away later, but at least they wouldn't interrupt him while he comforted Debbie.

She cried against his shirt. "I'm glad his mom is going to be okay, but I'm afraid I'm never going to get to be a mom."

"Yes, you will. Someday, you'll get to have the family you want."

"When? I'm thirty-six, Austin. Most women I know are done having kids by my age."

Austin buried his fingers in her tangled curls and cupped her head. "Have you thought about adopting?"

Debbie lifted her head but didn't loosen her hold around his waist. "I've applied, but single parents aren't usually a birth mother's first pick. And I have no idea when or if I'll get to foster again."

"Sure you will. You're a good mom, Debbie."

"You're just saying that to make me feel better."

"No, I'm not. Yes, I want to make you feel better but… Listen, for a solid week you've picked my kids up from school every day, fed them snacks, helped them with their homework, and swam with them. You've fed them dinner and come to their soccer games, where you take more pictures than I do. You've been more of a mother to them this past week than their own mother has been for the past five years."

Debbie pulled back, eyes wide. "Where is their mother?"

Austin wished he'd never mentioned Cheyenne.

He dropped his arms and stepped back. "Who knows? Spain? Italy?" He popped his knuckles. "She was too busy to visit last Christmas because she was cruising the French Riviera. And the year before that, she was in the Orient."

"When was the last time the kids saw her?"

Austin hated to admit that the kids hadn't seen their mother since the day she walked out on them. It wasn't so much that it painted Cheyenne in a bad light, it showed what an idiot he was for sticking with her so long and putting his kids through the emotional roller coaster ride their life with Cheyenne had been.

"So, do you think Noah will be okay? I mean, has his mother recovered enough to take care of such an active little boy?"

Debbie gave a sad smile. "His grandma flew in from Georgia and is going to stay and help out for a while." Debbie looked down at her fingernails. "I sent a little money with Gina, to help with the medical bills."

A little money? Knowing Debbie, she probably gave Gina enough money to not only cover the medical bills but to also keep Noah clothed until he was eighteen. The thought brought a smile to his face.

"I told Gina to be sure to tell Noah's mom that if she ever needed a break, I'd be happy to tend him." Tears filled her eyes again, and she wrapped her arms around herself. "But she said it doesn't work like that. It's too upsetting for the kids to keep going back to the foster home, because then they think their mom doesn't want them."

Austin pulled her into his arms again. "I'm sorry, Debbie. I know how much he meant to you despite being such a busy little boy."

Debbie buried her face against his neck as she wrapped her arms around his waist. "He was busy, but he was mine for a little while."

Her warm breath caressed Austin's neck, making his heart race like he'd just entered the Indie 500. His mouth dried up like the Sahara at the realization of how much he enjoyed holding her.

Austin didn't plan to fall in love again for a very long time, and he definitely didn't want to fall in love with a rich woman who had been married twice already. But he'd longed for a wife and a stable family life more in the past week than he had for the last five years.

Debbie finally loosened her hold and looked at him with tear-stained cheeks. "Sorry for being such a crybaby."

"You have every right to be upset." He held her tight with his left arm while he wiped away her tears with his right thumb.

Today, Debbie's gorgeous blue eyes looked like a stormy sea. Full of a turmoil that broke his heart a little. His thumb lingered on her jaw as his gaze dropped to her lips. They reminded him of the dusty pink roses lining the walk of his parent's home. The one place that had been a constant sanctuary in his life.

Debbie let out a soft sigh, and his head drifted lower. He didn't want to kiss Debbie. Didn't want to complicate their friendship. But he felt powerless to stop the pull her blue eyes and rosy lips had on him.

The front door opened and two men walked in.

"Are we finally building the gazeb—" The leaner and younger looking of the two auburn-haired men stopped talking at the sight of Debbie in Austin's embrace.

Heat filled Austin's face. He dropped his arms and stepped back, all thoughts of kissing Debbie gone.

Both men's brows furrowed as they took in Debbie's red eyes and tear-stained cheeks.

The one with the build of a linebacker balled his fists.

"You must be Debbie's brothers." Feeling anything but confident, Austin held out his hand to the brother he assumed was the oldest. "I'm Austin Reed. It's nice to meet you."

"Scott."

Right, the mechanic-slash-linebacker took Austin's hand.

Man, what a grip!

Austin resisted the urge to flinch and kept eye contact.

"Hi, I'm Rudy." The younger brother offered his hand after Scott finally released Austin's. "I work for the sheriff's department."

Was that Rudy's way of saying I may not have as tight of a grip as my brother, but I have a gun?

"Nice to meet you, Rudy."

Rudy blocked Austin's access to the sitting room doorway before releasing his hand. "What's wrong, Deb?"

"The social worker took Noah home last night."

"Who?" Scott asked.

"You know, the little hellion she's been fostering?" Rudy said.

Debbie smacked her brother's arm. "Don't call him that."

"Well, from the stories mom told us, the kid was quite a handful."

"Yeah well, you and Scott were tyrants when you were little too. Noah was just a... little busy."

Austin snorted.

Debbie scowled at him, but her voice softened as she continued. "He had the prettiest brown eyes, and he loved to snuggle and read books before naptime and bedtime."

Austin stared at Debbie. It amazed him sometimes how much Debbie loved children, even a child as rambunctious as Noah. No wonder his boys loved Debbie. Kids knew when an adult cared about them, and they usually reciprocated.

Scott cleared his throat, and Austin pulled his gaze away from Debbie. Heat again filled his face.

"So Austin, how did you meet my sister?" Rudy asked.

"We ran into each other at the grocery store. Literally." He grinned at Debbie. "And I drove—"

Debbie grabbed his arm. "I hired his daughter to paint a mural in the dining room."

Scott answered this with a grunt.

Rudy folded his arms across his chest. "What's his daughter painting a mural for you have to do with him hugging you?"

Debbie smacked Rudy's shoulder again. "Knock off the protective big brother act. You're my little brother, remember?"

Rudy sucked in a deep breath, drawing himself up to his full height. He puffed out his chest and propped his hands on his hips. "Yeah but we're bigger than you, Deb."

"Oh please. Get over yourself." Debbie rolled her eyes. "Austin and I are just friends."

Friends.

Right. He and Debbie were just friends, and you don't go around kissing your friends. That ruined friendships.

Ten minutes later, Rudy and Austin team-lifted one of the many boxes the gazebo kit was packaged in while Scott hefted a slightly smaller box onto his shoulder and walked out of Debbie's garage.

When they set their box down near the area prepared for the gazebo, Rudy asked, "So Austin, you have three kids, huh?"

"Yep."

"And where's your wife today?"

So much for dropping the protective big brother act.

"I'm divorced."

Scott and Rudy exchanged a look Austin couldn't interpret.

"How long have you been divorced?" Rudy asked.

"Five years. And yes I have sole custody because my wife moved to Europe after the divorce." Actually, she left the states with another man before the divorce was even final, but Austin wasn't about to reveal that information. "We've lived in Providence for about nine months now, but I work in the Tri-Cities area as a project manager for Cobalt Construction. My parents live in Boise and I have a younger sister who's married and lives in Billings, Montana. Anything else you'd like to know?"

Scott and Rudy exchanged another look.

Rudy broke the silence. "Yeah, what are your intentions concerning our sister?"

"I don't have any intentions where your sister is concerned." He couldn't believe he'd almost kissed her. "My daughter is doing a job for Debbie, and because I rely on Savvy to tend her younger brothers, Debbie has been gracious enough to bring the boys here after school each day until I can pick them up."

It was probably best he didn't mention the part about her feeding them dinner every night. It'd sound like he was taking advantage of Debbie.

And he was.

Scott gave another grunt, but Rudy's gaze stayed narrowed on Austin for a long moment before he nodded. "Okay then. Debbie may be our big sister, but we look out for each other in our family. And the last thing we want is someone taking advantage of her because of her wealth."

No wonder Debbie came home to this small town. Austin had no doubt the Wheeler men would mess him up if he hurt Debbie. It's a good thing he didn't plan on getting involved with her.

CHAPTER 14

*D*ebbie stared out the window at the men working in the backyard. As excited as she was to finally be getting the gazebo finished, it didn't bring the pleasure she thought it would.

The heartache over losing Noah was still too raw. How had she come to love him so deeply in just five days?

Trying to push aside thoughts of Noah, she headed to the shower. After shedding another round of tears under the hot spray, she decided it wasn't just Noah she missed. She'd let her dreams of having a family get out of hand. Having the Reed kids here as well all week had amplified the glimpse of familial bliss, and she loved it.

Okay, so it hadn't all been blissful. She couldn't help smiling as she recalled the laughter she and Austin shared while they cleaned up the olive oil. Debbie had been too stressed out to appreciate it at the time, but Austin had looked so comical standing on the counter, waving the dish towel at the smoke detector.

And he'd been so sweet to come back after the pool incident to comfort her and change the lock. He'd never understand how much it meant to her to have someone reach out to her like that. Her family was always there for her any time she called them, but it was nice not to have to make the call for a change.

Her pulse sped up as she thought about how quick he was to pull her into his arms this morning. For one brief moment, she'd thought he might kiss her, but then her brothers had walked through the door.

Debbie's phone rang as she finished dressing. She dropped onto her bed as she answered. "Hi, Mom."

"Hi, honey. How are you doing?"

"Fine," Debbie lied. Just the thought of telling another person Noah was gone brought tears to her eyes. She swallowed hard to clear the lump from her throat.

"Now honey, I know that's not true. Rudy texted me and told me Gina took Noah home last night."

Debbie sucked in a sharp breath. "I knew he'd have to leave eventually, but I just wasn't ready to say good—" Her throat tightened, cutting off her words.

"I know, honey. This kind of thing is never easy, especially for someone like you who loves wholly and completely. I was worried about you becoming a foster parent for that reason."

"Then why didn't you say something?" It wouldn't have changed Debbie's decision to foster, but she would have liked to know her mother had concerns about it.

"Because you had your heart set on it, and I just want to see you happy. You did finish the adoption paperwork too, didn't you?"

Debbie let out a sigh. "Yes, but I don't hold out much hope."

"Someday, honey, when the time is right. The Lord knows what he's doing."

"I know, Mom, but patience has never been my strong suit. You know that."

Her mom chuckled on the other end of the line. "Do I ever?"

"I was calling to see if you wanted to come to an impromptu barbecue this evening. Your dad's feeling cooped up, so he wants to do something. You probably don't feel like partying, but I think you need some distraction."

"I actually do have a distraction today. Scott and Rudy are helping Austin Reed build the gazebo."

Rustling noises and soft footfalls filled the line as though her mom moved to a different room. "Without your dad?"

"Austin works in construction. He knows what he's doing."

"I don't doubt that, but your dad will be sorry he missed out. He was looking forward to building the gazebo once he was back on his feet."

"I hope he's not too upset."

"He'll get over it. Maybe I can get him to build that pergola I've been wanting over the back patio." More rustling noises filled the line. "Why don't we have the barbecue at your house this evening?"

Debbie crossed to the window to check on the men's progress. At this rate, they'd be done by dinnertime no problem. She watched Austin's muscles bunch as he wiped sweat from his brow.

Talk about a nice distraction!

"Sounds good. Should we say six o'clock? Can you let Joy and Sheila know? I need to get some drinks for the men."

If Debbie called her sisters, she'd have to rehash losing Noah, and she couldn't handle that.

"No problem, hon. See you later."

Two hours later, Debbie watched Austin's Adam's apple bob as he chugged down the second round of lemonade she'd brought out.

The spring day had turned out warmer than they'd anticipated, and Austin had discarded his flannel shirt. The light gray t-shirt he wore hugged his torso like a second skin, and Debbie had a hard time keeping her eyes off his biceps.

Austin was hardly a bodybuilder, but he was built. Solid and strong. She'd noticed it when he held her the other night after the pool incident and again this morning. His embrace had been exactly what she needed both times, and she hadn't wanted to let go. She found more than comfort in his arms, she experienced a sense of wholeness.

"How come no one invited us to the party?" Joy's voice interrupted Debbie's thoughts.

Debbie turned to see Joy and her husband, Liam, approaching with Sheila and Mason right behind them.

"It's not a party," Rudy shouted down from his ladder. "We only invited the people who were willing to work."

Scowling, Mason stepped over and jiggled Rudy's ladder.

Rudy swore.

"Hey, watch your language," Joy said. "There are kids out here."

"Sorry." Rudy's face colored as he shot Joy, Sheila, and Austin an apologetic look. Then he looked down at Mason. "Grab that other ladder, and climb up here and help me."

After introductions were made, Debbie and her sisters stood and watched Austin, Rudy, and Mason start on the roof while Scott and Liam worked on the railing that would surround the gazebo. When Sheila started whistling and flirting with Mason up on his ladder, Joy dragged her and Debbie inside the house.

Dallas and Cody stayed outside with the twins and Joy's two sons. Logan was a year older than Dallas, and Lucas was the same age as Cody. Debbie's nephews were all close and got along well with each other. The cousins must have communicated with each other like their moms did, because all four boys brought the remote control cars Debbie gave them for Christmas last year.

Debbie saw the longing looks on Dallas and Cody's faces as they followed her nephews to the driveway. Now she wished she'd bought extra cars to keep here at the house.

Debbie turned on her sisters as soon as they stepped inside the house. "What are you guys doing here already? The barbecue isn't until six."

"Are you kidding? When Mom told us Austin was here helping build the gazebo, we had to come check him out." Joy turned and looked out the window. "Brooklyn went on and on about how good looking the guy at the park with Aunt Debbie was."

Debbie bit her tongue to keep from agreeing with her thirteen-year-old niece.

Sheila joined Joy at the window. "Tell me about it. Lizzy couldn't stop talking about the Zac Efron look alike."

"Mom! I can't believe you're telling them that!" Twelve year old Lizzy stepped around the wall that divided the dining room from the kitchen, followed by three more teenage girls. "I'm so embarrassed." She shot Savannah a quick glance before bolting down the hall.

Sheila's gaze darted between Debbie, Savannah, and the hallway.

Brooklyn scowled at Joy, looking like she might bolt too.

Joy's oldest daughter, Aubrey, who was just a year younger than Savannah, looked equal parts horrified and humiliated.

Joy stepped away from the window. "You must be Savannah. Debbie told me how amazing your painting is turning out. I'm sorry if we embarrassed you just now. Of course, you realize your dad is a handsome man."

Savannah's head jerked back; her brow furrowed, nose scrunched. She gave a disbelieving shake of her head.

"Ewww, Mom, stop." Aubrey pulled Savannah back into the dining room.

Joy and Sheila grimaced at each other. Then Sheila headed down the hall, mumbling something about Lizzy and hormones.

Debbie bit back a smile—glad she'd curbed her impulsiveness this time.

She went to the fridge and started pulling out lunch meat and cheese.

I hope I have enough bread to feed this crowd.

Joy walked out the front door and returned a few minutes later with several bags of groceries. She'd not only brought the makings for a salad for the barbecue, she'd brought a vegetable tray, chips, and sodas for lunch.

Sheila joined them a short time later with more sandwich makings and stuff for a fruit tray.

As they laid out lunch, Joy turned to Debbie. "I'm so sorry about Noah."

Debbie dropped the apple she'd been cutting and tapped her nails against the counter.

Don't cry! Don't cry!

Sheila stopped cutting the pineapple. "I'm sorry too, Deb. I guess it's best you lose him now rather than later, after you've had more of a chance to bond with him."

Debbie's mouth dropped open. How could Sheila say that? Debbie had never expected to get to keep Noah, but she *had* bonded with him the moment he fell asleep in her arms that first day. And she missed him like crazy!

Debbie turned and looked out the window, searching for a distraction. She needed fresh air or she'd end up saying something she'd regret. Spotting Cody sitting on the back patio with his elbows on his knees and head on his arms, she bolted for the door.

"I need to check on Cody."

She closed the door behind her on Joy's exclamation. "Sheila, how could you say that?"

Debbie sucked in a deep breath and dropped down on the step beside Cody. "What's the matter, buddy?"

"Nothin'."

Debbie stroked his back. "Come on, you can tell me."

Cody finally lifted his head. "They won't let me have a turn driving the remote-control cars."

His wet cheeks pulled at Debbie's heart, and a little burst of mama-bear anger shot through her. "They didn't share at all?"

"The big kid gave me a turn, but when I crashed it into the tire of my dad's truck, he took it away, and now, nobody will give me 'nother turn."

Debbie hugged Cody to her side. "I'm sorry, buddy. The boys are pretty possessive of their cars."

This was the kind of parenting Debbie had little experience with. It felt wrong to force the boys to share their cars. If Joy and Sheila were out here, they would insist the kids take turns, but as an aunt, Debbie wasn't sure it was her place. But she also didn't know what to say to a child who felt excluded.

Cody's posture remained slumped. "It's not fair. Dallas and I asked Santa for remote-control cars for Christmas, and we were real good too, but we didn't get them."

Debbie's heart split wide open as fresh tears filled Cody's hazel eyes. Why didn't Austin give his kids what they asked for? Did he consider gifts like remote-control cars frivolous? Some families were that way. Or could he simply not afford to buy his sons even the cheap cars?

With a father who worked as a handy man and a mother who worked in the school cafeteria, money had always been tight in Debbie's family, but her parents always found a way to provide them with a nice Christmas. Granted much of it was homemade.

She gave Cody a squeeze. "It's lunch time. How about we eat, and then we can swim in the pool." Debbie usually visited with her sisters instead of swimming with the kids, but today, she'd had her fill of adults.

Cody burst to his feet. "Yay! And this time we don't have to worry about keeping an eye on Noah."

Okay, maybe she didn't want to be with kids either. Maybe she should just lock herself away in her room for the rest of the day.

CHAPTER 15

"You are not!" Dallas's yell came from the family room.

Austin turned away from the stove where he was stirring the Hamburger Helper and looked at his boys.

"Am too," Cody countered. "Miss Debbie said so."

"No, she didn't. You're lying." Dallas's face grew red. A sure sign that things were about to get physical.

Austin loved his children, but sometimes being a single parent was exhausting. The last time the boys fought like this, it had been over the toilet. Cody had fallen in and had been mad at Dallas for days because he'd pushed him in.

On days like this, Austin longed for more adult conversation. That's probably why he enjoyed working with Debbie's brothers so much yesterday and spending time with her family. The whole day had been filled with laughter and good-natured teasing.

He'd ended up hitting it off with Scott and Rudy better than he'd expected as they talked about Debbie's family and her philanthropic activities. He'd learned she funded several programs and projects in the small town of Providence, including the rebuild of the sports complex where his boys played soccer, and the reading program they participated in at school.

Learning how truly generous Debbie was only strengthened his attraction for her.

He'd been leery when her parents showed up. Guilt ate at him for taking over as foreman on the project her dad had started.

Thankfully, Bill Wheeler had been content to sit in a nearby chair and watch. He'd given a few instructions from his spot in the shade, but for the most part, he let Austin run the show.

Austin visited with Bill while they ate dinner and learned he had a lot in common with Debbie's father. But where Austin had gone the commercial route, building multi-million-dollar apartment complexes, Bill had stuck with smaller, residential and renovation-type projects.

"No, I'm not!" Cody's voice reached a feverish pitch, pulling Austin from his musings.

"Boys!" Austin walked into the family room. "What is our rule about arguing?"

Both boys turned to him with a scowl.

"To not," Dallas mumbled. "But Dad, Cody says he's a better swimmer than me."

"Miss Debbie said I'm becoming an amazing swimmer." Cody propped his fists on his hips.

Dallas turned on Cody again. "That doesn't mean you're better than me. I'm a good swimmer too."

"Yeah, but she didn't tell you you're amazing."

Austin shook his head and dragged his hand down his face. Debbie didn't realize what praising one child and not the other would do to boys who were best friends yet still very competitive.

He put a hand on each boy's shoulder and guided them to the coat closet. He could send them to their room, but when he did that, the problem either escalated to throwing toys at each other or flopping on their beds and ignoring the other without ever working through their issues. In which case, the problem continued to simmer between them.

He released the boys long enough to pull the vacuum from the closet, then he pointed inside and looked at Dallas and Cody expectantly. The closet was too small to ignore each other but big enough they didn't have to touch.

They both scowled at him again.

"You can come out when you've worked this out and can communicate with each other respectfully." When the boys finally stepped into the closet with a groan, Austin added, "Remember to think about how your words make your brother feel."

He left the door partially ajar so they would have some light and returned to the kitchen where Savannah sat at the table doing homework.

"You know, Dad, one of these days, they are going to be too big to shove into the coat closet together."

"I didn't *shove* them in the closet." Austin shook his head then grinned. "But you're right. I guess we'll have to upgrade them to the bathroom at some point."

"Eww, Dad." Savannah pulled a face, and Austin laughed.

CODY RAN across the driveway and wrapped his arms around Debbie's waist. "Thank you, thank you, thank you!"

Tears filled Debbie's eyes. "You're welcome, buddy."

Though not as enthusiastic as his brother, Dallas hugged her next. "Thank you, Miss Debbie."

Debbie returned the embrace, relishing the moment. "You're welcome, Dallas. Now why don't you boys show me if these trucks can go as fast as the boxes say."

"Mine's not a truck. It's a jeep." Dallas picked up his remote control.

Debbie grinned. "Oh, sorry."

"I bet mine goes the fastest," Cody said as he pressed the lever on his remote control and backed the monster truck right into his shin.

Debbie and Dallas laughed. Contentment filled her as she watched the boys master driving their new vehicles. She took pictures of the smiles on their faces. Good thing she charged the batteries as soon as she got home from the store with the new toys, or she might have missed this joyful moment.

After a while, she reminded the boys to stay in the driveway and off the road then went inside to check on dinner. She peeked in the oven at the enchiladas then joined Savannah in the dining room.

"It looks amazing." Every day, Debbie studied the picture taking shape, trying to discern what Savannah had accomplished in her last painting session. And every day, Debbie spotted details that had been added where she thought the painting was already finished. Details that made the image practically jump off the wall.

Savannah blushed. "Thank you. I still have a lot to do."

"I can't believe how much you've accomplished in just a week."

Sure there were areas where the image was barely discernible, but Debbie knew what it would eventually look like, and Savannah was doing an incredible job.

The young girl turned away from the mural. "The boys were so excited for their trucks, I didn't get a chance to thank you for the art kit. It's really nice, but you shouldn't have spent so much money on me."

Debbie's heart sank. Savannah was too young to be worried about how much a gift cost. She wanted to reach out and pat Savannah's arm, but the girl was more reserved than her brothers.

"It was nothing really. I was just feeling a little lonely this morning and decided I needed to do something nice for someone else." Traitorous tears filled her eyes.

"You miss Noah, don't you?"

Debbie swiped at her eyes. "More than I thought I would. I mean he was such a little stinker and I didn't even have him very long."

"Do you think all moms miss their kids when they're away?" Savannah asked in a voice so quiet Debbie's heart split wide open.

These Reed children were going to be the death of her.

She had no idea how to answer. She wanted to assure Savannah her mother loved her and missed her no matter where she was, but Debbie couldn't understand how Cheyenne could walk away from her children. She ached to pull Savannah into her arms and tell her she missed her and her brothers like crazy when they weren't at her house.

Savannah's phone dinged, saving Debbie from having to answer the difficult question.

The girl set her pallet on the table and pulled her phone from her pocket. She let out a little squeal after reading the text on the screen.

"Is everything okay?"

Savannah's face split into the biggest smile Debbie had ever seen. "Yes!" she squealed again. "It's my friend Rainey."

"The one who used to like Caleb, but last week decided she now likes Justin?"

Debbie often visited with Savannah while she painted, and a lot had happened last week.

On Thursday, Justin had asked Rainey to Prom, and she decided she was in love with him, which gave Savannah and Debbie a good laugh.

Then on Friday, Savannah confessed to Rainey that she liked Caleb and that he'd been texting her. Rainey had been so excited for Savannah that she insisted they needed to go shopping for prom dresses together.

"She said Caleb asked her if I had a date for prom yet."

"I told you he likes you." Debbie gave Savannah a high five. "Boys don't change seats and ask girls for their number if they're not interested."

Her phone pinged again. "He asked Rainey for my address."

Debbie grinned. "He's asking you to prom, alright."

Savannah's smile faded.

"What's wrong?"

She chewed on her lip for a moment before speaking. "I'm not sure my dad will let me go."

"Why not? Doesn't he let you date?"

"He hasn't said I can't date, but I've never really been asked out." Savannah fiddle with the brush she still held. "It's just that he's pretty protective. I think he still views me as a little girl. I worry how he might react to my first date being prom."

"Perhaps if you mention to him that somebody might ask you out, it'll help prepare him for when it does happen."

Savannah grimaced. "Maybe, but I'm afraid he'll tell me I can't go because I'm too young to date or…"

"Or what?" Debbie asked gently.

Savannah lowered her gaze and shrugged. "We can't afford to buy a prom dress."

Debbie wrapped an arm around Savannah's shoulders. "I'd love to buy you a dress, Savannah. Don't let that keep you from accepting when Caleb asks you out."

"I can't let you do that." Savannah didn't pull away but she turned, effectively loosening Debbie's embrace. "My dad probably wouldn't allow it, anyway."

Debbie dropped her arm. "Why doesn't your dad like me?"

Savannah picked up her pallet and turned back to the wall. "It's not that he doesn't like you, it's just…"

"Just what?"

"He's just been burned too many times by wealthy people."

No wonder he was leery to let Savannah work for her and didn't like rich people. But he hardly knew Debbie. Just because she was wealthy, didn't mean she was a ruthless socialite. Yes, she may have acted haughty on occasion, but that was usually an act of self preservation.

Austin worked hard to support his family, but Savannah shouldn't have to miss prom just because he couldn't afford to buy his daughter a dress. It wasn't Debbie's place to interfere, and Austin would probably hate her even more than he already did for getting involved, but she only wanted Savannah to be happy.

"Would you like me to talk to your dad about letting you go to prom?"

Savannah turned, wide eyed. "Would you really? I mean, you wouldn't have to actually convince him to let me go or anything. But maybe if you bring it up, he won't be too shocked or upset when Caleb asks me out. And if he knows you're willing to pay for a dress, then he wouldn't stress about that."

"I can't guarantee great results, but I'll talk to him."

And hopefully, it wouldn't make him despise Debbie even more, because the more time she spent with the Reed children, the more she realized she liked their father.

Savannah dropped her pallet and brush and hugged Debbie. "Thank you."

Debbie squeezed her eyes shut against a sudden onslaught of tears.

CHAPTER 16

Austin's heart rate kicked up a notch as he neared Debbie's house. He shouldn't be so excited to see her again, but he'd enjoyed hanging out with her family last Saturday. She'd felt a little more approachable surrounded by people who fit his social class more than they did hers.

Austin made the turn into Debbie's driveway and slammed on his brakes to avoid running over a remote-controlled monster truck that zipped across the concrete.

Cody, monster truck in his arms, raced up to him as soon as he got out of the truck. "Look what Miss Debbie bought us, Daddy!"

Austin gave Cody a tight smile. "You mean she bought them for you to play with while you're here?"

Dallas walked over carrying a jeep. "No, she said we could keep them and take them home."

Debbie bought his sons remote control trucks? And not just any trucks. She'd purchased the expensive ones. Austin knew because he'd priced them at Christmas time. But there had been no way he could afford to buy two of them.

Heck, he couldn't even afford one. Which was just as well, because his boys would have fought over it.

Austin clenched his jaw as heat filled his body.

Who did Debbie think she was?

She had no right to give his sons expensive gifts without asking him first. Was she trying to buy their affection like Cheyenne's parents had? They'd spoiled his kids with expensive gifts, making him look like a loser in the process.

"Don't get too attached guys. You're not keeping them." Austin walked past the boys, ignoring their protests. He stormed through the front door without bothering to knock.

Finding Debbie in the kitchen, he walked right up to her. "What were you thinking?" The words came out a shout.

She flinched and took a step back. "What do you mean?"

"How dare you give my kids expensive gifts without consulting me first?"

"I—I wasn't thinking anything."

"Exactly. You rich people are all alike. You do whatever you please without even considering how it affects other people."

"That's not true!" Debbie squared her shoulders and glared at him.

"Isn't it?"

Austin was vaguely aware of Dallas and Cody coming into the house and Savannah entering the kitchen. He shouldn't shout at Debbie in front of his kids, but he was so angry with the beautiful, rich redhead, who made his pulse race every time he saw her, he couldn't think straight.

Despite his anger, he couldn't help noticing Debbie's fitted black slacks and ruby red blouse that accentuated her figure and fiery hair. She must be wearing lipstick today because her lips appeared much redder and fuller than on Saturday when he'd almost kissed her.

How could he be so angry with Debbie yet so attracted to her?

He propped his hands on his hips. "How do you think it makes me feel for you to give my kids a gift I can't afford to give them?" Out of the corner of his eye, Austin spotted Dallas and Cody whispering.

They'd better not be devising a way to convince me to let them keep the trucks.

"It's not my fault you couldn't afford them, so stop yelling at me."

"Dad—" Dallas pulled on Austin's sleeve, while Cody whispered something to Savvy.

"Not right now, Dallas. I'm talking to Miss Debbie."

"You're not talking to her. You're yelling at her, and we have a rule about arguing." Dallas pressed against Austin's back, pushing him to the other side of the kitchen.

"Stop it, Dallas. Sometimes grown-up discussions get a little loud."

"It's still arguing," Dallas said as he continued to push Austin.

"Yeah, Dad." Cody pushed Debbie across the kitchen where Savannah opened the pantry door and flipped on the light.

Dallas shoved Austin inside the large walk-in pantry. "That's enough, guys." He spun around to walk back out and crashed into Debbie who got pushed in by Cody.

"Wh—what's going on?" Debbie sputtered as she staggered sideways.

Austin wrapped an arm around her waist to steady her.

The door closed, and Savannah called, "At least it's not the coat closet."

Dallas's voice came through the door. "Make sure you think about how your words affect the other person."

Austin was one part amused, one part angry, and two parts tempted to kiss the woman whose body pressed against his. Her heavenly perfume wove a web around him, drawing him in—tempting and heady.

Stop it. Debbie overstepped the bounds. You're angry with her, remember?

He gave her a gentle shove and grabbed the doorknob. It twisted, but the door didn't move.

Dallas and Cody giggled on the other side.

"Very funny, guys. Let us out now." Austin shoved the door with his shoulder.

It didn't budge.

"I put a chair under the knob, Dad," Savannah said. "So be careful or you'll damage the door."

"You guys open this door!"

"You can come out when you're ready to communicate with each other respectfully," Dallas called.

"Agh." Austin slapped the door with his palm. He spun around and pointed a finger at Debbie. "This is all your fault!"

"My fault? You're the one who walked into my house shouting." She folded her arms over her chest. "What is this, anyway? Why did they lock us in here?"

Austin paced the cramped confines. He couldn't escape the scent of Debbie's perfume. "When my boys argue, I make them sit together in the coat closet—"

"You lock your kids in a closet?" Debbie's eyes widened, and her mouth dropped open.

"I don't *lock* them in. I don't even close the door. But I do make them stay there until they've worked out their differences."

Debbie snorted. "Fat chance of that ever happening. At least we won't starve in here." She grabbed a bag of pretzels and opened it.

"What do you mean?"

"Come on, Austin. I know you hate me." She pointed a pretzel at him.

"I don't hate you."

"Yes, you do. Or at least you hate 'people like me.'" She shoved the pretzel in her mouth so she could make air quotes with her fingers.

Austin let out a deep sigh. He *had* lumped her in with all other rich people he'd known. And he'd made it clear he didn't care for wealthy people.

Yes, she'd been out of line buying his boys such expensive toys without consulting him first. But he'd also learned from her brothers how selfless and generous she was. He hated that she could so easily give his kids what he couldn't. And he especially hated that he was so attracted to a woman that made him feel like an impoverished deadbeat.

He pulled a bucket labeled flour from under the bottom shelf and dropped down to sit on it, rubbing his hands over his face. "I don't hate you, Debbie. In fact, it's quite the opposite." He probably shouldn't have admitted that last part.

She pulled out the sugar bucket and sat beside him, facing him. "What do you mean?" Her thigh brushed against his, and he sucked in a sharp breath.

She really has no personal bubble.

It probably wasn't a good thing that he liked that about her.

"I find you very attractive, but I refuse to get mixed up with another wealthy woman."

"Another?"

Austin propped his elbows on his knees and stared at a stack of red and white striped popcorn buckets. "Cheyenne and I went to high school together. She was popular—head cheerleader, homecoming queen, and extremely wealthy. For most of our junior and senior years, she dated Tucker James. He was exactly the kind of guy people expected a girl like Cheyenne to date—all-star quarterback, the mayor's son, also very wealthy."

"Something happened between Cheyenne and Tucker halfway through senior year, though." Austin shrugged. "She caught him with another girl or something. Cheyenne was livid, and she broke up with him." He shook his head. "The next thing I knew, she was throwing herself at me."

He straightened and made eye contact with Debbie.

"I was totally out of Cheyenne's league. I lived on the opposite side of town. The side that's considered the wrong side of the tracks, if you know what I mean."

Debbie nodded, but didn't say anything.

"I knew she was on the rebound and was just using me to get back at Tucker. I even resisted for a while, but Cheyenne was persistent. She kept asking me out and dragging me to do stuff with her friends. I went from being a nobody to hanging out with the most popular crowds almost overnight." Austin popped his knuckles one by one as he recalled how vocally he'd attacked Debbie a few minutes ago. His stomach tightened.

"Her parents didn't approve of me, so we went behind their backs. It was almost as if finding Tucker with another girl flipped a switch inside Cheyenne, and she was suddenly bent on breaking all the rules." Austin lowered his gaze to his feet. "She ended up pregnant."

Debbie's hand rested on his shoulder, but he didn't lift his head.

"I was determined to do right by her even though her parents threatened to disown her if she married me." Austin shook his head. "Her father tried to pay me off. He begged me to dump Cheyenne and leave town. She was furious with her dad when I told her and insisted we elope. So we did, right after graduation."

"I went from working part-time in construction to full time and managed to rent a small one-bedroom apartment. Cheyenne got a job at a fast-food joint—which she detested—until Savannah was born. Money was tight, but we were happy. At least, I thought we were."

"What happened?" Debbie's gentle voice made him sit back and look at her. A frown marred her pretty face and understanding—or was it sadness?—filled her eyes.

"Cheyenne refused to go back to work after having Savannah, and I was okay with that. I liked the idea of our daughter having a stay-at-home mom. But things were really tight. I worked long hours to support us, but she resented me being gone all the time. I did my best to be an attentive husband and father when I was home, but it never seemed to be enough."

"When Savannah was about a year old, Cheyenne's parents decided they wanted to get to know their granddaughter. Instead of insisting they come to our apartment to visit, Cheyenne took Savannah over to her parents' mansion."

He stood and began to pace the few steps to the door and back. "I think she was embarrassed for them to see where we lived. Over time, Cheyenne visited them more and more frequently. Sometimes, even staying overnight. When she *was* home, she complained about everything; having to cook and how small and run down our apartment was."

"She always came home with new clothes and toys for Savannah from her parents. Then before long, it was new clothes and manicures for her." Austin's shoulders bunched as he recalled all the ways Cheyenne's parents spoiled her. "When Savannah turned three, her parents promised to pay for a nanny if she'd come home and live with them again. Cheyenne couldn't resist the life of luxury they offered, and she left."

"I'm so sorry, Austin." She reached out and grabbed his hand, surprising him.

He ceased his pacing and looked at their joined hands. Warmth flowed from her into him, administering understanding and comfort.

Debbie gave a quick squeeze then let go.

The contact was much too brief. He liked the feel of her dainty hand against his. He shook his head. "I refused to let her take Savannah out of my life. I showed up at her parents' house almost daily, which they hated. Her dad again tried to bribe me to walk away from my family. I made a concerted effort to court Cheyenne and win her back." He grinned. "I did her parents' trick and promised to build her a house if she'd give us another chance. I had shifted from working residential to commercial construction and became a project manager, so I was making decent money. She agreed to come back, but not until I had the house built. Because I did the bulk of the work myself with the help of friends, it took almost a year and half to complete. Thanks to Cheyenne's requirements, it ended up much larger and more expensive than I'd initially planned."

Austin straightened the soup cans on one shelf. "Things were pretty good for a while after we moved into the new house, but we had a hefty mortgage and finances were still pretty tight. Cheyenne hated having to live on a budget. It didn't matter that she had a beautiful kitchen, she still hated cooking. And she complained about the cleaning. I helped out when I was home, but the truth was, she expected to maintain the lifestyle she'd led at her parents' house."

"She sounds like Peter's daughter, Fiona," Debbie said with a grunt.

"She was. Her parents had totally spoiled her; and no matter what I did, I couldn't measure up. We argued almost daily." He grabbed a pretzel from the bag Debbie still held and ate it. "I kept remembering how happy we were when we first got married, and like an idiot I suggested we have another baby."

Debbie gasped and stood, dropping the pretzels on a shelf. "How can you say that? Hoping a baby will improve your marriage was the wrong reason to have a child; but bringing children into the world is never a mistake."

Austin dropped back down onto the flour bucket. "You're right, and I don't regret it for a minute. Dallas and Cody—who was a surprise—have done nothing but enrich my life. Unfortunately, Cheyenne didn't see them the same way. She resented what they did to her figure and how they tied her down. She became impatient and easily annoyed by every little thing they did."

Debbie sat again, but her posture remained stiff. With as badly as Debbie wanted children, hearing how Cheyenne resented their kids probably infuriated her.

"I frequently came home to find a babysitter tending the kids only to discover Cheyenne had been gone all day. She went to lunch with friends all the time and went shopping more and more often. She Doordashed dinner all the time. I knew we couldn't afford the lifestyle she was leading, but I also couldn't figure out how she was paying for it. Whenever I confronted her about her spending, she always said she'd found an amazing sale or that they were gifts from her mother." He plunged his hands into his hair as he recalled her lies. "She knew I hated her taking handouts from her parents, especially ones we didn't need. Cheyenne had two closets full of clothes she rarely wore."

"So, where was the money really coming from?" Debbie asked.

Austin's jaw clenched. Even Debbie could see through Cheyenne's lies. Why had it taken him so long to see the truth?

"She'd gotten two credit cards and maxed them out to the tune of sixty thousand dollars."

Debbie's brows shot up. "Seriously?"

Austin nodded. "She'd been using the cards to pay for a cleaning service along with all her other extravagances." He shook his head again. "She hid the statements from me so well I had no clue, until she decided she was tired of living a double life and left me for—" Humiliation choked off his words.

"For what?" Debbie asked gently.

Austin gave her a tight, humorless smile. "Turns out the friend she had lunch with so often was Tucker James. He got offered a job overseas and invited my wife to go with him." Austin popped his knuckles again. "Cheyenne walked away from her family, leaving nothing more than a note saying she hated being a mother and wanted to see the world. She's been jet-setting ever since. I got saddled with more than half of the credit card debt during the divorce proceedings because she'd forged my name on the applications. Needless to say, I lost the house, and we ended up moving in with my parents."

"Is that when Dallas stopped sleepwalking?" Debbie's perceptiveness surprised him.

"Yes, he had a lot of separation anxiety when he was young, and it manifested itself even when he was sleeping."

"If his mom was always leaving him with a babysitter, it's no wonder. Poor kid. I can see how the stability of living with your parents helped him overcome it."

Austin nodded.

"Has she ever come back to see the kids?"

"Not once."

Tears filled Debbie's eyes. "What kind of message has that given them?"

"It's better than her making promises and not keeping them." Austin's jaw clenched again. "Cheyenne's parents did that a lot, made plans to take the kids to an amusement park or someplace special then canceled at the last minute, telling them in a roundabout way they weren't a priority. Of course, that didn't stop them from buying the kids insanely expensive gifts we didn't have room for. I swear their only goal was to make me look like a failure as a father. I was so relieved when they moved to Arizona a few years ago. The kids rarely ask about them or their mom anymore."

"No wonder you dislike wealthy people."

"Yeah, well, besides my ex-in-laws, I've known plenty of other wealthy people—developers and investors—who stop at nothing to get what they want, regardless of what that means for the little guy."

"I don't want to be one of those people, Austin." Debbie put a hand on his arm. "I'm sorry I didn't consult you before buying your boys the remote control trucks." She let go of his arm and picked at her fingernails. "The house was so quiet today without Noah here, so I went for some retail therapy. All I could think about was how upset Cody was on Saturday when my nephews didn't want to share their remote-control cars with him. And well, I've told you how impulsive I can be." She grinned.

"Is that what he was so upset about?" Austin had noticed Cody sitting on the back patio crying and had been ready to go talk to him when Debbie sat beside him.

"Yes, and I was a little peeved with my nephews for not sharing with Cody, so I bought the bigger, better monster truck and Jeep for Dallas and Cody." Debbie raised her hand when he opened his mouth to protest. "You're right to be upset. It wasn't my place to buy such expensive gifts for your boys without checking with you first. My sisters have chewed me out for doing something similar multiple times."

"I'm sorry too. I shouldn't have yelled at you. My parents have chewed *me* out several times for being so da—dang prideful."

Debbie's musical laughter filled the pantry, and something inside Austin relaxed.

She clasped his hand. "Pride or not, you're a great dad, Austin."

"I don't know about that."

"You are. Your boys idolize you." She squeezed his hand and smiled so big her eyes lit up.

A surge of attraction shot through him at the contact. The temperature in the pantry skyrocketed, and Austin's heart rate kicked up a notch. She sat so close they could almost be considered one body. Austin wasn't usually the touchy-feely type, but he loved how Debbie wasn't afraid to show others she cared through touch.

Her perfume—more subtle than other days, but probably just as expensive—wrapped around him, drawing him in. His gaze locked with hers, and he saw the attraction he felt mirrored in her blue eyes. His gaze dropped to her lips—rosy and full.

He leaned forward, powerless to stop the pull she had over him.

Debbie's head tilted.

He paused for one brief moment, knowing this was a mistake but not caring, before touching his lips to hers. Her lips were softer than he expected and the feather-light touch he'd initiated wasn't enough. He leaned closer still until his lips melded with hers.

Austin's whole nervous system vibrated as a surge of electricity shot through his body. Bright lights flashed behind his eyes, leaving reflections bouncing around his brain.

When her lips parted, he didn't hesitate to accept the invitation. He tangled his fingers in her curly hair, enjoying its texture as her mouth moved with his. So many powerful sensations rushed through him, he feared his nervous system might short-circuit.

The grip she had on his hand tightened as she let out a little sigh. The whisper-soft sound against his mouth only ramped up his desire.

A sudden bump and scrape sounded on the other side of the door before it burst open.

"Are you being nice now, Daddy?"

CHAPTER 17

*D*ebbie felt herself slowly becoming intoxicated. Like the rush of free falling without a parachute. She was going to get hurt, but it was too late to do anything about it. Adrenalin surged through her heating every inch of her body.

She liked this man and his kids. A lot. But if he couldn't let go of his pride and accept her for who she was…

Cody's high-pitched voice filled the pantry, saying words Debbie's muddled mind couldn't decipher.

Austin pulled back so fast she fell forward a little. He jerked his hand from hers and was on his feet in an instant.

"Of course, I'm being nice, buddy." Austin cleared his throat as he escaped the pantry.

Yes, he was being very nice. Could the kids hear the breathlessness in their dad's voice like she could?

"Hey," Cody scowled at his dad. "You were supposed to be talking, not kissing."

Cheeks burning, Debbie stepped from the pantry to find Dallas pulling a face that clearly said "Eww." She looked at Savannah who stood nearby. The girl's eyes were wide and questioning, her mouth forming an O.

Was it only surprise? Or was Savannah as disgusted as Dallas to catch her dad kissing Debbie?

Debbie sucked a sharp breath. Austin kissed her. And she'd kissed him back.

"We did talk," Austin's voice pulled Debbie from her thoughts. He picked Cody up and plopped him on the counter. "And we decided that you can keep the trucks—" He held up a finger when the boys started to cheer. "*If* you do some chores for Miss Debbie to earn them."

We did?

Debbie's mind was still pretty muddled from that incredible kiss—in fact she couldn't see how Austin could stand there and pretend like nothing happened—but she knew they hadn't talked about the boys doing chores for her.

Austin looked at her; his brown eyes begging her to agree.

She cleared her throat. "I have lots of things that I need some strong boys to help with."

Well, she'd think of some anyway.

"Yes!" Both boys pumped their fists in the air, then Cody added. "We're good helpers, aren't we Daddy?"

"Yes, you are." Austin lifted Cody down. "Now, go get your backpacks and let's head home."

"But we haven't had dinner yet," Dallas said.

"Oh, right." Color flooded Austin's cheeks, and Debbie bit back a smile.

He was more flustered by their kiss than he let on.

"I guess you'd better wash up then and hope Miss Debbie and I didn't eat all of the food while we were locked in the pantry."

"Silly Daddy, dinner's in the oven." Cody turned and raced down the hall after Dallas yelling, "I wish we had a pantry, so Dad could lock us in it!"

"Me too," Dallas said. "I'd fight with you every day so he'd send us to the pantry."

Debbie and Austin both laughed.

Savannah still stood near the pantry, staring at the two of them.

Austin sobered and rubbed his hands on his jeans. "I uh... I'll set the table."

Debbie pulled the enchiladas from the oven, hoping they hadn't burned while she and Austin were imprisoned. She avoided Savannah's gaze while the girl washed out her brushes, and when they all sat around the table to eat, it soon became apparent that Austin was avoiding Debbie's gaze.

He didn't speak directly to her or even look at her once during the meal.

A horrible sinking feeling tightened Debbie's chest, and she pushed her half-full plate away. Austin regretted kissing her. She could see it on his face and in his body language.

What did you expect?

He said he refused to get mixed up with another wealthy woman. So why did he kiss her?

In Debbie's mind, telling someone you find them attractive then kissing them the way Austin kissed her was getting mixed up with them.

In fact, Debbie felt all kinds of mixed up.

As soon as the kids were done eating, she started clearing the table. A few minutes later, she found herself at the kitchen sink beside Savannah.

"So, did you talk to my dad?"

"Of course we talked," Debbie said defensively. Savannah didn't think she and Austin were making out in the pantry that whole time, did she? Not that Debbie would have minded.

"And what did he say?" Savannah bounced on her toes.

"About what?"

Savannah frowned. "About me going to prom with Caleb."

"Oh that." Debbie sighed. "We didn't get a chance to talk about that."

Savannah's face fell. "Right, because you were too busy kissing." She turned and walked away.

"Savvy, wait!" Debbie dried her hands and stood in front of

Savannah who stopped in the middle of the kitchen. "It wasn't like that, I swear."

"We all saw you guys kissing, so don't try to deny it."

Debbie put a gentle hand on Savannah's arm. "Yes, your dad kissed me, but it was only at the very end and for a brief moment." A moment Debbie would never forget. "I'm sorry if that bothers you. It's not likely to happen again, so don't worry."

"Why not?" Savannah's brow furrowed.

Did that mean Savannah would be okay if something developed between her and Austin?

Stop it! Don't get your hopes up.

"I think he regrets kissing me, so we'll probably forget it happened."

"What happened?" Austin asked as he walked into the kitchen.

Only the most amazing kiss Debbie had in over a decade. Had he forgotten the whole thing already?

"Nothing." Debbie grabbed Savannah's arm and pulled her down the hallway. "Listen, your dad and I talked about…you kids and how hard it is for him when I interfere. I planned to talk to him about letting you go to prom, but I didn't get a chance." She tucked a lock of hair behind Savannah's ear. "Even though he doesn't like me getting involved, I'm still willing to talk to him for you."

Savannah smiled. "Really?" Then her face fell. "I don't want him to get mad at you again, though." She wrinkled her nose. "But I don't want him to be upset with me either."

Debbie patted Savannah's arm. "Why don't you herd the boys out to your dad's truck and give me a few minutes to talk to him. If nothing else, my mentioning it will help pave the way for you to talk to him."

Savannah nodded. "Okay. Text me, though, so I know how it went."

They walked back into the kitchen to find the boys headed to the door with their backpacks. Savannah grabbed hers and rushed after them.

"Austin, wait." Debbie grabbed his arm as he was about to follow his kids out the door.

He sighed, closed the door behind Savannah, and turned to face Debbie. "Listen, I know I shouldn't have kissed you." He shoved his hands into his pockets. "I don't want you to think I'm leading you on or anything because I don't have any intentions of getting involved with som—"

"Someone like me?" Anger flashed in Debbie's chest and stung her eyes.

"What?" Austin shook his head. "No. I just meant I don't plan on getting involved with someone right now. My kids need to be my focus."

Debbie folded her arms. "Are you sure you don't want to get involved with *someone like me* because I might be a bad example to you kids? Or maybe you don't want to get involved with *someone like me* because it might hurt your pride?"

"No." Austin shuffled his feet. "Okay, yes. Do you have any idea how intimidating it is to be attracted to someone so wealthy when I'm struggling to make ends meet because I'm still trying to pay off my ex-wife's debts."

"Stop it," Debbie said.

"Stop what?"

"Stop saying you're attracted to me and then turning around and telling me what a turn off my money is."

"I didn't say it was a turn off, it's just—"

Debbie held up a hand. "Look, I don't want to argue with you anymore. Not about money. Not about the kiss." She definitely didn't want to hear that he regretted the kiss.

This was probably the worst possible time to bring up what she had to say, but she took a deep breath and forged on. "There's something I need to discuss with you concerning Savannah."

AUSTIN'S HEART STOPPED. "What about Savannah?"

So help me, if she wants to fire Savvy because the painting—that's turning out amazing—isn't up to her standards, I'll blow a gasket.

Debbie would prove to be just as bad as he had first suspected.

"First, I need to apologize." Debbie put a hand on his arm, and his traitorous heart started racing.

"For what?" His voice came out tight, his words clipped.

"When I bought the boys the trucks this morning, I bought Savannah an art kit as a gift."

Relief shot through Austin. "You bought Sav—"

Debbie held up a hand. "I'll make her work it off, like the boys, if you want me to. I actually have some other projects I'd like her help with when she's done with the mural."

More projects? The thought both discouraged and excited him.

He'd hate to see this time with Debbie come to an end when the mural was done, but he wasn't sure he could continue to have dinner with her every night without wanting to pull her into the pantry and kiss her senseless.

"And I promise, from now on, I will ask your permission before I buy your kids anything else."

Knowing Debbie, she probably paid hundreds of dollars for the art kit. It still rankled him that she didn't even think twice about dropping that kind of money on his kids. But now that she understood where he was coming from, he needed to let it go.

He took a deep breath and let it out slowly.

She grinned. "You might want to take one more deep breath, before I mention the next thing I need to discuss with you."

Austin's whole body tensed. "What do you mean?"

"I'd like to ask your permission to buy Savannah—or hire her to do additional work, if you'd rather—so she can buy her own—"

"Her own what?" the words came out louder than he intended.

"Calm down, or the kids will come lock us in the pantry again."

A car horn honked, reminding him his kids were just outside.

Austin took another deep breath. Heaven knows what would happen if he got locked in the pantry with Debbie again.

"Just spit it out," he said with a growl.

"I offered to buy Savannah a prom dress," Debbie blurted then hunched her shoulders as though bracing for impact.

Austin's gut clenched as adrenaline filled his system. "A prom dress? Savvy's not going to prom." She wasn't old enough for things like that. He balled his fists as his stomach twisted into knots. *No way is some boy taking my daughter to prom.*

Austin caught himself.

She is old enough.

She's almost seventeen. She'll be graduating next year.

"According to her friend, Rainey, there's this guy who wants to ask her out, but she's afraid you'll go ballistic."

Austin took a deep breath and asked, "Why is she afraid I'll freak out?"

Because you just did, idiot.

"Well, she says you're overprotective and—"

"I'm her father, I'm supposed to protect her."

"I know, and you're doing a fabulous job, but you have to let her grow up, too." Debbie put her hand on his shoulder, sending warm tingles zinging down his arm. "She's also concerned about being able to afford a dress."

Austin's jaw clenched. He hated that Savvy was so aware of their financial situation. And Debbie too.

He stepped away from her, for his sanity's sake. "So, I'm just supposed to agree to let her go out with some kid I know nothing about?"

"Of course not. There's plenty of time for you to get to know him before prom. Invite him over for dinner or something. Savvy really likes him."

"But they always have parties after these dances..." Austin's breath came a little faster. "I don't want her doing who knows what—" He shuddered as he remembered what transpired between him and Cheyenne after their senior prom.

"If it's okay with you, I'll offer to let Cheyenne's group of friends come here after the dance. You can help me chaperone while they swim and watch a movie, if you want."

He didn't know what was worse; teenagers running around half dressed or cuddling in a dark room downstairs. At least Debbie asked his permission this time before promising his daughter something. If he helped chaperone, then he could make sure nothing inappropriate happened.

A horn honked again.

He rubbed his tired eyes. "I'll think about it." He opened the door. "All of it."

Less than ten minutes later, Austin parked his truck in their driveway. He reached for Savannah's arm before she could climb out. "Hang on, Savvy." He looked over his shoulder at Dallas and Cody. "You boys go get ready for bed. I'll be there in a few minutes, after I talk to Savvy."

Savannah had been tense the whole ride home, almost cowering in her seat as if she feared him.

The thought saddened him. He never got abusive with his kids, even when he was upset with them, so why didn't Savvy feel like she couldn't talk to him about going to prom? Why did she need Debbie to act as a buffer?

"So, I hear some guy wants to ask you to prom."

Savvy turned toward him. "Caleb isn't just some guy, Dad. He's super smart and really nice."

Austin grinned. "Then why haven't I heard about him before now? I always thought you'd tell me when you got a boyfriend."

Even in the dim glow from the porch light, Austin could see a blush cover Savvy's cheeks.

"He's not my boyfriend."

"Yet." Austin couldn't resist teasing her. "But you want him to be, don't you?"

Savvy shrugged. "Maybe, but I'm not ready for a serious relationship."

Right answer, baby girl.

He put a hand on Savvy's shoulder. "Why didn't you want to tell me Caleb is planning on asking you to prom?"

She shrugged again. "I just figured you'd freak out. You always kind of get this panicked look in your eyes whenever I talk about college and things like that."

"Things that mean you're growing up," Austin said in a tight voice. "No matter how old you are, you'll always be my baby girl, Savvy. And I'll never be ready for you to grow up."

Savannah grinned. "Does this mean I can go to prom with Caleb?"

"I think you'd better wait for him to ask you before you get too excited."

"I know," Savvy giggled.

He pointed a finger at her. "And Debbie and I agreed that you're going to do additional projects for her to pay for your dress."

"Thank you, Daddy." Savvy leaned over and hugged him.

Austin blinked away the tears that flooded his eyes. Nope. He definitely wasn't ready for her to grow up.

"You know you can talk to me about anything, don't you, honey?" He said when Savannah pulled back.

She nodded but looked down at her hands. "I'm sorry I told Debbie before talking to you. She just happened to be sitting there when Rainey texted me. I was so excited, I just had to tell someone."

"I don't mind." He smiled. "I imagine she was much more excited for you than I would have been."

Savvy laughed. "Yeah she was." Then her laughter died, and she looked him in the eyes. "So, what's going on between you two?"

Austin's breath hitched. "What do you mean?"

"Come on, Dad. You two were kissing. You may not think so, but I listened when you gave me those talks about the birds and the bees and hormones. I remember the lectures on not kissing a boy until I was sure I really liked him and could picture a future with him. Does this mean you like Debbie?"

Of all the things for her to remember.

Yes, he liked Debbie. But he couldn't see himself ever letting go of his pride enough to make it work between them. Her money would always be a sore spot with him.

"You're not still waiting for mom to come back, are you?" Savvy asked quietly.

"No way." He clasped Savvy's hand. His heart hurt every time he thought about his eleven-year-old daughter's tear-stained face as she handed him the note Cheyenne had left on their bed.

Just when Savvy was becoming a woman and needed her mother most, she learned that her mom didn't want to be her mother anymore.

"Me either," Savvy said resolutely.

Over the years, Austin and Savvy had discussed Cheyenne many times. Without bad-mouthing Cheyenne, he made sure Savvy knew her mom wasn't rejecting her, she was simply searching for something that would bring her the kind of happiness she thought she wanted. It broke his heart that Savannah had memories—her brothers didn't have—of a neglectful, often absent mother.

"It's okay if you like Debbie," Savvy said quietly.

"What?" Austin didn't know what to make of her words.

Savvy shrugged like it wasn't a big deal, but Austin could hardly breathe. "She's really nice, and I think she'd make a good mom. I mean, she didn't even hesitate to jump in the pool after Noah." Savvy looked out the window. "She cried a little today when she talked about him."

Austin cleared his throat. "She would be a good mom, but I'm not planning on getting involved with her. Or anyone, for that matter."

Savvy turned back to him. "If you don't like her, then why did you kiss her?"

Austin rubbed a hand over his face. "I do like her, but things aren't that simple. Life is a lot more complicated when you're an adult."

Savvy rolled her eyes and reached for the door handle. "Whatever. You could uncomplicate it if you wanted to. Do you really want to end up all alone when me and the boys are gone?"

"Savvy—"

She was gone, and Austin didn't know whether to go after her or let it go.

Savvy was right. He could uncomplicate things if he really wanted to, but did he want to?

He doubted Debbie would be willing to downgrade to his lifestyle, and he could never live hers. Besides, if by some miracle, he and Debbie did get together, he didn't want his kids ending up spoiled like Cheyenne.

He wouldn't get his children's hopes up where Debbie was concerned. It was best if they all pretended the kiss never happened.

CHAPTER 18

*A*ustin's phone pinged as he climbed into his truck. He pulled it from his pocket. His heart skipped a beat when he saw Debbie's name on the screen.

No soccer game tonight, right?

Austin checked his calendar. Debbie was right. He'd forgotten the boys didn't have a game tonight. And he was actually getting off a little early, because the superintendent on this project canceled today's meeting. Which meant he and the kids could spend all evening at Debbie's house if they wanted.

Do I want to?

His heart screamed "Yes!" But his head said, "No!"

Tuesday night's soccer game hadn't been as uncomfortable as he'd expected, but once again, it had felt like he and Debbie were a couple as they sat on the sidelines cheering on Dallas and Cody together. A scene he could easily get used to.

Then last night had only been mildly tense as he and Debbie worked together to get dinner on the table. His heart only raced a little every time he glanced at the pantry door or stood too close to her.

When she touched him, though, intentional or otherwise, his pulse skyrocketed. He doubted she meant anything with her innocent touches. It was just the way she was, but it nearly drove him crazy. Every. Single. Time.

He texted Debbie: *No game tonight.*

She responded right away: *The boys are begging for a movie night. Do you care if they stay late?*

A movie night? In Debbie's dark theater room? The thought of sitting close to her sounded very appealing.

He started the engine and turned on the AC to cool the suddenly hot truck. At least she asked his permission before promising his boys something. If they started the movie right after dinner, it would finish about the time a soccer game would.

He lifted his phone. *A movie sounds fun.*

But he'd make it a point to sit as far away from Debbie as possible.

Checking the clock on the dash, he decided to hurry home and take a quick shower before heading to Debbie's. He wasn't trying to impress her or anything. He just felt especially grimy and had the time, so why not?

He turned his thoughts from Debbie to Savannah. She'd said she wasn't ready for a serious relationship, but she sure was excited last night when they arrived home from Debbie's house to find roses and chocolates on their front porch from Caleb, along with a cheesy poster saying, *Roses are red, Violets are blue, It sure would be sweet, To go to Prom with you.*

She'd taken a picture before touching the roses or chocolate to send to her friends—and he suspected, Debbie. Then she'd spent an hour on the phone with Rainey trying to figure out a creative way to respond. Austin had a feeling he'd be forking over some money once they decided on a plan.

Unless Savvy involves Debbie.

He couldn't decide whether to be upset that Debbie might step in and interfere again or be grateful that Savvy had a supportive woman in her life that she enjoyed sharing things with.

Traffic was lighter than Austin expected, and he made good time getting home.

Is this a sign?

He laughed at himself.

A sign of what? That I'm falling for Debbie?

No. He couldn't go there.

Not yet. Maybe not ever.

A silver Mercedes parked in front of his house caught his attention as he pulled into his driveway.

His stomach knotted at the same moment his heart leaped to his throat. He mentally reviewed the bills he had outstanding. He wasn't delinquent on any of them, so it couldn't be a bill collector. Besides, debt collectors didn't drive Mercedes. Did they?

He climbed from his truck with stiff movements, never taking his gaze from the car. He paused in the act of closing the door when a familiar, slender redhead stepped from the passenger side of the Mercedes.

Austin froze. A chill raced down his spine and spread throughout his limbs.

The pretty woman with a perfectly made-up face and long copper-colored hair smiled and waved. Her lashes were so thick and long he could barely see her hazel eyes, but he didn't need to see the color of her eyes to know they matched his sons' perfectly.

"What are you doing here?" He forced the words out through a dry mouth.

"Hello to you, too." Cheyenne sauntered toward him.

"Stop!" He held up a hand. "You don't get to waltz back and pretend you didn't destroy my—our lives."

Cheyenne folded her arms over a chest at least two sizes larger than it used to be. "Come on, Austin. Don't pretend you weren't as miserable there toward the end as I was."

"I was only miserable because you made my life that way." His stomach churned as he recalled all the lies she'd told, knowing she was keeping secrets but unable to figure out the truth. Then finding out she'd been intimate with another man while still sharing his bed.

He swallowed the bile that filled his throat. Sucking in a sharp breath, he squared his shoulders. "I repeat, what are you doing here, Cheyenne?"

She huffed and propped a hand on her hip. "I want custody of the kids for a while."

Heat rushed through Austin's body. His gut constricted, and acid burned his esophagus. He stifled the urge to curse and slammed his truck door instead. "No. I have full custody. You agreed to that. You can't expect to just show up and get something you don't deserve."

"I'm their mother, Austin."

"You haven't been their mother for the past five years. And you weren't much of a mother before that."

Cheyenne studied her ridiculously long fingernails. The move reminded him of Debbie. Except he could see the insecurity in Debbie's posture whenever she did it. It was how she deflected when something made her uncomfortable.

For Cheyenne, it had always been a show of superiority.

"Come on. We can settle this like reasonable adults. If we get the lawyers involved, it'll only get costly. Maybe even ugly." The words sounded like a threat. "You don't want to put the kids through that, do you?"

Cheyenne didn't care one bit about putting the kids through an ugly custody hearing. She'd do whatever it took to get what she wanted. Just like she always had. And she was counting on Austin's desire to protect his children to coerce him into going along with whatever she had planned.

The question was: What did she have planned? Why did she want the kids? He refused to believe Cheyenne had suddenly developed a maternal longing.

No, that kind of yearning made women jump into the pool without hesitation to save a little boy who tested and tried her patience again and again. Not subject them to an ugly custody hearing.

The driver's door of the Mercedes opened, and an older version of Boise's golden boy and all-star quarterback stepped out dressed in a charcoal power suit.

How dare he show up here?

Austin's fists balled, and he clenched his jaw as he envisioned knocking out one of Tucker James's perfect teeth.

No matter how badly he wanted to punch the man who tore his family apart, Austin was smart enough to know it would only cause him more problems. Actually, he should thank Tucker. Other than his financial situation, his life had been much more pleasant the last five years without Cheyenne than the previous twelve had been when he'd tried so hard to keep her happy.

Tucker wrapped an arm around Cheyenne and locked gazes with Austin. He gave a curt nod, which Austin ignored.

He stared at Cheyenne. Austin couldn't afford a costly custody battle, but there was no way he'd let Cheyenne march in and upset their lives. "Sorry, I don't give in to idle threats anymore."

"Idle?" Cheyenne laughed. "If I sue for custody, Austin, who do you think will win?" She put a hand on Tyson's chest. "Their mother and stepfather, who is a man of considerable means? Or their blue-collared father who can't afford to rent anything better than this... dump." She sneered as she pointed at the rental house they'd called home for the past nine months.

Perspiration stung Austin's brow, and his mouth may as well be stuffed with cotton for how dry it was. He couldn't lose his kids, especially not to this conniving woman. He resisted the urge to roll his neck and rub the tension from his jaw.

He prayed Debbie would forgive him for the lie he was about to tell. "As it just so happens, my fiancé's wealth is..." He forced a laugh. "Well, let's just say it makes *considerable means* look... paltry."

Cheyenne's eyes narrowed in disbelief.

Knowing he needed to sell the lie, he kept talking. "We haven't set a date yet, but I know she'd have no problem getting married right away if she felt it was in the kids' best interest." That part was true anyway. Debbie would do anything for his kids. Of that, he had no doubt.

He coughed to clear the acid burning his throat and shrugged. "Legal fees won't be a problem."

Cheyenne laughed. "Austin Reed, the proudest man on the planet, accepting money from a wealthy woman? I'll believe that when I see it."

Austin sucked in a sharp breath. "It's easy when said woman is more generous than anyone I've ever met." That was true too. "And never uses her money to manipulate other people to accomplish her own agenda." That part he was still a little unsure about, but he wanted to believe it was true of Debbie.

Tucker cleared his throat. "Perhaps the four of us could discuss the kids over dinner."

Austin stared at the other man like he was speaking a foreign language. Tucker James had no right to suggest anything concerning Austin's children.

He shook his head.

Cheyenne stepped away from Tucker and stood so close to Austin he could smell her expensive perfume—heavy and cloying. "I'm not trying to take the kids away from you. I'd just like to see them. Maybe spend a day or two with them."

A crawling sensation raced across his skin, and he wished Cheyenne and Tucker would disappear to wherever they'd been for the last five years. He flexed his fingers then balled his hands. He ached to punch Tucker and curse and shout at the woman who'd hurt him and his children more than anyone ever could. He needed to get to his kids and find a way to keep them safe from the storm headed their way.

"Why?" The single word came out clipped and harsh. When she didn't answer, he asked again, "Why now, after five years?"

He couldn't for one second believe Cheyenne had anything other than selfish motives for wanting to see the kids.

"Discuss it with your fiancé. Let's have dinner and talk." Cheyenne gave him the syrupy-sweet smile she had always used on her parents to get what she wanted.

She'd used it on him too many times to count. And he'd given in to her more often than he'd like to admit.

"Call me. I haven't changed my number," she said before turning toward the Mercedes.

That knowledge surprised him. He'd assumed she'd changed her number the day she'd shaken off her old life and walked away from it.

"I don't remember it. I deleted it after you walked out, and well, five years is a long time." He gave a shrug that probably looked stiffer than he intended.

Austin *had* deleted her number, but he still remembered it.

Cheyenne smiled over her shoulder. "Good thing you haven't changed yours then. I'll text you."

"You should have called and saved yourself a trip," he said to their backs.

Austin hated to think to what lengths she'd gone to know not only where he lived but also that he hadn't changed his number. She'd probably had some private detective following him for the past month.

He remained rooted to the spot until his unwanted guests drove out of sight.

He slumped against his truck, still fighting the urge to punch something. Turning, he propped his elbows on the side of the bed and scrubbed his hands over his face then plunged them deep into his hair.

He needed to fix this.

But how?

Still struggling to take a deep breath, he climbed back into his truck.

A THRILL SHOT through Debbie when a knock sounded on her front door. She shouldn't be so excited to see Austin again, but the thought of spending the evening with him and his kids without the chaos of the soccer fields made her happier than she'd been since Noah left.

Getting too attached to his family was dangerous. When Savannah was done with the mural and the other projects Debbie wanted her help with, she'd never be able to fill the void they'd leave.

Austin had made it clear he wasn't interested in getting involved with her, so she needed to keep her growing feelings for him and his kids in check.

Like I can control that.

She took a deep breath before opening the door. No need for Austin to know how excited she was to see him.

One look at the man on the other side of the door, and the air whooshed from her lungs. "Austin, what's the matter?"

He often looked exhausted when he arrived for dinner, but something about his posture and the look on his face tonight went beyond fatigue. The fine lines around his eyes were deeper and longer than usual. His hair stood on end, and his shoulders hunched.

He stepped through the door and grabbed her hand. "I need to discuss something important with you."

Debbie's stomach dropped at the seriousness in his voice. She studied his face.

He was worried about something. Something serious.

Was it financial problems? Debbie would help him in a heartbeat if he'd let her.

"Daddy's here!" Cody ran at Austin with his arms open wide.

Austin swept his son up and hugged him.

Is that a tear on his lashes?

Cody squealed. "You're squishing me, Daddy."

"Sorry, buddy." He set Cody down and pulled Dallas, who stood nearby, into his arms for a hug.

Debbie frowned. What's up with him tonight?

He always greeted his kids with a hug when he came home, but tonight there was a desperation in the way he held them.

After Austin released Dallas, he went straight to the dining room. Debbie followed.

He wrapped an arm around Savannah and pulled her tight against his side. "It looks amazing, honey. Have I told you how proud I am of you?"

"Thanks, Dad." She laid her head on his shoulder, and a little zing of warmth shot through Debbie's chest at the scene.

Austin cupped her head and pressed a kiss to her hair. Tears filled Debbie's eyes. This single father had a great relationship with his children.

Savannah lifted her head and looked at her dad. "What's wrong?"

He chuckled, but it sounded forced. "What makes you think something's wrong?"

Savannah put down her brush and pallet and folded her arms. She stared at her dad with a furrowed brow.

He let out a heavy sigh, his shoulders drooping with the action. "There's something I need to talk to you about." He cast a glance toward Debbie and the boys. "Later, tonight. Okay?"

The confused girl nodded, but her face showed the same bewilderment Debbie felt.

Austin turned toward Debbie. "What can I do to help with dinner?"

They spent the next few minutes finishing preparations while the boys set the table. The meal was filled with Dallas and Cody's usual chatter, but a tension surrounded the table that the boys seemed oblivious to.

Savannah cast as many concerned glances at Austin as Debbie did. Each one was answered with a tight smile.

Thanks to Austin's unusual behavior, Debbie didn't have much of an appetite. Judging by the food he pushed around his plate, he didn't either. When the boys finally finished eating, Debbie wasn't sure who hurried the clean-up process more; her or Savannah.

Austin stood at the back door the entire time, hands deep in his pockets, staring out into the evening shadows.

"Yay! Movie time!" Cody shouted.

Austin shot Debbie a frustrated glance, and Savannah hovered nearby, as though wondering if she'd be forced to watch the movie before finding out what bothered her dad.

Austin turned to Debbie. "Is it okay if Savannah and I pop some popcorn while you take the boys downstairs and get a movie started?"

Was he dismissing her? Or did he just want a few minutes alone to talk to his daughter?

He ruffled the boys' hair. "I need to talk to Miss Debbie about something, so I'm afraid we won't be able to watch with you tonight. But Savvy will join you in a little bit, okay?"

"Okay," the boys said in unison as they darted toward the stairs still unaware of the tension filling the kitchen.

Austin caught Debbie's arm as she turned to follow the boys. "Give me a few minutes with Savannah, please."

She nodded and headed down the stairs. Exercising great patience, she listened to the boys argue then finally settle on which movie to watch. She showed them how to work the recliners and got them blankets to snuggle with. Then Debbie lingered a little longer, figuring if Austin and Savannah were done talking, she would have come downstairs by now.

Unable to stand it any longer, Debbie crept up the stairs. She couldn't hear any voices in the kitchen. Finally, she stepped around the corner to find Savannah in Austin's arms with her head on his shoulder.

Austin spotted Debbie and gave her another tight smile. He loosened his hold on Savannah and lifted her chin. "Are you going to be okay?"

She shrugged as she stepped out of his embrace. "I have to be, don't I?"

"Savvy, you know I don't want—"

"I know, Dad." She wiped at the tears on her cheeks. "I don't want to either. But if you feel that's what's best, then we'll do it." Savannah shot Debbie a quick glance then looked back at her dad. "But I think you should do that other thing we talked about, too."

Austin cupped his daughter's cheek and pressed his forehead to hers. "Don't tell the boys yet, okay. This isn't going to be pleasant, but we'll get through it together."

Savannah nodded before pulling away again. She stepped to the sink and splashed water on her face before patting it with a paper towel.

The raw emotion filling father and daughter's faces pulled at

Debbie's heart strings. Could she convince Austin to let her help with whatever was going on?

Wait.

He wasn't going to force Savannah to stop working on the mural, was he? She was getting so close to finishing, and Debbie loved it. She loved the artist and her brothers even more.

Debbie sucked in a deep breath. She'd tried to tell herself not to get too attached to the Reed children, but her mother was right; Debbie loved wholly and completely.

Savannah gathered the popcorn buckets and headed toward the stairs.

"Savannah, wait." Debbie darted to the pantry and grabbed an additional popcorn tub and filled it with juice boxes, licorice, and some miniature candy bars.

"Thank you," Savannah said when Debbie handed her the bucket. She glanced at her father who stood at the back door again with his hands in his pockets then leaned closer to Debbie. "Please say yes," she whispered, then she darted down the stairs.

Say yes to what?

Debbie turned to find Austin staring at her. He looked more guarded and upset than he did when he first arrived. She took a hesitant step toward him.

He jerked his head toward the family room and walked out of the kitchen.

Debbie followed, feeling like she was headed to her own execution.

Austin sat on the leather sofa, so she did the same, but he was back on his feet in an instant, pacing the length of the room.

Debbie wanted to tell him to just spit it out, so she could help him with whatever was bothering him, but she bit her tongue. He'd tell her when he was ready.

He finally paused his pacing and looked at her. "I stopped by my house after work and...found Cheyenne and her—" He cut off his words. "Cheyenne and Tucker were there."

Debbie scooted to the edge of the sofa. "What? Did she let you know she was coming? What does she want?"

"No. I had no idea she was going to be there. She wants to see the kids." He resumed his pacing. "She wants to take custody of them."

"Then why did she come instead of having her lawyer contact you?"

He shook his head. "I don't know. At first, she asked if we could just work something out, but when I told her she had no right to see them she threatened me with a costly, maybe even ugly, custody battle."

Debbie was on her feet. "No, Austin, you can't let her do that. Imagine what it will do to the kids."

He shoved his hands into his hair. "I know, but I can't stop her if that's what she wants. When she pointed out that she's their mother and emphasized how," he made finger quotes, "well-to-do her husband is, I kind of snapped."

"What did you do?"

Please don't let it be something that will hurt his chances to keep his kids.

"I lied to Cheyenne." Austin stopped pacing and took her by the shoulders. "Please forgive me."

Debbie would have been thrilled at the contact if his words weren't still filled with desperation.

"Forgive you for what?" she asked a little breathless regardless.

"I told her my fiancé was extremely wealthy and that legal fees wouldn't be a problem. I also hinted that she would be willing to marry me in a heartbeat if it would help my custody case." Austin cringed as he finished speaking.

He may as well have thrown ice water in Debbie's face. She couldn't have been more shocked. "You're engaged?" She pulled away from him. How could she have not known this about him after all the time they'd spent together?

And he kissed me!

"No, not yet anyway." He gave her a pointed look and a sheepish grin.

Debbie sucked in a sharp breath. "You mean me?"

I'm supposed to be the fiancé who would marry him in a heartbeat to help him keep his kids.

Debbie pressed one hand to her stomach and the other to her throat. She would do anything to protect those kids from an ugly custody battle. But marry their dad?

She was incredibly attracted to him, but to marry a man just to keep his ex-wife from getting custody was wrong. A marriage built on deceit didn't have a chance.

Austin was a good father, who didn't deserve this nightmare though.

Savannah's whispered, *"Please say yes,"* filled Debbie's head. Did that mean she wanted Debbie to pretend to be her dad's fiancé? Debbie felt she and Savannah had grown close over the past week and a half. Did the girl feel the same closeness?

Tears filled Debbie's eyes. Savvy would rather have Debbie in her life than her own mother.

Warmth flooded over her at the thought of becoming Austin's fiancé. She was more than half in love with the man already, so selling the relationship wouldn't be hard. Except he only wanted a pretend fiancé.

He's not in love with me. He'd never marry someone like me.

As badly as Debbie wanted a family, she didn't want to marry again for anything other than love. She'd tried to come to terms with the fact she might never marry again, even though the thought still depressed her. *If* she was fortunate enough to have that opportunity a third time, it would only be because she was certain it was the kind of love that would last. Like her parents.

But still…if she could help Austin keep his kids—make this situation easier on the children—she'd do it.

He began to pace again. "I know I'm asking a lot. Tucker suggested the four of us sit down and discuss the kids. He's the last person in the world I want to talk to about my kids, but I'm afraid if I don't—" Austin choked on the rest of his words.

"You're afraid if you don't, he and Cheyenne will turn this into an ugly custody battle." Debbie took a deep breath and stepped in front of Austin, putting a stop to his pacing. "He's right. Cheyenne and Tucker need to meet your fiancé. When they see how wealthy I am, they'll know threatening you with a costly custody battle won't work, which will give us the upper hand."

Austin's eyes widened, and he grinned so big it sent Debbie's heart into a tailspin. "Does this mean you'll pretend to be my fiancé?"

She swallowed down the disappointment that the word *pretend* triggered in her. There was no way she'd walk away from a fake engagement unscathed.

"On one condition." She poked his chest. It was all she could do not to gasp at the firmness of the muscles behind his t-shirt. She jerked her hand back as the urge to splay her hand across his chest hit her.

"Anything," Austin agreed without hearing her terms.

"If this *does* end up going to court, then I get to pay all legal fees."

His brow furrowed, and a mixture of emotions raced across his face. He was trying to think of other options, Debbie was sure of it, but she was determined to hold out. He would never willingly let her help him financially, but he had more than his share of financial problems, so she needed to make him commit to letting her pay the legal bills if she was going to do this.

If there was one thing she'd learned from Sofia it was to use any advantage she had to get what she wanted. And right now, she wanted to help Austin and his kids, even though she might get her heart broken in the process.

CHAPTER 19

Austin smoothed back his damp hair before knocking on Debbie's door. He'd taken off from work early today to get a haircut and shower before coming over. He may as well have not bothered going into work at all for as effective as he was.

Dallas and Cody had taken the news that their mother wanted to see them much better than he'd expected. Neither of them really remembered Cheyenne, so it didn't mean much to them.

They showed little emotion when Austin told them about their mother, but when he told them he and Debbie were engaged the boys went ballistic, cheering and jumping on the furniture like a couple of hyperactive monkeys.

"You mean we can swim everyday and watch a movie whenever we want?" Cody yelled as he jumped off the couch.

"Does this mean I'll get my own room?" Dallas ran and did a flip over the end of the sofa.

Naturally the boys assumed they would all move into Debbie's house after the wedding.

Except there isn't going to be a wedding.

It had about killed Austin to agree to let Debbie pay any legal fees that might arise with a custody battle, but that didn't mean he would accept handouts from her. He hoped this never went to court, and he certainly didn't expect her to support his family.

That's my job.

If he got into a relationship with Debbie, he had a feeling she'd expect to continue to live with the same level of comfort and convenience she did now. Like Cheyenne had when she came back to him. Austin could never afford that.

He was already in a relationship with Debbie, though. Sort of.

The door opened, and Austin's mouth dropped open.

Debbie wore a blue satin and lace dress that made her eyes brighter and bluer than ever before. Her minimal makeup made her lips look redder and more kissable than he'd ever seen. The sweetheart neckline of her dress surrounded a sapphire and diamond pendant that probably cost more than Austin made in a year. The reminder of her wealth caused a tightness in his chest.

The hi-lo hemline of her dress and silver strappy heels showed off her slender legs and complimented her curves. Her heavenly perfume hit him, ramping up his attraction. How did she always make the expensive fragrances smell so good when they had always been so nauseating on Cheyenne.

Debbie grimaced. "It's too much isn't it?"

Austin snapped his mouth closed. "No. You look great."

"I needed a little confidence boost, I guess." She gave him a shy smile as she smoothed the dress over her hips.

He smiled back as he adjusted his sports coat. He only ever dressed this nice for church. "Me too."

Cheyenne and Tucker would probably be dressed in a suit and evening gown that cost thousands of dollars each, but Austin didn't care. He'd let Cheyenne know long ago he wasn't impressed by money. That hadn't changed.

His only goal tonight—he still couldn't believe he'd let Debbie talk him into meeting with them twenty-four hours after they showed up at his house—was to let Tucker and Cheyenne see how wealthy his fiancé was and for him and Debbie to present a unified front.

Guilt rushed through him, tying him in knots, every time he

stopped to think about how he was using Debbie and her wealth to impress his ex-wife.

"So why did you ring the doorbell?" Debbie asked as she led him into the house.

"Well, I know I've let myself in a couple of times but it's your house, so—"

Debbie grabbed his arm. "You're my fiancé now, so you don't need to knock." She lowered her voice to a tone he found rather seductive. "If we want to convince Cheyenne, we need to act the part."

Austin snaked an arm around her waist and pulled her against him. A little practice couldn't hurt.

"Did you say fiancé?" a female voice asked as they entered the kitchen. "Oh my goodness! Congratulations, Debbie!" A pretty curly-haired blond, wearing an apron, circled the island and wrapped her arms around Debbie, who grimaced at him over the woman's shoulder.

Austin was still trying to figure out what was happening when Debbie pulled back and made introductions.

"Amy, I'd like you to meet Austin Reed, my— fiancé." Debbie gave him an apologetic look. "Austin, this is Amy Young. She works at Charity's Diner. I asked her to cook and serve dinner for us tonight."

Amy thrust out her hand. "I didn't realize this would be an engagement party. I would have made something a little fancier."

"It's not an engagement party." Austin shook Amy's hand and gave her what he hoped looked like a friendly smile before turning back to Debbie. "You're not cooking tonight?"

She forced a laugh. "I've been so nervous today, I was afraid we'd have a repeat of the lasagna disaster."

Austin chuckled. "Yeah, that wouldn't make a good impress—" He stopped himself and shook his head. "Why am I worried about impressing Cheyenne?"

Debbie smiled at Amy. "Would you excuse us, please?" She took his arm and guided him out of the kitchen. "Sorry for calling you my fiancé in front of Amy. I know we discussed keeping this pretend engagement quiet."

He waved away her apology. "I told the kids last night, so I'm sure word will get around. I figured it wouldn't look good if Cheyenne said something to one of the boys about us being engaged and they were clueless."

"Right." Debbie smoothed her dress again. "Listen, Austin. When you have money, people expect you to act a certain way. *You* don't need to impress Cheyenne, but she and Tucker will examine everything *I* do. And if she finds me lacking, we'll both hear about it." She waved her hands at him, flashing sparkling rings and red fingernails—nails that were pink yesterday. "That's why I got a fresh manicure today and hired Amy to cook and serve dinner tonight. That's also why I had the cleaning company that usually only comes twice a month make an extra visit today."

Debbie uses a cleaning company?

Of course she does. This house is huge. It's too much work for one person to clean.

He sighed. "I'm sorry I dragged you into this. You shouldn't have to go to extra lengths to impress my ex-wife."

"I'm not sorry." She grabbed his arm. "I'd do anything for your kids. Just promise not to hold anything I say or do tonight against me."

"What do you mean?"

"If Cheyenne gets catty, I'll probably reciprocate to an extent. Just remember I'm playing a part and that's not who I really am."

The hairs stood up on the back of Austin's neck. What was he getting into? Cheyenne could be vicious. He wasn't worried about the kids seeing that side of their mother, but he didn't want them to view Debbie in a bad light. Good thing they wouldn't be here tonight.

"Which of your sisters did you saddle the kids with?"

"I asked Joy first, and she said yes. Then she decided to invite Sheila's family over too and make a party of it."

"Did you tell them why we wanted them to watch the kids?"

"I told them you needed some moral support while you met with your ex-wife and her husband."

"But you didn't tell them we're engaged?" The collar of Austin's shirt suddenly felt too tight even though he hadn't bothered to wear a tie. A white lie was so much easier to get away with when you kept it to yourself.

"No, but if you told the boys, I'm sure they'll know before the night's over." Her brow furrowed as she grimaced again.

He shoved his hands into his pockets. "Yep, and I told Savvy she can't tell anyone the truth. Cheyenne and Tucker aren't from here, but all they'd have to do is ask a few questions around town, and they'd figure out we aren't really engaged."

Debbie stepped closer and smoothed the lapels of his jacket. "Then we need to make sure we're convincing."

Her heavenly perfume surrounded him like a gentle, seductive cloud, drawing him in. He slid his arms around her waist and pulled her against himself.

She fit so nicely in his arms.

His gaze locked on her brilliant blue eyes, spotting the green spokes there. No one would doubt his attraction to Debbie. He had a feeling it showed on his face.

Debbie was an amazing woman with so many admirable qualities. If she wasn't so wealthy—no, if he wasn't so hung up on his pride over her net worth—Austin could totally picture a future with her.

A twinge of guilt raced upward from his abdomen, tightening his chest, over the reminder that he was using her.

Debbie's velvety red lips parted in a smile as her hands slid up behind his neck to play with the hair there. "Your hair looks nice." Her voice was soft and sincere.

Again, Austin couldn't help thinking how seductive it sounded. Electric tingles raced down his spine at her touch. He lowered his head.

Her brothers are going to kill me!

The thought came out of nowhere.

He released Debbie and jerked back.

Her eyes shot open, and a frown covered her face. "Is something wrong?"

"No. I'm sorry." Austin rubbed the back of his neck where his skin still tingled. "I just... Maybe we should save the displays of affection for our intended audience. You know, since this is only pretend."

Debbie's face fell. "Right, of course." Her voice was tight. "We don't actually need practice. I mean, it's not like we haven't kissed before."

She thinks I don't want to kiss her.

Nothing could be further from the truth. He'd thought about the kiss they shared in the pantry a lot this week and desperately wanted to do it again. But he didn't want to kiss Debbie solely because Cheyenne had pushed him into this situation.

He grabbed her hand and tugged her toward him. "Debbie I—"

The ringing of the doorbell cut off his words.

He swore under his breath. Austin didn't want to eat dinner with Cheyenne and Tucker and have to act civil. He wanted to spend time with Debbie. Alone.

Maybe they could find some common ground, besides the kids, to build a relationship on. Something that didn't make the massive discrepancy in their financial statuses feel so insurmountable.

Debbie pulled him toward the front door. "That'll be our guests." She stopped at the edge of the kitchen and gave him a push. "Go open the door like it's your own home. I'll come right behind you and greet them."

Austin's shoulders bunched as he approached the front door. He certainly didn't feel at home. He paused to roll his shoulders and erase the scowl from his face before opening the door.

"Austin." Cheyenne pranced in on four-inch heels. "I have to say, I'm shocked. I didn't expect to hear from you so soon. And I can't believe you're actually engaged to whoever owns this gorgeous home."

"That would be me," Debbie said as she slid her hand into his.

He tightened his fingers around hers as his chest swelled with gratitude for this woman's willingness to stand beside him through this ordeal. He didn't know what he'd do if he had to face Cheyenne and Tucker alone.

Debbie introduced herself to their guests and invited them into the sitting room before he could find the words to make introductions.

He put an arm around Debbie as they sat on the sofa. She leaned into him, like he'd hoped she would.

Cheyenne perched on the edge of the love seat. Her green satin dress hugged her figure so tightly, she might pop a seam if she tried to sit back and relax. She looked at him. "Looks like you have a thing for redheads."

Austin took his time admiring Debbie's deep red curls that reminded him of ripe cherries. Most of her hair was pulled up in a sophisticated style this evening, but he reached out and wrapped one of the loose locks around his finger.

"I think you may be right."

Debbie put a hand on his thigh and gave him a dazzling smile. If he didn't know better, he'd think she was in love with him.

It's just an act. We're both playing a part.

That's why he fingered her hair. Not because he'd dreamed about burying his fingers in it a million times this week.

"So, how long have you two been engaged?" Tucker asked.

"Not long," Debbie answered before Austin could decide what to say. "But the attraction between us was pretty instantaneous. At least on my part." Debbie smiled at him again.

"Same," was all he could say because when Debbie smiled at him like that, his brain turned to mush.

Cheyenne ran her hand along the arm of the love seat as if inspecting the quality of the upholstery.

Austin had no idea what kind of furniture this was other than it looked nice and was comfortable. It easily rivaled anything that had been in Cheyenne's parents' house though.

"I'm surprised you even looked twice at a woman with this kind of wealth, Austin."

As if she actually knew how rich Debbie was. Austin didn't even know that.

Cheyenne's better-than-you-attitude grated on Austin's nerves. "Oh, I looked twice alright, and even a third time, before I found out how wealthy she was. Good thing Debbie has a lot of redeeming qualities."

He meant it as a joke, refusing to let Cheyenne and Tucker get to him, but when Debbie quirked an eyebrow at him, he feared he'd offended her. He should probably apologize later.

"Your engagement ring is beautiful, Debbie. Did Austin actually buy that for you?"

Scowling, Tucker leaned toward Cheyenne. "That's not a very appropriate thing to say."

Cheyenne just scoffed and waved his comment away.

Engagement ring?

Austin didn't buy Debbie a ring, engagement or otherwise. Even if he had the money to do so—which he didn't—he hadn't had the time since getting engaged last night. It hadn't even crossed his mind that Debbie should have a ring.

Debbie tensed beside him. She held out her left hand and admired the ring on her third finger; a sparkling solitaire that had to be at least a carat sat surrounded by a delicate weave of white gold strands and additional tiny marquis-shaped diamonds.

No way could he afford a ring like that. Did she splurge on it today on her shopping trip? Or had one of her previous husbands given it to her? His chest tightened at the thought, and acid crept up his esophagus.

Debbie lowered her hand. "We haven't had the chance to go shopping together since we got engaged, but I was so excited to make it official that we picked this ring from my collection of jewelry for me to wear until he can buy me one."

At least she stuck mostly to the truth. If the ring was part of her collection, it was probably from one of her previous marriages. He doubted her jerk of a first husband could have afforded a ring like that when they got married at eighteen. So that left Peter, the billionaire.

Cheyenne snorted. "You may as well get used to that ring, because Austin is too much of a penny pincher to buy anything close to that nice."

"Cheyenne!" Tucker hissed through clenched teeth.

Austin tensed, his heart thundering in his ribcage. He was about to let loose a few choice words when Debbie put her hand on his chest. The action only made his heart race a little faster.

"I don't need a fancy ring, I have plenty of those. I'll count myself lucky to wear whatever ring Austin gives me. I know he'll provide me with something beautiful as soon as he's able."

She said the words with such sincerity, he wanted to do exactly that.

Except this isn't a real engagement.

Debbie continued, "You know, after he finishes paying off the debt he got stuck with in the divorce." Debbie's voice was syrupy sweet but there was an undercurrent of hardness there that Austin did not want directed at him.

Cheyenne gave Tucker a brief, tight smile before dropping her gaze to her hands.

Amy stepped into the doorway of the sitting room. "Dinner is served."

They all made their way to the dining room where Debbie pointed out Savvy's artwork. "Savannah has been painting a mural for me."

Tucker's gaze drifted from the mostly finished area to the part that still needed a lot of work. His brow furrowed. "It's uh…"

"It's not finished yet," Austin said before he could pass judgment on Savvy's skills.

"It reminds me of this coastal village we stayed at in Sicily a couple of years ago," Cheyenne said, turning away from the wall. "It was so beautiful there. I loved the white-sand beaches with water so blue you couldn't help but fall in love with the place."

Heat filled Austin's chest. Cheyenne hadn't changed one bit. She only ever thought about herself. She couldn't even appreciate how gifted their daughter was. He was glad he'd insisted the kids not be here this evening. Savannah would have been so disappointed by her mother's reaction—or lack of—to her painting.

"Sicily *is* beautiful," Debbie said, "but Greece stole my heart." She placed a hand on her chest as she studied the wall. "Savannah's painting touches something deep inside me. It feels so life-like, I can practically smell the salty air and feel the sun on my face."

Cheyenne studied the wall again, and Austin waited for a compliment on Savvy's work. Instead, she turned to Tucker with a pout. "We should visit Greece someday."

Really?

He stepped forward—jaw clenched—ready to tell Cheyenne she could forget trying to get custody of the kids.

Debbie leaned into him, sliding her arm around his waist, as if sensing his need for a calming influence. "I'm so amazed by Savannah's talent. She's inspired me to finally decorate the house."

"I thought your walls looked a little bare." Cheyenne looked around with a frown, scrutinizing every piece of decor, which was minimal, while Tucker closed his eyes for a long moment and shook his head.

Austin always thought Debbie was a minimalist and that's why her house was sparsely decorated. He'd never considered that she simply hadn't had the desire. He'd always felt it was a family that made a house a home. Did Debbie feel the same way?

Had decorating not been a priority since what she really wanted was to fill her house with children rather than expensive things?

"I'm starting to develop a vision of what I want and have commissioned a few pieces of art that I think are going to be amazing." Debbie pulled him toward the table.

She insisted Cheyenne and Tucker sit in the seats that faced away from the painting, and Austin wanted to hug her for it. He'd much rather look at Savvy's unfinished painting than their dinner guests. And he certainly didn't want them to have the opportunity to scrutinize and find fault with Savvy's painting.

As they ate their salads, Debbie and Cheyenne continued to talk—with occasional comments from Tucker—about the exotic places they'd visited. Debbie had traveled much more extensively than their guests. Yet Cheyenne's tone remained boastful while Debbie's held a note of gratitude for being able to experience so many amazing places.

Austin had never been interested in traveling the world, but the awe with which Debbie described the Parthenon, the Egyptian pyramids, and the Incan ruins made him want to visit those places. With her.

After Amy brought out the main dish of filet mignon, Debbie shifted the topic of the conversation. "Tucker, what kind of work do you do?"

Austin focused on the delicious food in front of him and partially tuned out Tucker for the next twenty minutes while the man talked about working for an international consulting firm. The kind that often dismantled struggling businesses only to put them back together again, but costing thousands of people their jobs in the process.

For the first time, Austin noted that they were eating from fine china and drinking from crystal goblets. Debbie really had pulled out all the stops tonight.

As Tucker continued to drone on about all the companies he'd worked with throughout the world, Austin found correlations between Tucker's work and the cities Cheyenne boasted about visiting.

She travels with him.

They may have traveled all over the world, but they hadn't paid their own expenses. Tucker may make good money doing what he does, but Austin doubted he had the kind of wealth Debbie did.

For some reason, that pleased him.

He almost laughed out loud when Amy brought out thick slices of chocolate cake for dessert. The same decadent cake Debbie served him the first time he came to talk to her. Was that really only two weeks ago?

So much had happened over the past couple of weeks that he felt like Debbie had always been a part of their lives. Warmth spread through his chest, and he sucked in a deep breath. He couldn't lose sight of the fact that there were too many major differences between them.

Remembering Debbie's reaction the last time she ate this cake, he watched her face as she took her first bite.

She didn't disappoint him. Her eyes drifted close, and she hummed a soft, "Mmm."

He was still staring at her when she opened her eyes again. She turned to find him watching her. She grinned, and her lashes dipped, hooding her eyes. He couldn't decide whether she looked guilty or embarrassed, but she definitely looked adorable.

His gaze focused on a speck of frosting on her lip. The urge to kiss it off swept over him. He tightened his grip on his fork to keep himself from reaching out and pulling her into his arms.

"So, Debbie, how many servants do you have?" Cheyenne's high-pitched voice broke the spell Debbie had over Austin.

He dropped his fork and balled his hands into fists. The fork landed on his plate with a clatter.

Could the woman be any more inappropriate?

Tucker's face colored as he gave a tight smile. He leaned toward his wife again. "That's none of our business, honey."

Austin was so fed up with Cheyenne, he wanted to kick her and Tucker out. But it wasn't his house. However, Debbie said he should act like this was his home.

Debbie put a gentle hand on his arm as if sensing he was about to do something they might regret. "I don't have any servants."

When both Cheyenne and Tucker's brows rose, Debbie continued, "I *employ* people to help with specific jobs from time to time. Other than a handful of lawyers, accountants, and investment brokers I pay to help manage my late husband's fortune, I only employ one teenage boy who cleans the pool and cares for the yard."

Cheyenne's eyes widened. "You have a pool?"

Austin ignored his ex-wife's surprise and turned to Debbie. "Let me guess, Eli is your pool boy?"

Debbie winked. "I made him an offer he couldn't refuse."

Austin laughed out loud. Debbie's wealth overwhelmed him to the point of making him feel horribly inadequate, but he loved the way she helped others with her money. He looked at Cheyenne unable to keep himself from making comparisons between the two women in which his ex-wife came up lacking. He was fed up with her pretenses and arrogant attitude.

"Even though Debbie can afford to pay someone to cook like this every night, she doesn't need to, because she's an amazing cook. You should taste her lasagna."

It was Debbie's turn to laugh. She leaned over and bumped his shoulder with hers. "Shh... You weren't supposed to tell anyone about that."

He grinned. "I didn't tell them the lengths you go to to get such a unique flavor."

"Aren't you two so cute?" Cheyenne's voice had turned nasally. A sign Austin recognized as jealousy.

Not what he was aiming for by flirting with Debbie, but he'd take it. He'd had enough of the couple across from him. It was time to wrap this evening up.

He narrowed his gaze on Cheyenne. "Why are you here?"

"W-what do you mean?" Cheyenne sputtered as Tucker tugged at his collar.

"You said you wanted to discuss the kids, but you haven't even asked about them tonight, or for the last five years, for that matter." He motioned to the wall behind them. "You can't even be bothered to express appreciation for your daughter's talents. The only thing that seems to interest you is Debbie's money." He shook his head. "I don't know what you hoped to accomplish by showing up so unexpectedly, but there's no way Debbie and I..." he took the hand of the woman who'd played an exemplary role tonight, "will let you take the kids away."

"I'm their mother—"

"Then why haven't you acted like it over the last five years?" His voice rose.

Tucker put a hand on Cheyenne's arm. "Let's just tell them." His voice was firm and deep.

"Tell us what?" Austin asked with an edge of steel in his voice.

Cheyenne and Tucker stared at each other for a lengthy moment before she whispered, "Fine."

Tucker looked directly at Austin. "We don't want to take full custody. We don't even want temporary custody—"

"Then what the he—" Austin bit back a swear word. "What are you doing here?" His patience was wearing thin.

"We just want to take the kids for a couple days."

"Take them where?" Debbie said at the same time Austin said, "Why?"

Cheyenne leaned forward. "Tucker's company is having a two-day family event at a resort in Florida."

"So?" Austin said.

"Well, Tucker's company is very family oriented, and he's up for a promotion—"

Debbie looked at Tucker. "You want to use the kids to make your bosses think you're the perfect man for the job just because you have a family?" Revulsion filled her voice.

Tucker tugged at his collar again and winced as he lowered his eyes to the table.

"A *step* family," Austin corrected. There was no way he would let these two take his children thousands of miles away.

"I know it's asking a lot, but if Tucker gets this job, he'll be making twice as much as he does now and—"

Austin shook his head. "It's always about the money with you, isn't it, Cheyenne?"

She pouted. "You know I can't live an impoverished life, Austin. I'm sure Debbie understands how I feel. Once you have money, it's difficult to go without."

"Even at our poorest, we never lived in *poverty*," Austin said through clenched teeth. He hated how inadequate she made him feel.

Debbie piped up. "I think you're confusing ability with desire. It's not that you aren't capable of living a lesser lifestyle, Cheyenne, it's that you aren't willing to. And the fact that you expect to use your children to accomplish your selfish purposes proves how truly shallow you are."

Austin put his arm across the back of Debbie's chair. It was his turn to settle Debbie down. The woman was so passionate about children, especially his children, that it must kill her to discover their own mother doesn't feel the same way about them.

"Debbie's right. It's horribly inappropriate for you to use the children this way. Showing up after five years of no contact, using them for a weekend, then disappearing again. What kind of message does that send to the kids?"

Tears filled Cheyenne's eyes. "I do want to see them and spend time with them, but I… I know I'm not a good mother. I don't have much patience, and even though I know it's selfish, I enjoy my freedom." She dabbed at her eyes with her napkin. "I felt really guilty after I left, but I never pursued shared custody because I didn't want to subject the kids to my poor mothering skills. And I—" She looked at Austin and sucked in a deep breath before continuing. "I didn't want to come to resent them again. It was easier to stay out of their lives, knowing you'd take good care of them."

"Maybe you need to see your children again," Debbie said quietly.

Austin's rib cage tightened, squeezing the air from his lungs.

What is Debbie doing?

He withdrew his arm from the back of her chair and scowled at her.

She put a hand on his thigh and looked at Cheyenne. "The boys aren't needy toddlers anymore, and Savannah is almost an adult. You might find you feel differently now."

Heat filled Austin's veins at Debbie's betrayal. He scooted his chair back and bolted to his feet so fast everyone jumped. "Would you excuse us for a minute?" He grabbed Debbie's hand and practically dragged her from the dining room.

When he spotted Amy in the kitchen near the sink, he kept walking and pulled Debbie into the sitting room. "What do you think you're doing?"

Twin furrows formed between Debbie's brows as she tugged her hand from his. "She's their mother, Austin. No matter how neglectful she's been, she should see that her children are healthy and happy." Her scowl turned to a grin. "Once Cheyenne spends a few hours with Dallas and Cody, she'll see how energetic and rambunctious they are.

I mean, they only get loud and boisterous when there's something exciting going on."

And Cheyenne would hate that.

Austin laughed. "You are a genius, you know that?" He grabbed her hand again and drew her toward him. "It was amazing the way you put Cheyenne in her place at every turn. I can't believe I ever thought you were as bad as her."

"I'm just glad things didn't get really nasty."

He tucked a lock of loose hair behind her ear and dragged his finger along her jaw. "Have I told you how beautiful you look tonight?"

Debbie's breath hitched as rosy spots colored her cheeks, making her all the more attractive. She put her hands on his chest.

His heart thudded hard and fast against her palm. This woman brought out the strongest emotions in him. Ones he didn't want to fight. "I'd like to kiss you now, if that's okay?" His voice came out husky and rough.

"But we don't have an audience." Her words were breathless.

"Good." He wrapped one hand around her waist and the other behind her neck before lowering his lips to hers.

CHAPTER 20

*D*ebbie melted against Austin as his lips covered hers. She'd been wanting this all week. Ever since he gave her that glimpse of heaven in the pantry. She felt like an adrenaline junkie, craving that next big rush.

Every time Austin touched her or held her, her blood heated, and her limbs vibrated with an intoxicating awareness. More. She only wanted more of Austin. Of his kisses. His arms holding her.

Austin deepened the kiss and the stress of the day slipped away. She wrapped her arms around his neck and clung to him. She hadn't kissed a man with this kind of passion for over a decade, and it did all kinds of crazy things to her nervous system.

She'd thought she could be happy if she could adopt a couple of children, but it suddenly became clear in order to fill the emptiness in her life, she needed a man. And not just any man.

She needed a hardworking and strong man who respected women, and loved children. One who could drive her crazy with his ki—

A masculine cough sounded behind Debbie, and Austin pulled back but didn't release her.

"See, I told you he wasn't angry with her," Tucker said.

Cheyenne propped a hand on her hip. "You said he just wanted to talk to her in private. But clearly he wanted to do more than talk."

"Can you blame me?" The deep timbre of Austin's voice sent goosebumps down Debbie's spine.

Austin released Debbie and stepped away.

She immediately missed the contact of his strong warm body against hers.

"Listen, Cheyenne, I can't agree to let you just take the kids to Florida, but I do agree with Debbie that maybe you should meet the kids and spend a little time with them. Then maybe we can go from there."

Debbie could sense the tension in Austin—as she had all evening. Facing his ex-wife and the man who stole her away and considering letting them back into his children's lives must be horribly difficult for him.

Her heart swelled with pride in the man who was making such a monumental effort. As crazy as it sounded, she was glad he'd asked her to pretend to be his fiancé. This whole ordeal might break her heart, but she loved seeing how fiercely he cared for his kids and the lengths to which he would go to protect them.

"It's a start, I guess." Cheyenne gave a triumphant grin. "How about Tucker and I take the kids out to lunch tomorrow?"

"No!" Austin stepped forward. "I said you can meet them, I didn't say you could *take* them."

Debbie slid her hand into Austin's again. It seemed to be a good anchor for him this evening. "The boys have a soccer game tomorrow morning. Why don't the two of you come watch the game then you can join us back here for lunch?"

Belated, Debbie remembered she and Savannah were supposed to go shopping for prom dresses tomorrow after the game. They would just have to postpone that for a couple hours.

Austin's hand tightened on hers for a moment before he relaxed and nodded.

Tucker and Cheyenne looked at each other for a moment then finally Tucker nodded.

"Great! We'll see you tomorrow." Cheyenne offered her hand to Debbie. "Thank you so much for having us. Maybe tomorrow, you can give us a tour of your beautiful house."

Debbie watched the muscle in Austin's jaw twitch as he shook Tucker's hand. Did Austin even say two words to the other man tonight?

She heaved a sigh of relief when Austin closed the door behind the other couple.

He pulled off his sports coat. "Can you believe the nerve of those people?"

Debbie let out a heavy sigh. "Unfortunately, I've met way too many people like them. Some even worse, if you can believe that."

"I've known my share of people like them too, and I can't say that I care for any of them."

A grin spread across Debbie's face.

"What?" he asked.

"Does this mean I've graduated?"

"What do you mean?"

"Instead of saying *people like you*, meaning me, you said *people like them*." She pointed at the door. "Please tell me you don't still consider me one of those kind of rich people."

Austin smiled. "I was wrong to judge you by all the other rich people I've known. Forgive me?" She nodded, but his smile faded. "Seriously, thank you for pretending to be my fiancé and not making me face them alone."

Debbie's own smile faded.

Right. We're only pretending.

That kiss felt so real it made her forget Austin didn't mean any of this. His pride hadn't suddenly disappeared. If anything, it was stronger than ever after Cheyenne practically accused him of making her live in poverty.

"You're welcome." She forced a smile as she changed the subject. "I'll make sure the boys' remote control trucks are charged for tomorrow."

He laughed. "I never knew you could be so devious." He stretched and turned toward the door. "I guess I'd better go get the kids."

"Do you want me to come with you?"

"Maybe I'll just send you." He grimaced. "I'm not sure I want to face your sisters."

Debbie frowned. "Yeah, I don't want to face them either. Should we go in together and try to convince them this is real? Or do I face the firing squad alone?"

He rubbed his neck. "Are your brothers likely to be there?"

"No, why?"

"I have a feeling they are going to kill me when they find out we're engaged."

Debbie huffed out a breath. "They didn't drop the big brother act last Saturday, did they?"

Austin shook his head. "But I can't blame them. If my sister got engaged to some guy she'd only known for a couple of weeks, I'd run him out of town."

Debbie sat on the sofa in the sitting room and slipped off her heels. "I've made enough crazy life choices that even though my family will be surprised, they won't be too shocked."

"Right. They'll just think you're impulsive and insane, while I look like a gold digger."

"Oh please, we both know you don't want anything to do with my money."

"Yeah, but everyone else doesn't know that."

She stood and smiled at him. "Then I guess you're going to have to work extra hard to convince everyone you're really in love with me."

DEBBIE PICKED up the remote and stretched out on the sofa in her living room. She'd shed the satin and lace dress as soon as Austin and Amy left and donned comfy pajamas. The longer she continued to dress casually the more she enjoyed it.

Dressing up in nice clothing and jewelry made her feel pretty and special, but Austin's gaze had barely taken in those things when he first arrived tonight. He'd stared at her face, and she'd never felt more beautiful.

Debbie sighed. That was nothing, though, compared to the way she felt when he kissed her.

Austin seemed like the perfect man. Why did he have to have such an aversion to her money?

For the first time since marrying Peter and becoming wealthy, she considered giving it all up. She could easily sign over large chunks of Peter's fortune to various charities and be done with it, but she'd promised him she would bless as many people as she could for as long as possible. And she enjoyed helping others.

In the end, she'd let Austin go to Joy's house alone. He'd admitted he planned to text Savannah to tell her he was there and to bring her brothers out.

Debbie didn't blame him for being a coward, since that was exactly the reason she'd decided not to go. If they'd try to sell her sisters on their relationship, she'd not only feel like a fraud, she'd end up longing even more than she already did for his touch and kisses.

The doorbell rang just as she turned on the TV. She turned it off again and braced herself for the inquisition she knew was coming.

Joy and Sheila rushed in as soon as Debbie opened the front door.

"Please tell me it isn't true and that Cody was just telling lies," Joy said.

Sheila swatted Joy's arm. "Of course he wasn't lying. Even Savannah confirmed it."

They both stared at Debbie.

She stood frozen as heat flooded her cheeks. Maybe it would have been easier to have Austin beside her to help convince her sisters.

"Well?" Joy propped a hand on her hips.

"Well what?" Debbie's voice squeaked.

"Why didn't you tell us you and Austin are engaged?" Sheila grabbed Debbie by the shoulders and shook her.

"It's a new development," Debbie said.

"I'll say." Joy shook her head. "You guys barely met two weeks ago. How can you be engaged already?"

Debbie gave a shrug she hoped looked nonchalant and looked away from their gazes. "I actually met him three weeks ago. And there's a lot of chemistry there."

It wasn't entirely a lie. On her part, anyway.

"I don't doubt that." Sheila fanned herself. "Austin's a hottie, and you're so pretty and classy he can't help but be attracted to you."

"You think I'm pretty?" Debbie asked.

"Absolutely," Joy said.

"Of course, you are," Sheila added.

Debbie had always felt plain compared to her curvy sisters. Her augmentation had helped her self esteem, but she wasn't as confident and photogenic as they were. Her hair was a darker red than theirs, but she still had pale skin and plenty of freckles.

Joy shook a finger at her. "Stop fishing for compliments and trying to change the subject."

I need chocolate.

Debbie headed to the kitchen, knowing her sisters would follow. Opening the freezer, she grabbed a carton of rocky road ice cream then pulled three spoons from the drawer. She'd only taken a few bites of her cake before Austin dragged her from the dining room, and Amy had cleaned the table and thrown away the leftovers by the time their guests left.

"Yes, it's fast, but there's just something about Austin..." Debbie let the sentence hang because she wasn't sure how to finish it and just thinking about him made her warm all over.

"But two weeks?" Joy's brows raised. "Who asks someone to marry them after only two weeks?"

"Three weeks," Debbie said.

"And who says 'yes' after only knowing someone that long?" Sheila added.

Debbie didn't bother to respond, because the answer was obvious. *Only impulsive, irresponsible Debbie does that.*

Joy picked up a spoon and pulled the carton of ice cream toward her. "Wait a minute." Changing her mind about scooping ice cream, she pointed her spoon at Debbie. "You got engaged to Austin last night and had dinner with his ex and her husband tonight?"

"Oh." Sheila gasped. "I see now. Austin didn't want his wife to think he hadn't moved on and gotten over her."

"That's not why he asked me to be his fiancé," Debbie defended.

Austin could care less what Cheyenne thought about him.

"*Asked* you to be his fiancé?" Joy's gaze narrowed on Debbie. "Don't you mean he asked you to *marry* him?"

Oops.

Now they'd know for sure that her and Austin's engagement wasn't real.

Sheila grabbed the ice cream since Joy didn't seem very interested in eating it. "Duh, if she's his fiancé she's going to marry him."

"Austin doesn't strike me as the type to need to save face with his ex. There's more going on here, isn't there?" Joy's gaze narrowed on Debbie. "Why is his ex-wife in town?"

Debbie pulled the ice cream toward her and took her time digging out a bite and eating it. The cool, sugary concoction did nothing to soothe the warmth that seemed to have settled in her face and neck.

"Well?" Joy asked.

"She wants custody of the kids for a while." The admission did nothing to ease the tightness in her throat.

Sheila gasped again. "He asked you to be his fiancé, thinking it'll keep him from losing his kids."

"How would being engaged guarantee he wouldn't lose his kids?" Joy finally scooped out a bite of ice cream but focused again on Debbie.

"She threatened him with a costly and messy custody battle. He needed to let her know an expensive court case wasn't a threat." The words came out in a rush.

"He's using you for your money?" Sheila frowned. "Wow, I never thought he was that type."

"He's not. He could care less about my money. But he needed to do something to protect his kids." Debbie held up a hand. "You guys can't tell anyone the truth. If his ex finds out, it could really mess things up for him." Debbie picked at her fingernails. "And don't tell Mom and Dad, please?"

"Why not?" Sheila asked.

Joy nudged Sheila's shoulder. "Why do you think? She's afraid they'll be disappointed in her."

Bill and Alice Wheeler had always loved their children unconditionally, but there had been a few times in Debbie's life where the choices she'd made had disappointed them. Choosing to marry Keith at such a young age instead of going to college had been one of those times. Marrying Peter had been another one, because they thought she'd only done it for the money.

Not only would her whole family think she was impulsive, they would think she was irresponsible and foolish. Nothing screamed desperate like getting engaged to a man she'd only known for a few weeks.

Sheila gave her a sympathetic look.

Joy dropped the spoon that still held ice cream on the counter and grabbed Debbie's left hand. She studied the ring on her finger. "So this is all pretend?"

No doubt joy and Sheila recognized the ring as one Debbie used to wear frequently before she decided to make some lifestyle changes.

Debbie pulled her hand away before nodding and lowering her gaze. She didn't want to see her sisters' disappointment.

Sheila let out a dramatic sigh. "I'm sorry, Sis." She waved a hand in the air as she continued to talk. "I still think getting engaged after only knowing someone for two weeks is crazy, but you and Austin would make the perfect couple. And he already has kids. You'd finally get to be a mom."

Debbie had already considered that. She couldn't help herself. If this engagement was real, she and Austin would end up getting married, and she could be a mother to the three kids who made her days richer and fuller than she'd ever dreamed. But if the last eighteen years had taught her anything, it was that life rarely turned out the way you wanted.

She'd had her share of disappointments over the years, and the last thing she wanted was to open herself up for more, but she couldn't help wishing she and Austin and his children had a future together.

Joy finally picked up her spoonful of ice cream and put it into her mouth. A glint filled her eyes as she savored the sweetness.

Debbie braced herself. Joy only ever got that gleam in her eyes when she was planning.

"It's only pretend *for now.*"

Debbie did not miss the emphasis Joy placed on the last two words.

"This will give you even more opportunity to spend time together, *acting* like an engaged couple. Who knows what feelings might develop."

"Yes!" Sheila clapped her hands. "Just like all of those romance novels where a couple falls in love while they're pretending to be in a relationship."

Debbie rolled her eyes at Sheila. Her sister was such an incurable romantic. She had read her share of romances over the years, but each time she missed her chance at her own happily ever after, she'd become more and more disillusioned.

While her sisters plotted and planned ways Debbie could win Austin over by throwing herself into her role as his fiancé, she searched for ways to protect her heart from the man and children who held the power to break it.

CHAPTER 21

*A*ustin resisted the urge to pop his knuckles yet again as Debbie slid forward on her camp chair and rotated her body to look around. He knew who she was looking for, and he also knew she wouldn't find them.

"Are you sure you gave Cheyenne the right address?"

"Yes."

"And you told her I'd have extra camp chairs for them?"

"Yep." He'd also told Debbie not to bother, but she hadn't listened.

"But it's almost half time. They should be here by now."

"Mmhmm."

"Maybe you should call them."

"No way."

Debbie finally settled back in her seat and crossed her legs. Today, she wore some sort of wine-colored, flowing, silk pants with high heels and a floral blouse that brought out all of the shades of red in her hair. She looked downright sexy yet ridiculous sitting in a camp chair at the park dressed like a supermodel, wearing diamonds and rubies, but Austin was glad she was here. In case Cheyenne and Tucker did show up.

He did his best to appear relaxed even though he seethed inside.

He knew Cheyenne wouldn't show, yet the disappointment that filled him on his boys' behalf nearly consumed him. Telling the kids last night that they would be having lunch with their mother tomorrow had been one of the hardest things he'd ever done.

The boys had handled it better than Savvy. He'd talked to her for a long time after the boys went to bed and let her know she was almost an adult, and no one would make her do anything she didn't want to. He also tried to prepare her to face her mother by reminding her how self-centered Cheyenne still was.

"Should *I* call her?" Debbie asked.

"No."

"How can you just sit there acting like you don't have a care in the world?"

"I stopped worrying about Cheyenne the day she walked out on me, leaving me with three children to raise." That wasn't entirely true, but Austin had realized long ago he was better off without his ex-wife in his life.

For the hundredth time in two days, he wished Cheyenne had never shown up on his doorstep. He pulled his phone out and checked the time. "Knowing Cheyenne, she's just getting out of bed."

Debbie's brow furrowed. "You knew she wouldn't come to the game."

He gave a curt nod. "I know Cheyenne, and I know she can't be bothered with children's extracurricular activities. If it wasn't for Tucker's promotion, she wouldn't be here at all."

Debbie let out a heavy sigh as she folded her arms over her chest. "I thought she was at least a little bit sincere when she said she really did want to see the kids."

"She'll do whatever she needs to to get Tucker his raise."

"Are they likely to bail on lunch too? If so, you'll have a lot of food to eat. I placed an order for finger sandwiches, two different salads, a fruit tray, and a cheesecake assortment from Charity's Diner first thing this morning."

Austin's mouth began to water even as he wished Debbie hadn't gone to so much effort and expense. Between paying Amy to cook and serve that fancy dinner last night and now lunch, it'd take him a month to come up with the funds to pay her back. Not that she'd let him.

He shook his head. "Cheyenne wants a tour of your house too badly."

"You haven't even had a tour of my house."

"Not a guided tour, no. But I searched your whole house for Noah, remember?" Austin recalled the discomfort he felt as he rifled through her closet.

"That's right. Can you believe that was only last Monday?" She grinned, and his heart tripped in his chest. "It feels like so much has happened since then."

"Yeah, we got engaged." He gave her a sly grin.

They'd already been congratulated on their engagement twice this morning by random people he didn't know, but Debbie did. She'd confessed that her sisters knew the truth behind their engagement, but she also said they wouldn't tell anyone.

He hoped she was right. Amy must have told some people last night after she left Debbie's house though. Otherwise, no one would know he and Debbie were engaged.

The thought both warmed him and terrified him. Part of him wished their engagement was real. He liked the idea of a future with Debbie. One where his children had a caring mother. The other part of him knew he could never measure up to the kind of man she deserved.

She needed someone who was financially comfortable and didn't get intimidated by wealth every time they turned around.

"So, um… which of your previous husbands gave you the ring?"

"Which ring?" She held out her hands, displaying four separate rings. All different than the ones she wore last night, except the one on the ring finger of her left hand.

"The one you're pretending is your engagement ring." The words came out through a tight throat.

She fingered the ring. "I bought this ring for myself years ago because I fell in love with it the first time I saw it."

JILL BURRELL

"You bought it for yourself?" Austin wasn't sure why that pleased him, but it did.

"Have I mentioned that I can be impulsive? Having the money to buy whatever I want doesn't really help me curb my impulses."

That was the problem with him and Debbie? Would there ever come a day that she ran out of money? If they were together, would she expect him to support her impulsive habits?

A whistle blew on the field and the next thing Austin knew his boys were at his side drinking from their water bottles.

Forty minutes later, he followed Debbie into her driveway. He itched to call Cheyenne and tell her lunch was canceled since she didn't bother to show up for her sons' soccer game. But Debbie had already picked up enough food to feed a small army.

He helped her carry bags and boxes into the house as the boys raced to the playroom. Then he paced the opposite side of the island as she arranged the food on pretty platters.

A soft psst caught his attention. He looked at Debbie.

She tilted her head toward the doorway between the kitchen and dining room where Savvy stood with her arms wrapped around herself.

Austin stepped toward her.

Uncertainty filled Savvy's eyes. "Is it okay if I hang out with the boys in the playroom? You know, until they come."

His stomach hardened at the vulnerability in his daughter's voice, and for the hundredth time, he cursed Cheyenne for showing up out of the blue.

Debbie rounded the counter and gave Savvy a quick hug. "It's going to be okay. Lunch will be over before you know it. Then we can go shopping for your prom dress." This brought a small smile to Savvy's lips.

Austin pulled Savvy into his arms when Debbie released her. "Remember, no one is going to force you to do anything you don't want to do. That means you don't have to—"

"Hug her, I know." Savannah nodded. "It's just lunch, right?" She put on a brave face, but beneath her mask, Austin could see the insecure little girl who had been hurt deeply by her mother's abandonment.

Savannah walked out of the room, and Austin dropped into a chair and hung his head. "Please tell me this isn't a mistake. That my kids aren't going to suffer for my decisions."

Debbie knelt in front of him and smoothed back his hair. "You're just doing what you feel is best."

If he wasn't so distressed, Austin would have welcomed her touch. But he couldn't afford to let his attraction to Debbie distract him from doing what his children needed him to do.

He lifted his head and leaned back. Not far enough to insult her but enough so he could concentrate. "Please just stay by my side, and help me protect my kids from her."

The doorbell rang, and Austin tensed.

Debbie stood and pulled him up. "We're only doing them a favor, remember? You hold all the cards."

Austin let Debbie guide him to the front door. He opened it when she pushed him forward. Was she trying to help him act like the man of the house? Because he sure didn't feel like it. Not of this house anyway.

Cheyenne and Tucker breezed in like they hadn't already committed an unpardonable sin today. Cheyenne looked like she'd dressed for afternoon tea with the Queen of England in a mid-calf, lilac-colored, chiffon dress with a sequin-covered bodice. And Tucker wore business casual as though he planned to spend the afternoon at the country club.

"We missed you both at the soccer game this morning." Debbie smiled and waved their guest into the sitting room, but Austin detected a tension in her voice that wasn't usually there.

Cheyenne waved a hand in dismissal. "We booked a hotel in the Tri-Cities area last night instead of making the drive back to Boise, but I didn't have anything appropriate to wear for lunch today, so I had to go shopping this morning."

Of course, shopping was more important than her kids.

Austin flexed his fingers, resisting the urge to double up his fists and punch something. Better yet, someone.

Debbie leaned against his side and slid her hand into his.

How does she always manage to soothe my irritation with a simple touch?

"Well," he said, "I'm sure you're ready for lunch and to meet the kids. Debbie and Savannah have plans this afternoon, so we—" Austin stopped himself from saying we may as well get this over with. "We should probably eat."

"Oh, we just ate breakfast not too long ago," Cheyenne said with a wave of her hand. "I'd love a tour of this fabulous house before we eat."

"Maybe you should meet the children before we take a tour. That is why you're here, isn't it?" Debbie's words carried a hard edge. Apparently, his fiancé—*pretend fiancé*—wasn't any fonder of his ex-wife than he was.

He gave her hand a quick squeeze before standing. "I'll go get the kids."

As badly as he wanted to protect his children from their mother, the sooner she met them and realized she didn't really want custody, the better. Cheyenne would disappear as soon as she got what she wanted, so the quicker they helped that happen, the sooner he could say good riddance.

Savannah looked up as soon as he stepped into the playroom. "Are they here?"

"Yes." Austin wished there was some way to make this easier for his daughter. But she would have to face her mother at some point. He'd rather it be while he was by her side to protect her.

Savvy stood, and the boys followed her from the room. They walked much slower and quieter than their usual run-and-scream-at-the-top-of-their-lungs pace. Perhaps they were more upset about meeting their mom than Austin realized.

Dallas slid his hand into Austin's.

He squeezed his son's hand, then put his arm around savvy's shoulder and pulled her close, keeping a close eye on Cody who walked ahead of them.

DEBBIE GAVE Cheyenne and Tucker a tight smile as Austin walked out.

He better come back.

It wouldn't surprise her if he decided to take the kids and sneak out the back door. What kind of woman promises to attend her sons' soccer game then goes shopping instead? And how on earth can Cheyenne be more interested in touring the house than seeing the children she hasn't seen for five years?

Cody walked through the wide doorway into the sitting room first.

Cheyenne leaned forward on the sofa. "Oh my goodness. Dallas, you're so big."

"I'm not Dallas."

"Oh, then you're…" Cheyenne faltered as though she couldn't remember the name of her youngest son.

"I'm Cody." He said the words with an air of defiance then walked over and sat by Debbie.

She wrapped an arm around his shoulder and pulled him close.

"Cody. Right. I can't believe how big you are. You were just a little guy the last time I saw you."

And whose fault is that?

Dallas walked through the door next.

"Oh, there you are, Dallas. Wow, you sure have grown too."

"I'm almost ten." A note of contempt filled Dallas's voice.

Was that his subtle way of reminding his mother how long she'd been gone?

Even though Dallas could be as hyperactive and as loud as Cody, he had a much more serious and reserved personality. He was only four when his mom left, but was it possible he remembered her neglect while she was still there? He plopped down on the couch on Debbie's other side.

She wrapped her other arm around him. Tears flooded her eyes when he leaned into her.

Dallas wasn't usually as cuddly as Cody.

Cheyenne stood when Savannah walked into the room. "Look at you Savvy. I can't believe how grown up you are."

Savannah froze when Cheyenne took a step forward.

Debbie tensed, wanting to tell Cheyenne she didn't have any right to expect her daughter to welcome her with open arms. Austin stepped up beside Savannah, wrapping an arm around her shoulder, and Debbie sighed in relief.

Cheyenne stopped her advance. "You're such a beautiful girl, Savvy. You remind me of myself when I was your age."

Austin looked at his daughter. "Really? I think she looks like my mom. She definitely has Grandma Reed's strawberry blond hair and button nose."

Debbie bit back a smile at the way Austin put Cheyenne in her place.

He and Savannah joined them on the couch, and Debbie reveled in the feel of them being one big happy family.

Cheyenne introduced the kids to Tucker, who tugged at his collar repeatedly and greeted the children with, "How do you do?" and "It's nice to meet you."

Debbie wasn't certain if he shared Cheyenne's aversion to children, but he clearly wasn't comfortable around kids.

"So what grade are you in, Savvy?" Cheyenne asked.

"I'm a junior." Savannah's voice came out quieter than usual.

"I remember when I was a junior. That was the year our football team took state, thanks to Tucker here. Me and my cheerleader friends had so much fun flirting with all the football players on that long bus ride. Are you a cheerleader?"

"No. I'm an artist."

"Right. I saw your painting last night."

That's it? No compliment about her daughter's talent?

Heat filled Debbie and it was all she could do not to spring to her feet and tell Cheyenne and Tucker to leave.

"I can't believe how incredibly talented Savannah is," Debbie said. "I love her style, and I'm very pleased with how beautiful her painting is turning out."

"I'm so proud of her," Austin said.

"Oh right. It's a very nice painting. I'm sure it'll be beautiful when it's finished."

Seriously?

Debbie pushed herself to her feet. "Well, as Austin said, Savvy and I have plans this afternoon. So what do you say we get the tour over with and eat lunch?"

So I can get you out of my house!

Austin would hate Debbie for what she was about to say next, but she needed to get away from Cheyenne or she'd likely do something they'd both regret. "Austin, honey, would you mind taking our guests on a tour of the house while Savannah and I finish getting lunch ready?"

Austin looked at her with wide eyes. His surprise gradually turned to a scowl as his brow lowered.

She gave him a pleading look before turning to their guests. "Like I mentioned last night, I haven't done much decorating and the furniture, at this point, is pretty minimalistic. I mean half of the bedrooms are still empty." She gave a light laugh. "So don't expect too much."

Debbie guided Savannah to the kitchen so she could try to build the girl up without it being obvious she was compensating for her loser of a mother.

CHAPTER 22

Austin had no idea what he was supposed to say to his ex-wife and her husband as he walked them through the house they assumed he'd soon be sharing with Debbie.

He paused at the doorway to each room and let them go in and look around. The rooms were spacious with large closets, but like Debbie said, many of them were empty. When they reached a room that had sturdy wooden bunk beds with steps that doubled as a storage area, Cheyenne's interest piqued.

"Is this the boys' room?" She feigned a shocked expression. "Are you and the kids sleeping over already?"

"Debbie's nephews sometimes sleep over." He only knew this because Easton and Weston begged their mom to let them sleep over last week after the barbecue. "Dallas and Cody have their hearts set on finally getting their own rooms."

It would never happen, because he wasn't marrying Debbie, but she certainly had plenty of bedrooms.

Cheyenne didn't say much again until they reached Debbie's bedroom. She wandered around the master suite taking in every detail, her head slowly nodding.

With approval or acceptance? Austin wasn't sure, nor did he care.

He was too distracted by the king-sized bed covered in a blue and gray comforter with splashes of yellow. The colors fit Debbie's personality perfectly. Serious and dependable, yet lively.

Instead of being over the top, the carefully stacked decorative pillows appeared inviting, giving the bed a comfortable and cozy feel. He couldn't get the image of her laying in that huge bed out of his head.

This was the only room in the house with a personal touch. In the corner sat a leather armchair beside a small table. A reading lamp and an open book gave the spacious room a homey feel. Everywhere he looked, he saw glimpses of the woman he was falling for. A mixture of her expensive perfumes lingered in the air, making his blood pump a little faster.

He resisted the urge to follow Cheyenne and Tucker into the ridiculously large bathroom, even when Cheyenne oohed and awed. He'd taken note of the roomy glass shower with double shower heads and sunken tub when he searched for Noah last week. Both large enough for two people. The last thing he needed was to imagine Debbie in either one.

He heaved a sigh of relief when Cheyenne and Tucker finally decided they were finished ogling every little thing in the master suite. They'd spent so much time in Debbie's massive walk-in closet, Austin suspected Cheyenne had inspected all the brand names of Debbie's clothing and accessories. Maybe even tried on her shoes.

He hoped Debbie had her valuables locked away in her safe.

Austin fought the urge to roll his eyes as the unwelcome guests continued to display appreciation over the theater, game, and exercise rooms downstairs. The envy that filled Cheyenne's nasally voice as they wandered the heated indoor pool area told Austin that despite her bragging about Tucker's wealth and their worldly travels, they didn't own a house like this.

Unfortunately the tour made him more acutely aware of Debbie's wealth and the fact that he didn't belong in a home like this. A headache formed with the thought, because as much as he liked

Debbie, he wasn't sure he would ever be comfortable living with this kind of wealth and leisure.

Despite losing his appetite over the course of the tour, he was so relieved to finally sit down at the table on the covered patio with Debbie and the kids that he overfilled his plate.

Between eating lunch outside and the promise of playing with their remote control trucks afterward, the boys were especially loud. They giggled over the funny-looking finger sandwiches and complained about having to try both of the salads.

"Do we really have to eat everything?" Dallas asked.

Their noise irritated Cheyenne and Tucker, Austin was sure of it, but he didn't even try to quiet them. Telling them to use their inside voices wouldn't do any good while they were outside.

"So, Savannah, what is your favorite subject in school?" Cheyenne asked.

Good. She's finally making an effort.

"I like art of course, but I really like my math teacher too. He makes learning fun, and I'm good—"

"I was never any good at math," Cheyenne interrupted. "But Science was the worst." She looked at Tucker. "Do you remember Mr. Pick His Nose?" She turned back to Savannah and laughed. "That wasn't his real name of course. It was Pickens but he had allergies and always blew his nose so loud it scared everyone. He often stuck his handkerchief and finger so far up his nose I thought it was going to get stuck."

Austin leaned back in his chair and stared at his ex-wife. What had he ever seen in Cheyenne? Had she always been such an egotistical narcissist? Did she forget that he was the one who sat beside her in Mr. Pickens's earth science class? Not Tucker.

He looked at Tucker, who gave him a tight smile. The man didn't say much, and that was fine by Austin. It's not like Cheyenne actually gave him much opportunity.

"Savannah, why don't you tell your—" Debbie cut off her words. "Tell Cheyenne and Tucker what you'd like to study when you go to college."

Austin was grateful Debbie had pulled the conversation back to his daughter. He was also glad he wasn't the only one who had a hard time referring to Cheyenne as his children's mother.

"I'm going to study graphic design."

"You mean like the kind of art in those graphic novels? Aren't those just for children? Don't you want to do something more meaningful with your life?"

Like you have any room to talk.

Tucker ducked his head and rubbed his forehead as though he had a headache coming on. Either that or he was embarrassed by his wife.

Austin bit back a smile. He really ought to thank the other man for putting him out of his misery. The rejection he felt for himself and his children had been unbearable at the time, but looking back, he realized life had been much more pleasant without having to worry about Cheyenne's self-absorbed, insensitive, ignorant ways.

Tucker turned to Dallas and Cody. "What do you boys like to do when you're not in school?"

"I like to swim," Cody said in a much louder voice than necessary.

"I like to play soccer," Dallas said more quietly.

"I like soccer too." Cody bounced in his seat as he talked.

The boys continued to speak over one another as they continued talking about their favorite activities, including video games. They got louder with each thing they listed. Normally, Austin would have reminded them not to interrupt each other, but today, he didn't particularly care about manners. They couldn't get much worse than their mother.

Before long, Tucker looked like he regretted engaging with the boys and fell silent.

No matter what topic came up in conversation, Cheyenne had something to say, always bringing the discussion back to herself, finding new ways to brag about the lifestyle she lived.

Austin tuned her out until she said his name, and he realized she was talking to him.

"Excuse me?"

"I said what are you going to do after you and Debbie get married?"

"What do you mean?" Was this a test? Did she know he didn't intend to actually marry Debbie?

"I know how important it is to you to 'support your family.'" She made air quotes. "But it's not like the measly income you make working construction can support Debbie and all of this." She waved her hands in the air to indicate their surroundings. "So, are you planning on getting a real job or something?"

Tucker grimaced as he wrapped an arm around Cheyenne's shoulders. "That's none of our—"

Cheyenne waved him away and looked at Austin expectantly.

A real job?

Austin doubled his fists under the table. She sounded like her father. *"When are you going to get a real job so you can take care of my daughter like she deserves?"* No matter how hard he worked or how much money he made, it had never been good enough for Cheyenne and her parents.

Would Debbie think he was good enough?

Debbie leaned forward in her seat. "You do realize this house was built by construction workers, don't you?" She shook her head. "Not that it's any of your business, but what makes you think I expect Austin to support me? Marriage is a two-way street. It's each person giving one hundred percent." Debbie grabbed his hand and squeezed.

He bit his tongue. Letting a woman defend him wasn't in his nature, but he and Debbie needed to present a united front.

"Plenty of women work to help support their families. Just because I'm independently wealthy and don't need to work in order to contribute, doesn't mean that Austin's additions to our family's finances won't be welcome and sufficient."

Debbie's words made Austin feel ten feet tall but also filled him with doubt. Compared to her wealth, his income was truly insignificant despite the raise he'd received when he'd made the move to project manager last fall.

Debbie's voice took on a hard edge as she continued. "Tell me, Cheyenne, what do you do to contribute to your marriage?"

Cheyenne's mouth dropped open, and she sat back in her seat. "I—I support my husband fully in our marriage despite his frequent need to travel."

"Yes, by traveling *with* him," Debbie supplied. "But when was the last time you fixed him dinner or did his laundry?"

Cheyenne's face turned red, and she looked to Tucker for help. The other man's lips curved slightly before pressing into a thin line as though he held back a smile.

"Can we be done?" Dallas asked while Cody's cheeks still bulged with his last bite.

Relief filled Cheyenne's face at the interruption.

"Yes!" Austin and Debbie said in unison.

She must be as eager to get rid of our guests as I am.

"Leave your plates for now," Debbie said. "Bring your trucks out here to the patio to drive them, so we can keep an eye on you guys."

"Ahh," Cody said. "But the driveway is bigger and funner."

"I know, but you need to spend time with your mom while she's here."

Lunch couldn't wrap up fast enough for Austin. When the noise level surrounding them climbed with the buzz and whine of the remote control trucks, he did nothing to quiet the boys. He simply focused on his food, knowing he'd be miserable later for eating so much.

When Savannah pulled her phone out and started texting at the table, he didn't correct her either. Her table manners couldn't possibly get worse than her mom's.

His phone vibrated in his pocket. He pulled it out to read a text from her.

Can Debbie and I go shopping now?

Another one came through as he read the first.

Please!!!

He looked at his daughter. She was miserable. He could see it in her frown and the tilt of her eyebrows. Her shoulders drooped so low he had to bite back the urge to correct her on her posture.

He swiped a response.

Soon.

"Savvy, will you please help the boys load their plates in the dishwasher?" He said, giving her an excuse to leave the table.

She bolted from her chair so fast Austin almost burst out laughing.

After a lengthy silence that quickly grew uncomfortable, Debbie dropped her napkin on the table. "It's great that you two were able to visit, but Savannah and I are going shopping for a prom dress this afternoon."

"A prom dress?" Cheyenne perked up.

Debbie grimaced, regret flashing across her face.

"I'd love to go shopping with you. In fact, I saw a gorgeous dress this morning in a cute boutique in Kennewick that would be perfect for Savvy."

Savannah stepped back out onto the patio at that moment. Her brow furrowed as her gaze darted from Cheyenne to Debbie to Austin.

"I thought you wanted to spend some time with the boys," Austin said. "You know, to get to know them." The last thing he wanted was for Cheyenne and Tucker to stick around, but he also didn't want her ruining what should be a fun experience for Savvy.

Cheyenne looked at Dallas and Cody who had gone right back to driving their remote control trucks. A look of distaste crossed her face, leaving a slight frown.

"I'll have plenty of opportunities to get to know them later. But Savvy is so grown up already."

"Yes, but Debbie and Savannah have been planning this girls' outing for a while now." He tried again. "It's a good chance for them to bond."

Cheyenne affected a pout. "What about my chance to bond with my own daughter? I haven't seen her in years."

"And whose fault is that?" The words were out of Austin's mouth before he couldn't stop them.

Tucker grabbed Cheyenne's arm, but she shrugged away from him.

"I'm sorry I'm not the kind of mother you think I should be, Austin, but I really want to do this one thing with my daughter."

As far as Austin was concerned, she wasn't any kind of mother at all.

"I'm afraid we won't have room for you," Debbie said in a sweet voice that was as fake as Cheyenne's ridiculously long eyelashes. "We planned to drive my Porsche, because Austin promised to take my SUV in to get the oil changed."

She just bought the SUV; it didn't need maintenance already. Austin looked at Debbie whose eye twitched in the semblance of a wink.

"That's right the Cadillac is overdue for an oil change."

"So, why don't you change it yourself?" Cheyenne gave him a doubtful look. "You used to always do that to save money."

"Yes, but we never owned a car that cost a hundred grand either."

"Well, Tucker and I can drive. There's room in our Mercedes," she threw out the make of their luxury car as though she thought it would impress someone, "for Debbie and Savvy to ride with us."

"Actually, I promised Savvy she could drive the Porsche."

He knew what Debbie was trying to do, but it was all Austin could do to stay in his seat. Savvy had her driver's license, and she was a good driver, but she hadn't had much opportunity to drive on the interstate at higher speeds. He certainly didn't want her to do it in a car that cost more than he made in a year.

"Oh, well, we can just follow you so we can shop together then."

"I have some work I need to do this afternoon, Chey," Tucker said.

She waved a hand of dismissal. You can do it in the car while we shop. Like you always do." Cheyenne turned to Savannah. "Wouldn't it be nice to have your mom as well as your soon-to-be step-mom with you when you pick out your first prom dress?"

"What makes you think this is my first prom?" Savvy's voice lacked the confidence Austin figured she was aiming for.

"Because I know your dad, and I'm pretty sure he would have thought you were too young to go to prom last year."

Austin rose and stepped to Savannah's side. "You don't have to do thi—"

"I know," she lowered her voice, "but if I don't, is she going to cause more problems?"

"I don't know, honey." Austin hated that his daughter was forced to make this kind of decision.

Savvy turned to Cheyenne. "I guess you can come, but I'm going to ride with Debbie." Then she turned and walked into the house.

Debbie was on her feet in an instant, grabbing her own plate and Austin's. "Looks like I'd better get lunch cleaned up then, so we can go."

"You don't have your hired help today?" Cheyenne asked.

Debbie turned a tight smile on the other woman. "I don't *need* her today. I'm perfectly capable of cleaning up. Besides, Austin and the children are great helpers."

That was his cue. He stepped back to the table and grabbed his and Debbie's lemonade glasses.

"Wait," Cheyenne grabbed his arm. "We've met the kids. Can we make arrangements to take them to Florida now?"

"No way in he—" He bit his tongue. "No. You cannot make arrangements to take my kids to Florida." He set down the glasses, propped his fists on the table, and glared at his ex-wife. "Maybe, just maybe, if you had come here acting like you truly wanted to see the kids and given me even a glimpse that you actually cared about them, I might consider it. But you are so self-absorbed that you can't be bothered to discover what amazing children you have."

Cheyenne was on her feet in an instance, all semblance of niceness gone. "I'll get the lawyers involved if I have to, Austin. And I'll demand visitation and shared custody right away."

"Now, honey, settle down." Tucker wrapped an arm around Cheyenne. "We've got plenty of time to work this out with Austin and Debbie. There's no need to involve the lawyers." He gave Austin an apologetic look.

Austin couldn't help but wonder whether Tucker was truly happy with Cheyenne. It appeared that she took advantage of him and his wealth every bit as much as she had Austin's—except he didn't have any wealth. Of course, that hadn't stopped her from spending money.

Cheyenne stamped her foot. "I know but the sooner we get this squared away, the sooner we can get out of this hick town." The words were meant for Tucker, but Austin heard them.

"We'll go back to our condo in Boise tonight and we'll follow up with Austin and Debbie next week."

Condo?

Was that the only residence they had? No wonder Tucker was eager to avoid calling the lawyers. He either traveled so much he didn't need a bigger residence or he didn't have nearly as much money as Cheyenne wanted them to believe.

"DEBBIE, WAIT." Austin hurried across the garage when Debbie opened the door to her Porsche. Without warning, he pulled her into his arms.

She tensed despite her racing heart. Was this just a demonstration for Cheyenne and Tucker's benefit since they had a clear view of them from where they stood beside their Mercedes? When Austin ducked his head toward her neck, she wrapped her arms around his waist. She'd love to melt into him and let him wipe away the tension that filled her.

After that ordeal with Cheyenne, she needed a confidence boost. Especially considering the afternoon she faced.

Austin's arms tightened. "Look out for Savvy, please. Cheyenne is the type to steam-roll a soft-spoken person over, and Savvy would never dare to stand up to her mom."

His warm breath against her ear sent shivers coursing down her neck and back. She wanted nothing more than to stay in his arms forever. Again, she toyed with the thought of giving away all her money. If it meant she could have Austin and be wrapped in his arms everyday, she'd do it.

Debbie nodded. "Okay, but who's going to look out for me?"

He pulled back to look at her. "You're hardly soft spoken, and I love that about you."

Hearing the L word out of his mouth sent a surge straight to her heart. Loving her and loving something about her weren't the same thing, but maybe her sisters were right. Could she make him fall in love with her during this fake engagement?

Debbie didn't want to lump herself in the same category as Cheyenne, but she was selfish. She wanted Austin's attention. She wanted him to kiss her again.

She grinned. "No, I'm worried about who's going to bail me out when I get arrested for assaulting Cheyenne."

He threw back his head and laughed, and warmth flooded over her. His laughter was rich and full and made her feel light and bubbly.

"I certainly wouldn't blame you if you did." His arms slackened as though he intended to let her go.

Debbie didn't release him. "Is that it?"

"What do you mean?"

"We have an audience that we are trying to convince we are in love, and you're not going to see me for hours. Shouldn't you be loath to let me go?"

Yep. I'm selfish alright.

He smiled as he tightened his embrace. "Right. We shouldn't pass up this opportunity to convince them."

Convince.

The word made her heart sink a little, but then Austin's lips were on hers, and her pulse skyrocketed.

There was nothing hesitant about this kiss. His lips claimed hers and moved with a gentle yet determined motion that made a million little fireworks explode inside her body. Sparkler-like flashes of electricity raced along her nerve endings, filling her with the most incredible sensations. Weightlessness. Euphoria. Heaven.

Splaying her hands across his broad muscular back, she kissed him with everything she had, enjoying the moment, in case she never got another one.

Austin pulled her more firmly against his body, readily accepting all she offered and giving in return. He ran his hands up her back, leaving a trail of fire under her silk shirt. Burying one hand in her hair, he cupped her head. The other traveled back down to her hip.

"Ew, Dad." Savannah's voice came from inside the car. "Enough already."

Austin's lips turned up in a smile, effectively ending the kiss. He kept his head close to Debbie's however. "I think we grossed her out." His voice was rough and gravelly.

Another little shiver shot through her. This man did things to her that she hadn't felt in a very long time. Things she wanted to feel more of.

"Yes, and if that wasn't convincing, I don't know what would be." Her voice still sounded breathless.

He lifted his head and brought his hand up to stroke her cheek. "That was..."

"Nice," she whispered.

"Yeah."

"Dad, can we go already?" Savvy's voice had taken on a note of impatience.

Austin's hold on Debbie loosened. "Good luck."

"I think I'm going to need it." She climbed into the car and looked at Savannah slumped in the passenger seat. "Are you sure you don't want to drive?"

"I'm not in the mood today. I'd probably wreck your car. That's all I need with *them* following us."

"I'm sorry I let it slip that we were shopping for a prom dress," Debbie said as she backed out of the driveway, trusting Austin would lock up her house when he left.

"It's okay." Savannah shrugged. "It's not like we've been able to connect on any other level. Shopping's my mom's favorite activity, so...who knows, it might end up being fun." She didn't sound very convinced.

"The lack of connection is not your fault. You know that, right?" Debbie put the Porsche into first gear and took off down the two-lane highway.

Savannah gave another shrug.

Debbie put a hand on the girl's arm. "You don't need to impress your mom or try to prove yourself to her in any way."

"I know, but…"

"But what?"

Savannah shrugged again. "I know girls whose moms are their best friend. I guess I kind of always wanted that."

"I imagine her leaving was really hard on you. Especially as you were coming into your teen years."

"It was, but it's not like she'd been home much before she left."

Debbie recalled Austin saying he often came home to find a babysitter taking care of the children. She had always had a good relationship with her mother and sisters, so it broke her heart to realize that Savannah had never had that.

"What kind of experiences do you wish you'd had with your mother?" Debbie asked. Maybe she could do some of those things with Savannah. It wouldn't be the same as doing them with a mother who loved her, but maybe it would let the girl know how much she cared about her.

Savannah scoffed. "Nothing now. I mean, I always kind of wondered what it would be like if she came back. I guess I had forgotten how self-centered she was."

"She is quite the narcissist, isn't she?"

"Can we not talk about her anymore, please?" Savannah asked.

"Gladly," Debbie said with a laugh.

"What would you like to talk about? We have a long drive, it'll pass faster if we talk about something fun."

When Savannah didn't say anything, Debbie took on a teasing tone. "Should we talk about Caleb?"

Savannah had been so excited on Thursday when she told Debbie that Caleb had asked her out already. After finishing homework with the boys and without Noah to keep an eye on, Debbie talked with Savannah a lot while she painted. It had become the highlight of her days.

She was about to ask Savannah if she'd decided how to respond to Caleb yet when the girl gave her a serious look.

"Do you like my dad?"

Warmth filled Debbie's face. Her and Austin's kiss had been for Cheyenne and Tucker's benefit, but she should have remembered they had another audience too. She debated how to answer Savannah's question. If she said "yes" would that upset the young woman? And if she said "no" would Savannah be disappointed.

She darted a quick glance at Savannah and decided the girl deserved the truth. "I like your dad very much. But you do know we're only pretending to be engaged, right?"

"Yeah, but..."

"But what?" Debbie prompted. She really wanted to hear what Austin's daughter thought about all of this.

"I've never seen him kiss anyone besides my mom. But he never kissed her like *that*."

The warmth that had filled Debbie's face spread throughout her body as she remembered how passionate their kiss had been. She could understand why Austin never kissed his wife like that in front of the kids. Kisses like that usually led to other things that weren't appropriate with an audience.

What might have happened if he'd kissed her like that without an audience?

Stop.

She couldn't go there. It'd only make her want things she couldn't have right now. And maybe never would.

"Hasn't he dated over the last five years?" Debbie asked, trying to change the direction her thoughts had headed.

"No."

"Really? Not at all?" Debbie didn't know why, but that pleased her.

"I asked him once why he didn't date, and he said he just wanted to focus on us kids. I told him he was going to be lonely when we all left home, and he said he had yet to meet anyone he was interested in getting to know better. I thought maybe he was still in love with my mom, but he let me know that wasn't the case."

Cheyenne was certainly a beautiful woman, but if their relationship had been as tumultuous as he'd described in the pantry, their love had probably faded long before she left. Debbie and Austin weren't exactly dating, and he'd been forced into proximity with her because of the job she hired Savannah to do, but was she the kind of woman he'd like to get to know better? Did finding her attractive equate to wanting to get to know her better?

Or did her wealth negate any attraction he might feel?

She handed Savannah her phone. "Here, find us some music to listen to."

~

"How about this one?" Cheyenne held up a form-fitted burgundy sheath with a slit clear up to the hip and a plunging neckline.

Debbie fought the urge to roll her eyes. She'd worn her share of skin tight clothing with low necklines, but she'd never worn anything that provocative. She couldn't believe Cheyenne suggested it for her sixteen-year-old daughter.

"Um...that's not really my style," Savannah said before turning and slowly wandering around Debbie's favorite dress shop.

A few minutes later, Cheyenne held up another dress that had no back. "Look at this gorgeous green one."

The emerald-colored satin was pretty, but Austin would kill Debbie if she bought his daughter a dress like that. She breathed a sigh of relief when Savannah shook her head.

"Oh, I've got one." This time Cheyenne held up a sparkling white dress that was even lower cut than the first one and possibly see-through.

"Seriously?" Debbie couldn't hold her tongue any longer. "That's not an appropriate dress for Savannah."

Cheyenne surveyed the dress then looked back at her daughter. "I suppose you're right. She's not busty enough. Too bad you're not as endowed as Debbie and I are." Then she headed to the dressing room with the white dress.

Debbie stepped close to Savannah. "Don't listen to her. You're perfect the way you are. Besides, her boobs are just as fake as mine."

Savannah snorted as she tried to smother a laugh.

Debbie put her hands on her hips and stuck her chest out. "If my boobs were real, I'd have the curvy hips to match them, like my sisters." She tilted her head toward the dressing room. "Trust me, I know implants when I see them. I suspect your mother had a tummy tuck as well."

Savannah laughed again.

They'd ended up doing a lot of that on the drive here. Their discussion of music, friends, and boyfriends had morphed into sharing their daydreams and most embarrassing moments. Austin had tried to deter Cheyenne by telling her this shopping trip was meant to be a bonding opportunity for Debbie and Savannah, but she hadn't expected the bonding to happen so easily.

She felt a closeness with this girl that surprised her. Even more so than she did with her own nieces. Savannah reminded her so much of herself when she was a teenager full of hopes and dreams that were often overshadowed by insecurities. Trying to find her place in the world while being responsible for younger siblings wasn't easy.

Even though the conversation circled around to Austin occasionally, Debbie was careful not to let it linger on him for too long. Otherwise she might admit to Savannah that she was in love with her father.

Savannah finally found a dress to try on but decided she didn't like the way it looked on her, so she returned to the floor to look some more.

Cheyenne continued to suggest dresses that weren't appropriate for a teenage girl, including a little black dress that was so short it hardly left anything to the imagination.

Debbie looked around in frustration. There were plenty of pretty dresses here that could be considered modest, but Savannah didn't seem interested in any of them. Not that she was interested in any of the ones her mom was picking out either. Thank goodness.

It didn't dawn on Debbie until now that although this shop had all kinds of formal dresses, it catered to the more mature woman. There was nothing here that fit the fairytale type dream of a young girl going to her first prom.

She pulled out her phone and did a quick search for dress shops.

A few minutes later, Debbie had to intervene as Cheyenne tried to insist Savannah try on a purple, satin, strapless dress.

"It reminds me of the dress I wore to senior prom." Cheyenne guided Savannah over to one of the floor-length mirrors and held the dress up in front of her. "Your dad couldn't keep his hands off me that night. Of course, I couldn't keep my hands off him either. Have you ever seen him in a tux?"

"That's enough," Debbie said. "We're done here." She took Savannah by the arm and headed for the door, trying desperately not to picture Cheyenne in Austin's arms. "There's another shop I think we should check out."

"Wait!" Cheyenne called. "I want to buy this white dress before we leave."

Fifteen minutes later, Debbie knew she'd made the right choice in bringing Savannah to a different store when the girl's eyes practically lit up as they walked through the door. The racks were full of gorgeous floor-length satin and chiffon dresses in bright jewel-toned and pastel colors. It was every young girl's dream. Any girl who ever dreamed of being a princess, that is.

Savannah's smile dimmed as she checked a price tag.

Debbie hurried to her side. "Don't worry about the price. I have a plan for you to earn the money, remember? You just find the dress that's right for you, okay?" She'd even taken time to pull cash out of the bank yesterday so she could hand it over and let Savannah pay for her own dress.

Savannah nodded and pulled the dress from the rack. It didn't take her long to gather a selection to try on.

Debbie stood near the dressing rooms and gave appropriate compliments each time Savannah came out in a new dress. She wanted to smack Cheyenne for her negative comments.

Too plain. It washes you out. Boring. It's not very flattering.

Debbie tried to follow up each of Cheyenne's criticisms with something positive, so Savannah didn't take her mother's words to heart. Her breath caught when Savannah stepped out of the dressing room in a beautiful misty blue dress. The fitted bodice was covered in lacy embroidered flowers accented with tiny silver, hand-sewn beads. The flower design tapered off just past her hips where the A-line chiffon skirt curved out in a graceful bell shape.

The dress was neither too poofy or plain. It fit Savannah perfectly, and she looked simply beautiful in it. Out of all the dresses she'd tried on, Savannah liked this one the best. The smile on her face attested to that.

"You look beautiful, Savannah." Debbie whispered.

Cheyenne regarded her daughter. "It's pretty, I guess. But it makes you look like a little girl playing dress-up."

Savannah's smile faltered.

Debbie grabbed her hand and made eye contact with her in the mirror. "Don't listen to her. You look like a princess. Besides, prom is the funnest ball to play dress-up for."

Savannah's smile returned, and she studied her image in the mirror for a long time. Before she returned to the dressing room, Debbie insisted they find some accessories to go with the dress.

She toyed with the idea of letting Savannah borrow her diamond necklace, earrings, and bracelet, but she figured Austin would have a fit. He looked like he might have a heart attack when she mentioned letting Savannah drive the Porsche.

Debbie made plans to ask Austin if he'd let her arrange for a manicure and hair trim and styling for Savvy for prom as they selected a delicate rhinestone-covered headband, cubic zirconia jewelry, and silver low-heeled sandals.

When Savannah headed to the dressing room to change, Cheyenne stopped her.

"Savvy, wait!" She approached with a crimson-colored dress similar to the ones she'd tried to get Savannah to try on at the previous store. "I think you should try on this one. It would totally bring out the red in your hair, and I think it would be very flattering to your figure, straight as it is."

"She's already chosen a dress," Debbie said through clenched teeth. Where had the woman been for the past twenty minutes?

Cheyenne propped a hand on her hip. "Well, if I'm going to pay for a dress, I think I should have a say in what dress my daughter gets."

"You're not paying for the dress." Debbie's head began to pound. She'd had about all she could take of this woman today.

"I know you have plenty of money, but you're not her step-mother yet, so it's not really your place to pay for it."

Debbie bit back a comment about it not being Cheyenne's place either, because she hadn't been much of a mother for the past five years. Instead, she forced a smile and said, "Savannah will be paying for her own dress."

"Oh." Cheyenne's eyes widened. "I didn't think Austin had that kind of money."

"She earned the money herself by working for me." Debbie nudged Savannah toward the dressing room, turning her back on Cheyenne.

And I'll make sure I slip her the cash as soon as we're out of Cheyenne's sight.

They couldn't get out of the store fast enough to suit Debbie. When they walked out, Tucker still sat in his car. Still on the phone, like he was at the last store. Where that man found enough patience to put up with Cheyenne was beyond her.

After putting the dress box and accessories bag into her trunk, Debbie turned to Cheyenne. "Well, it's been..." Debbie found herself at a loss for words. She couldn't say fun, because it wasn't. She couldn't even say pleasant, because it had been the exact opposite.

Cheyenne pulled Savannah into a hug. "Thanks for letting me tag along. Maybe next time I'll buy you the red dress."

Debbie took in Savannah's stiff posture and wondered if she needed to rescue the girl.

Fortunately, Cheyenne stepped back after a brief moment. "Well, we have a long drive back to Boise tonight. I'll probably see you both sometime next week." She slid into the Mercedes next to Tucker.

"I hope not," Debbie said through tight lips as she tried to hold a smile that she hoped looked cordial.

Savannah snorted again as she burst into laughter beside her. "Me too."

Debbie hooked her arm through Savannah's. "I need chocolate. And ice cream. Rich chocolate ice cream. Are you in?"

Savannah smiled and nodded.

"Good. Then afterward, you can drive the Porsche home."

CHAPTER 23

Austin dumped the cooked spaghetti noodles back into the pan and drizzled olive oil over them to keep them from sticking. Memories of dropping Debbie's olive oil and both of them getting splashed filled his mind.

Her shocked face looked so cute. Then when she dissolved into giggles while trying to clean the floor, he couldn't help but join her.

Cody saying Debbie's name in an excited voice that was at least ten decibels higher than it should be caught Austin's attention.

"And she has this really big house."

Austin looked over his shoulder to see Cody waving his arms in the air to demonstrate how big Debbie's house was for his Grandma and Grandpa Reed who'd only arrived half an hour ago.

"It's ginormous!" Dallas added.

"It's got a swimming pool and a movie room." Cody's voice got louder each time he spoke.

"And a game room." Dallas's voice rose in pitch too. "And we get our own rooms after Dad marries Debbie."

"What?" Austin's parents said in unison.

Austin froze.

Shoot.

He'd forgotten to tell the kids not to mention that. Of course, they would tell their grandparents about the most exciting thing to ever happen to them.

Within seconds, both of his parents stood in the kitchen staring at him.

"Since when are you engaged?" His mom spoke first.

Austin gave them a tight smile. "Dallas and Cody, go play in the backyard for a while, please."

"But Nana and Papa just got here," Dallas said.

The kids loved their grandparents. They'd grown close while Austin and the kids had lived with them for a year after his divorce. Since their move to Providence, the kids' contact with their grandparents was limited to Sunday video calls, so having Nana and Papa here for Easter was a special treat.

"I know, and you can visit and play games with them after dinner. But right now, I need to have a grown up talk with them."

"Okay," Dallas said. He grabbed Cody's t-shirt and pulled him to the sliding glass door.

"No fighting," Austin called to them as they closed the door behind them.

He turned and covered the noodles and turned the burner under the simmering spaghetti sauce off before facing his parents.

"I can't believe you didn't tell us you were dating someone," Mom said, her voice an octave higher than usual.

"I'm not." He held up a hand when his parents started to protest. "I mean, I wasn't."

Technically he and Debbie still hadn't dated even though they'd kissed three times.

Austin sat at the table and motioned for his parents to do the same.

"What's going on, son?" Dad asked as soon as he'd settled into a chair.

Austin sucked in a deep breath. "I haven't been dating anyone. It's not what you think. I'm not really engaged."

"Then why did the boys say you were getting married?" His dad's heavy eyebrows lowered.

Austin looked at the ceiling for a moment before sighing. He couldn't lie to his parents. "Cheyenne showed up here a few days ago. She wants to take custody of the kids."

"What?" Mom's face registered panic.

"Why now?" Dad said, his brows lowering even further.

"Apparently, Tucker is up for a promotion. He works for a family friendly company, and they want to use the kids to show that they're dedicated to their family." The derision in his voice grew sharper with each word.

"I always knew if Cheyenne showed up again it'd be because she was up to no good." Disapproval filled his mom's face.

"Tell me about it."

Savannah had been near tears when she came home and told him about the horrible shopping trip with her mom. He had a feeling if it wasn't for Debbie the whole day would have been absolutely miserable. He hated to think how horrible it might have been for Savvy if Debbie hadn't been there to build her up and cheer her up with ice cream and the opportunity to drive one of the most expensive sports cars in the world.

Now she was in her room with Rainy, gushing over her dress and the pretty accessories Debbie helped her pick out.

Seeing Savannah behind the wheel when the Porsche pulled up outside only an hour ago nearly gave him a heart attack. Then Debbie climbed out of the car, and their kiss came flooding back to him, and it was all he could do to breathe while his heart raced a hundred miles an hour. It had taken every ounce of his willpower to keep from walking outside and pulling her into his arms again. Instead, he smiled and waved at her through the window and waited for Savannah to come in.

For a moment, he thought she might follow Savvy inside after his daughter hugged her, but she just smiled and waved back. Then she slipped into her car and drove away.

Dad shook his head. "I'm sorry to hear Cheyenne's back, but I don't understand what that has to do with you getting engaged."

Austin told his parents how he'd panicked by lying about being engaged to a wealthy woman when Cheyenne first threatened him with an expensive and messy custody battle. He left out the part about said woman being willing to marry him for the sake of the children.

"And this Debbie just agreed to be your fiancé?" Mom asked. "Isn't she the one Savvy's doing the painting for? Why would she agree to such a hair-brained idea?"

"We've become pretty good friends, and she loves kids. The boys really like her."

I like her.

Did kissing her in the pantry make them more than friends?

"I'll say," Dad said. "They wouldn't shut up about how nice and pretty she is and how big her house is."

Now mom's brow creased. "I understand why you felt she'd be a good safeguard against Cheyenne, but are you sure you know what you're doing getting mixed up with another wealthy woman?"

"I'm not getting mixed up with her. This whole engagement is just pretend." Maybe if he said it enough he'd believe it. Because each time they kissed, an electric charge shot straight through his veins. It felt reckless and dangerous yet exhilarating. It filled him with a magnetic charge that made him never want to let her go.

Crap. I'm totally mixed up with her.

"Tell that to your sons," Dad said.

"I can't. I can't risk them telling Cheyenne the truth." Not that she even bothered to talk to them today.

Austin rubbed his hands over his face. He really should have considered how a fake engagement would affect the boys, especially when the threat from Cheyenne was over, and he ended the relationship.

And he had to end it. His pride wouldn't let him marry a woman who was so rich it would feel like she was supporting him and his family.

"It's nice of Debbie to be willing to help you out," Mom said, "but I worry that you might fall for another rich woman. Don't forget how miserable you were trying to keep Cheyenne happy."

He'd never forget how difficult life was with Cheyenne, but he was definitely falling for another rich woman, and there wasn't a single thing he could do about it. Especially if they kept kissing.

"Debbie's different. She's not spoiled and selfish like Cheyenne. She actually grew up as the oldest of a large family with modest means."

It was so easy to defend the beautiful redhead, so why couldn't he accept her wealth?

"How did she become so wealthy?" Dad asked.

"She inherited the money when her second husband died." He wouldn't bother telling them how old Peter was. His parents would think Debbie was a fortune hunter.

"She's been married twice already?" Disapproval filled his mother's voice.

Austin rubbed his neck. He wasn't surprised that tidbit of information bothered them. It still bothered him a little, even though he knew her marriage to Peter was in name only. It made it sound like Debbie didn't take marriage vows seriously.

But he didn't intend to marry Debbie, so why was he still so jealous of her previous relationships?

"How far is this thing with Cheyenne fighting for custody likely to go?" Dad pulled Austin's wandering mind back.

"I don't know. She wants to take the kids to Florida for a weekend for some sort of corporate family retreat."

Mom gasped. "Florida!"

"Yes, and every time I dig in my heels, she threatens to call her lawyer."

"You can't afford that, son."

"I know." Austin didn't bother to tell them of his promise to let Debbie pay if it came to that.

His pride couldn't take that kind of hit. It had been hard enough to borrow money from his parents and to rely on them so much over the years. He couldn't tell them he'd agreed to let a woman he'd only known for a couple of weeks pay for his legal fees.

"I can't believe I'm saying this," Mom said, "but you need to do whatever it takes to keep Cheyenne from getting the kids. I doubt her mothering skills have improved over the past few years."

"No, they haven't. If anything, they've worsened."

"How far is this Debbie woman willing to go to help protect the kids?" Dad asked.

Austin shook his head. "I don't know."

He'd been up front with Debbie about the lie he'd told Cheyenne, and she still agreed to pretend to be his fiancé. If it came down to it, would they go through with it? A fake marriage sounded even less appealing than a real one, because there would be no doubt in either of their minds that he was using her for her money. Besides, he didn't think he could live in the same house with her without wanting her in a very real way.

If letting Cheyenne take the kids to Florida was the only way to keep this from going to court, he had to agree. But how could he subject his children to that?

JOY SIDLED up to Debbie as she speared a slice of ham. "So, have you told Mom and Dad yet that you're engaged?"

"No." Debbie's gaze darted around, ensuring neither of her parents were near.

"You know they're going to be even more upset if they find out from someone else."

"I know. I'd hoped this whole thing would stay quiet, but Amy Young overheard us talking about it and must have told someone because two different people stopped to congratulate us at the soccer game yesterday."

"I'm surprised no one said anything at church today," Joy said as she scooped up potatoes.

"Me too. I guess everyone was too excited about it being Easter."

Debbie had been tempted to sit by Austin and the kids, but when an older couple she suspected was Austin's parents joined them, she decided to sit with her own parents. But their gazes had locked for a moment, and a tingling warmth flooded over her.

"I say rip the bandage off and just get it over with." Joy patted Debbie's shoulder before grabbing one of their mom's homemade rolls and walking away.

Debbie turned and searched for a place to sit.

Her whole family had come over to her house for a change, mostly because her big yard would make for a fun easter egg hunt. After lunch, the women would help the kids color hard-boiled eggs while the men hid candy filled eggs outside.

Today's weather wasn't quite as nice as yesterday's, but they'd still chosen to eat outside. Her dad and brothers had set up extra tables out on the back lawn while the women finished getting the food ready.

Although tempted to sit by Joy and Sheila, Debbie walked over to where her dad and brothers sat. Two empty chairs remained at their table, one for Debbie, the other for her mom.

Mom always sat by Dad. It was just the way they were. Always searching each other out. Each of them making sure the other had everything they needed. They frequently touched and flirted with one another like they were still newlyweds regardless of who was around.

Debbie wanted a relationship like that. She wanted a man who worried about whether she was comfortable. One who wasn't afraid to pull her into his arms and kiss her silly even though there were people around. Like Austin did yesterday.

Her face grew warm as she slid into the chair across from her dad. Every time Austin kissed her he rocked her world, but there had been a hunger in yesterday's kiss that spoke of passion and promises.

Mom was always the last one to serve herself, but Debbie didn't have to wait long for her to join them. She played with her food, drawing designs in her mash potatoes with her fork. There was no way she could enjoy eating until she got this weight off her chest.

When she realized she was drawing a heart, she knew she was in trouble.

"Is there something wrong dear?" Mom's gentle voice made Debbie jump.

She sucked in a deep breath. "There's something I need to tell you and dad."

Scott and Rudy must have sensed her apprehension because they both looked up from their food and gave her a wary look. They looked ready to bolt. With three older sisters who openly discussed hormones and female problems, they had been exposed to many discussions they would've liked to avoid. Her dad looked like he'd rather be anywhere but there during most of those conversations too, but he always stood beside her mom, offering his mostly silent support.

Just get it over with. Quick. Like a bandage.

Debbie braced herself and blurted, "Austin and I are engaged."

"What?" A chorus sounded around the table.

First from her dad, then her brothers.

"Wh-when did this happen?" Mom's voice was an octave higher than usual. "Didn't you just barely meet him like two weeks ago?"

"Three weeks," Debbie said, like an extra week made all the difference. "W-we got engaged Thursday night."

"Oh, honey," Mom said in a quiet voice. Her tone was soft but it was filled with disappointment.

Dad hung his head and shook it back and forth.

Gah.

Debbie hated disappointing her parents.

Mom reached out and clasped Debbie's hand. "I know you're desperate to have a family, sweetheart, but throwing yourself at the first man you meet who has kids isn't the right way to go about it."

"I didn't throw myself at Austin!"

I just threw my tampons at him. Three times.

"Maybe not, but you hired his daughter, and you insist on feeding his family dinner every night."

Mom only knew that last part because Debbie needed dinner ideas a few days ago.

"I only did that so that Austin would agree to let Savvy paint my mural. He relies on her to tend the kids and fix dinner on the nights he works late."

"I know. You explained that the other day, but I still fear your generosity has made you a target of a desperate man."

"It's not like that," Debbie insisted. Although it was more like that than she wanted to admit.

Debbie sat back in her seat and crossed her arms. She looked over at Joy, seeking support.

Joy mouthed, "Tell them the truth."

The less people who knew this engagement was fake the better. All Austin needed was for someone to let it slip and for Cheyenne to find out. She'd use that to her advantage if all of this resulted in a custody hearing.

But Debbie hated lying to her parents.

"Okay, the truth is…" She leaned forward and braced her elbows on the table. "I'm only pretending to be Austin's fiancé because his ex-wife has threatened to sue for custody. She's a despicable person who only wants to use the kids for her own advantage. He's trying to protect his children from her."

Dad and Mom both scowled.

Scott's brow furrowed as he tilted his head to the side.

Rudy's eyebrows raised. "The only way for you to truly help him protect his kids from his ex-wife is to actually marry him and provide a stable home life for the children."

Trust Rudy who was smart as a whip and had a degree in criminal justice to put the pieces together in this manner.

"We're hoping it doesn't come to that." Not that she wouldn't mind marrying Austin for real.

"You're hoping?" Dad said.

Debbie let out a long sigh. "We thought that once his wife saw that he had a wealthy fiancé she'd see that threatening him with a costly custody battle wouldn't work."

"So he's using you for your money?" Contempt filled Rudy's voice. Scott squared his shoulders and doubled his fists.

"No!" Debbie said. "Well, yes he is but not like… The truth is, he doesn't like rich people. If it wasn't for my money, he might actually like me. I mean, like me for me." Tears pricked Debbie's eyes, because she wanted Austin to do more than like her. She wanted him to fall in love with her, like she had him.

She blinked away the tears and cleared her throat. "You guys can't tell anyone. If his ex-wife finds out we're not really engaged, it could cause a lot of problems for Austin, and the kids will be caught in the middle." She stared at Rudy.

If anyone at this table was going to let the truth slip, it would be him. He was more social than most of the rest of the family, and he loved to talk. Mom and Dad may not approve of what she was doing, but they'd support her. And she definitely didn't have to worry about Scott telling anyone. He wasn't much of a talker, and he definitely didn't gossip.

Mom's hand found hers again. "What happens when the ex-wife is no longer a threat?"

Debbie shrugged. "We'll probably break the engagement off."

Why did saying those words hurt so badly?

"But you love him. And you love those kids."

If Mom had formed it as a question, Debbie could have tried to deny it, but she couldn't. So she just nodded.

"And what happens when Savannah's done with her painting? Will they keep coming around? Is there a possibility this relationship can grow properly?" Mom held up a hand. "I mean in a few more months."

Debbie shrugged again. "I have some other projects in mind that I want Savannah's help with, but I meant it when I said he doesn't like rich people. He's been burned and manipulated too many times by them."

"That's stupid," Scott said, surprising them all. "You're doing a lot of good with your money. If he can't see beyond your wealth, then he doesn't deserve you." He said the words with such conviction, they brought new tears to Debbie's eyes.

She smiled at him. "Thanks, but he's a really proud man who's been through a lot."

Mom squeezed her hand before releasing it. "If it's meant to be, it'll all work out."

Debbie sure hoped her mom was right. And that it was indeed meant to be.

CHAPTER 24

"What is she wearing?" Savannah asked in surprise.

Debbie stared as Cheyenne swept out of the car, as graceful as ever, in a skin-tight, full-body, burgundy jumpsuit that encased her right arm in one long sleeve but left the other shoulder completely bare. A gauzy split skirt flared out from her hips, billowing around her as she walked. Sparkly four-inch heels kept the skirt from dragging on the ground.

In any other setting, Debbie would compliment her on her attire, but here at the park, she simply couldn't. Cheyenne's outfit looked more appropriate for the red carpet than a grassy field. She couldn't understand this woman. Was she so obsessed with flaunting her affluence that she had to show off every chance she got?

Debbie thought about the jewelry and expensive, form-fitting clothing she used to wear. Had she appeared that arrogant and pretentious?

"I don't know," Debbie said, "but I hope she doesn't have to go to the bathroom while she's here."

Austin and Savvy laughed, and he slid a strong hand around Debbie's waist. Warmth flooded her body as butterflies swarmed her stomach. After a full week in which there had been no hugging or kissing, not even hand holding, Debbie's traitorous body welcomed the contact.

Austin had been under tremendous stress at work as deadlines approached, and he'd worked late every night this week, often arriving at her house exhausted and irritable. She'd tried not to put much stock in what felt like rejection and enjoyed every moment she had with the kids, but she'd concluded that despite the sparks present during their kisses, to Austin, they had only been a show for Cheyenne and Tucker's benefit.

Cheyenne's heels clacked on the concrete as she and Tucker approached. "Really, Austin, did we have to meet at a park? Why couldn't we have met at Debbie's house again?"

The arm Austin had around Debbie's waist tensed. "Because the boys wanted to spend the day at the park. If you want to get to know them, you need to do it in their environment." His tone held a challenge.

Debbie figured the boys would have been content spending the day at her house again, but she had a feeling Austin wanted to make Cheyenne and Tucker as uncomfortable as possible.

Judging by the scowl on his ex-wife's face, he'd succeeded. She glared at him for a long moment before looking away. Her gaze drifted to the table with the food, and her nose wrinkled. "You were serious about eating pizza?"

"Of course I was." Austin shook his head before turning to help the boys serve themselves.

Lunch was a stilted affair with Cheyenne taking the smallest slice of pizza possible that she hardly touched, because she was too busy complaining about the weather.

"What do you mean?" Austin said. "This is the nicest weather we've had all week."

He was right. In fact, Tuesday night's soccer game had been canceled due to rain and cold temperatures. But it didn't surprise Debbie that Cheyenne was cold with one whole arm bare.

Tucker, being the gentleman he was, gave his wife his sports jacket to wear. He was still mildly overdressed in Khakis and a polo shirt but didn't look as out of place as Cheyenne.

"But it'll hide my cute outfit," Cheyenne complained as she slipped the jacket on.

Debbie rolled her eyes as she recalled how she'd occasionally suffered discomfort for the sake of the outfit she'd wanted to show off. Now, seeing how ridiculous she must have appeared, she was grateful for the changes she'd made.

Cheyenne made little effort to talk to the kids, so Debbie and Austin took turns encouraging the boys to tell their mom about their teachers, friends, and favorite video games. She winced occasionally as their volume grew with their excitement. By the time they started arguing over who'd built the best house on Minecraft, she looked like she'd tuned them out altogether.

Neither Debbie nor Austin tried to pull Savannah into the conversation after last week's fiasco. They figured they were fortunate she'd agreed to be here at all.

"Can we play soccer now?" Dallas asked after shoving the last half of his cookie in his mouth.

Austin shook his head. "Give the rest of us slow pokes a few more minutes to finish eating, bud."

"I brought some gifts for the kids." Cheyenne motioned for Tucker to go to the car. "They should open them before they run off and play."

When he returned a few minutes later with three large gift bags, Austin tensed beside Debbie.

The boys fairly bounced with anticipation when Cheyenne handed Savannah her gift first.

Savvy's hands shook a little as she accepted it. Her shoulders hunched as she peered inside, as though expecting a snake to strike her, before pulling out a bulky red and silver case.

Debbie recognized the logo of an expensive makeup brand on the side.

Before Savvy even had the chance to open the case and discover for herself what was inside, Cheyenne leaned across the table. "This is one of the best brands of makeup out there, and the nice thing is it's an all-in-one kit. It's got everything you need to make yourself look beautiful."

"She's already beautiful," Debbie insisted, wrapping an arm around Savannah who sat beside her. "She doesn't need makeup for that." Debbie loved that Savannah was comfortable with who she was and didn't feel the need to wear a lot of makeup to try to fit in. She wished she had learned that lesson sooner.

Cheyenne waved a hand. "I know, but I thought she might like to start wearing a little more makeup. You know, so she can really get the guys' attention. And I thought maybe next week, we could go to a salon in the Tri-Cities area and get extensions put in your hair."

A low growling sound erupted from Austin on Debbie's other side.

She put a hand on his arm and pasted on a smile. She turned toward Cheyenne. "Savvy and I already have an appointment to get manis and pedis before Prom." She picked up a lock of Savannah's hair. "Extensions would only weigh down the body in her gorgeous hair."

Debbie had nearly cheered when Austin agreed to let her take Savannah to get her hair done before prom. Of course, he'd insisted Savvy work it off.

"I suppose you're right. You'll have to let me know when you plan to get your manis and pedis. I'll see if I can join you." Cheyenne wrinkled her nose and smiled at Savannah like they were best friends. "Wouldn't that be fun?"

Savvy's forced smile said it'd be anything but fun.

Debbie kept her own smile in place but remained silent.

Finally, Cheyenne handed Dallas and Cody their gifts. They tore into them without hesitation.

"Cool!" Cody cried as he pulled out a Star Wars BB8 Sphero Robot. The kind that needed a smartphone or other bluetooth device to operate it.

"Oh no," Austin said, rubbing his forehead.

Dallas's brow wrinkled as he pulled the box from his bag. "What is it?"

"What is it?" Incredulity filled Cheyenne's voice. "Only the best and most expensive virtual reality headset available."

Dallas looked at his mother like she was speaking a foreign language. "What do you do with it?"

"Wha—"

"Cheyenne!" Austin interrupted her exclamation. "My boys get a very limited amount of screen time that they have to earn. They do not have phones or any other kind of smart devices to run those things."

"Well, why not?"

"Because young boys with the kind of energy they have don't need those kinds of…toys. They need to run and play and just be kids."

"Well, all kids nowadays have smart devices."

"Not all kids," Debbie said as she slid her hand into Austin's. Her own sisters resisted getting their kids phones until they were teenagers.

Cheyenne turned to Tucker. "I knew we should have just bought them the iPads."

"No, you shouldn't have." Austin said.

Tucker shook his head. "We should have gotten them dart guns, like I said. Austin's right. Young kids don't need expensive electronics."

"Since when do you know anything about kids?" Cheyenne glared at Tucker.

"Well, obviously you don't know your own kids very well." Tucker returned her stare for a long moment before shaking his head and looking back at his empty plate.

Apparently, there was trouble in Cheyenne's paradise. Maybe Tucker was tired of her spending all his hard-earned money on over-the-top, frivolous things.

Tension thick enough to cut with a knife filled the air. Debbie searched for a way to ease it, yet do what was best for everyone involved.

"Why don't I take the boys' gifts to my house. Then after they are done with their homework on Monday, instead of playing the Xbox, they can use my iPad to play with their new toys." She squeezed Austin's hand and gave him a pleading look, begging him to agree so things didn't escalate any further.

After a long, tense moment, Austin finally nodded.

Dallas shrugged and set the VR box on the table. "Can we play soccer now?"

Before long, Austin and his kids had spread out on the grassy field. Austin and Cody against Savannah and Dallas. Debbie didn't think Savvy was all that interested in playing soccer, but she obviously preferred it to talking with her mother.

Debbie closed the remaining pizza box and cleared the table before heading onto the field.

"Wait, where are you going?" Cheyenne asked. "You're not actually going to play soccer, are you?"

Feeling peeved and not wanting to spend any more time with Cheyenne than necessary, Debbie propped her hands on her hips as she turned back. "I came to spend the day with the kids, so if they want to play soccer, then I'm going to play soccer."

"But what are we supposed to do?"

Debbie walked over and propped her hands on the table, leaning over until her face was only a foot from Cheyenne's. "If you want Austin to consider letting you take the kids to Florida, you'll get out there and play soccer too." When Cheyenne jerked back, her face filled with disgust, Debbie went on. "I don't care if you hate every second of it. You will make the effort to get to know your kids." She shifted her gaze to include Tucker. "Or you can say goodbye to your raise." Again, Debbie started to walk away.

"But I can't play soccer in heels." Indignation filled Cheyenne's voice.

Heaving a sigh, Debbie pivoted. "What size shoe do you wear?"

"Seven and a half."

She forced another grin. "You're in luck." Debbie toed off her own tennis shoes, slipped off her socks, and stepped out onto the grass.

When she was young, she went barefoot all the time. She couldn't count the number of times she'd argued with her mom before school and church because Mom insisted she needed to wear shoes. She still enjoyed going barefoot in her own home, but she rarely went barefoot outside anymore.

The damp grass pressed between her toes, and Debbie gasped. It was colder than she'd expected, but she kept walking. At least the grass was finally greening up and was no longer dry and crunchy, thanks to the rain they'd received this week.

Everyone stopped playing as she walked onto the soccer field. Austin met her halfway. "Why are you barefoot?"

"Because Cheyenne can't play soccer in her heels."

His brow furrowed. "Cheyenne doesn't play soccer."

"She will today, because I told her there was no way you would even consider letting her take the kids to Florida if she didn't get out here and make an effort to bond with her kids."

They both looked at the pavilion where Tucker and Cheyenne now argued.

Austin took Debbie's hand and led her toward the others. "How much do you want to bet she doesn't step one foot off the cement?"

Debbie laughed. "Oh, a betting man, are you?"

"Only when it's a sure thing."

"I don't know. I think you'd better get ready to pay up." Debbie had made her words to Cheyenne sound enough like a threat that she was pretty sure the other woman would eventually join them whether she wore Debbie's shoes or came barefoot. If anything would entice that woman to do something, it was money. "How about the winner gets a kiss?"

Austin stopped walking and turned to her with raised eyebrows. A slow grin spread across his face. "We'd both win, in that case."

Debbie shrugged. "I don't mind sharing my reward with you."

"Deal." His hand tightened around hers, and a gleam filled his eyes as he took a step closer.

Eager for a preview, she leaned toward him.

"Come on, Debbie, you can be on mine and Savvy's team." Cody grabbed Debbie's other hand and yanked her away from Austin.

His gaze followed her as they joined the others, and warmth filled her. At this point, she couldn't care less what Cheyenne did, she just wanted to collect on that kiss.

"Cody, show Debbie where that hole is so she doesn't step in it and twist her ankle." Austin pointed to the far sideline.

Although Debbie stayed active by swimming and exercising, she wasn't very graceful or athletically inclined. She did her best to keep up with the rest of them, though. The first time she kicked the ball, she had to stifle the urge to swear. She hit it with the side of her foot, like her nephews' soccer coaches taught them, but it hurt worse than she expected. It didn't help that her feet were half frozen from the cold grass.

After about five minutes, Tucker walked out onto the field.

Austin froze and stared at him so long, Debbie feared they might come to blows. Then he nodded his head for Tucker to join him and Dallas. It was another ten minutes before Cheyenne came out wearing Debbie's tennis shoes. Again, Austin stopped playing, his mouth dropping open. He turned to Debbie and grinned, then tossed the ball he'd been holding to Tucker.

Their gazes remained locked as he walked toward her with a purposeful stride.

Her hands and feet prickled with anticipation, and she found it difficult to take a deep breath.

"You're amazing, you know that?" he said in a low voice as he reached her. He cupped her face in both hands and lowered his mouth to hers.

A rush of sensation filled her when his lips met hers. Tingly, fluttery, sparkling sensations, sending a rush of messages to her brain to pull him closer. She parted her lips and leaned into him, wrapping her arms around his waist.

Austin let out a soft moan as he pressed his lips more firmly against hers, sliding one hand into her hair and the other behind her back.

Ripples of warmth cascaded over her. She didn't realize how chilled she was until a spark ignited in her that quickly turned into a blazing fire, radiating warmth from head to toe. A sense of wholeness and belonging enveloped her. This was what she'd been longing for her whole life.

But this is only pretend. It's only for show.

Sadness rushed over, even though Austin's lips were still on hers. Fighting the melancholy, she focused on the man who held her so tightly. Not for the first time, she considered giving away all her money. If she could enjoy this every day for the rest of her life, she'd still be the richest woman in the world.

"Come on, Dad. We're supposed to be playing soccer," Dallas yelled.

"Yeah." Cody shoved his way between Austin and Debbie, pushing them apart. "Get back on your own side, Dad."

The same disappointment Debbie felt filled Austin's face, but he quickly hid it with a grin as he walked backward. "I'll make a bet with you anytime, as long as the stakes are the same."

She laughed, savoring the warmth that lingered in her limbs.

Cheyenne stood mostly off to the side holding her flowing skirts off the ground with both hands as the game resumed. At one point, Tucker kicked the ball to her, but his aim was too high. She released her skirt and blocked her face with her hands as she screamed.

The ball hit her forearms.

"No hands!" Dallas and Cody yelled in unison.

"I didn't hit it with my hands." Cheyenne's face turned red as she defended herself.

"Hitting the ball with your arms is the same as hitting it with your hands," Dallas explained with exasperation.

"I didn't hit the ball. It hit me." Her voice became shriller with each word.

Austin put a hand on Dallas's shoulder and pulled him back. He grinned at Cheyenne. "Next time try hitting it with your head. That's legal."

They continued to play for some time, and Debbie could tell the men were taking it easy on them. After a while, it became obvious both Austin and Tucker were trying to get Cheyenne to engage by repeatedly kicking the ball her way.

She gave an excited squeal the first time she managed to actually connect with the ball, which made everyone laugh. Eventually, she started to chase the ball, fighting Cody for the chance to kick it. In her excitement, she let go of her skirts. She shrieked as she tripped over the flowy fabric and went down.

Tucker raced to her side while everyone else approached more slowly. Debbie grimaced, fearing how Cheyenne might react.

"Are you okay?" Tucker helped his wife to her feet.

"Yes, but my outfit is ruined." Distress filled her voice, raising it an octave.

"No, it's not. We can have it dry cleaned."

She inspected her skirts. "Did I put a hole in it?"

He helped her examine the gauzy material before wiping a smudge of dirt from her bare arm. "It's fine. And we can go shopping to get you some new clothes for the drive home."

Cheyenne's face brightened. Tucker had said the magic word. Shopping.

"Okay, but I don't think I want to play soccer anymore."

"We can play Frisbee!" Dallas said. He raced over to the pavilion to get the Frisbee.

If Cheyenne was bad at kicking a soccer ball, she was even worse at catching a Frisbee. Of course, Debbie wasn't much better, but she had a blast trying to beat Austin and Dallas to the flying disc every time it came her direction. Ten minutes into their game, she was so intent on trying to catch the throw that Savannah had sent high and wide that she didn't pay attention to where she was running. Her right foot landed in the hole Austin and Cody had warned her about and twisted as she came down hard on her ankle.

She let out a cry of pain, and it was Austin's turn to race to her side.

"How badly is it hurt?" he asked as he gently lifted her foot.

Debbie sucked in a sharp breath. "It's pretty bad, but I'm sure it's only a sprain."

"I think you need to be done playing." He helped her to her feet and lifted her into his arms. "We need to get some ice on your ankle."

"Do you have any ice packs in the cooler?"

"Only the hard kind that I use in my lunch box."

"They'll have to do." Debbie didn't relish putting ice packs on her already cold feet.

"No, we need to get you home. Better yet to the doctor."

She grabbed Austin's arm as he set her on the bench of the picnic table. "No, we can't leave yet." She lowered her voice so the group that had followed them from the field wouldn't hear. "Cheyenne is actually making an effort to engage with the kids. I'll be fine."

Shaking his head, he tucked two small ice packs around her ankle. "Your feet are freezing. I hope you don't catch a cold from this."

He grabbed two jackets from his truck and wrapped the larger one —an insulated flannel that smelled like him—around her shoulders and the smaller one that belonged to one of the boys around her feet.

Although Debbie loved the attention, she shooed him away. "Stop fussing over me. Go back out and play, or Cheyenne will use this as an excuse to call it a day."

Even though she enjoyed being surrounded by Austin's scent and snuggled in his jacket, it wasn't enough to distract her from the pain that throbbed in her ankle as she watched the others play. She should ask Savannah to drive her home so she could elevate and better ice her foot, and more importantly, take a pain reliever.

The game ended abruptly a few minutes later when Cheyenne missed the Frisbee and it struck her in the face. She wailed as Tucker guided her to the pavilion, holding her face with one hand and her skirts with the other. She freaked out when he dabbed a napkin to her face, and it came away with blood on it.

"I'm bleeding?" Her voice rose again. "Is it going to scar?"

"No, no." Tucker assured her. "It barely broke the skin. You're going to be fine."

Debbie caught a glimpse of Cheyenne's eye the next time he pulled the napkin away. An angry red mark marred her cheekbone just below her left eye. It wouldn't scar, but Cheyenne might end up with a black eye.

A commotion ensued when Cheyenne said she was done, and

Austin agreed that their time at the park was over. Dallas and Cody didn't want to leave yet, but Austin insisted on getting Debbie home so she could better care for her ankle.

Cheyenne and Tucker left with barely a goodbye, while Austin and Savannah carried stuff to his truck. Dallas and Cody continued to grumble, but Debbie was in too much pain to console them. Before long, she was on the couch in her family room; Austin had driven her home while Savannah drove his truck.

He lingered long enough to make sure she had an ice pack, a water bottle, and some pain reliever. About the time he tucked a blanket around her and handed her the remote, the boys asked if they could go play video games.

Austin shifted from one foot to the other and rubbed his hands down his thighs. "No, we should go so Debbie can rest. I'll come back and check on you a little lat—"

"Don't worry about me." She waved him away. "I'll call my parents if I need something."

"But we don't want to go yet," Cody said.

Austin put a hand on each of the boys' shoulders and pointed them to the front door. "You guys have chores to do at home, and I need to do some grocery shopping."

He turned back before stepping out of the family room and pressed a quick kiss to her forehead. "Are you sure you're going to be okay?" When she nodded, he straightened. "I'm sorry about your ankle. I hope it feels better soon. Let me know if you need anything."

"Okay." Debbie smiled and gave his hand a quick squeeze before he backed away. Within seconds, he was gone, and she was left alone in a quiet house.

She did need something. She needed Austin and his kids to stay. She wanted their noise and the chaos their presence created. She didn't want to be alone. More than ever, she wanted a family. The Reed family.

∼

AUSTIN PUT his plate in the dishwasher then turned to Savannah. "Hey, honey, will you take the boys downstairs to the game room for a little bit. I need to discuss something important with Debbie."

Savvy grinned and got a knowing look in her eyes. "Discuss something? Yeah, right. I bet that's all you want to do."

He snatched the dish towel off the counter and swatted her backside as she walked away. He couldn't blame her for thinking he had ulterior motives after she witnessed that kiss on Saturday. He may have gotten a little carried away. In fact, it was a good thing they'd had an audience or who knows what he might have done.

There was just something about Debbie that made him want to lose control.

"I want to play basketball," Dallas yelled, already on his way downstairs.

"No, let's play ping pong," Cody shouted equally as loud.

"What's wrong?" Debbie asked as soon as the kids were out of earshot.

She only limped a little as he led her to the family room where he plopped down on the couch. Thankfully, her ankle hadn't been injured as badly as he'd feared. She sat next to him, much closer than he'd anticipated.

It had taken all of his self control this evening to keep his hands off her. In fact, when he only greeted her with a smile when he first arrived, instead of the kiss he wanted to give her, a flash of disappointment covered her face. She quickly hid it, but he still felt bad. He didn't dare let himself touch her though.

He pulled his phone from his pocket and showed her the text he received from his ex-wife Sunday evening. "Cheyenne texted me last night. She promised not to get the lawyers involved if I agree to let her take the kids to Florida in three weeks."

"She sounds desperate."

"I don't think Tucker is nearly as wealthy as Cheyenne lets on."

"It doesn't help that she enjoys spending money." She shook her head. "I can't believe she's acting like she holds all of the cards."

"She's always been that way. It's her way or the highway."

Debbie squared her shoulders. "Not anymore. Let her call her lawyer. And I'll call mine."

"No, wait. I don't want a custody battle."

Austin had hardly slept last night because the thought of letting Debbie pay for a lawyer and court fees didn't sit well with him. But more than that, he didn't want to subject the children to the whole ordeal. Especially knowing Cheyenne didn't really want them.

"I appreciate you being willing to pay the legal fees, but think about what a custody battle will do to the kids? Cheyenne threatened to request immediate custody. If she gets a hearing right away and the courts allow her visitation, she'll likely end up with the kids in three weeks anyway. But then what?"

"What do you mean?"

"The next time Tucker takes a trip to Timbuktu, she'll cancel on her weekend with the kids, inadvertently telling them they aren't as important as the lifestyle she's living."

Debbie slumped back into the couch. "You're right, but she shouldn't be allowed to just use them for her own selfish purposes."

"I agree. The thought of sticking them on an airplane and sending them thousands of miles away to spend the weekend with her makes me sick. She truly has no idea how to care for children."

"I'll say." Debbie shook her head. "It makes me so angry the way she treats Savvy."

Austin propped his elbows on his knees and shoved his hands into his hair. He felt like he was stuck between a rock and a hard spot. No matter what decision he made, the children would suffer.

Debbie stroked his back in a comforting gesture, creating slow rhythmic circles.

He quickly became aware of the warmth of her hand seeping through his shirt. His nerve endings tingled and sent crazy messages to his brain to take his shirt off and pull her into his arms and pick up where they left off with Saturday's kiss.

He sprang to his feet and began to pace the room. Now was not the time to give in to his crazy urges. But he couldn't think straight with Debbie touching him.

"I've got it!" Debbie was on her feet now and right in front of him.

"What?" He took a step back. He used to like the fact that she didn't have a bubble, but not anymore. She was too much of a temptation.

"We'll fly to Florida with the kids. You can find out the name of the resort where Cheyenne and Tucker plan to take them, and I'll book a suite for us. The kids can go to whatever activities they need to with their mom, but then they can come back to our rooms and stay with us."

It was a great idea, but there was no way Austin could afford to stay in some fancy hotel, let alone buy airline tickets for five people. He knew Debbie wasn't suggesting he pay for it, but letting her pay for him and his family to make such a trip somehow felt wrong.

"Debbie I can't—"

"Stop it!" She grabbed his shoulders and shook him. "Set your pride aside for one minute. This isn't about you and what you can and can't afford. This is about your children. I know you love them and want to protect them, but you can't do that if you're thousands of miles away." She slid her hands down his arms and clasped his hands. "This way, you can be right there if anything happens."

She stared up at him with such an earnest expression, it took his breath away. Thanks to the baby blue blouse she wore, her eyes looked like the sky on a summer day. Hopeful and playful.

A mini vacation on the beaches of Florida could be fun. If they gave Cheyenne what she wanted, this fake engagement could be over in a few weeks.

Then what?

A large part of him never wanted it to end, but he couldn't let go of that part that felt degraded every time he thought about how wealthy Debbie was.

He squeezed her hands. "Okay. I'll find out which resort they're going to be at, and you can book a suite."

"And the airline tickets?"

"We could make Tucker pay for the kids' tickets."

"Yes, but then we may not end up on the same flight as them."

"You're right. Okay the airline tickets too." He held up a finger as a grin spread across her face. "But we're flying economy."

She frowned then opened her mouth like she planned to argue but closed it again. "Business class," she finally said.

He locked gazes with her for a long moment, attempting to put his foot down in a figurative way.

She didn't flinch. In fact, she smiled. Just like Dallas did a few weeks ago.

"Fine. You can book business class."

"Yes!" She threw her arms around his neck, and the next thing he knew his lips were on hers.

His surprise quickly dissipated and he gave in to the temptation, circling his arms around her waist.

"Dad, I need to get home!" Savannah walked through the arched doorway of the family room. "Rainey's coming over so we can study for our Chemistry test."

Austin pulled away from Debbie and looked at Savvy. She rolled her eyes and shook her head at him.

He cleared his throat. "Right. Go get your brothers."

"I already sent them out to the truck."

"Okay. I'll be right out."

Savvy narrowed her gaze on him and folded her arms. "I'm not sure I can believe you."

He gave Debbie's hand a quick squeeze before walking out of the room. Pausing in the doorway, he said, "I'll let you know what Cheyenne says, so you can make arrangements." Then he stepped back into the room. "But don't tell the kids. I don't want them to know yet."

"Okay." Debbie smiled, and he had to fight the urge to pull her back into his arms.

"Thanks for dinner. I'll see you tomorrow." He turned and hurried toward the front door.

Savvy was right behind him. "Don't tell us what?"

"Nothing."

The last thing he needed was to get the kids' hopes up about going on vacation when he wasn't sure how things with Cheyenne might turn out.

～

"Okay, boys, go take a bath," Austin said as they walked through the door Friday evening.

"Do we have plans tomorrow, Dad?" Savannah asked as she dropped her backpack near the door.

"Well, your mom was supposed to come visit again this weekend, but she canceled this afternoon."

Big surprise.

Austin knew she'd end up flaking out. Especially since he'd agreed to bring the kids to Florida.

"Good." Savannah mumbled the single word under her breath, but he heard it.

He knew Savvy often felt left out among her friends because she didn't have a mom. For that reason, he'd half hoped she and Cheyenne could build some sort of relationship, but it didn't look like that would ever happen. He was just relieved Savvy wasn't hurt by the fact that her mother didn't seem interested in a relationship with her.

Instead, she seemed to have formed a bond with Debbie. The two of them apparently talked about everything, lately. And Savvy had gained celebrity status at school because she was working for and friends with the richest woman in town.

Well, maybe not the richest. He'd heard rumors that the rancher's wife at the Double Diamond Ranch inherited a bunch of money a few years ago.

Debbie had worked her way into his life so completely he feared his kids liked her more than they did him most days. He both loved and hated it. Loved it because the kids enjoyed being around her. He'd come to realize that even though they loved going to her house, when they talked about Debbie lately, it was always about the things she'd done with them and how she made them laugh.

He hated it because he still didn't feel like he could accept her money. Despite Debbie's kindness and generosity, he'd never felt so inadequate and impoverished in his life. Well, except for all those years he was married to Cheyenne.

He was going to break more than his own heart when he ended this engagement. He'd been careful all week to make sure he and Debbie were never alone. He didn't trust himself to keep his hands off her. And when he left each evening without kissing her goodnight, she looked as disappointed as he felt, but he couldn't lose sight of the fact that this was supposed to be a pretend engagement.

Savvy had finally finished the mural at Debbie's house and it had turned out amazing, but come Monday, she would start some other smaller projects in other rooms to pay for her prom dress. Although Austin enjoyed going to Debbie's house for dinner each evening and getting to know her despite the boys' chatter, he'd be relieved when Savvy was done working for her.

"Dad?" Savvy said at the same level Cody usually talked at.

"What? Why are you shouting?"

"Because I said your name three times, and you didn't answer." Exasperation filled her voice.

"Sorry, I guess my mind was elsewhere."

"I'll say. I bet I can guess exactly where. Or maybe I should say with whom." Savvy gave him a teasing grin.

"That's enough." He shook a finger at her. "What do you want?"

"Can Caleb come over tomorrow? You said you wanted to meet him before prom, and that's next weekend."

Austin's stomach tightened. He always reacted this way when he thought about Savvy growing up and having a boyfriend.

"Yeah, he can come over. What time are you thinking?" Austin tried to think of what he needed to do tomorrow, now that Cheyenne had canceled.

Savannah shifted from one foot to the other. "Is it okay if he comes over for dinner...and maybe stays to watch a movie...or something?"

Austin debated teasing his daughter about her boyfriend, but decided against it since he didn't want her teasing him about Debbie. Savvy said she wasn't ready for a real relationship yet, but she'd sure seemed to like this Caleb kid. Austin needed to make sure he was good enough for his daughter.

"Sure. Dinner and a movie. Sounds fun."

And I can make sure Caleb keeps his hands to himself.

Savvy headed to her room, but she turned back. "You could invite Debbie over to join us, if you want."

"What?" Austin's head popped up.

She shrugged like it didn't really matter. "Maybe it's your turn to cook for her for a change." Then she disappeared into her bedroom.

But she'd planted a seed that took root so fast Austin knew he was crazy for considering it. How would Debbie react to eating dinner with them at their small kitchen table? He knew she grew up with humble roots, but had she become so accustomed to her lifestyle that she'd be uncomfortable in his?

He pulled his phone from his pocket and flipped it around in his hands half a dozen times before turning it on. He pulled up Debbie's name then paused. Did he really want to do this?

Yes, I do.

But what kind of message would he be sending her? Would she think it meant more than it did?

He swiped out a quick text before he could talk himself out of it.

Do you have plans tomorrow evening?

Her response came quicker than he expected.

Since Cheyenne canceled, I was thinking about celebrating with a bubble bath.

She probably meant it as a joke, but there was nothing funny about the image that popped into his head of her in a bubble bath.

Kidding! What do you have in mind?

He shook his head to rid it of her and bubbles.

Savvy invited Caleb over for dinner and a movie tomorrow.

I'm glad you finally get to meet him.

Yeah.

So... was there an invitation in there somewhere?

Shoot!

It had obviously been a long time since he'd dated. He had no idea how to do this.

Wait! Do I want this to be a date?

Sorry. Would you like to join us for dinner? It's my turn to cook for you for a change.

That depends. Do you know how to cook? I was under the impression Savvy does most of the cooking at your house.

Austin laughed. Was Debbie flirting with him via text messages? They didn't exactly get a lot of opportunities to do that when they were surrounded by the kids.

Yes. I know how to cook.

In that case, I'd love to come.

Austin grinned. He shouldn't be so happy that she'd agreed to come to dinner, but he was.

So… any special reason?

Austin stared at his phone, debating how to answer.

I mean, am I coming as your fiancée? Or something else?

Did she want to come as his fiancée? From the way Debbie responded to his kisses, he was pretty sure she didn't mind pretending they were a couple in love. But he didn't want to encourage that when he wasn't sure they had a future.

Can it just be a friends thing this time?

Hopefully, she wasn't as disappointed by that question as he was.

CHAPTER 25

*D*ebbie took one last look at herself in her rear view mirror before climbing from the Escalade. Even though it was an expensive vehicle, it felt less pretentious than the Porsche.

This was the first time Austin had invited her to his house, and she didn't want to do anything to mess it up. That's why she wore jeans and a t-shirt even though she wanted to dress up for him.

She still wasn't sure why he'd invited her, but there was no way she'd say no. Yes, she'd experienced a momentary pang of disappointment last night when he asked if this could just be a friend thing. But she'd quickly responded with, "Sure."

Unsure whether he intended this to be a date or just two friends hanging out with a bunch of kids, she was determined to keep it casual and follow his lead.

She took a deep breath, detecting the smell of wood smoke in the air, before knocking on the front door.

"Imma get it!" Cody's voice came from the other side of the door, and Debbie smiled.

Talk about deja-vu. Wow! So much had happened since the last time she'd knocked on this door.

"Hiya, Debbie." He smiled, showing the edge of his front tooth that had started growing in.

"Hi, Cody. How are you." She still wanted to tuck him in her pocket and take him home with her. If for no other reason than his dad would have to come pick him up.

"I'm tired." He let out a dramatic sigh.

She crouched a little to look him in the eyes and put her hand on his forehead. "Why are you tired?" Was he coming down with something?

"Because Dad made us clean the whole house today! So we could make a good 'pression."

"Cody!" Austin's deep voice coming from behind the open door sent shivers racing down Debbie's spine. "You're supposed to invite Debbie in. Not make her stand on the porch all night."

Austin stepped into view, and she had to catch her breath. He'd skipped shaving today and the two-day stubble on his jaw looked incredibly sexy. Not to mention the dish towel he had slung over his shoulder.

Sheila always insisted there was nothing sexier than a man with an apron and a dish towel. Debbie had to agree. Of course, Sheila also joked that a man was sexiest when he wore nothing but an apron.

Heat filled Debbie's face as she pictured Austin's broad, naked chest peeking out behind an apron. She stopped her imagination there, before it could wander any further.

Austin leaned toward her, a concerned look on his face. "Are you feeling okay? You look flushed."

Debbie forced a laugh. "I'm fine. So are you going to invite me in? Or do I have to stand on the porch all night?"

Cody had disappeared, but Austin's body now blocked the doorway. There was no way Debbie could get in without pressing impossibly close to him. Nothing about that move would say, "Just friends."

"Right. Sorry." He stepped back and waved her in.

"So is Caleb here?"

"He just arrived a few minutes ago." Austin led Debbie into the kitchen to the sliding glass door. He motioned outside where Dallas,

Savannah, and a tall boy sat around a fire. Cody was already making his way to the others.

"Ooh, he *is* kind of cute," Debbie said. "So, what do you think of him?"

Austin shrugged. "He seems nice. Respectful. But it's obvious he didn't come to see me." Austin held out a cookie sheet loaded with hot dogs, buns, and condiments. "Would you mind carrying this out for me?" Then he picked up a crockpot and walked out.

"We're eating outside?"

"Is that a problem?" Austin turned and regarded her with raised eyebrows.

Was this some kind of test? If she said the wrong thing, would she fail?

She smiled. "Not at all. But you promised to cook for me. Making me cook my own hot dog over a fire is cheating."

"I did cook for you." He held the crock pot up. "We're having chili dogs. Unless you're one of those boring people. In which case, you can have a bowl of chili with a hot dog on the side." He winked at her before making his way to the fire pit.

Debbie spotted a card table off to the side of the fire pit, holding paper products and roasting sticks. She set the cookie sheet on it.

The next thirty minutes were filled with lots of noise and laughter while Austin helped the boys roast their hot dogs and stack chili on them. Because there were only three roasting sticks, Debbie sat back and waited. She enjoyed watching Austin help his children. There was something about a man that loved kids that melted her heart. And a good-looking man with strong, broad shoulders and an easy-going personality was enough to make her fall head over heels.

She looked up in surprise when Austin handed her a plate with a roasted hot dog on it. He winked. "Now you can't say I didn't fix you dinner."

Debbie laughed and accepted the plate. She'd never been a fan of chili dogs because they were so messy to eat. In fact, Cody wore as much as he'd consumed, but he was happy as could be. Accepting

Austin's challenge, she piled chili on top of her hot dog then followed it up with a sprinkle of cheese.

After making her way back to her seat, she debated on the best way to eat the concoction without ending up like Cody. Finally, she just picked it up and went for it. The rush of flavors that filled her mouth—savory and slightly spicy—made her smile. She looked up to find Austin watching her.

"Delicious," she mumbled as she chewed her food.

He smiled in return, and her heart leaped in her chest. This man affected her in ways no other man had. Not even her first husband Keith, whom she had been so in love with, made her feel like this.

After finishing her chili dog, and only using two napkins in the process to keep from looking like Cody, Debbie went back for another bowl of chili. Sliding back into her seat beside Austin, she said, "This is amazing. Did you actually make it from scratch? Or is it from a can?"

"It's my mom's recipe."

"I'm impressed. I've never met a man who knows how to cook like this."

"Well, don't be too amazed. I don't have a very large variety of skills in the kitchen. I have about six dishes that I can make well. The rest usually comes from a box."

They continued to share small talk as they ate, then she helped him carry the food back into the house, only to return with the makings for s'mores. More fun and laughter ensued until Cody's marshmallow started on fire and ended up black.

Big tears welled in his eyes. "But I don't like burned marshmallows."

"Can I have it, Cody. I like them that way," Debbie lied.

She and Austin had just been discussing how they liked their marshmallows toasted to a golden brown.

"You don't have—"

"It's so nice of you to toast a marshmallow just for me." Debbie cut Austin off and put her arm around Cody's shoulders.

She pulled the charred ball of sugar from Cody's stick and stuck it in her mouth. "Mmm...so good."

"I can cook one for you too," Dallas said.

"Thank you, Dallas. What a gentleman." She looked at Austin who stared at her. "I think he's had a great example."

Austin smiled and mouthed, "Thank you."

She and Austin continued to visit around the fire for some time while the kids played tag. Debbie enjoyed every minute of it, especially the fact that Caleb at nearly six feet tall was willing to let little Cody tag him once in a while.

Debbie leaned toward Austin. "I like Caleb. He seems like a good kid."

"Yeah, he does," Austin said, watching Caleb pick up a giggling Cody and run after Savannah. "I'm glad he turned out to be nice because I think Savannah really likes him."

"She does."

He turned toward her at this, bringing his head within inches of her own. "Has she told you how much? I mean, do I need to worry about a serious relationship forming here. Savvy's only sixteen."

Debbie leaned back a bit. Not because she didn't enjoy being close to Austin, but rather, if she didn't, she'd end up kissing him like she did a few nights ago when he agreed to let her book plane tickets and a suite in Florida.

"She talks about Caleb with the same respect she talks about you. In fact, that's one of the things she likes about him; he reminds her of you."

Austin grimaced. "I'm not sure that's a good thing."

Debbie laughed. "It is. Trust me."

They continued talking, mostly about the kids, until the sun set. As darkness settled in, Savannah approached them.

"Dad, can we go in and watch a movie now? Caleb has to be home by ten."

"Yes, but make sure it's one your brothers will enjoy too."

Savannah rolled her eyes, but said, "Okay."

Determined to follow Austin's lead, Debbie waited for him to follow the kids into the house. When he didn't move, she looked at him. He wasn't watching Savannah and the boys as she'd expected, he was watching her.

"Aren't you planning on chaperoning?" she asked, nodding her head toward the others.

He looked to where Caleb was giving Cody a piggy back ride into the house. "I think they have enough chaperones tonight. I'd much rather stay out here with you. That is, if you don't mind." He gave her such an intense look that a shiver raced down her spine.

She gave an involuntary tremble. "I don't mind."

"You're cold. Let me put some more wood on the fire."

He piled three more logs on, and soon, flames rose, and warmth emanated from the fire. He pulled out his phone and sent a quick text to someone then slipped it back into his pocket. Before sitting down again, he shifted his chair to a ninety degree angle with hers. His leg pressed against hers when he dropped into his seat again.

"This way, I can look at you without kinking my neck."

Debbie let out a little sigh. Between the fire and the warmth his nearness triggered in her, she could stay here all night.

Dallas came running out with a throw blanket in his arms. "Here, Dad."

"Thanks, bud." Austin took the blanket and leaned close to Debbie to spread it across her. "There, now I don't have to worry about you getting chilled."

She chuckled. "Are you afraid I'm going to get up and leave?" If she did, it'd only be because she didn't want to end up doing something impulsive and ruining everything. If Dallas hadn't brought the blanket out, she could have pretended she was still cold and used it as an excuse to sit on Austin's lap.

"I just thought it would be nice for us to talk. You know, without kids around to repeatedly interrupt."

"That sounds nice. Do you think we can remember how to converse like two adults?"

He laughed. "It might take some work, but I think we can figure it out."

She joined in the laughter, but soon, the sound of crickets and the crackling fire filled the otherwise quiet night.

"So, what did you want to talk about?" she asked.

He shrugged. "Anything. Everything. We're supposed to be engaged, but I don't even know your favorite color."

"My favorite color is blue." Debbie continued to share snippets of information about herself with him, finding out interesting things about him as well.

The conversation turned much deeper than she expected as each of them shared how devastated they were following their respective divorces and what it had done to their self-esteem. She'd always wanted to help people, that's why she got a nursing degree. And he saw building homes and apartments for people as his way of providing a better world for his kids.

Austin surprised her when he started talking about his financial struggles.

"Every time I feel like things are going good and that I'm making progress on Cheyenne's debts, something happens that sets me back."

"Like what?" Debbie asked. She'd love nothing more than to help him with his debt, but he was too proud; he'd never accept a handout.

"Like an investor backing out of a project, stiffing me and all of the other contractors on a month's worth of wages and leaving me without a job. Or the truck that I'd driven since I was seventeen repeatedly breaking down and finally dying altogether." He popped his knuckles as his agitation grew. "And of course with three kids, there have been plenty of medical bills. Some bigger than others, like when Savvy's appendix ruptured last fall right after we moved here and Cody getting pneumonia and having to be hospitalized for three days back in December." He raked a hand through his hair. "I'll be paying on those for a while yet."

Again, Debbie wanted to offer to help him, but she bit her tongue. Tonight was going so well, she didn't want to say anything to mess it up.

As if uncomfortable with the direction their conversation had taken, Austin changed the topic back to trivial things. They soon realized their birthdays were exactly a month apart, and that Debbie was older than Austin.

"Does that bother you?" she asked.

"Does what bother me?"

"That I'm two years older than you. Most men don't like to date women that are older than them. Not that we're dating or anything." She rushed to add that last part.

He grinned as he shook his head. "No, we're just pretending to be engaged." He studied her. "Does it bother you?"

"You're asking a woman who was married to a man thirty-eight years her senior if it bothers her to be engaged—I mean, pretend to be engaged—to a man two years younger than her?"

"I take that as a no. Good to know." He opened his mouth to say something else, then closed it again. He stared at the fire for a long moment before turning back to her. When he did, it was with such intensity it took her breath away. "What was it like being married to a billionaire?"

Debbie sucked in a sharp breath. She didn't talk about her marriage to Peter much, because most people didn't believe that she hadn't married him for his money. Nor did they understand that being married to such a wealthy man was hard.

AUSTIN'S QUESTION hung in the air for a moment before Debbie rolled her eyes. "Peter wasn't a billionaire."

"Sorry, millionaire. Although judging by your house, which I assume is paid for, there's more than one number in front of the comma that denotes millionaire status."

Did he sound bitter or jealous? He was neither, but there was a tightness to his words he feared Debbie might interpret in a negative way. He wasn't sure why he felt the need to know exactly how wealthy she was, but he did. Not that it would do anything other than making him feel more inadequate than he did already.

"Yes, my house is paid for," she said. "And yes, Peter's net worth was on the high end of the millionaire spectrum." She paused for a moment before continuing, "It was a lot harder being married to him than you might think."

"Really?" Austin felt his eyebrows raise. He couldn't fathom how having an endless supply of money could be a hardship. Unless…

"I know you told me it was in name only, but did you ever…?" He wasn't sure how to finish that sentence

"Sleep with him? No. We did attend a handful of social functions together where he asked me to play the part of a devoted wife. On those occasions, I kissed his cheek or he kissed mine, but our relationship never went beyond that."

That relieved Austin for some reason. "Was that weird?"

"No, he never gave off a creepy old man vibe. He felt more like a doting uncle. At least, that's how I thought of him. I was just a companion to him, but I did grow very fond of him. It was difficult seeing him suffer there toward the end." Debbie's gaze focused on the dancing flames, and her face took on a faraway look.

"Why was it hard being married to him then?"

"You mean besides having to learn how to spell my last name?" she said with a chuckle.

"What was your last name?"

"Lukaszewski." She spelled something that sounded nothing like what she'd just said.

He chuckled. "No wonder you went back to your maiden name."

Debbie shook her head. "I still suffer with the hardest part about being married to him and becoming suddenly wealthy."

"What's that?"

"Impostor syndrome." She studied her nails.

"What do you mean?"

"I did nothing to earn the money he'd worked his whole life for, so I felt like a fraud. Of course, it didn't help that the people in his social circles thought I was nothing more than a gold digger. I already struggled with my self image, being constantly criticized didn't help. As I'm sure you're aware, wealthy people can be pretty vicious." Debbie shifted the blanket across her body as though adjusting a shield. "Then after Peter passed away, certain people were suddenly nice to me, and I came to realize it was because they all wanted something from me. I didn't know who my real friends were." She shrugged. "I guess that's why I've surrounded myself with family."

"Do you ever regret marrying him? I mean, do you find being wealthy a burden?"

She stared at the fire for a moment. "There have been times when I've wished I never promised Peter I'd bless as many lives as I could for as long as possible with his money. His accountants see to most of the donations given to dozens of large charities each year. Most of which just ends up padding the pockets of the board of directors and doesn't really make it to those who need it most." A hint of disgust entered her voice.

"I guess that's why I always feel like I need to do more for the people around me." A slow smile spread across her face. "When I feel like I've made a difference in someone's life, being wealthy no longer feels like a burden." A look of reverence crossed her face.

"Scott and Rudy mentioned a few of the things you've done for the community in general, but what kind of differences do you like to make in others' lives?"

Debbie spoke slowly, as though choosing her words carefully. "I used to think I needed recognition for my good deeds. A carry over from my Sofia days, I guess. Don't get me wrong, it's great seeing families enjoy the new park and appreciate other programs I'd funded, but it's helping people like the Duncans that makes me feel like having money is a blessing instead of a burden."

"Who are the Duncans?"

"They're a young couple who had twins about a year and a half ago. Adriana was put on bed rest at twenty weeks and had to quit her job. The babies came twelve weeks early and were in the NICU for eight weeks. Nick, the father, had just changed jobs, and his insurance benefits hadn't kicked in yet, so they were swamped with massive medical bills." The corners of her lips turned up in a hint of a smile. "Helping them not only felt good, it made me feel like I'd made a difference in those babies' futures."

"I'm sure you did."

Some days, Austin felt overwhelmed with the debt he'd been struggling with for so long. It occurred to him that Debbie could help get rid of it all if he'd only ask her. But he'd never be able to bring himself to do it. It would emasculate him worse than Cheyenne's infidelity had.

"What would you do to help others if money wasn't an issue?" Debbie asked, surprising him.

Austin mulled her question over for a minute. Unfortunately, he'd never been in the financial position to help others like he'd like to, but a long time dream of his came to mind.

"As a builder, I've always wanted to build affordable housing for lower income families without the builders and contractors having to sacrifice their incomes."

"You mean like apartment buildings?" Debbie leaning forward in her seat, a new light sparking in her eyes.

"Apartments and small homes. I've worked on a few Habitat for Humanity homes, and I know what you mean by how amazing it feels to help someone you've come to know personally."

"Isn't it the best feeling?" She grabbed his hand. "Tell me more. How many apartments would you build and where? How big could you build the homes and still keep them affordable?"

Austin hadn't felt cold until her warm hand settled over his, then he wanted to pull her onto his lap and soak up her heat. He laced his fingers with hers, but he wasn't content to leave them there, so he dragged his fingers through hers, caressing her knuckles and up to her wrist before reversing the motion.

Debbie sucked in a sharp breath and her gaze met his. Hers reflected the light of the dancing flames in a flirtatious way that he found all too provocative.

He was playing with fire, but he didn't care. Smiling at the pun, he kept exploring her delicate hand.

She held it steady, returning his caresses when his movements allowed her to.

Forcing a calmness he didn't feel, he talked about what it would take to build the kind of housing he had in mind. Enjoying the physical connection with her, he let himself ramble on about blueprints, permits, and contractors.

Debbie listened, but the inviting light in her eyes soon turned glassy, and he realized he'd over done it.

"I'm sorry." He slowly withdrew his hand from hers.

"About what?" Disappointment filled her face.

"For boring you."

"You weren't boring. Distracting? Absolutely. Boring? Not in the least."

He grinned at her, but it quickly faded with her next words.

"I've had an amazing time tonight, but it's getting late. I think I should go home before I—"

"Before you what?" He prodded. He didn't want her to leave, even though letting her go was the smart thing to do. Otherwise he might pick up where they left off with that mind-blowing kiss last Saturday.

She gave a tight smile. "Before I do something impulsive."

He stood at the same time she did, bringing them face to face with mere inches between them. He grabbed her hands before she could move away. He wouldn't mind her being impulsive and ignoring any personal boundaries tonight.

They locked gazes.

"Did I pass the test?" she asked breathlessly.

"What test?"

She gave a slight shrug. "The way you watched me all night made me wonder if you expected me to pitch a fit about eating chili dogs around a campfire."

"I watched you all night because I can't seem to keep my eyes off you." He tugged her forward until her body barely brushed his. "And yes, a small part of me wanted to know if you'd be horribly uncomfortable here."

"I'm not, so did I pass?"

"That depends." He dragged his fingers up her arm, feeling goosebumps form in their wake.

"On what?" her words came out low and breathy.

"If we can share a goodnight kiss as friends without screwing this relationship up. Fake engagement aside, of course." He dipped his head a fraction, giving her a chance to pull away.

She lifted her chin a little, bringing her lips within inches of his. "We can if we define our relationship as friends with benefits."

"I like benefits." He closed the gap between his mouth and hers in a gentle kiss.

She wrapped her arms around his neck and raised on tip-toe, pressing her lips more firmly against his.

Encircling her in his embrace, he deepened the kiss. It was so easy to get lost in the passion with her, especially after the things they'd shared with each other tonight. For the first time, he felt like maybe they could find a way to overcome their differences.

"Dad!" Dallas yelled. "The movie's over, and Savvy wants you to come say goodbye to Caleb."

He pulled away from Debbie and swore under his breath.

"My sentiments exactly," she said with a chuckle.

"Every. Single. Time." He spat the words out.

Debbie laughed and pulled away. "I think that's my cue to leave."

He caught her hand in his. "I'll walk you to your car, but apparently, I need to see Caleb off first."

CHAPTER 26

Austin's heart leaped in his chest when Debbie walked into church the next morning wearing an emerald green dress that hugged her figure in all the right places. He wasn't planning on making a public statement concerning their relationship, but he couldn't stop himself from waving her over to sit with him and the kids.

Sitting there in God's house with her on one side, her hand in his, and his kids on the other side felt perfect.

His enthusiasm dimmed when the minister announced two tragedies that had occurred last night and invited the congregation to pray for those affected; The Crawfords, whose house burned down—thankfully, no one was injured—and the Duncan children, Lucia and Mia, whose parents Nick and Adriana, were killed in a car accident late last night.

A collective gasp rippled across the congregation. This was news to most of them. Horrible news.

Debbie pulled her hand from his to press to her lips. Of course she knew the deceased couple. Communities like this were close-knit, and everyone knew everyone else.

Wait. Nick and Adriana Duncan?

Those were the parents of the twins that Debbie helped pay the medical bills for. She'd done her best to make sure the girls had a good start in life, and now they'd lost their parents.

He tightened his hold around Debbie's shoulders as she continued to softly weep.

When the sermon ended, she sprang to her feet. "I'll be right back."

She made her way to the front where she waited along with the rancher from the Double Diamond and his wife to speak to the minister.

The Crawford family was about to get more help than they knew what to do with. But what could any of these wealthy people do to help the poor orphaned girls?

When Debbie returned, she still had tears in her eyes.

He took her hand. "Would you like to come over for lunch? We're having leftover chili."

"That's sweet of you, but I don't feel like eating right now."

"I understand." He pulled her into his arms and gave her a tight hug. "Let me know if you need anything."

She nodded then pulled away. He followed her outside and watched her climb into her SUV and drive away.

Four hours later, as he dozed on the couch his phone dinged. He tapped his screen to find a text from Debbie.

Guess what? Gina just dropped off the Duncan girls for me to foster.

Austin smiled. Although their parents' death was a horrible tragedy, hearing that Debbie was being allowed to foster the little girls that she already loved so much created all kinds of emotions in him.

I feel so bad for those little girls. I'm glad you get to be there for them. How long do you think you'll get to keep them?

He remembered how broken up Debbie was when Gina took Noah home.

Indefinitely. Their mom grew up in an orphanage in Mexico, and their father was raised by a great aunt who is 85 now and not in good health.

Another text came through before he could respond.

They don't have any other family. That means that my chances of being able to adopt Lucia and Mia are really good.

Debbie finally had a family of her own.

What a tough, but amazing opportunity for you all.

He really was happy for her, but that little inkling in the back of his mind that had been contemplating making Debbie a part of their family freaked out a little bit. It was one thing to consider bringing one person into their family but to bring three more?

Debbie would never expect him to support their family in the way he'd always felt like he needed to, especially with the level of upkeep a house the size of hers would require. But the need to protect and provide for those he loved was so deeply ingrained in him he didn't know how to let it go.

Austin wasn't sure what to expect when he arrived at Debbie's house Monday evening for dinner, but it wasn't the mad house that he walked into.

Debbie stood in the middle of a kitchen that looked like a disaster zone, holding a crying toddler on each hip, and Dallas and Cody arguing in front of her. The sink overflowed with dirty dishes, and spilled cereal and sippy cups littered the countertops and floor.

"Is not!" Cody propped his hands on his hips and scowled at his brother.

"It is too your fault," Dallas said.

Debbie bounced trying to soothe the crying girls she held. "That's enough boys." Her normally loose curls were tangled and in disarray, and dark shadows ringed her eyes.

"But I didn't do it on purpose," Cody insisted. His little face had turned red, and he looked like he was near tears.

Austin stepped over a few toys as he approached his sons and put a hand on their shoulders. "Calm down, now."

Cody turned and wrapped his arms around Austin's waist. "I didn't mean to hurt her, Daddy."

"Hurt who, buddy?" He patted Cody's back.

Was that why the girls were crying? Had he hurt them? If that was the case, there would be some serious consequences.

"Cody was supposed to be helping Lucia down the stairs, but she pulled her hand from his and fell halfway down." A tremor filled Debbie's voice as she continued to try to soothe the toddler who held a hand to her forehead. "And then Mia started crying because her sister was upset."

Austin disengaged himself from Cody and stood in front of Debbie. He studied the two beautiful little girls in her arms. Both had the biggest brown eyes he'd ever seen—even bigger than Noah's—and soft wavy dark brown hair. He searched for something to help him tell them apart. He finally spotted a pink bow in the hair of the one he suspected was Lucia and a purple bow in the other girl's hair.

"If Lucia fell and bumped her head…" He gently rubbed the back of her head in a soothing gesture. "Then this must be Mia." He put a hand on the other girl's shoulder. "Will you let me hold you while Debbie helps your sister feel better?"

The little girl leaned into Debbie's shoulder.

"It's okay, Mia, Austin is my…good friend"

Austin smiled at her hesitation. He liked being her good friend, but he wanted to be so much more than that. His thoughts concerning Debbie often went way beyond friendship.

Finally, Mia held her arms out to him, and he lifted her up.

"Thank you," Debbie said as tears filled her eyes.

"Hey." He wrapped his free arm around her. "Are you okay?"

She nodded as she blinked away the tears. "Just tired and feeling overwhelmed, I guess. They've been really upset, of course, and didn't sleep well last night. They've cried most of the day, and I have to hold them to soothe them, which means I don't get anything done."

"It's going to be a big adjustment for all of you." He pressed a quick kiss to her forehead before releasing her. "But I've no doubt you can handle this." He turned and picked up the tongs and stirred the spaghetti noodles that looked like they were about to boil over. "I mean if you can handle Noah, then you can handle these two little cuties."

"True." She chuckled as she pulled ice cubes from the freezer and wrapped them in a paper towel. "Even though there are two of them, they aren't nearly as busy as he was." She sat on a kitchen chair and helped Lucia hold the ice to her head. "It's just hard knowing how to comfort them and then to get drinks or food with both of them in my arms... It's overwhelming."

Austin continued to help Debbie finish getting dinner ready, each of them with a child on one hip, because every time they tried putting the girls down, they cried. Then they both ended up eating with a child in their lap, as they tried to coax the girls to eat something.

"I really think part of their tears at this point is exhaustion. They haven't slept more than two hours at a time, and one or the other woke up every couple of hours last night, which of course woke her sister up."

"Where are they sleeping? You don't have them all the way upstairs do you?" He hated to think of a sleep exhausted Debbie tumbling down the stairs.

"They slept in my room with me last night, but Scott and Rudy are coming over tonight to help move the playroom upstairs and set up the toddler beds my parents picked up for the girls today in the room across from mine."

"Good. I'll help."

"You don't have to do that. You've done enough already tonight."

Austin contemplated saying it was the least he could do for the woman he was in love with but Dallas piped up. "I'll help too. I can carry the toys."

"Me too," said Cody.

He grinned at Debbie. "I guess it's settled then."

True to Debbie's word, Scott and Rudy arrived a short time later. After a brief, tense moment where Debbie's brothers were clearly surprised to find Austin and his kids having dinner with Debbie, noise and pandemonium ensued.

Lucia and Mia started crying again, upset by more strangers, and

Dallas and Cody were so eager to help that their voices reached new levels.

After asking Savannah to help Debbie out by loading the dishwasher, Austin finally managed to get the boys focused on carrying the toys from the old playroom to the new, and Debbie took the girls to her bathroom, hoping a bubble bath would calm them down and keep them out of the way.

The whole time they worked together, Austin half expected Debbie's brothers—well, Rudy, since Scott rarely talked—to give him a hard time about taking advantage of Debbie and her generosity. When neither of them did, Austin decided he had a guilty conscience. Debbie provided free babysitting and dinner for his family every night and what did he give her in return?

Nothing. Except more work.

It was late by the time they had all of the furniture moved and the youth beds assembled, but Austin lingered long enough to make sure the beds were made up with the new bedding Debbie's parents had bought. The last thing he did after telling his kids to go get in the truck was carry down a twin mattress from one of the bunk beds to lay on the floor of the girls' room for Debbie, in case they had more rough nights.

Debbie walked into the room holding a girl with each hand as he straightened the bedding on the twin mattress.

Tears again filled her eyes as she smiled at him.

He straightened and walked over to her. "Hey, it's going to be okay."

"I know. Thanks for being so thoughtful." She gave him a watery smile.

"I didn't want you to have to sleep on the floor if you felt like you needed to stay with the girls."

She released the girls' hands and wrapped her arms around his neck.

He gave her a brief hug and planted a quick kiss on her cheek before releasing her. "I'd better go. I need to get my own kids to bed." He bent down to the girls and gently stroked their cheeks.

"Goodnight, little angel one and little angel two. You sleep well, okay?"

One girl—he wasn't sure which one, since they no longer wore different colored bows—gave him a shy smile. The other just stared at him with solemn eyes.

As he let himself out of the house, he determined tomorrow he'd have Debbie teach him how to tell the girls apart, because if those little darlings came as a package deal with Debbie, he was in.

CHAPTER 27

Debbie checked the clock as she pulled the chicken and rice casserole from the oven. Austin would be here soon, and she wanted to make sure dinner was a hundred percent ready. It still embarrassed her to remember what a mess he walked into on Monday. And how she nearly burst into tears.

Yesterday was only marginally better, but dinner still wasn't quite done when he arrived to find the boys not yet dressed for soccer. Debbie had totally spaced it because she was still living from minute to minute in a state of overwhelming exhaustion.

One part of her felt so blessed to be able to foster these two beautiful little girls, but every time she thought about what they'd lost for her to have this opportunity, her heart broke, and she had to fight the depression.

Austin had been amazing. Again. He'd quietly told the boys to go get ready for soccer, then he'd helped her in the kitchen, unloading the dishwasher between helping with dinner and juggling the clinging girls. He managed to get most of the dirty dishes loaded before they were ready to sit down to eat.

Because of how late it was, the poor boys had to eat so fast they probably got indigestion while running up and down the field. She'd opted to stay home with the girls because the weather had been windy and cold.

But there was no soccer tonight, and the girls had been slightly less clingy today and were, at this very minute, upstairs in the playroom with Dallas and Cody. And dinner was ready. If all went well, she and Austin could share more than a brief hug and a peck on the cheek.

Hearing the front door open and close, she turned and greeted him with a big smile. But something about his demeanor made her smile fade and her arms remain at her sides.

She studied his face trying to figure out what was wrong. Exhaustion filled his features, like usual, but there was something in his hooded eyes that she couldn't interpret. The fine lines around his eyes were more prominent than usual, and he fairly scowled.

"What's wrong?" When he didn't answer, she tried again. "Did someone die?"

"I wish," he said under his breath.

Debbie frowned. "What do you mean? What's going on?"

Her mind darted in all kinds of crazy directions. Had something happened to Austin's parents? Did he lose his job? Her heart lurched at that one. Austin would not handle that kind of setback well.

"I got a text—"

"Dad's home!" Cody yelled as he ran down the stairs.

Dallas lagged behind, making sure Lucia and Mia, who scooted down backwards on their tummies, reached the bottom safely. He gave his dad a hug after Cody, then the two little girls followed his example and wrapped their arms around Austin's legs.

Austin's features relaxed as he picked up first one girl and then the other. "How are my little sugar plums today?"

The girls giggled which brought a smile to Debbie's face. On Monday, he'd called the girls cuties and little angels, then yesterday, he called them his little princesses.

Did he plan to come up with a different endearment every day?

Debbie hoped he'd eventually run out of endearments because he spent so much time here.

She didn't have a chance to find out what was bothering Austin because of the craziness they'd come to call dinner. At least the food was ready tonight, and the girls cooperated by sitting in their highchairs, which gave Debbie ample opportunity to watch Austin and wonder what was bothering him.

He caught her looking at him more than once and gave a slight shake of his head each time. Even though the girls had put a smile on his face, it hadn't stayed, and his posture remained rigid.

As soon as dinner was cleaned up and the dishes done, Austin asked Savannah to keep an eye on the kids in the playroom for a few minutes so he could talk to Debbie.

"But Dad, I have homework tonight."

"I know, honey. And I promise I won't take long, but I need to talk to Debbie about something important."

"That's what you said last time, and I came down and caught you guys kissing."

"That's only because you came down too soon," Austin joked but the smile he gave Savannah as he guided her to the stairs didn't meet his eyes.

Debbie soon found herself in the family room with Austin. "Okay, what's going on that's making you so ornery?"

"I'm not ornery."

"Well, you certainly aren't happy."

He scrubbed his hands over his face and dropped onto the sofa. "I know. I'm sorry. Having to deal with Cheyenne always puts me on edge."

"Cheyenne? What has she done now?" Debbie sat down beside him.

"She sent a text saying Tucker got the big promotion sooner than they expected, so don't worry about bringing the kids to Florida next week."

"What?"

"Tucker got the—"

"I heard you the first time. I just can't believe that she is so incredibly shallow that she doesn't want anything to do with her kids now they don't serve her purpose."

"I can. This is why I didn't want to tell the kids about the trip. Deep down, I knew Cheyenne would either back out altogether or do something vindictive just for the sake of it. I should have known she'd never change."

Debbie shook her head. "How did you put up with her for twelve years?"

He shook his head. "It wasn't easy, nor was it pleasant most of the time."

She put a hand on his arm. "I'm so sorry. So, do we take the kids to Florida anyway just to spite her?"

He took her hand in his before shaking his head. "I don't know. A vacation would be fun, but I'd rather they not miss a day of school. And I certainly don't want to take the chance of running into Cheyenne and Tucker there. Besides, now you have the little ones to worry about."

"You're right. I hadn't even thought about what we'd do with them." She frowned. "I'm not sure if I'm even allowed to take them out of the state." Shaking her head, she continued, "I probably couldn't book two extra seats at this point, and the trip might be too much for them right now anyway." She let out a sigh that she hoped didn't sound too disappointed. She'd been looking forward to having two days with Austin on the beach. "I'll cancel all the reservations tonight after I get the girls into bed."

He caressed her hand like he did last Saturday, sending tingles all the way up her arm. "Maybe we can plan some sort of outing for next Saturday. Heck, we could just spend the day here, swimming and watching a movie, and the boys would think they were in heaven."

Debbie grinned. She loved that he wanted to spend his day off with her. And she loved how his fingers were slowly driving her crazy. Fearing the answer, she asked the question that had been on her mind ever since their fake engagement started?

"So what now?"

His brow furrowed. "What do you mean?"

"What do we do about our engagement?" She lowered her gaze,

fearing that despite the attraction between them, Austin didn't really want a long-term relationship with her.

He shifted a little, rotating his body toward her. His warm, calloused fingers lifted her chin. "Seeing as how our engagement was made public by Amy, I think I'd like to let it stand."

"Really?" The word came out in a quick huff of air as Debbie released the breath she'd been holding.

"Really. I've been falling for you for a while now, and your two beautiful daughters have kind of gotten a hold of my heart strings too."

Tears clogged Debbie's throat and flooded her eyes at those two words. "My daughters?"

Austin wiped away the tears that spilled onto her cheeks. "They'll be all yours someday. I'm sure of it. You've waited long enough for a family."

A mild pain filled Debbie's chest as her heart expanded, and more tears spilled over. She'd been trying not to get too emotionally attached to the twins, because she couldn't bear it if, for some reason, she didn't get to keep them. But the thought of them really being hers someday filled her with such joy she couldn't contain it.

He wiped away her tears again. "Now quit crying, woman, because I have about three minutes before Savannah comes downstairs. I plan to spend the first minute kissing you and the other two rubbing your shoulders."

Debbie laughed and brushed away the last of her tears. As he started to lean in, she leaned back. "What if I want to forgo the shoulder rub?"

Heat filled his gaze as he slowly continued to lean toward her. "Three minutes of kissing? That's enough time for a serious make-out session. Keep it PG, the kids could walk in on us any minute."

Debbie's giggle was smothered by his lips.

CHAPTER 28

Austin rolled over and stretched. Sunlight filtered through his curtains already. He looked at the clock. Nine o'clock. He hadn't slept this late on a Saturday for years.

Of course, they'd come home late last night. He'd let the kids talk him into staying later than usual at Debbie's to watch a movie. He'd agreed mostly because he wanted to spend more time with the woman who had burrowed her way inside his heart. And he may have used the children's distraction with the movie as an opportunity to steal some kisses from Debbie.

An odd tremor pulsated through his abdomen every time he thought about how rich she was. He couldn't deny her wealth still bothered him. If he married Debbie, his children might turn out like Cheyenne. But he was beginning to feel like he couldn't live without her either. He could honestly say he'd never been happier in his life.

Austin climbed out of bed and wandered to the kitchen. He should probably get the kids up and moving soon. They planned to go to a petting zoo today with Debbie and the girls. Then they'd spend the afternoon swimming at Debbie's house.

His lips turned up at the thought of Debbie in a swimsuit. That would be a glorious form of torture, because with the kids around, he wouldn't get much time alone with her.

He picked up the stack of mail he'd dropped on the table last night. Mostly bills, like usual. His hands stilled as he spotted an envelope with Providence Medical Center on the return address. He'd just made a payment last week and shouldn't get another bill for another three weeks.

What if they didn't get my payment?

He couldn't afford late fees. He tore open the envelope and searched for the balance due and the payment due date.

Balance due: $0.00

Wait, what?

He scanned the paper, finding each of the measly payments he'd made over the last six months listed. At the bottom, he saw a payment made by an anonymous donor for the exact amount he still owed. The payment was made five days ago. Two days after he told Debbie about his difficulty in paying for Savvy's and Cody's medical bills.

What was she thinking?

Debbie knew he hated handouts.

And he hadn't asked for her help. Heat rushed through his body. Hadn't he become more to her than just another charity case?

Austin hurried to his room and threw some clothes on. Then he knocked on Savvy's door. He opened it to find her just getting out of bed.

"I need to leave for a bit. Make sure the boys get some breakfast when they wake up."

"But, Dad, Caleb is coming to pick me up in an hour."

"Why?"

"Hello, today's prom. We're going hiking for our day date."

Right. Prom. He'd forgotten.

"Don't worry. I'll be back in less than an hour."

It wouldn't take but a few minutes to give Debbie a piece of his mind. He was done with rich people and their meddling.

He was so focused on the words he planned to say to Debbie, he was lucky he didn't get in an accident on the way there. After ringing the doorbell, he balled his fists, crumpling the statement he held. He resisted the urge to swipe away the sweat that pricked his brow. It was a chilly morning, but heat still coursed through his veins.

The door opened.

"You're ear—"

Austin stepped inside, getting right in her face. "I told you not to make decisions for my children…for my family without consulting me first."

She stepped back. "I didn't."

"Then what's this?" He waved the statement from the hospital at her.

Her brow furrowed. "I have no idea."

"You don't know when to quit, do you? You think just because you're rich you can do whatever you please. Just like Cheyenne."

Debbie reeled back. "How can you say that? I'm nothing like Cheyenne. I care more for your children than she ever did."

"Then why don't you respect their father?" The volume of his voice rivaled Cody's when he got excited. "Why do you have to strip away my dignity by going behind my back?"

"What do you mean?"

"I've tried to let go of my pride and not hold your money against you, but just when I finally thought maybe things could work between us you *have* to interfere."

Debbie's chin dropped as she shook her head. "Calm down." She reached out as though she meant to put a hand on his chest, but he stepped away from her. "I don't even know what you're talking about."

"Don't tell me to calm down! If I'd wanted your help paying my bills, I would have asked for it. A man has an obligation to protect and provide for his family. That's exactly what I've been trying to do, and yes, my kids have had to do without a few things, but we were doing fine until you came along and made them want all kinds of things they can't have." Tightness seized his chest as he realized how badly he'd wanted all those things too.

I should have known it couldn't happen with another rich woman.

Debbie reeled back again as though he'd struck her. Then she propped her hands on her hips and scowled. "I've already apologized for buying the remote-control trucks."

"This isn't just about the trucks. The boys can't stop talking about getting to live in a big house and finally getting a mom."

"Really?" Debbie pressed a hand to her chest.

"Only they aren't getting a mom. Our engagement was fake, remember?"

Tears filled her eyes, and her words came out husky. "You said you'd like to let it stand."

"I guess that was a mistake." Austin knew he was being a class A jerk, but he couldn't let this go. "That was before you stuck your nose where it didn't belong. *Again*."

Cries came from the kitchen, tightening his chest even more. He was going to miss those little girls.

Anger sparked in Debbie's gorgeous blue-green eyes. "I didn't stick my nose anywhere. And unless you can stop shouting at me, and explain what's going on, then I think you'd better leave."

He lowered his voice as he waved the statement in her face. "I'm talking about you paying Savvy's and Cody's medical bills."

She shook her head. "I didn't pay any medical bills."

"Then why does it say anonymous donor right there." He stabbed at the paper with his finger.

Debbie winced, and her shoulders slumped. "I'm not the only one with money in this town who likes to do a good deed now and then."

Austin took a deep breath, but it didn't calm him like he'd hoped. She was right, but he hated that someone had thought he was in need of charity. "Right. Because bailing out us poor people makes you feel good."

Her eyes continued to glisten as she backed toward the kitchen where the cries had intensified. "You're such a hypocrite, you know that. You chew me out for buying your boys a gift, then turn around and use me and my money to *bail you out* with your ex-wife."

Austin's stomach clenched, joining the tightness in his chest. "I was trying to protect my family."

"So was I." Vehemence filled her voice. "That's why I agreed to pose as your fiancé."

Of course, she'd done it for the kids.

But at some point things had changed between them. His feelings had grown stronger, and he was sure hers had too, but he couldn't help but resent her right now. He couldn't let go of the feelings of inadequacy that filled him. The insecurity warred with defensiveness and annoyance inside of him.

Silence fell between them broken only by Lucia's and Mia's cries.

She really had been selfless in helping him protect the children from Cheyenne. Debbie loved his kids. He could see it in everything she did for them. They loved her just as much, but Austin wasn't sure he wanted this lifestyle for himself and his children. He had thought they could make it work, but this one little thing felt insurmountable to him right now. What about the next time he became resentful and upset over something to do with money?

His kids were going to hate him for what he was about to do, but he simply couldn't overlook the way her money made him feel so insecure and agitated.

"Well, there's no need for that anymore is there?" He turned and walked out the door.

∼

"Dad, why did Debbie text me and say you need to drive me to my hair and nail appointment?" Savannah asked as soon as she walked through the door after the hike. "Is something wrong with one of the girls?"

Shoot.

Austin had totally forgotten that Debbie had promised to take Savvy to get her hair done for prom tonight. He'd blown into her house and said the things his pride needed him to say, and he'd burned bridges in the process.

He leaned back from the table where he played a game with Dallas and Cody. It wasn't much of a consolation prize, but it was the best he could offer when he told them their plans with Debbie had been canceled.

Austin owed his kids the truth. Otherwise, they would keep asking when they could go to Debbie's house again.

He cleared his throat. "Debbie and I had a fight this morning. She won't be watching you after school anymore, and we won't be eating dinner at her house again."

"What?" Dallas asked.

"Why? said Cody.

Savvy's face fell, and her eyes glistened. "But she has two more projects she wanted me to do."

"You're done working for her. I told you rich people can sometimes demand too much of their employees, and this proves it."

"But she hasn't demanded anything of me, and she's paid me a lot. I still owe her work because she paid for my prom dress and for the hair and nail appointment."

Austin ground his teeth together. The fact that Debbie had gone ahead and paid for Savvy's hair and nail appointment even though they weren't together anymore rubbed him wrong. He'd had enough time to think, and he'd realized she probably hadn't been the one to pay the hospital bill, since she'd been busy with the twins all week. He couldn't bring himself to apologize to her, though, because he still felt too apprehensive about how her money would affect their lives.

"I made a promise to Debbie." Savvy raised her chin even though tears fell on her cheeks. "I can't back out now. You of all people should know that. What kind of work ethic is that?"

Austin rolled his neck. His daughter had a point, but he couldn't go to Debbie's house every day to pick up his kids and pretend nothing was wrong. Nor could he expect her to continue to tend his boys and feed his family.

"Fine." The word came out clipped. "Let Debbie know you'll have to finish her projects on Saturdays when I can be home with the boys."

"But—"

Austin held up a hand and cut off the boys' protests.

Savvy's lips pressed into a thin line, and her shoulders slumped. She gave a slight nod before walking out of the room.

The bathroom door slammed, and Austin jumped.

Great. How do I repair my relationship with my daughter after something like this?

At least Rainey's mom had insisted on the after party being at her house where she could chaperone, and he didn't need to worry about taking advantage of Debbie any more than he already had.

"I want to go to Debbie's house after school," Cody said. He folded his arms and affected a pout.

Dallas's arms were folded too, but he stared down at his lap.

Austin let out a heavy sigh. "I know you do, but we won't be going over there anymore, so you'll just have to get used to the idea." He picked up the dice and passed them to Dallas. "Let's finish our game before I have to take Savvy to get her hair done."

"I don't want to play anymore," Dallas mumbled before getting up and walking out the back door.

"Me either," Cody swiped a hand across his money, knocking most of it to the floor, and followed his brother.

Austin resisted the urge to shove the whole game off the table.

How did our lives go from almost perfect to perfectly miserable in a matter of hours?

CHAPTER 29

A flash of guilt filled Debbie's chest as her mom bent and picked up four dirty diapers from the family room floor. She'd been meaning to get to those. Just like she'd been meaning to do a lot of things this past week. She usually used the girls' nap time to do some cleaning, but she hadn't been able to get herself to do more than cry or watch Netflix lately.

"When was the last time you ate something?" Mom asked after returning from throwing the diapers away. When Debbie didn't answer, she went on. "Please tell me you at least ate some of the macaroni and cheese you made for the girls."

Debbie grimaced. She was not a fan of most of the convenience foods the girls seemed to prefer, but she couldn't find the energy or desire to cook anything else.

Mom knowing she made mac & cheese for the girls for lunch reminded her she still needed to wipe off the kitchen table and sweep the floor. And load the dishwasher. She pulled the laundry basket she'd deposited in the family room last night up onto the couch beside her.

Why did all the daily tasks she used to enjoy doing suddenly feel like such a chore?

The cleaning service was due to come tomorrow, for which Debbie was grateful, but she would be embarrassed if they found two-day-old food on her floors.

"That's what I thought," Mom said, propping her hands on her hips and shaking her head. "It's a good thing I brought over some freezer meals. I put two of them in the freezer and the other two in the fridge to start thawing."

"Thanks," Debbie said, mustering a smile.

Mom sat down on the other side of the laundry basket and picked up a cute little jumper. Despite Gina bringing over some of the twins' clothing from their house, Debbie couldn't resist buying some new outfits for the girls. Even though she wanted to buy *all* the cute clothes, she'd shown great restraint, because she knew the girls would outgrow them so fast.

"Is motherhood supposed to feel like this?" She asked her mom in a quiet voice.

"Like what, honey?"

"Like I'm...drowning." Debbie blinked back the tears that filled her eyes. She couldn't even blame her pendulum of emotions on post postpartum depression like most new moms, or even sleep deprivation, since the girls were sleeping much better now.

Mom caught her arm as she reached for a pair of pajamas. "Any mom with twins often feels overwhelmed. Heck, one child is enough to do that to you, as I'm sure you realized with Noah."

A hint of a smile pulled at Debbie's lips as she thought about the busy little boy who'd stolen her heart so quickly, yet tested her patience to the limits.

Compassion filled her mom's voice as she went back to folding more clothes. "Being a mom can be hard, being a single mom... Well, that's even harder."

"I thought if I just got a couple of kids of my own, then I'd be happy, but..." Debbie couldn't finish her sentence around the lump in her throat.

"Once you've enjoyed ice cream, it's hard to imagine a life without it."

Debbie frowned at her mom. It wasn't surprising her mom would use ice cream in an analogy—that's where Debbie got her love for ice cream, after all—but she wasn't sure what Mom was saying.

"Honey, you've had a glimpse of being a part of a whole family, with a strong supportive man by your side."

Conflicting emotions filled Debbie as she recalled telling her mom how kind and helpful Austin had been last week when she was adjusting to having the twins. Despite the chaos, it had been the happiest week of her life. And she'd fallen even deeper in love with him Friday night when he read the girls a bedtime story.

Then only a few days later, she'd turned around and told her mom how angry Austin was when he thought she'd paid off his hospital bills. That had hurt Debbie deeply. She wanted nothing more than to help Austin with his financial struggles, but she understood how important it was to him to provide for his family. She'd never do anything to undermine that.

It hurt that he'd had so little faith in her. That he'd immediately lumped her right back in with all of the other rich people who'd hurt him. Comparing her to his self-centered, egotistical, narcissistic ex-wife had been the worst insult he could throw at her.

"He'll come around," Mom said confidently.

"Don't hold your breath. He's never liked my money. It's always been a source of contention between us."

"Maybe, but someday he'll realize that having you in his life is more important than his pride."

Debbie picked at her fingernails. "What makes you so sure?"

"I saw the way he looked at you during the barbecue a few weeks ago. He couldn't keep his eyes off you." Mom gave her a knowing look. "He may struggle to accept your wealth, but his love for you will win out eventually."

Debbie wished she had her mom's confidence. Austin had said he was falling for her, but he'd never said he loved her. And she'd never told him she was in love with him.

She'd suffered enough rejection over the past few years that the last thing she wanted to do was make him feel like she was rushing things and end up pushing him away. So, she'd kept her mouth shut and she'd lost him anyway.

∼

BANG!

Austin jolted at the booming sound and struggled to keep his truck in his lane as it pulled to the right. As soon as it was safe to do so, he pulled over to the shoulder of the highway. He swore and smacked the steering wheel with his fist.

A flat tire was the last thing he needed to deal with right now. He was already late coming home as it was.

He got out and checked the front right tire. Sure enough. Blown. Practically shredded.

He swore again and kicked the tire for good measure. He'd needed new tires for a while now, but he just hadn't had the extra money, so he'd kept putting it off.

He put in a quick call to the neighbor down the street whose son played on Dallas and Cody's team to see if she could get his boys to soccer. Then he sent a text to Savvy to let her know he'd be late, and that Mrs. Johnson would take the boys to their game.

Thirty minutes later, he swore again and threw the tire iron on the ground. The lug nuts had been so stubborn, he'd broken a bolt.

He pulled his phone out again and looked up numbers for a tow truck. There were exactly two repair shops in Providence: Knight's and Decker's. Although Decker's specialized mostly in quick oil changes, he called them first, because Debbie's brother, Scott, worked at Knight's Repair Shop.

Three minutes later, Austin disconnected the call with Decker's mechanic. Their only tow truck was out on a call and wouldn't be available for two hours. Rolling his neck, he dialed the number for Knight's.

"Knight's Repair Shop," A deep voice answered on the fourth ring.

Scott.

Austin had only ever heard Debbie's linebacker of a brother say a dozen words, but he was sure it was him on the other end of the line.

He cleared his throat. "Yes, I need a tow truck. I'm about fifteen miles south of Providence, Northbound, on highway 395."

Scott rattled off several questions, wanting to know the make and model of his vehicle and the reason for needing a tow.

Austin paced beside his truck as he supplied the information Scott needed. When Debbie's brother asked for his name, he froze.

It's a small town. You're bound to run into Debbie's family eventually.

"This is Austin Reed."

You know, the man who used your sister and broke her heart?

Silence filled the line for a long moment, and Austin feared Scott might refuse to help him.

"Give me fifteen minutes," Scott said, then the line went dead.

Half an hour later, after listening to Scott do lots of muttering about the condition of his tires and watching him shake his head while he inspected the broken bolt, Austin found himself riding in the tow truck with the mechanic.

The radio played a country station on a low enough volume that it should have been easy to converse, but Austin couldn't think of a single thing to say, especially around the tightness in his chest and abdomen.

And Scott was hardly a great conversationalist.

Finally, as they exited the freeway, Austin couldn't stand the silence anymore. "If you've got something you want to say to me, let's hear it."

"What do you want me to say?" Scott's voice was deeper than it had been while he'd been muttering about the tires, as though he repressed some emotion.

Probably anger. At me.

Austin shrugged. "I figured you'd have something to say about what happened between me and your sister."

Scott's grip on the steering wheel tightened until his knuckles turned white. "I don't know exactly what happened between you and

Debbie, but I figure if you can't love her for who she is, she's better off without you."

"I do love who she is. I love how generous and giving she is. I love how patient she is with my kids." The words were out before Austin could stop them. He'd never said the "L" word aloud in conjunction with Debbie. He tried to backpedal. "But I can't..."

Scott shot him a quick glance before returning his gaze to the road. "Can't what? Man up and admit that you need her?"

"I don't need her money," Austin said with force.

"I never said anything about her money." The other man looked at him again, longer this time, before making the turn onto the road that would lead them into Providence. "That's your problem right there."

"What do you mean?"

"You can't separate your feelings for Debbie from her money. And you seem to think accepting her and her money as a package deal manifests some sort of weakness in you. You say you love how generous and giving she is. Her money helps her to be that way. And she's able to be patient because she doesn't have to worry about how she's going to provide food, shelter, clothing, and a college education for your kids like you are."

Austin stared at Scott. He'd never heard the man speak so many words at once. The linebacker had a wisdom that belied his quiet nature.

"Why are you making a relationship with Debbie one-sided? Did you ever stop to think about what you have to offer her?"

Austin snorted. "Like what?"

Scott shrugged. "Don't you think she ever gets lonely or scared living all alone in that big house out on the remote highway? Maybe she'd appreciate having a competent man around so she wouldn't have to call her dad or brothers every time she wants a piece of furniture moved or has a leaky faucet or a clogged drain."

Austin's mind raced. Did he really have something he could offer Debbie besides debt?

"I'm sure she'd love to let someone else worry about changing the light bulbs in the vaulted ceiling." Scott started ticking things off with his fingers. "And taking care of the pool maintenance. How about the upkeep on her vehicles and the yard."

"Eli takes care of the pool and the yard."

"Only until he leaves for college next fall. But Eli also works at the garage with me and as a busboy at Charity's Diner. Debbie doesn't always get his help as soon or as often as she would like."

"She can easily afford to hire someone to replace Eli."

Scott shook his head. "Maybe, but finding someone to take turns getting up in the middle of the night with a sick toddler isn't as easy."

Austin turned to Scott. "Have the girls been sick?"

The muscle in Scott's jaw tensed as he shook his head again. "All Debbie has ever wanted is a family. You can give her that. That's something her money can't buy." When Austin didn't respond, he added, "It was never Debbie's dream to be a single mother."

Austin wasn't sure how Scott knew what Debbie's dream was. But he was right.

No one ever dreamed of being a single parent. It was the hardest thing he'd ever done in his life, and now Debbie was experiencing how difficult it was.

But it had been easier when Debbie was sharing the burden with him. He never had to worry about his children when they were with her. Even when she'd been exhausted and stressed out. She'd still made sure they were fed and their homework was done.

Having her back in his life—in his arms—meant swallowing his pride. Could he do that?

A tightness seized his chest, squeezing the air from his lungs. His mouth dried up like the Sahara desert, and his own heartbeat grew so loud in his ears that he could no longer hear the radio playing.

Could a man physically choke on his own pride and suffocate to death?

Or will I be the first?

CHAPTER 30

"You can't give it to her!" Dallas yelled from the family room.

"Yes, I can!" Cody's voice reached new decibels.

Austin sighed and rolled off his bed. He'd been attempting to rest on this Sunday afternoon, but obviously that wasn't happening anymore. At least he'd taken the kids to church today, which was more than he could say about last week.

They'd arrived late and left early, so he didn't have to worry about crossing paths with Debbie. But that hadn't stopped his heart from racing when he spotted her flaming red hair near the front by her parents.

Then she'd taken Lucia—at least he thought it was Lucia—out to change a diaper, and their gazes had locked for one long moment before she looked at the boys on either side of him. A sheen of tears filled her eyes before she hiked up her chin up and hurried down the aisle.

"But she's not your mom, dummy!" Dallas's voice had risen too, but then it dropped with his next sentence. "We're never going to have a mom."

Pain, sharp and swift, pierced Austin's chest. He'd never intended to raise his children without a mother. No one had ever interested him, though. Until Debbie. Most days, he thought they were doing fine, but then other days, his children felt the lack of a mother in acute ways. And it had only become worse since they'd experienced Debbie's motherly love.

"Boys, what's our rule about arguing?"

Cody turned to him, red-faced and eyes glistening. "I don't want to go in the closet, Dad. I wanna go see Debbie." He stomped his little foot.

"I know, but—" Austin had been about to say that he needed to fix things with Debbie first, when Dallas cut him off.

"I told you. You may as well just throw your present away, like I did."

"What present?"

Cody held out a piece of yellow card stock; a picture frame with his grinning freckled face inside. The splotches of color around the edges made it obvious his son had painted the flowers, decorating the frame himself. "I told Ms. Jeffries, the art teacher, that I didn't have a mom to make a card for. So she told me to make it for my grandma or whoever I wanted. I want to give it to Debbie."

"But she's not your mom, so you can't." Dallas propped his hands on his hips and leaned his upper body forward.

Austin's heart twisted. Had he overlooked how badly Dallas had been hurt by Cheyenne's abandonment? He'd always been such a quiet and thoughtful child, Austin had no idea he was keeping so much emotion bottled up. The recent development with Debbie had made it all come to a head.

Austin was vaguely aware of Savannah entering the room as he sat on the couch and looked Dallas in the eye. "Did you make a picture too? Would you like to give it to Debbie?"

Dallas's gaze darted toward the garbage can, but his voice was tight—still bordering on angry— when he spoke. "Ms. Jeffries said everyone had to make one."

Austin walked over to the kitchen trash can, praying he hadn't dumped something in there unknowingly and ruined Dallas's picture.

He heaved a sigh of relief when he spotted a picture of Dallas surrounded by a blue picture frame.

Austin picked it up. "You did a great job, bud. Blue happens to be Debbie's favorite color. I think she'd love to receive such a special gift for Mother's Day."

"But she's not my— mother." Dallas blinked rapidly to rid his eyes of the tears that flooded them when his voice broke.

Debbie could be their mother if Austin would just stop being so stubborn. He rehearsed his conversation with Scott two days ago. Maybe he had more to offer Debbie than he thought. Something more valuable than her jewelry, expensive cars, and house. Something irreplaceable.

He could offer her not only his love but his childrens' too.

But would she take him back after he'd been so horrible to her?

Austin sat back down on the couch and pulled both boys into his arms. "Debbie may not be your mom, but she loves you guys like you were her own children." He squeezed them tight. "I'm the one who screwed things up with Debbie. I never meant for it to hurt you kids." He looked at Savvy so she would know his apology was meant for her too.

She gave a small smile and blinked back tears of her own.

"I want to fix my mistakes, but I'm not sure Debbie will forgive me."

"She will," Savvy said with a smile. "And I have a gift for her too."

"I hope you're right, but I'm going to need you all to help me."

A chorus of "Okay," filled his ears, and before Austin knew it, he was pulling into Debbie's wide driveway.

He looked up at her house. Its size still overwhelmed him, but man, he'd missed this place. Especially all of the laughter and fun they'd had inside.

The boys opened their doors, but Austin stopped them. "Wait a minute!"

They both let out a dramatic sigh, but they obeyed.

"Now remember, if Debbie doesn't want us to stay, we're going to be respectful and leave. No whining. No throwing a fit. I know she'll be happy to get your gifts, but I'm not sure she'll be happy to see me."

"We know, Dad. You already told us." Exasperation filled Dallas's voice.

"Right." He'd talked during the whole drive, partly to hide his nervousness, and partly to prepare his kids for the disappointment if things went badly. He turned to Savannah. "I meant it when I said you're going to have to give me and Debbie some uninterrupted time together. That is, if she doesn't boot me out."

She put a hand on his arm. "It'll be okay, Dad. You'll see."

The kids slid from the truck eager to see Debbie again, but Austin's chest tightened as he stared at the file folder on the center console.

Time to swallow my pride.

WHEN DEBBIE'S DOORBELL RANG, she got up off the floor and stretched her stiff joints. She'd spent more time on the floor these last two weeks than she had in the last thirty years.

She couldn't help herself. She wanted to be right there with the girls, experiencing everything with them. They'd already grown and changed so much, and she didn't want to miss a thing.

After a full week of moping, she'd shaken off the blues the best she could, determined to enjoy the gift that she'd been given. It had been a lot harder to do than she'd expected, but she was trying.

Debbie let the girls trail behind as she headed to the door. Thankfully, they'd adjusted and weren't as clingy as they used to be.

She opened the door to find the four people she loved most besides Lucia and Mia on her doorstep. Her heart stalled in her chest for one long moment then pounded out an irregular rhythm against her ribcage.

Her gaze met Austin's who stood at the back of the group.

His brow wrinkled a little and he chewed on the edge of his bottom lip.

"Hi, Debbie." Little Cody swept through the doorway. "I made a Mother's Day card for you."

Cody's words swept all the air from her lungs. And when he thrust a yellow paper in her hand and wrapped his arms around her waist, a rushing, tingling sensation filled her body.

She wrapped her arms around him and hugged him back. "Oh, Cody. I love it. I can't wait to hang it on my fridge."

"I made you one too." Dallas stepped in and hugged her next.

A sudden rush of emotion clogged Debbie's throat and threatened to spill out of her eyes. The pain she'd been experiencing the past week of a broken heart suddenly reversed, and her ribcage grew tight as her heart expanded.

She studied Dallas's picture as she returned his embrace. "How did you know blue was my favorite color?"

He pulled away. "I didn't when I made it, but Dad told me today."

She looked up at Austin who still stood out on the porch.

He gave her a soft smile.

Before Debbie could say anything, Savannah stepped inside. "I have something for you too."

Savannah held out two watercolor paintings that didn't show features but there was no mistaking Debbie's red curly head next to Noah's black hair. The second image blurred as Debbie lost her struggle against the tears, but she recognized her red hair again, this time tucked between two dark-haired toddler girls; one dressed in pink, the other in purple.

"They're beautiful, Savvy." She pulled the girl into her arms.

"I've missed you," Savvy whispered.

"I've missed you too. Thank you for sending me pictures of your prom. You looked absolutely beautiful."

She'd been relieved when Savannah texted her to tell her that her dad had agreed to let her continue working on Debbie's paintings on Saturdays. The text, even though it excited Debbie, had made her cry. Because she didn't just want Savvy to come work on her projects, she wanted the whole Reed family.

This was the first time she'd seen Savvy, though, thanks to prom and Debbie's family celebrating Mother's Day yesterday, because her sisters were out of town today.

"Please forgive my dad," Savannah whispered before pulling back.

Debbie released her and looked at Austin again who still stood at the edge of the porch, holding a file folder in his hand.

He cleared his throat. "May I come in and talk to you?"

A swarm of butterflies erupted in her stomach, making her nauseous. She stepped back and waved him in. As he stepped inside, his masculine scent combined with fresh air, sunshine, and fabric softener hit her. Her heart pounded so hard she was afraid he could hear it.

Of course she would forgive him, because she loved him. But he'd hurt her deeply by believing she'd intentionally do something that she knew would hurt his dignity.

"Savvy." Austin nodded his head to the kids surrounding them.

Savannah nodded and picked up Lucia and turned to Dallas. "You bring Mia upstairs."

Within seconds, Debbie stood alone with Austin in her wide entry way. She shifted her weight from one foot to the other. Did she invite him to sit in the living room?

No. That's too formal.

The kitchen. It's supposed to be the heart of the home.

She turned and walked toward the kitchen, hoping he would follow.

When Austin didn't say anything, she busied herself by digging in her junk drawer for magnets to put her first ever Mother's Day gifts up on the refrigerator.

When there was nothing left to distract her, she turned to him.

"Do you mind if I get myself a drink of water?" Austin tugged at the collar of his t-shirt.

"Help yourself?" Debbie waved a hand toward the cupboard that held the glasses.

A good hostess would get it for him, but she held back. He'd come here for a reason, and he was obviously uncomfortable. Maybe he'd feel more at home if he helped himself, like he used to.

He left the file folder on the counter while he got ice water from the fridge. When he turned around, she kept the counter between them.

If she didn't, she might throw herself into his arms before he had a chance to say whatever it was he'd come here to say.

She pointed at the folder. "So is that another Mother's day present for me?" She joked, but her own laughter fell flat.

He slowly pushed the folder toward her. "This is me swallowing my pride." When she reached for it, he kept his long, strong fingers on it, holding it in place. "First, I need to ask for your forgiveness. I said some horrible things to you last week, and I'm sorry."

She opened her mouth to say he was forgiven, but he kept talking.

"This…" He tapped the folder before pulling his hand back. "Is me asking you for help. I'm tired of being in debt. Tired of feeling inadequate and deficient. I want a relationship with you because I'm madly in love with you, but I don't want to go into it feeling incompetent and defective."

The butterflies in her stomach turned into thousands of hummingbirds darting every which way looking for sweet nectar. Their fluttering pushed upward, causing her chest to swell. So many emotions filled her; she didn't know what to address first.

"You are in no way defective or deficient," she said vehemently. "I've never doubted your abilities as a father or as a provider, and you shouldn't either."

He acknowledged her words with a nod, then pointed to the folder. "I'm laying all my cards on the table. The most recent credit card statements with their balances are in there along with my bank statements, and pay stubs. Oh and my truck desperately needs new tires."

She put her hand on the folder and leaned over the counter. "I don't care how much you make or what you owe. I'll gladly help you in any way I can."

"Thank you."

"I know how difficult this was for you. It means a lot to me that you would ask me for help."

He cleared his throat. "The truth is… it's not your money I want—except maybe for new tires." He ducked his head briefly before raising it again. "I want you. In my life. Forever."

She grinned as she slid the folder to the side. "Well, since I forgive you and because I love you too, I'd really like to hear more about this relationship you'd like to have with me."

He rounded the counter so fast he took her breath away. Grinning, he pulled her into his arms. "I want a relationship that lasts forever and involves lots of kissing, hugging, and…" He lowered his voice to a seductive whisper. "And other things."

She laughed. "That sounds like exactly what I'm looking for."

His lips met hers, and a million tiny sparklers ignited inside her, flooding her whole body with the most amazing sensations. She wrapped her arms around him and kissed him back with everything she had.

He groaned and tightened his embrace, pinning her against the counter.

After another long moment, she pushed back, gasping for air. She burst into laughter. "I've missed you so much."

He buried his face in her neck and inhaled. "I missed you too. I never thought I'd say this, but I missed the smell of your expensive perfume and your big house where we can send the kids upstairs—or downstairs—so we can be alone together."

His breath tickled her neck, sending shivers down her spine. It wasn't long before his lips were on hers again, and warmth filled her body from head to toe.

When they finally pulled apart, Debbie let out a lengthy sigh. "I have an investment opportunity I'd like to discuss with you."

His brow furrowed as he pulled back to look at her. "Investment? You realize I'm broke, don't you."

"You have three beautiful kids who love you. You're wealthier than you realize." She gave a soft smile before waving a hand. "Anyway, I want you to partner with me to build some affordable housing here in Providence."

Austin's eyebrows rose. "Really? Like apartments?"

"Small homes, apartments, whatever you think would be best to meet the needs of the community."

He gave a little chuckle before shaking his head. "I'm sorry. It's a great idea, but I'm not interested in talking about apartments right now. I'd much rather discuss being partners. Lifelong partners."

"Oh, I like the sound of that." Debbie leaned in for another kiss, but he resisted, pointing a finger at her.

"But I don't want our kids spoiled, like Cheyenne. They need chores and responsibilities."

"Fine. We'll come up with a list of jobs together." She grinned as she pulled him closer. "But I'm going to spoil our kids Austin. I'm going to shower them with love and affection. I'll read stories to them every night, play games with them, make them cookies after school, tickle their backs, and—"

Austin's lips cut off her words.

She let out a lengthy sigh and leaned into him, determined to enjoy every second they had together.

Until the kids interrupted them, that is. And then she would make cookies with her family.

EPILOGUE

Tires screeched to a halt outside the open garage door.

Scott lifted his head and looked out front.

Rudy climbed from his patrol car and marched toward Scott. "What are you still doing here? You're supposed to be on your way to pick up Debbie and Austin from the airport."

"I know." The words came out a grunt as he strained to tighten the final lug nut on the Ford Focus. He straightened. "But Mrs. Jacobson needed new brakes before her trip tomorrow."

"That's right she's going to help her daughter who just had a baby."

It didn't surprise Scott that Rudy knew about Mrs. Jacobson's trip. He was the most talkative and friendly deputy in the sheriff's department. Rudy knew everything about everyone in Providence—good and bad.

"Well, it looks like you're done now, so get moving. I'll go pick up Mrs. Jacobson and bring her to get her car."

Scott nodded and headed to the bathroom to wash up. "Rudy—"

His brother turned. "I know. I'll get payment from her. Don't worry, I'll give her the old-lady-on-a-fixed-income discount." He waved his arms overhead. "And I'll be sure to lock up."

"Thanks."

Scott didn't know what he'd have done these past three years without Rudy and Mary, the manager of the gas station and convenience store attached to the repair shop. The two of them had repeatedly stepped in to help Scott as manager of Knight's repair shop. They verified his parts orders, checked his bookkeeping, and helped with all the paperwork.

They both knew what a struggle it was for him to make sense of blocks of texts and numbers on a page or computer screen, but they also knew he didn't want to let down Charity Knight who'd put so much faith and trust in him to run the shop that her late husband had built.

After washing up and throwing on a clean shirt, Scott jumped into Debbie's Cadillac Escalade and headed to the freeway. He still couldn't understand why Debbie insisted he bring her SUV. She and Austin could have fit in his truck just fine.

As he drove, he thought about their wedding two and a half weeks ago. If it hadn't been for the monkey suit Debbie made him wear, it would have been the funnest party the town of Providence had ever seen. Even though he felt stupid in his tux, Dallas and Cody sure looked sharp in theirs.

Lucia and Mia had been adorable little flower girls in their matching ruffly, pink dresses, and Savannah was a beautiful maid of honor. Her friend Caleb sure thought so too, judging by the way he couldn't take his eyes off her.

Both Debbie and Austin had looked so happy, it had almost made Scott want to get married. Almost.

He couldn't think about that yet though. He needed something to offer a woman first. Few women aspired to marry a mechanic with dyslexia. The simple fact he relied on others to help him do his job proved he wasn't exactly a catch.

Austin's parents, Alex and Nora Reed, had been gracious enough to stay at the house and take care of the kids while the newlyweds honeymooned in Greece and Italy. Scott's parents had also helped by shuttling the kids to and from school and other activities. But Debbie and Austin's two week honeymoon got extended four more days, and Austin's parents had to return to Boise.

So his mom stepped in to take care of the kids. Dad had planned to pick up the newlyweds, but he ended up having a building inspection scheduled for today on the house he'd been renovating. And Rudy was on duty. Hence the reason Scott was on his way to the airport, despite being swamped at the garage since Eli left for college two weeks ago.

His phone rang just as he exited the freeway. "Hello."

"Scott. Where are you?" Debbie's voice came over the phone.

"I'm two minutes out. Be right there."

"Okay, we'll see you at passenger pick up. I can't wait to show you our surprise." Her last words came out as a squeal.

"Surprise?" What kind of surprise did a couple bring home from their honeymoon, other than gifts for their five children?

"I can't wait to show everyone!"

Muffled sounds filled the line, then Scott heard Austin say, "Let the man focus on his driving," before the line went dead.

As Scott pulled into the passenger pickup, it wasn't hard to spot his sister's unique fiery red hair. Her face glowed almost as much as her hair.

Marriage definitely agrees with her.

Scott popped the trunk and climbed out to help Austin load the suitcases. The man fairly beamed. The honeymoon had obviously done him some good too. Scott turned to grab the last bag by Debbie's feet only to find she'd picked it up and was holding it with an arm hooked through the handle.

Wait. That's not a suitcase. It's a baby carrier.

"What—" Scott shook his head in disbelief.

"Surprise!" Debbie squealed.

"That's why you extended your honeymoon?"

No wonder she asked me to bring the SUV.

"Yes. The day before we were supposed to come home, I got a call from the National Adoption Agency that I applied to months ago. So we took a detour through New York on the way home." She turned the baby carrier and lifted the blanket so he could see the tiny, sleeping infant inside. "Meet your nephew, William Alexander Reed."

ACKNOWLEDGMENTS

Thank you to my local critique group for helping me work out the kinks and figure things out with this story. Thanks to my online critique group (Gisele, Charlene, Rebekah). You ladies are the best! You kept me going when I wasn't sure where this story was going. I couldn't have done this one without you.

Special thanks to my beta readers, Jenessa and Rebekah. Your input was invaluable! And special thanks to Kelli Ann Morgan at Inspire Creative Services for this amazing cover and her patience with me while I decided what I wanted my cover to look like. And finally, thank you to Megan Walker for her thorough job in proofreading.

As always, thank you my wonderful husband and family for your unfailing support. And the biggest thanks ever to my awesome readers. You make it all worth it!

ABOUT THE AUTHOR

Jill has always been an avid reader, and romance has always been her favorite genre. If she's not writing or folding laundry her head is usually in a book.

When her father told her, "I've got a story I want you to write," she didn't think she'd ever actually do it.

But after twenty years of being a stay-at-home mom with seven children, the idea of writing and publishing a book sounded less terrifying than entering the workforce again. Boy, was she wrong!

Keep in touch with Jill Burrell
www.jillburrell.com

- amazon.com/author/jillburrell
- facebook.com/authorjillburrell
- goodreads.com/authorjillburrell
- bookbub.com/authors/jill-burrell

Made in the USA
Middletown, DE
19 August 2022